A
DARKNESS
ABSOLUTE

Also by Kelley Armstrong

Casey Butler
City of the Lost

Cainsville
Betrayals
Deceptions
Visions
Omens

Age of Legends
Forest of Ruin
Empire of Night
Sea of Shadows

The Blackwell Pages (co-written with Melissa Marr)
Thor's Serpents
Odin's Ravens
Loki's Wolves

Otherworld
Thirteen	*Broken*
Spell Bound	*Haunted*
Waking the Witch	*Industrial Magic*
Frostbitten	*Dime Store Magic*
Living with the Dead	*Stolen*
Personal Demon	*Bitten*
No Humans Involved	

Darkest Powers & Darkness Rising
The Rising	*The Reckoning*
The Calling	*The Awakening*
The Gathering	*The Summoning*

Nadia Stafford
Wild Justice
Made to be Broken
Exit Strategy

Stand-alone novel
The Masked Truth

A DARKNESS ABSOLUTE

KELLEY ARMSTRONG

MINOTAUR BOOKS ✖ NEW YORK

A DARKNESS ABSOLUTE. Copyright © 2017 by KLA Fricke, Inc. All rights reserved. Printed in the United States of America. For information, address St. Martin's Press, 175 Fifth Avenue, New York, N.Y. 10010.

www.minotaurbooks.com

The Library of Congress Cataloging-in-Publication Data is available upon request.

ISBN 978-1-250-09217-5 (hardcover)
ISBN 978-1-250-09220-5 (e-book)

Our books may be purchased in bulk for promotional, educational, or business use. Please contact your local bookseller or the Macmillan Corporate and Premium Sales Department at 1-800-221-7945, extension 5442, or by e-mail at MacmillanSpecialMarkets @macmillan.com.

First Edition: February 2017

10 9 8 7 6 5 4 3 2 1

A
DARKNESS
ABSOLUTE

ONE

We've been tracking Shawn Sutherland for almost two hours when the blizzard strikes. That's the common phrasing. A storm hits. A blizzard strikes. Like a left hook out of nowhere. Except that's not how it usually happens. There's always warning. The wind picks up. The sky darkens. At the very least, you sense a weight in the air. When the snow starts, you might curse at the suddenness of it, but you know it wasn't sudden at all.

This blizzard is different. Deputy Will Anders and I are roaring along on our snowmobiles, following a clear set of footprints in newly fallen snow. I'm glad Sutherland's prints are obvious, because it's such a gorgeous day, I struggle to focus on my task. The sun glitters off snow and ice as I whip along, taking my corners a little too tight, playing with the machine, enjoying the ride on what has become a rather routine task.

Rockton is a secret off-the-grid town, a safe haven for people in hiding. If a resident keeps his head down and doesn't cause trouble, we don't notice him. Until last month, that was Sutherland. Then the first snow came, and he snapped, declaring that he wasn't spending another winter in this town. He's run twice since then. Our boss—Sheriff Eric Dalton—warned Sutherland that if it happened again, he would spend the winter in the jail cell instead. Protecting citizens is our responsibility, even when it means protecting them from themselves.

Yesterday, Dalton flew to Dawson City on a supply run and, yep, Sutherland bolted again. But he's too afraid of the forest to actually leave the path, which makes him very easy to track after a light snow-fall. Hell, I'd have taken the horses instead if Dalton wasn't due back before nightfall; I need Sutherland caught by then. Given that the sun starts setting midafternoon, we don't have much time.

We're ripping along when I catch sight of a dark shape ahead. Anders doesn't see it—he's gawking at something to the left, and I flip up my visor to shout at him. Then I see what he does: a wall of white. It's on us before I can react, a cyclone of driving snow and roaring wind, and I hit the brakes so hard my ass shoots off the seat and nearly sends me face-first through the windshield.

The sled's back slides—right into a tree. I curse, but on a path this narrow, striking a tree is damn near inevitable. I'm just lucky *I* wasn't the one hitting it.

I hear Dalton's voice in my head. *Stay on the sled. Get your bearings first.*

When I lift my leg over the seat, I hear him say, *Stay on the sled, Butler.* I ignore him and twist to look around.

White. That's all I see. Blinking against the prickle of ice pellets, I close my visor. Even with it shut, I hear the howl of the wind, an enraged beast battering at me.

I slit my eyes, turn my face from the wind, open my visor, and shout "Will!" but the storm devours my words. When I open my mouth to yell again, the wind whips rock-hard ice pellets into my face, and I slap the visor shut.

The first lick of panic darts through me, some primal voice screaming that I'm blinded and deafened, and if I don't move, don't do *something*, I'll die in this wasteland, buried under ice and snow.

And that's exactly the kinda thinking that'll get you killed, Casey.

Dalton's voice in my head again, a laconic drawl this time. He switches to my given name as his temper subsides, knowing all I need is a little bit of guidance from the guy who's spent every winter of his life in this forest.

I take a deep breath and then try the radio. Yes, that should have been the obvious first response, but four months up here has taught me that our radios are about as reliable as the toy versions I used as a kid. The second I pull off my helmet, the driving snow has me closing my eyes, hunkering down, and blindly raising the receiver to my ear.

"Butler to base," I say. "Anyone there?"

Static answers.

"Anders?" I say. "Will? You copy?"

I'm not surprised when silence answers. Unless his helmet is off, he won't hear his radio.

I squint in front of me, where he'd been only minutes ago.

He's there. He must be. I just can't see through this damn snow. "Will!"

The howl of the wind responds.

I put my helmet back on and push the ignition button. As soon as the engine fires up, I know that's the wrong move. Anders was in front of me. I risk bashing into his sled. Or into *him*.

Dalton would tell me to stay on the sled. But if Anders is doing the same thing, maybe five feet away, we'll freeze to death out here.

Which is why I told you not to go chasing Sutherland. Maybe if he loses a few fingers to frostbite, that'll teach him.

Okay, so I screwed up. Live and learn. But I need to do *something*, because there's no way in hell I can sit tight and pray this blizzard ends before I die of exposure.

Hanging on to the handlebars, I pry my ass off the snowmobile, fighting a wind that wants to knock me into the nearest tree. My snowmobile suit billows, and threatens to send me airborne. The snowsuit is militia gear, meant for guys twice my weight.

I fight my way off the sled. Gripping the seat back with one glove, I open the saddlebags and root around until I find the rope. Then I remove my gloves, and the moment I do, I can't feel my fingers and panic starts anew, every cold-weather warning about exposed skin racing back and—

As long as it's snowing, it's not actually that cold.

Dalton's voice rattles off statistics about northern temperatures and windchill and snowfall. I manage to tie the rope on the seat back. I stop to rub my hands briskly before double-checking the knot. Then, gloves on, I set out, hunched and hanging on to the rope, my oversized snowsuit snapping around me like a sail. A gust whips down from the treetops and the next thing I know, I'm flat on my back, staring into swirling white as I struggle to catch my breath.

Up, Butler. This isn't the time for snow angels.

I flash Dalton a mental middle finger and roll onto my stomach. Then I crawl, my head down against the gale.

They did not prepare me for this in police college.

Yeah, yeah. Move your ass.

I'm a homicide detective, not a tracking hound.

Well, then, maybe you shouldn't have tried tracking him.

I grumble and keep inching along as the rope plays out behind me. I spot an elongated dark shape ahead. Anders's snowmobile. I pick up my pace, and as if in answer, the gale picks up too, snow beating from every direction. I grit my teeth and keep going, focused on that dark shape even as snow piles on my visor. Finally I'm there and I reach out and—

Something grabs my hand. Grabs and yanks, and I fall with a yelp. I look up, ready to give Anders shit, but when I wipe my visor, all I see is the dark shape of his sled.

The wind dies, just for a second, and I hear a whining. The wind? I spot something whizzing past right in front of me, and it takes a moment to realize I'm seeing the snowmobile track running. The sled is on its side. The track is what "grabbed" my hand—I'd reached out and touched it.

Sled. On its side. Still running.

I struggle to my feet and yank open my visor, yelling, "Will!" as I stumble forward. I grab the nearest part of the sled that *isn't* the running track belt and fight that wind to get around the snowmobile. That's when I see the windshield. The broken windshield. And I see the tree that the sled almost skimmed past, the left side hitting just hard enough to stop the snowmobile dead, and Anders . . .

Anders did not stop.

There was a six foot two, brawny man riding that snowmobile, without any restraints, and when it hit the tree, the force flung him through that windshield into the endless white beyond.

TWO

I stumble forward, following the trajectory from the sled, trying to run, which only makes it worse. I'm staggering, and I can't see a damned thing, and then I pitch forward, tripping on what I think is a branch or a root, and I go down, sprawled over Anders's leg.

When I look again, all I see is that one dark spot, where I tripped over his leg. Otherwise, he's covered in snow. Buried in it.

I find him and feel my way up until I'm at his helmet. He's face-down, the helmet neck opening and vents snow-covered. I clear them fast and then check the pulse in his neck. It's beating strongly, which only means his heart is pumping. Only means he's alive.

I grew up in a family of doctors, and I know I shouldn't just flip Anders onto his back, but right now making sure he's breathing is the important thing. I still try to do this with him prone. I shift position, and my shoulder hits something hard. I reach out to feel a tree. Which he'd hit. Headfirst.

Shit, shit, shit!

I awkwardly tie the rope around my foot, so I don't lose my way. Then, equally awkwardly, I dig under his helmet, my gloves off, to unhook his chin strap—

Anders jumps as my ice-cold fingers touch his bare throat. He flails and then scrambles to sit up, sees me, and blinks.

"Hold still," I say as he removes his helmet. "You hit your head."

I take his chin in my hand, apologizing for my cold fingers, and check his pupils. They look normal. I examine his head next, which should be easy enough—he wears his hair buzz-cut short, as if he's still in the army—but dark hair over an equally dark scalp makes looking for blood and cuts a whole lot tougher. I don't feel any, though.

"You seem okay. I'm just worried about—"

"Intercranial injury. Yeah. Well, I'm conscious. I can recite the Pledge of Allegiance if you like."

"That would require me knowing the Pledge of Allegiance."

He chuckles. "Yeah. How about Hamlet's soliloquy." He runs through it.

"Impressive."

"Not really, considering I had to say it every night for two weeks in my junior year. Which was . . ." He looks up as he thinks. "June 1994. Proving I can access personal memories, too. How do my pupils look?"

"Same size and not dilated."

"I should be fine, then."

Anders was pre-med when he decided to serve his country. The US Army had started training him as a medic before they both realized he was better suited to military policing.

The wind has died down again, falling snow entombing us in white. I retrieve the first-aid kit and a flashlight from Anders's saddlebags. I shine the light up and down his snowsuit, looking for rips or tears, any sign of injury.

"How fast were you going?" I ask.

"I hit the brakes as soon as the snow blew in. Hit them too fast. Lost control. Skidded. Sudden stop, and I went flying. I wasn't going more than few miles an hour by then. Just enough to send me through the damn windshield."

He rubs the back of his neck. "I'm going to be sore as hell in the morning, but it wasn't a high-speed impact."

I nod. That's the biggest concern—he could have done serious damage to his spine.

He rolls his shoulders and moves his back, testing. "I should be good to go. How far are we from town?"

"About five clicks."

"Shit."

Under normal conditions, that's a couple hours' walk along the winding path. With a storm, it'll be several times that.

I check my watch. "We've got less than two hours of daylight left. If you call this daylight." I wave at the steady snowfall, the sky beyond already gray. "I'm going to say we collect our stuff from the saddlebags and find shelter for the night."

"Yeah. Eric'll be pissed, but it's not like he'll be flying home in this. With any luck, he won't be able to radio in either."

"We'll start out at daybreak. Which means about, what, ten in the morning?"

A wry smile. "Welcome to the north. Okay. Let's see if I can stand."

I take his hand, and he's shaking his head, mouth opening to tell me that helping him up isn't a wise idea. I place his hand on a tree instead—it can support his weight. He chuckles, and he's carefully rising when I say, "Down!" pushing him to the ground as I cover him, my gun drawn.

"What the—?"

I clap a hand over his mouth and gesture with my chin. There's a figure on the path, appearing from nowhere, just like the one I saw before the storm hit. When Anders sees, I move off him and he flips over, his gun out, gaze fixed on the figure.

The falling snow is a shimmering veil between us, blurring everything more than an arm's length away. I'm presuming the figure is a man, given the size, but I'm on my stomach, and it's at least twenty feet away, and all I can say for sure is it's standing on two legs.

"Shawn?" I call. With the wind dropped, my voice carries easily. The figure doesn't move. "Sutherland?"

"*Shawn!*" Anders snaps with the bark of a soldier, nothing like his usual laid-back tone. Every time I hear it, I jump. He gives a soft chuckle.

The figure doesn't move. I can't see a face, but I can tell he's wearing a snowsuit not unlike ours—a bulky one-piece, dark from head to toe. According to the guy who saw Sutherland run, he was dressed in hiking boots, jeans, a ski jacket, and Calgary Flames toque. I whisper this to Anders before I shout, "Jacob? Is that you?" Dalton's younger brother lives in these woods.

"Jacob?" I call again, and Anders stays quiet, knowing a shout from him would send Jacob running.

"Jacob?" I say. "If that's you, we've had an accident. We're fine, but we can't get back to town in this weather. We need to find shelter. Do you know of anyplace nearby?"

When he doesn't respond, I know it's not him. As shy as Jacob is, he knows I'm important to his brother, and he'd help me.

This might be a hostile. There are two kinds of former residents out here, residents who left to live in the forest. Some we call settlers, which is what Dalton's parents were, people who moved into these Yukon woods to live off the land. They stay out of our way, like Jacob does. Then there are the hostiles, those who went out there, snapped, and have become the most dangerous "animals" in these woods.

"Hey!" I call. "You know I'm talking to you. Maybe you can't see through this snow, but I can see enough to know you're not holding a gun on me. There are two trained on you, though. If you think we're easy prey, just raise your hand, and I'll be happy to demonstrate my marksmanship."

"That means she'll put a bullet through your damn shoulder," Anders calls, giving me a look that says I might need to take the diction down a notch. "That'll be the first bullet. Her warning shot. I don't give warning shots. I'm not good enough for that. Mine goes through your chest."

Which is bullshit, on both counts. He's a better marksman *and* more likely to aim a nonfatal shot. But he's also the big guy with the booming voice, which makes him a helluva lot more intimidating than me.

The figure takes a lumbering step forward. It's more of a shamble than a walk, and seeing that, an image flashes in my mind. Before I can speak, Anders whispers, "Are we sure that's a man, Case?"

No, we are not. The memory that flashed is of a walk with Dalton after a particularly rough day. There may also have been a bottle of tequila involved, and some hide-and-seek, the sun falling as we goofed off, me darting around a tree fall . . . and startling a grizzly pawing apart the dead timber for grubs.

I've faced armed gunmen and not been as terrified as I was when that beast reared up, all seven feet and seven hundred pounds of him. Now I look at this figure through the snow veil. It's a tall, broad shape on two legs. Dark from head to toe. Taking another lumbering step toward us.

I hear Dalton again, from that evening in the woods.

Don't move. Just stay where you are.

My first instinct is to shout, as it was back then. But I'd had the sense to whisper the idea to Dalton before I did.

It's not a black bear. Make a lot of noise, and you'll only antagonize it. Speak calmly and firmly so it realizes you are human.

I do that now, but I stay stock-still. Anders does the same, both of us straining to see, but the thing is only a dark shape against a quickly darkening backdrop.

Just don't move, Casey. You're fine. I've got my gun out. Perfect trajectory to the snout. That's where you want to hit if you have to shoot.

Dalton couldn't help turning even a stare-down with a grizzly into a teaching moment. But the reality was that he'd been calming me. A grizzly bear less than a meter away? No big deal. Let's take what we can from this. He'd also been calming himself, the strain clear in his voice. Now, remembering his words, I adjust the angle of my gun, whispering to Anders, "I'll go for the upper chest. You take the head. Just wait until we can see it. We have to be sure."

He nods, but my warning is more for me than him. Stay calm. Be certain before I pull the trigger. My gun isn't meant for shooting bears—I don't haul around a .45.

But you know what's even better than shooting? That canister in your pocket. Pull it out as slowly as you can—no sudden moves.

Gun in my right hand, my left slips into my pocket and removes a small can. Pepper spray.

The problem here is that we're lying on the ground. There's no way to spray it in the bear's eyes from this position. I'm not even sure Anders can fire a bullet at its face with enough accuracy.

As long as it's upright, you're good. It's unbalanced on two legs. It's just checking you out. The trouble comes if . . .

The shape drops to all fours, and beside me, Anders lets out a hiss. We're both trying to make out the bear's head, but its whole body has turned to a dark blob. Anders backs onto his haunches, gun in one hand, the other pushing himself to a crouch. I do the same. I know not to leap up. Again, if it was a black bear, that'd be the right move— show it you're bigger. But with a grizzly, we're not.

"I'll spray first," I whisper. We will give this bear a fighting chance. That's Dalton's rule. He never hesitates to kill an animal if it's a serious threat, but he won't if he has the option.

We're waiting for the bear to charge. That's why it dropped to all fours. It's taking longer than we expect and then it rises again.

Anders makes a soft growling sound that has me nodding in agreement. The beast is toying with us. While we don't exactly want to deal with a charging grizzly, neither of us is good with just waiting, unable to see enough to be sure it's a bear, not daring to shoot if it isn't, not even particularly wanting to shoot if it is.

The sun is dropping farther with every second. We need to get to shelter before nightfall, need to be sure Anders is okay after his collision, and it's not enough that we're trapped by a freak blizzard, we're stuck in a standoff with a damned grizzly.

"Just go," Anders mutters to the bear. "Nothing to see here. Run along home."

When the bear turns around and starts ambling off, I have to stifle a snicker at Anders's expression.

"Well, that was easy," he says.

"Bears." I shake my head. This was how my last grizzly stare-down had ended, too. When that bear showed no signs of charging, Dalton advised me to take slow steps back, and as soon as I was far enough away, the bear snorted and returned to digging for grubs, satisfied that I'd been suitably intimidated.

This bear is gone, but we stay crouched and watching until Anders's wince tells me his back didn't escape that collision uninjured.

"I'll stand guard," I say. "You empty the saddlebags."

He does. Then we head for my sled to do the same. The snowfall's still heavy enough that I'm grateful for the rope, guiding me through that endless white. As we near the spot where the bear stood, I spot something red under a layer of new snow. I brush the snow aside and uncover a woolen hat. A bright red, gold, and white one with a flaming C on the front.

Sutherland's Calgary Flames toque.

I remember the figure standing here, watching us, and then bending over.

Not a bear preparing to charge.

A man, placing this on the ground.

I turn over the hat in my hands, and as I do, something dark smears on my gray gloves. I lift one hand to my face for a better look, but even before I catch the smell, I know what it is.

Blood.

THREE

I clear the spot where the toque lay. More blood. I position the hat on my hands and can see the blood is on the back. Consistent with a blow from the rear. I shine my flashlight into the toque. There's hair. Light brown, like Sutherland's. What I'm really looking for, though, is brain matter. There's none of that. A blow hard enough to draw blood, but not crush the skull.

As I fold the toque, Anders points. He knows what I'll want next and has uncovered boot prints under a thin layer of snow, confirming we had indeed been looking at a man and not a bear.

Anders takes off one of his boots and lowers it next to the print. It's the same size.

"Eleven," he says, but I know that already—we've done this before. In Rockton, crime solving is decidedly low-tech.

I compare the tread and make mental notes for later.

There's no question of going after the guy. His footprints are already covered. Yes, that toque suggests something happened to Sutherland, but I won't risk our lives running pell-mell through a darkening forest in hopes of finding him. Shawn Sutherland brought this on himself. Yes, that's a cold assessment. It's also the same one Anders makes, without any discussion. This forest isn't a whole lot different from a war zone. If one of your comrades disappears on a mission, you'll move heaven and earth to find him. But if he goes AWOL? Screw him. He made his choice.

We'll look for Sutherland when it's light. And we'll come back again to search with Dalton, even if by then we'll be looking for a body. Right now, though, we need shelter, or there'll be *three* bodies lying frozen in the snow.

We continue on to my snowmobile. It has Dalton's saddlebags, removable, easily converted into a backpack. We stuff everything in, and Anders insists on carrying it while I lead.

"I can bench-press my own weight," I say. "I can carry that bag."

"But you're the one who knows where we're going," he says.

"Uh, no, I don't. Bear Skull Mountain is just to the north, where we might find a cave, but that's all I've got."

"I don't even know which direction is north."

I could point out that we have a compass, but Anders isn't just directionally challenged—put a compass in his hand, and it starts spinning, as if his very physiology foils him.

"North is to our right," I say.

He lifts his hands, checking for the L that indicates left. I sigh. He grins and hefts the bag as we head out.

I find the mountain. Anders finds the cave. He's a spelunker, which is not the hobby for a guy who can't tell his left from his right. As compensation, he draws amazing maps of cave systems, but Dalton still insists that he never go caving without a more directionally adept partner, which these days is often me.

Anders can look at a mountain and, in one sweep, find the most likely places for a cave entrance. By the time we reach the mountain, the snow is light enough that he's able to point out two spots. We pick the one with a natural pathway leading to it.

The first time I entered a cave was with Dalton, visiting a local recluse. I'd seen the small opening under a rock ledge and thought, *That's not a cave.* To me, a cave is the sort of place a bear might make a den, with a wide opening. Most entrances to a system, though, are more like this: a gap that doesn't look big enough for even me to squeeze through. As always, perception is deceiving, and Anders makes it inside without even snagging his snowsuit on the rocks.

It opens wider past the entrance, but it's still not a stereotypical cave. The first "room" is maybe six feet in diameter with a ceiling just high enough for Anders to sit without scraping his head.

Caves maintain a constant temperature year-round, so Anders can remove his snowsuit without fear of frostbite. Halfway through examining him, as sweat drips into my eyes, I strip out of mine, too.

His collar is bruising where the helmet slammed down, but the bone is intact, and he accepts only one of the two painkillers I offer.

We spread out the contents of my bag. In winter, Dalton assigns one of the militia guys to check the saddlebags daily to make sure they're fully stocked. It always seemed like overkill, but now I send him a silent apology as we find everything we need: flashlights, extra batteries, a full water canteen, meal bars, flares, emergency blankets, waterproof matches, and a first-aid kit.

"You want to see if we can get in farther?" Anders says when a stray gust sets me shivering.

"Good idea."

Exploring an uncharted cave takes time. Anders wiggles through one tight passage, only to have to back up when it narrows. After maybe half an hour, we find a decent cavern, tall enough to kneel in, long and wide enough to sleep in.

We kill time by talking. Anders is the chatty one, but with a friend, I can give as good as I get. When we're tired enough to sleep, I set my watch alarm for first light and stretch out on the blanket.

The moment quiet falls, I hear something deep in the cave.

It sounds like scraping. I picture a grizzly sharpening its claws on the wall, and I have no idea if they do that, but that's exactly what it sounds like. A rhythmic, long, and slow scratching.

Anders whispers, "You hear that?"

I nod and then realize that's pointless. Another thing about caves? Unless there are direct vents to the outside world, there's no light. Absolute darkness. I remember the first time Anders showed me that, admitting he snuck out sometimes to sit in the complete dark and complete silence. Alone with his thoughts. Alone with his darkness.

At the time, I hadn't understood. Oh, I understood the appeal—I felt it, that mix of incredible discomfort and incredible peace. Absolute dark and absolute clarity, reaching into the darkness inside me. But there seemed to be nothing dark in Anders. I know better now. It took some time for me to come to terms with his past. And then more time to realize that the person I'd befriended wasn't a mask he wore in Rockton. It's all him, the dark and the light.

I turn on my flashlight and tell him I do hear something, and he says, "Scratching?"

"Um-hmm."

"Bear?"

I mentally flick through my local critter list, courtesy of the naturalist who shares my bed. Around here, most predators will take shelter in a cave if that's what presents itself, especially in bad weather.

"Probably bear," I say.

"Black, right?"

"The blacks stay in the forest."

"Of course they do. Grizzlies. It's always grizzlies."

"Could be a mountain lion."

"I'll stick with grizzlies."

As for how a bear or mountain lion would get in—it's a cave system, which means there are bound to be bigger entrances. We're safe in here, though. This cavern only has two openings, and both were barely big enough for Anders.

"So we stay?" I ask, when he says we'll be safe.

"You okay with that?"

"I will be after I double-check the perimeter."

He chuckles. "Good idea."

He makes his way along the walls, ensuring we didn't miss an opening. I crawl to the back passage and push my head and shoulders through.

I call, "It's not big enough for a bear or cat. We're—"

A voice echoes through the passage. I hesitate, thinking it's my own. But the voice comes again, and it's definitely not mine.

I withdraw quickly and whisper, "Listen."

He pokes his head in. After a moment, he pulls back, swearing under his breath.

"I'm not imagining it, then," I say.

"No. Guess we're making a moonlight trek to Rockton after all."

He's right. Even if it's only settlers, we can't take a chance. Time to pack and go.

As I roll up my blankets, the voice comes again, and this time I catch "*Hello?*" It sounds like a woman.

I motion to Anders that I'm going to crawl farther along that passage. He nods. The voice is too far away to be an immediate danger.

I reach a turn and shimmy around it, which requires a move Petra calls "humping the wall." In other words, rolling onto my side and, well, making that particular motion to wriggle around a ninety-degree angle. The moment I turn the corner, I can distinguish words.

"Hello?" she calls. "I heard voices. Please, if you can hear me, *please,* I need . . ."

The rest trails off. I lie on the floor, listening and considering. Then I shimmy past that corner again and back all the way out.

"It's a woman," I say. "She heard us talking, and I think she's calling for help."

"Shit." Anders rubs a hand over his face.

"Have the hostiles ever lured people in like that? As a trap?"

"Not since I've been here. But there's always a first time."

I echo his curses.

"Either way," he says, "we might not even be able to get to her. I say we see how close we *can* get and assess the situation."

FOUR

First, Anders struggles to hump the curve. Then we hit a squeeze even I don't dare try. We back up and resume packing to leave, but I still hear that voice, and even if I can't make out the words, my imagination fills them in.

"There was a passage off the one we came in through," I say.

"You want to give it a try?"

"I'm a chump, right?"

He smiles. "Then we both are, 'cause I was just going to suggest we try to find another way before we give up."

"It's probably a trap."

"Yep."

"That path up the hillside . . ." I say. "At the time, I was crowing about our good luck, finding a natural path straight to the cave entrance. Now I'm thinking it was a little too lucky."

"Yep."

"So we try to get closer?"

"Yep."

We take the other passage. It's slow going. We catch the occasional sound of a voice, but it echoes too much to track. Each time we try a new route, we mark it so we don't get lost. We crawl around for at least an hour, and the woman has gone silent. I'm about to say we should just give up when I catch soft crying. Then I see light.

We flick our own light off fast. In front of me, Anders picks his way toward the crying until I see an opening ahead, and he stops so fast I bash into him. He drops onto his stomach so I can see over him. The passage ends in a cavern, and in that cavern, there's a coiled rope and an old wooden crate. The light, though, seems too dim to be coming from there.

Anders motions that he's going to check it out, and he crawls on his belly, knife in hand. Then he stops. At least a minute ticks by as I watch him leaning and peering before he inches through.

I creep along until I can see the cavern. It's no bigger than the first one we'd stopped in. There's the crate and the rope and . . . a hole in the floor. That's where the light is coming from—that hole. Anders is edging around it, trying to peer down without leaning over.

As I crawl through, I realize the rope is attached to an old metal hook, driven into the rock. It's knotted for scaling down the hole, but right now it's coiled at the top. Yet that soft crying comes from below. From inside the hole.

It's a trap. It has to be. Otherwise . . .

In the city, I'd think this was a hostage situation. But out here, that makes no sense.

If it's not a trap, then someone *is* trapped. A settler or a hostile, or even just an adventurer, too naive to realize she's a few months out of season for adventuring.

There. A logical explanation. Either a trap or an accident. As for that shiver up my spine, the voice whispering that isn't what this looks like? Clearly mistaken.

I motion to Anders that I'll take a closer look. I try to peer down that shaft without being seen, but there's no way to position myself in shadow—the light is right in the center of the hole. When I peek over the edge, she sees me. And I see her, and the second I do, I know my brain has made a mistake. My gut did not.

She wears what looks like men's clothing, oversized and ragged, and she's standing at the base of a drop at least fifteen feet straight down to a cavern no more than five feet in diameter, the bottom covered in furs. There's a crate, like the one up here. Hers has a candle burning on it. Nothing more. Just a woman and furs and a crate and a candle. Her long hair is matted, her face streaked with dirt, tear tracks running through it.

She could still be a hostile. This could be her home, and we've been lured here. But when she looks up and sees me, she bursts into fresh tears.

I've heard that expression before. *Bursts into tears.* I've never really seen it, though, like never I'd never seen a storm *strike* before today. This is exactly what it sounds like: a dam bursting, tears coming so fast they leap from her cheeks as she falls to her knees, face upturned to mine.

"Oh, God," she says. "Please be real. Tell me you're real."

Anders crawls to the edge. "Just hold on. We're going to get you out—" He stops. "Nicole?"

She's looking up, blinking as hard as she can. "Will?"

"Holy shit," he whispers. Then, "It's me, Nicole. Will Anders. Just hold on. We're going to get you out of there."

She grimaces, as if she's trying to smile. Then the tears come again, body-racking sobs of relief as she falls to the floor.

FIVE

As we lower the rope, Anders whispers to me, "Nicole Chavez. She disappeared last year in the fall. We found—We *thought* we found her body. We were sure of it. The clothing—"

He shakes his head. Time for that later. We've lowered the rope, and Nicole reaches for it but misses. Anders shines his light down and says, "Nicki?" and she looks up straight into the beam and yelps, hands going to her eyes.

"Sorry," he says and turns the flashlight aside. "There. Light's off. Just take hold of the rope. Good. You've got it. Now put your foot on the first knot . . ."

He coaches her, and she tries—damn it, she tries so hard, and every time I say, "Here, we'll come help," she says, "No, I've got this." But she doesn't have it. She's too weak.

I look at that hole, not even big enough to stretch out in, and I hear Anders's words

Disappeared last year in the fall.

My stomach heaves.

"Nicole?" I call. "Just wait. Will's coming down."

Anders shakes his head at me. "You should be the one."

"She knows you."

"But I'm probably going to need to haul her up."

"Right. Okay."

I climb down the rope. When I reach the bottom, I say, "I'm Casey Butler."

"Pleased to meet you, Casey Butler." She hiccups a laugh that turns into a sob and falls against me. I enfold her in a hug, and she's so thin I could have hauled her up that rope myself. I tell her it'll be all right, she's safe now, we found her. Then she pulls back suddenly.

"We need to go."

"It's okay. We're the only ones here."

She starts to shake, her fingers gripping my arms. "No, we need to go. Please. Quickly. Before he . . ."

She can't even finish, and I try to calm her, but she's too agitated. Help has finally arrived, and she needs to get out *now*.

I fix the rope around her waist and knot it as well as I can. Then I give Anders the go-ahead. He pulls her up, and I help by boosting her.

She's just beyond my reach when she convulses, saying, "No!" and I yell, "Will! Hold on!" and she's kicking, and I'm trying to grab her, telling Anders to lower her again. He gets her down, and the moment her feet touch the furs, she's scrambling for the crate, saying, "Sorry, sorry, sorry. I just—I need—" She reaches it and drops to her knees and pulls off the cover. Inside are two books with battered bindings. As she pulls one out, pages fall, and I see handwriting and realize they're journals. Filled journals.

"I'm sorry," she says as more pages fall. "I just need—I have to take them. Please."

"Of course," I say, and I gather the pages, and she says, "I know I should leave them. I can't. I'm sorry."

"It's okay. We have a bag."

She lets out a shuddering sigh and then, hugging the journals to her chest, she lets Anders pull her up.

When I climb out, Anders is examining Nicole, and she's staring at him, tears rolling silently down her cheeks.

"You look just like I remember," she says. "You're so . . ." She flushes and drops her gaze with an awkward laugh. "Sorry. I've been dreaming of someone rescuing me for so long that I can't help thinking this must be one of those dreams, because if I ever get rescued, it's going to be by a couple of miners who haven't seen a shower in weeks."

"Oh, I'm not nearly as clean as you think," Anders says. "You just can't *see* the dirt. And Casey scrubbed up before she climbed down to rescue you. She's such a prima donna."

Nicole laughs, a real one, and looks up at him. "I remember that about you. You were always funny and kind, and I wanted to get to know you better." Another flush. "Not like that. I just mean you seemed nice."

Her hands flutter on her lap, and as Anders examines her, he keeps teasing, that gentle way of his, but even as he does, he sneaks me looks that tell me this is not the woman he remembers. She's dangerously thin, and up close, I can see signs of malnutrition, her hair patchy, rashes on her skin.

"Can we leave now?" she says. "Please? I'm not hurt, and I'd really like to get out of here. I can make it. Just show me the way."

Anders and I look at each other. I say, "It's the middle of the night, and there's been a storm. We'll go if that's what you absolutely need, but it'll be much safer to wait until morning."

She starts to shake, and I hurry on. "If you need to get out of here, we completely understand. But you are safe. We have guns, and we're both police officers."

"Both?" She looks from me to Anders. "Oh. I know Will likes caving, so I thought you two were out doing that. I didn't realize it was night." Another twist of a smile. "Or winter."

"It is," I say. "We were—"

I think of what we were doing. Of that bloodied toque. Of the man in the path. I'm not telling her that, so I say, "We were on patrol when the storm hit, and it was late in the day, so we holed up here. The point is, we have supplies, and we're armed. We'll be fine until morning. One of us will stay awake, and we'll leave at the first *hint* of light. But if you need us to go now, we can do that."

She nibbles her lip and looks at Anders.

He nods. "Casey's right. You want to get out of here as fast as you can. We totally get that, and we'll do our best to make that happen. But it is safer in the daytime."

She squares her shoulders. "He won't come tonight. If he does . . ." She looks, not at Anders, but at me. "Will you shoot him?"

"With pleasure."

SIX

We return to the cavern where we left our things. Anders sits guard at the entrance while I unpack for Nicole. I hand her two energy bars, and she stares at them and says, "Chocolate?"

"Well, supposedly. It's not exactly Godiva."

Tears well again. "I used to turn up my nose at Godiva. Clients would buy us baskets, and I'd tell my co-workers that if you've had real Swiss chocolate, Godiva wasn't any better than that cheap stuff you get at Easter. Do you know how many times I dreamed of those baskets?" She opens a bar and inhales. "No fancy chocolate can touch this. Not today."

She takes a bite, and the sheer rapture on her face makes *my* eyes well.

"Were there Saskatoon berries in Rockton this year?" she asks. "I remember Tina's jam. On Brian's bread. That was heaven."

"Tina made jam," I say as I hand her the water pouch. "And Brian is still baking bread. You'll get all you want tomorrow."

"So Tina and Brian are still there," she says. "What about—" She stops herself. "I'm sorry. You need to sleep."

"Nah, Casey never sleeps," Anders says. "You want to know who's still in Rockton? Let's see, there's . . ."

———

Anders doesn't list everyone. There are nearly two hundred people. A few months ago, I couldn't have imagined a town that small. Now it feels huge, as I struggle to remember names. This is community policing, where every resident expects you to know their name. More importantly, I need to know them all because policing in Rockton isn't like law enforcement anywhere else in the world.

Rockton is supposed to be a place of refuge for those in need, those whose very lives depend on escaping the world—escaping an abuser, escaping false charges, escaping an impossible situation or a stupidly naive mistake. The town is financed by also admitting white-collar criminals who've amassed a fortune and are willing to pay very well to lie low until they're forgotten. Then there are those like me and Anders, on the run for something we did, something that *does* deserve retribution, but the council has decided our crimes aren't the types we're liable to re-commit and they are otherwise in need of our skills.

So that's Rockton. Or that's what it's supposed to be. There's a deeper ugly truth, the one that means they *really* need people like me and Anders. Modern Rockton, established as a haven by idealists in the sixties, is now run by investors who aren't content to take a cut of profit from white-collar crime. They accept massive admission fees from actual criminals, giving Dalton false stories, which leaves him trying to uncover the real criminals to protect the real victims.

These criminals are exactly what Anders and I discuss once Nicole is asleep. She's snoring softly, telling us she's definitely out, and we slip into the next cavern, our voices lowered as we talk. We discuss the possibility that Nicole's captor isn't a settler or a hostile but a monster much closer to home.

Before she fell asleep, I'd asked her, as carefully as I could, if she could tell us anything about her captor. She said that the whole time she'd been in there, he'd covered his face. She knew only he was undeniably male. As for how she knew that . . . I know the answer. But I wasn't making her say it.

"I want to say it's not possible he's from Rockton, but—" Will runs a hand over his hair. "Shit."

"It wouldn't be easy. Presumably he's coming up at least once a week, likely twice, with food and water. It'd be a long hike in bad weather, but if he left Rockton in the early evening and got back in time for his work shift in the morning, no one would be the wiser. It's not as if residents can't sneak past the patrols."

Rockton isn't a walled city. They've tried that—it only makes people rebel. Residents aren't prisoners. The rules against wandering into the forest are for their own good, and most people know enough to stay put.

"I'll need a list of everyone who has been in Rockton since before Nicole disappeared," I said. "I'll cross-reference it against those who've been caught out at night, but really, we're going to be looking at every able-bodied male." Which encompasses most of the population. Less than twenty-five percent is female, and you don't get into Rockton if you aren't "able-bodied"—we just don't have the resources.

"Anyone on Eric's list who might be good for it?" Anders asks.

I *wish* it was a list. It's a book filled with details he's gathered on every resident he knows or suspects is in Rockton under false pretenses. Most of it is suspicion, but in Rockton, it's guilty until proven innocent. It has to be.

We discuss a few possibilities. I don't tell Anders what Dalton suspects them of. Anders knows we have criminals in Rockton. Hell, technically, he's one of them. I'm one of them too, but I'm not in the book because Dalton alredy knew my crime when I arrived. I've convinced Dalton that Anders needs to know what we're dealing with, but he's never seen the book and doesn't want to.

What I tell Anders is names only, and he gives me his thoughts on each. Two of them arrived after Nicole disappeared. We discuss the others.

"Personally, I like Mathias for it," Anders says, leaning against the cave wall as we sit, side by side, blanket drawn over our legs.

"Mathias isn't on my list."

"He should be."

"He isn't even on *Eric's* list."

"He should be. Crazy butcher Frenchman should be on every list."

"I like Mathias."

"You like weird. Look at the company you keep."

I bop my head against his shoulder. "Don't be so hard on yourself."

"I meant Eric. I am the picture of normalcy and mental health."

There was a time pre-Dalton when Anders and I flirted with the idea of, well, flirting. On paper, he's perfect—gorgeous, funny, smart, sweet. Finding the deeper and darker parts should have made him even more perfect for me. Instead, it made him *too* good a fit. Even before that, it would have felt like flirting with a brother. So very wrong.

"Nicki doesn't suspect it's someone from Rockton, does she?" Anders says.

"She doesn't seem to, considering she's eager to get back there. Which might mean she somehow knows it's not a resident. But more likely, she just doesn't think it could be. Because that's not the kind of person we let in."

Anders shuts his eyes. "I liked Rockton a lot better when I thought I was the only exception."

"You're not that special. Sorry."

He smiles and squeezes my hand under the blanket. "So how are we going to handle this? Taking her back to the very place where her kidnapper might be waiting."

"Very, very carefully."

We crawl out of the cave at eight thirty the next morning. It looks like 2:00 A.M., not even a hint of gray to the east.

"It'll be light soon, right?" Nicole says. "I know it takes a while for the sun to come up, but it gets gray long before that." She manages a smile. "I'm used to gray."

As she says that, a realization hits, and I turn to Anders and point at my eyes. Nicole has been in candlelight for . . .

I keep avoiding the question of how long she's been down there. I cannot comprehend the idea of being in that hole for a year. Even thinking it sends my brain spiraling, unable to process. I hold on to a fantasy that she left Rockton and was living on her own, and her captivity was recent.

However long she's been down there, though, she cannot be out

here in full daylight. It would be like looking into an eclipse, permanently damaging her retinas.

We can work around that. Put on a helmet, the visor tinted. Blindfold her if we need to. But while I look at that darkness and know "gray" isn't coming anytime soon, I also know how much she wants to leave—*needs* to leave. If it were me, I'd run until I collapsed. Get away, as far as I could, as fast as I could.

We set out.

SEVEN

The compass leads us back to the path. We find the snowmobiles and dig them out. Then we discover a problem I feared.

"It's dead," I say as I try—again—to start Anders's snowmobile.

"Is that the technical term?" he asks.

I mouth an obscenity, and Nicole chuckles. Dalton has been teaching me basic mechanics, but there hasn't been time for more than having him explain while he fixes something.

As I head to open the hood, my foot kicks at the snow and the smell of fuel wafts up.

"I think the technical term is 'out of gas,'" Nicole says.

She's right. When the machine ended up on its side, it started leaking fuel through a cap that must not have been screwed on properly.

"We can siphon some from the other sled," Anders says.

"We don't have a hose," I say. "And I'm not sure lack of fuel is the only thing keeping her down. You had a collision and a wipeout. Take mine with Nicole. I'll follow the path on foot."

Anders shakes his head. "If you walk, we all—"

"No." I catch his eye and shoot a look toward Nicole. I made her sit while I examined the sled. She's winded, and there's no way she can walk to Rockton.

"Then you two take the snowmobile," Anders says.

I wave the compass. He gestures at the path. I wave the compass again. He sighs.

"I'm not even going to ask what all that means," Nicole says.

"Casey is reminding me I can't find my way out of a shopping mall. I'm pointing out that I have a path to follow. She's not buying it."

"If it was a straight line to Rockton . . . ," I say.

"Yeah, yeah. But I'm not leaving you out here. All three of us can ride. I've doubled up with Eric."

"It's a matter of space not weight," I say. "Stop arguing, and get on the damn sled. You'll be in Rockton within the hour. You can send Kenny back for me."

Nicole is shivering convulsively. She's wearing my snowsuit and Anders's sweater, but she's having trouble regulating her body temperature, a combination of semistarvation and living in a controlled temperate environment. As soon as she sees us looking, she straightens and says, "I'm fine. Just caught a chill. I can walk."

Anders looks at me. "You're taking the backpack and my snowsuit."

"Bag, yes. But that snowsuit? I'll be lucky if I don't face-plant every five paces, tripping over it. I'm fine."

"Nicki? We're going to switch suits, okay? Mine probably smells more than Casey's, but it's a sexy, manly smell."

I snort at that, but it gets a glimmer of a smile from Nicole. We find a sheltered spot, and he strips first, and we help her switch as fast as possible. After a few last words, they're on the sled and roaring to Rockton.

I start walking. It's five kilometers. I can do that in a couple of hours. I have to laugh at the thought. In the city, if someone told me it'd take me two hours to travel that far, I'd wonder if I had to get on all fours and crawl.

I'm not a runner—muscle damage means I can't do more than dash from point A to point B. But down south it wasn't unusual for me to walk this far to work in good weather, and I could clock it in under an hour easily. Walking in a snowy forest is a whole different thing. Which is why humans invented snowshoes, to emulate animals with oversized feet as an adaptation to winter travel. And, yes, that's another Dalton tidbit, squirreled away in my brain. He's been taking me snowshoeing, though I'm not sure if it's more for my education or his amusement.

I'm thinking of the last time we went out, a week ago, heading into the forest with the fixings for a bonfire and—

A twig cracks to my left.

I spin. Even as I do, I'm mentally rolling my eyes. It's going to take more than four months up here to stifle the city girl in me. I still need to pay attention. But the startle response—hand going to my gun—isn't required . . . unless I have a hankering for venison or rabbit.

A wash of gray to the east promises sunshine, but it's no more than a promise, and I need to shine my flashlight into the forest. I expect to hear more twig snapping as some curious woodland creature beats a hasty retreat.

Instead, I hear silence. An eerie one I'd have noticed earlier if I hadn't been amusing myself in pleasant-memory land.

Quiet's not good in a forest.

Um, it's always quiet in the forest.

I said that once, and Dalton made me stop talking, close my eyes, and identify five sounds, not unlike a drill sergeant making me drop and give him five. It'd been a lesson, too. I easily heard the sounds, even if I needed help identifying them. Quiet isn't silence. When the forest goes silent . . .

There's a predator nearby.

Right. *Me.*

But even as I reason that, I'm still shining that flashlight, and the hairs on my neck are still up. I'm just a human. Wildlife steers clear, but it doesn't stop what it's doing and wait for me to pass.

I consider. Then I take a step in the direction of the noise. I stop. Silence. Another step. Still silence. Another . . .

The wind whips past in a sudden gust, startling me again, and I get a face full of blowing snow. Then an eerie whine cuts through the trees and another blast of wind hits, driving icy pellets into my face.

That's why the forest went quiet. A fresh storm blowing up.

I turn back toward the path, mentally calculating how much farther I have to go—

A figure stands ten feet away. Wearing a snowsuit, a dark balaclava, and goggles. The first thing I process is that he's roughly Dalton's size. But then he moves, and that movement tells me it's not Dalton. The balaclava and goggles aren't something he would wear while combing the woods for me . . . and it's exactly what was wrong about that figure on the path yesterday, one reason we'd mistaken it for a bear, our eyes failing to see a human face.

I remember what Nicole said about never seeing her captor's face. How it'd always been covered.

I raise my gun. The figure dives into the undergrowth. I fire a warning shot, the sound echoing, some creature to my right barreling through the trees in escape.

I'm looking around, both hands on my gun, having dropped the flashlight when I aimed. It's on the ground behind me, lighting the scene, but a visual sweep shows nothing, and the wind swirls madly now, ice beating my face, stinging my eyes as I struggle to keep them open and—

I sense something behind me. I spin and see a metal bar on a collision course with my skull. I duck, and it glances off my ponytail. There's a grunt, and the man lunges, metal bar in flight, poised to strike me as soon as I run. I don't run. I wheel and kick.

It's a crappy kick. Guys on the force always expected me to be some kind of martial arts expert, given my Asian heritage. I do have a black belt . . . in aikido. Kicks aren't my thing.

But I kick now because it's the best move, and while my foot connects, there's not enough power—my messed-up leg again. It's enough to knock him off balance, though. I go in for the throw down, and I grab the arm holding the bar, but a whiteout gust slams us at that very moment, and I can't see what I'm grabbing for. I glimpse something dark, and my fingers close instead around the metal bar. It starts to slide, too smooth for a decent grip.

I twist, thrusting the bar up and getting under it. My motions match his rather than opposing them, and he gives another grunt of surprise. His grip loosens, and I wrench on the bar, and then it's mine, which is nice, but not really what I want.

I whip the bar as far away as I can. I don't go for my gun, though. The snow is swirling around us, and I can barely see a guy who isn't more than two feet away. I'm as likely to lose my weapon like he just lost his. So I keep the gun holstered and punch instead, an uppercut aiming for the highest point of the dark figure.

My fist connects with a *thwack*. The figure reels, and I swing again, a right jab this time. It's a glancing blow, my knuckles grazing his snowsuit as he dodges. And then he's gone.

He's retreated only a foot or two, but it's enough. He disappears behind the snow veil. I lunge, swinging, and I'm moving slow enough that I keep my balance when my fist strikes air. I do, however, hit a tree. Pain rips through my arm, and I keep moving, wheeling, to put that massive trunk at my back. I press up against it, fists raised, watching for movement through the swirling snow.

I wait. And then I wait some more.

There's not a damn thing else I can do. I can't see through the snow. I can't hear over the howl of the wind. I am frozen here, quite literally starting to freeze as snow pelts my face and melts and freezes again, and then it's not melting; it's coming so hard and fast that it's piling on me, and still I don't move.

I think of that hole where Nicole was held captive. It's all I can think of, and I know if I make the wrong choice here, that's where I'm going.

My brain screams that I'm an idiot for letting Anders leave. I'd been focused on protecting Nicole, keeping her out of that hole. The thought that I could end up there myself did not occur to me until now, as I stand against this tree, letting the snow pile over me as I blink to keep my eyes clear of snow because I do not dare shut them for a second.

EIGHT

I stand there as the snow piles up, and my muscles whine and then screech in complaint. Yet I do not, for one second, think, *Oh, I'm sure he's gone by now.* I can't take that chance.

So I stand there until distant gray on the horizon fulfills its promise. While I don't see the sun—the storm still rages, and its rays can't pierce the clouds—it becomes light enough for me to distinguish shapes, and that's all I need. To be sure there isn't a man in a snowsuit standing right there, waiting. I drop to a crouch and peer at the ground. Through the snow, I see the indentations of our fight. On the other side is his exit path. Those footprints haven't filled with snow, meaning he did stand there, waiting, as blind as me, ultimately deciding I'd slipped away.

I crawl through the woods. Part of that is staying close to the ground so I can follow those fast-filling footprints. Part is so, if I find him, I won't be an upright human shape, easy to spot.

The footsteps lead to an open area, and I lose them as the forest cover opens and the snow dumps down.

I straighten. I still can't make out more than the dark shapes of trees. The storm shows no sign of letting up, and now that I've lost my attacker, I need to hole up and wait for help. Anders will have reached Rockton by now. Once the storm subsides, they'll be out searching, and I need to be ready.

I head in the direction I'm certain will lead me to the path. But I'm moving slowly, and I can't judge distance, and it feels as if I've been walking forever, while at the same time, it feels as if I haven't slogged more than fifty feet. There's no sign of the path. I pull out the compass. The glass is completely fogged. I hold it at every angle and knock it against my leg, to no avail. I scan the forest, squinting, searching for at least the distant swell of mountains, but there's nothing.

I swing left, hoping to find the path I made and follow *it* to the main trail, but soon I know I've gone too far, my crawl-trail filled with snow. And that's when I drop. I just drop, my ass hitting the ground, snowmobile suit whispering against the snow. I sit there, and I stare out, and it's as if that hour of standing in place and holding myself so tight finally hits in a wave of complete mental and physical exhaustion.

I have no idea which way is north, south, east, west. The snow continues to fall, cold and wet, and I can't feel my face, can't feel my toes. Even my glove-covered fingers are numb.

I'm lost. In so many ways. Lost and defeated.

The north has won. The forest has won. I thought I could do this. Thought I could adapt, learn not to fight nature but work with it. That was Dalton's one overarching lesson. The forest isn't the enemy. It's not trying to kill you. It just doesn't particularly care if you live or die.

Well, I'm going to die. Maybe that should seem ironic—I escaped my attacker only to perish in the forest. But if I have to go, I'll take this. A simple and painless death. I can feel lethargy creeping over me, and I know it's hypothermia. Just get sleepy and drift off.

I swear I hear Dalton snort at that. Snort and shake his head and settle in to watch, not the least bit concerned because he knows that simple and painless is not the way I'll die. I'm just sulking.

Better hurry it up, Butler. You sit there much longer, you might get that easy death whether you want it or not.

I've spent twelve years refusing to feel sorry for myself. Whatever problems I faced in life, I brought them on myself. Self-recrimination instead of self-pity. Yet one is as pointless as the other. I'm learning to indulge in emotions I've kept tamped down so long—anger, outrage, grief, and yes, self-pity. So I wallow in poor-me for another minute. Then I push to my feet, ignoring the muscles that scream for me to stop, just sit down, take it easy, it's not like I'm going anywhere while this storm rages.

Which I'm not—going anywhere, that is. I won't waste my energy when I might very well end up walking *away* from Rockton. I have a plan, which I was formulating while sulking. I might have allowed myself those moments, but that doesn't mean I allowed them to be unproductive.

Step one? Send up a silent thank-you to Anders, for the god-awful scarf he gifted me with a few weeks ago.

Some Rockton residents earn extra credits with cottage industries, like knitting. And they're stuck with whatever materials they can convince Dalton to bring back. Dalton—whose idea of high fashion is blue jeans, T-shirts, and cowboy boots—sees nothing wrong with grabbing whatever is in the bargain bin at the textiles shop. When I complained about my secondhand smelly scarf, Anders outdid himself, buying one that was a truly flattering mix of neon green and bright orange.

He'd made me wear it yesterday by hiding every other option. Now I climb a tree, wrap the scarf between two limbs and leave the most perfect flag imaginable, one I can see even through the snow.

Under that tree, I've created a shelter from a downed limb, covered with one of the emergency blankets. It's little more than a windbreak, but it'll do. Then I hunker in my shelter, with my back to a tree, gun at the ready, waiting for rescue or attack, whichever comes first.

The storm hasn't abated, but it did die down while I built my shelter, as if cutting me some slack. Forty-five minutes pass. A few more hours of daylight remain, which means I have a decision to make— do I use those hours to find my way back?

The damn compass hasn't cleared. I still can't see the mountains. But my shelter isn't enough for night. Nor is it safe. *He's* out there. Possibly waiting for dark, now that I've sent up a flare to helpfully pinpoint my location.

I'll give it thirty minutes more. And as soon as I think that, I hear the now-familiar distant whine of the wind picking up.

"No. Hell, *no*."

I scramble out of the shelter and peer around. The snow is still falling, but it's light enough that I could have been walking. *Should* have been walking.

Walking where? In circles? Farther into the forest?

I'm listening to that wind, and I'm squinting up into the sky, as dark as twilight now, and I channel Dalton in an endless string of expletives to describe exactly how bad a decision it feels like. I watch the storm roll in, feeling like the idiot standing in a field, spotting a funnel cloud and thinking, *Huh, guess I should have gotten indoors when that siren started.*

But this *isn't* a funnel cloud. I can't get out of its path. Ultimately, I did make the right choice. It just feels passive, waiting for rescue instead of getting off my ass and wandering deeper into the forest to collapse of exhaustion and freeze to death.

I take out another flare and light it. I watch it soar into the air, and there's this little part of me that almost hopes it will bring the guy in the snowsuit, because at least then I can *do* something. He'll come, and I'll be waiting, and I'll shoot his ass and use his still-warm corpse to construct a new shelter until the storm passes.

It's an awesome plan. And proof, maybe, that I've been out here a little too long.

I light another flare.

The storm hits then. And hit it does, even if I had warning. There's the darkness and the whine of the wind and then it really is like that imaginary funnel cloud striking, an incredible gust of wind that knocks me clear off my feet. I have to fight to get back up, the storm raging already, as if, like me, it needed a break and is plenty pissed by that show of weakness, coming back full force. I'm grabbing saplings and dragging myself to my shelter, and with every inching step, I'm cursing myself for building the damn thing in a clearing. I reach it and—

Something hits me full in the face, and I scramble back, clawing. A bag. There's a plastic bag over my head, and I can't breathe, and I can't pull it away, and my gloves keep slipping on the plastic, and I'm panicking too much to take them off.

I manage to catch a fold in the plastic, and I yank and find myself holding the emergency blanket that formed my shelter. I fight my way back, but there's no way this blanket is staying on again. Not with this wind.

I need to take shelter, even if shelter is no more than hunkering down behind a fallen tree and wrapping the blanket around me.

I turn to leave the clearing, and he's there. The man in the snow-mobile suit. Standing less than a meter away. I can't run in snow. He's too close for me to pull my gun. I swing at him. It's all I can do. I drop the emergency blanket and swing. He grabs my arm in an aikido hold, but it's not quite right; his grasp is a little too high.

Lower, Eric. You can't get a proper fulcrum point there. All I have to do is . . .

I twist, as I did then, and I break free, and there's no thrill of victory, no follow-up swing. I know it's no coincidence that I'm thinking of Dalton. As I break away, I catch a glimpse of his face, lit with a fury that makes me suspect I'd be better off facing the guy in the snowmobile suit.

"Eric."

NINE

Dalton propels me from the clearing like I'm a five-year-old being marched from the mall after a tantrum. Four months ago, I'd have thrown him off and warned him against ever laying a hand on me again. Then I'd have added it to the list of "Things That Prove Sheriff Eric Dalton Is an Asshole."

That list included locking residents in the cell, tossing them into the horse trough, and marching them through town, arm behind their back. A power-drunk bully with a badge, who fancied himself some kind of Wild West sheriff, two seconds from ordering miscreants to a noon showdown in the town square.

That's what I used to think. Some residents still do. But most know better, and they understand that's how he maintains order in a town where he *is* the only law. Today, I see the sheen of sweat on his face, hear him still catching his breath, and I know he saw that flare and came running full speed from wherever he'd been searching. He's still in a panic, and anger is how he channels that. No "thank God I found you, Casey," but "Goddamn it, Butler, this was the fucking stupidest stunt you've pulled yet."

He marches me through the forest, not a glance at his surroundings, not a glance at his compass, knowing exactly where to find the sled. He strong-arms me onto the back of it and then takes the front and clicks the ignition. The engine roars to life . . . and the snow-mobile goes nowhere. He gives it gas. The tread spins.

I get words then. A string of expletives barely audible over the wind. He climbs off. I try to do the same, but his hand slams down on my shoulder, as if he might lose me again. I give him a look, lift his hand, and climb off the sled.

There's at least two feet of snow on the path. Heavy snow from the earlier downfall with a layer of lighter stuff from the new storm. Our combined weight is too much to make it through that.

He turns the sled around to use the tracks he made coming out. We climb on, but the treads just grind deeper into the snow.

Dalton hands me the keys and points. I hand them back. He glowers. I shake my head. He reaches out, as if to put my ass on that sled, whether I want to go or not.

"It's too slick," I say, shouting to be heard over the wind. "I'm not a good enough sled driver, and I'll ride right off the path and then we'll be back where we started, me stranded in the forest in a snowstorm."

He glares, knowing I'm playing into his fears. Then he looks up and down the path, hand shading his eyes.

"We need to find shelter," I say. "It'll be dark soon."

He gives me a no-shit look, but I'm still not getting conversation. If he opens his mouth, he'll want to ream me out for leaving Rock-ton against his orders, and that's hardly productive.

Dalton keeps looking around. Assessing and comparing data to the map in his head. He's got his hood pulled up, dark toque almost hiding his light hair. He normally wears it almost as short as Anders, but he's been letting it grow out for winter, when every bit of in-sulation helps. He's also letting his beard grow out from its usual can't-be-bothered-to-shave-every-day stubble. Yet he keeps it trimmed, assessing my reaction. That's the side of him most don't see, the side that isn't quite so fuck-you, is even a little bit self-conscious, making sure his lover likes what she sees.

There's plenty to like. Dalton isn't gorgeous. I'd say he's pleasant-looking if that didn't seem like damning with faint praise. But there's something to be said for pleasant, for a face that's easy to look at. Crow's-feet hint at the corners of his eyes despite the fact he's two months younger than me. Those wrinkles come from spending as much time as possible outside and not wearing sunscreen or sunglasses as often as he should. I bought a coconut-based sunscreen, and when he wore it, I may have commented on—and demonstrated—how good he smelled. I may also have let my gaze linger a little longer when he was wearing the Ray-Bans I bought. Yep, I'm playing him shamefully, but if it saves him from skin cancer, it's worth it.

Dalton finds the direction he wants and, still without a word, unloads his saddlebags. He'd grabbed mine from the clearing before hauling me off, and now he stuffs his supplies in. I don't offer to carry it, partly because I know he'll refuse but also because offering seems like begging for his attention, his forgiveness.

We hike back to the clearing, and he starts gathering snow. While I have no idea what he's doing, I say, "Tell me what I can do, Eric." He doesn't answer at first. Being pissy, though, isn't going to get this accomplished. Dark is falling fast, and we need shelter.

He motions for me to help him pile snow layering the soft and the hard until we've constructed a massive mound. Then we wait. Dalton doesn't say we're waiting. He rummages through his bag and finds water and bars and makes me eat and drink while he keeps checking the snow pile. Finally he starts hollowing it out.

It's dark by the time he's finished. I won't say he constructed an igloo. It's more rudimentary than that, and honestly, when I see what he expects us to do, I hesitate.

I remember when my parents caught me digging out a snow fort with a friend, and I was grounded for a week and forced to read the medical file on two kids who'd suffocated in a collapsed snow fort. That was life with my parents—when I tried something dangerous, I didn't get a lecture, I got coroner's reports. Which put me in good stead for being a homicide cop, however much they'd hate to think they helped me into a career so obviously beneath me.

My parents were . . . difficult. That's really all I can say. They died in a small plane crash a few years ago, so there's no point in being angry or bitter. If a part of me finds a small irony in the fact that they'd died doing the kind of thing they'd warned me off . . . Well, I don't dwell on it. I loved my parents in my way, and I think they loved me in theirs, but I'll never know for sure, and there's nothing I can do about that.

As for what Dalton wants me to do now, the question comes down to this: do I trust him? The answer is: unequivocally. When it comes to safety, he can be as paranoid as my parents, but he deals with that through education—not the kind that comes with coroner's photos but the kind that says, *If you're going to build a snow fort, here are the ways to make it safe.* When he sees me looking skeptically at his shelter, he finally does speak, grunting, "Roof's only a foot thick. It collapses? You can dig out."

We go inside, and he turns on the flashlight and motions for me to give him my hands. When he pulls off my gloves, I say, "They're fine, Eric. I can feel them," but he examines my fingers and then my toes, warming them with his body heat, careful not to rub. Then he checks my eyes, which feels like he's checking a horse, pulling up my lids and peering in without a word.

He hands me the water, and I drink some more. As our bodies heat up the insulated shelter, he pulls off his snowsuit. I do the same, and he sits there, cross-legged, ignoring the water pouch as I hold it out. Instead, he runs his hands over his face and through his hair and exhales as if he's been holding his breath all this time.

I crawl over to him, and when he looks up again, my face is right there. I say, "I'm sorry," and his hands are in my hair, lips on mine.

I lift my mouth to his, my lips soft, but it's not that kind of kiss. It's the kind that says he's been going out of his mind since he flew back into Rockton and found me lost in the woods, midstorm, with the psycho who captured Nicole.

Now I'm here, and I'm safe. He's built this shelter, and I'm finally safe.

So, no, it's not a quiet kiss, or a soft kiss. It's the kind that has me flat on my back in two seconds, and undressed in not much more. It's hunger and need, edged with residual terror and panic. And I feed right back into it, my own terror and panic of the last twenty-four hours finding release in rough kisses and rougher hands and finally, proper release, deep and shuddering as I collapse onto the snow-packed ground.

Dalton hovers over me, breathing hard, his eyes closed. I reach up and put my hands against his cheeks. When he opens his eyes, I say, "Hello."

He chuckles. "Missed that part, didn't I?"

"Kind of."

"I was worried."

"I know."

He rolls onto his back and flips me onto his chest.

"I hate worrying," he says. "Fucking hate it."

"But you're so good at it."

He pushes my hair back, and I feel the tremor in his fingers as he says, "You were gone, and the storm and then Will and Nicole and . . ." He swallows. "I was so fucking worried."

I bend down and kiss him. "I'm sorry. I really am. Sutherland bolted, and I wanted sex."

He sputters a laugh at that.

"Well, not with Sutherland, obviously," I say. "But I wasn't able to go to Dawson City with you this time, and it was a *long* three days."

"You missed my scintillating conversation."

"Nah, just the sex. So, see, the problem was this: if you came back and Sutherland was gone, we'd have had to go after him right away."

"It could have waited five minutes."

"It'd been three days, Sheriff. I wanted more than five minutes."

"Pretty sure you didn't just *get* more than five minutes."

"I made an exception for your mood. You owe me. I will collect. Anyway, the point is that I went after Sutherland so I could get sex when you came back."

"Not because you wanted to impress me? Have him waiting when I returned?"

"Mmm, yes. That, too. But the sex excuse is funnier." I stretch out on him. "I made an error in judgment. The weather was good when we left. Perfect, in fact. Now I know not to trust that. It literally changed in a heartbeat."

"It does that." He pulls one of the emergency blankets over us. "I overreacted, and *I'll* apologize for that. Obviously, I can't insist you stay in town. That's not right."

"As my lover, no. As my boss, you totally can. I distinguish between the two just fine, Eric."

"Are you telling me you wouldn't have done the same under your old boss?"

"I didn't want sex from my old boss," I say with a smile, but then add, "No, I would have still left. This was simply employer-employee insubordination. Feel free to punish me for it. As for *how* you punish me, you *can* blur the employer/lover line there."

A sudden laugh vibrates through him.

He shakes his head. "You punished yourself enough. Lesson learned. All I cared about was finding you. That storm blew up, and I started thinking of how big this forest is and how I might never—" He takes a deep breath. "Enough of that shit. You found Nicole."

"Right. Good change of subject." I start to roll off him, saying, "I'll let you get comfortable," and he says, "This *is* comfortable," pulling me back on and adjusting the blanket over us. "If you get cold, let me know," he says.

"Weirdly, despite being naked in an igloo, I'm not cold." I purse my lips. "Except maybe my toes. I'm putting on my socks." I do that, and I put his on him, too, which makes him smile, and then I stretch back out on his chest, cuddling into his body heat as I say, "So, about Nicole . . ."

"I fucked up. I—"

I press my fingers to his lips. "You thought she was dead, so you stopped looking for her. Will said you found a body. That's not fucking up, Eric. I know you're good at taking blame. Even better than me."

"Nah, I'm minor league. You're pro."

I stick out my tongue and then say, "Well, as a pro, let me speak from experience and stop you right there. Skip it and move on, Sheriff. Tell me about Nicole."

He does. Nicole Chavez came to Rockton eighteen months ago and hadn't made much of an impression. That's not a bad thing. She wasn't a troublemaker, kept to herself.

She disappeared last year. It was late October, and the weather seemed fine, not unlike yesterday, but Dalton could read the signs that told him a storm was brewing. Come morning, Nicole's roommate reported she'd been out all night.

That wasn't uncommon in Rockton. We're the Vegas of the north, with population stats that are clearly in the ladies' favor. If Nicole wanted overnight company, she'd have no problem finding it. But that wasn't normal for her, so Dalton set the militia checking door-to-door while he and Anders headed into the forest. When the storm hit, they hauled ass home. The moment it cleared, they went back out again.

After three days of searching, they gave up. The roommate admitted Nicole sometimes snuck past the town boundary, taking time for herself. Dalton figured she went walking and got lost. He kept looking, but he knew as time passed, the likelihood of finding her alive plummeted.

Come spring, they found a woman's badly scavenged and decayed body at the foot of Three Peaks Mountain. Her skull and spine showed signs of trauma, and our town doctor Beth had ruled that she'd been climbing, maybe searching for shelter from the storm, when she'd slipped and fallen. The corpse had matched Nicole's hair color and size, but with the condition too bad for a proper ID, Dalton would still never have leapt to the conclusion it *was* Nicole . . . if the body hadn't been wearing her clothing.

"Her captor set it up," I say. "He found a corpse—a settler or hostile. He might have even killed a woman who roughly matched Nicole. He staged it so you'd stop looking."

"And I fell for it."

"Yeah, you messed up. I mean, obviously, if a woman goes missing out here and you find a body matching hers and wearing her clothing, your first thought *should* be that she was kidnapped by a crazy person who staged her death."

When he hesitates, I roll my eyes. "That's sarcasm, Eric."

He says nothing.

"You're still going to blame yourself, aren't you?"

"So would you." He shifts, arm going under his head. "Tell me about finding her. I didn't get much from Will. He was filling me in as fast as he could while I got the sled going."

I tell him about the man in the snowsuit and about finding Sutherland's toque. I plan to hold off on my up-close-and-personal encounter with the guy today, but he says, "And you didn't see any sign of him after that?" and I won't lie. Not to him.

I admit that snowmobile-suit guy came after me, and with every word, Dalton tenses and by the time I finish, it's like I'm lying on a wooden plank. I decide it's time to crawl off and get my clothes.

"He's long gone," I say as I dress. "I was careful when I set off the flares. I knew I might draw him in. I was ready."

"I know that. I just . . ." He takes a deep breath. "Are you okay?"

"He didn't hurt me."

"I don't mean that, Casey. Are you . . . ?" He trails off and rubs his mouth. "Stupid question, right? You're going to tell me you're fine, even if I'm sure you're not."

I want to brush it off. *No, really, I am fine.* But I'm trying not to do that with Dalton. "It did freak me out. I kept thinking of Nicole and that hole and . . ." I inhale. "Can we talk about something else? Please?"

He nods, pulls on his jeans, and takes bars from the bag, saying, "Ran into an interesting guy in Dawson City."

I smile. "Shocking."

"No shit, huh." He roots in the bag and hands me another bar. "This particular guy caught my attention because he was running down the street stark naked, which, in summer, wouldn't be all that strange, but at this time of year, even for Dawson City, it seemed a little odd. So I went out to see what was going on and . . ."

TEN

Dalton and I have fallen asleep. We're half dressed—better for sharing body heat—and I'm curled up against him in my bra and jeans, one emergency blanket under us, two more on top, snowsuits stretched over as makeshift comforters.

It's a sound sleep, both of us exhausted, and when I do wake, it's only because Dalton insisted I drink most of the water to rehydrate and my bladder is screaming for mercy. I pull on my jacket, not bothering with my shirt. Boots next, and then I crawl from the shelter to find actual sunlight seeping through the trees. I look up toward it, smiling . . . and see a figure standing five feet away.

I'm still half asleep—and unarmed—and I scramble back into the shelter. Dalton's up, gun in hand as he dives past me through the exit and then . . . "Fuck."

"Sorry, Eric. Didn't mean to spook her."

The snow shelter muffles the voice, but I recognize the accent. Dalton has traces of it. I used to think it was regional. It isn't. It's the vocal tics of someone raised apart from the world, out here with his family.

"Good morning, Jacob," I call.

Dalton's younger brother mumbles something that might be a greeting. He reminds me of kids when I did school visits, those who weren't quite sure how to talk to a police officer and hedged their bets by mumbling, gazes fixed on their sneakers.

I let Dalton go first and then slip out behind him and hightail it off to privacy as he calls, "Not too far!"

When I come back, I resist the urge to play hostess. *Would you like anything, Jacob? How about an energy bar? Water? Do you want to come inside where it's warmer?* I'm reminded of when my friend Diana drove me crazy trying to win her ex-husband's parents' approval. That's what I do with Jacob. It's not that he disapproves of me. He's not sure what to make of me. And then there's the fact that I bear scars from our first encounter, when he'd been drugged and out of his mind.

I remember when he spotted one of the scars once as it was healing. I'd tried to make light by joking that it wouldn't be noticed, pulling up my sleeve to show that I had plenty more from the beating that nearly killed me twelve years ago. And yep, that joke went about as well as one might expect. Awkward humor isn't my style, but Jacob brings out that too, in my desperate need to make a connection with the guy who matters most to Dalton.

I say, "I'll go in and pack while you two talk," but Dalton shifts into my path, forcing me to stay.

Jacob looks like his brother, enough that the first time I saw him, there was a moment when I thought he was Dalton. The main difference is the shoulder-length hair, and at this time of year, he's sporting an impressive beard. When he looks in my direction, I'm reminded of the second biggest difference—the gaze that won't meet mine, ducking away, shy and uncertain.

Dalton says, "Jacob was just telling me he saw you out with Will. He went looking for you guys after the storm. He caught the flares yesterday, but by the time he got here, I had the shelter built. So he stood watch."

"You've been out here all night?"

Jacob shrugs and mumbles that it was no big deal, then says, "You okay? Eric says there was a guy."

"I'm fine, thanks. You didn't happen to see anyone, did you?"

He shakes his head.

"Walk back with us," Dalton says. "See if you and I can get that sled going. If not, I'd appreciate you accompanying us to Rockton, in case this guy shows up."

We don't get Dalton's sled going. So we walk. Jacob leaves us near Rockton. I know we're close even if we can't see the town. It's kept hidden by methods that grow increasingly high-tech and expensive, as the world outside becomes someplace where you can't hide a settlement, even in the Yukon. Disguised at both ground level and aerial, it uses everything from structural camouflage to technology that I suspect even the average reclusive billionaire can't get his hands on.

What I spot first are the hints I've learned to look for, and then there's a smile on my lips and a quickening of my steps, the sense most people would instantly recognize as the feeling of returning home. I've always felt the relief of closing my apartment door behind me, but this is more. It's a sense of place, of belonging, and it scares me a little. I've only been here four months. I don't know that Rockton *is* home, that it *can* be home, that I'll have that choice to make.

We're still on the outskirts when I spot Anders. We radioed ahead, and he's waiting with a thermos of coffee.

"Figured you'd want this at the first possible moment," he says, handing it to me.

"Best deputy ever." I pour a cup and then hand the thermos to Dalton, who drinks it straight. As I resume walking, I say to Anders, "Okay, what's up?"

"I brought you coffee. If you're complaining, then maybe you won't want these cookies Brian baked for you this morning." He pulls a wrapped bundle, still warm, from his pocket.

I take them. "Something's up, and it has nothing to do with why you're bringing gifts. You just do that because you're awesome."

"Can I get that in writing?"

"Casey's right," Dalton says. "Not about the awesome part. That depends on what condition my town's in. Something's up, and it's making me think I might not be awarding you that awesome certificate anytime soon."

"There's a certificate?"

"I have a stack of them," I say.

"That's because you're sleeping with him."

"Will," Dalton says, "what's going on?"

Anders makes a face. "I know the last thing you need is to be plunged into a fresh crisis—"

"Spit it out, Will," a voice says, and I glance up to see Isabel striding toward us.

Isabel Radcliffe. She's forty-five, dressed in a sealskin coat and mukluks, with no makeup or hair color—both being nonpriorities in Rockton—and she still manages to be one of the most glamorous women I've ever met.

Isabel is a former psychologist. Here she's the local bar owner. And brothel owner. I have issues with the latter, but we have become what one might call friends.

She continues, "If you think Eric and Casey are not perfectly capable of leaping from crisis to crisis, clearly your brain has frozen, soldier boy."

"I'm going to tell them," Anders says. "I'm just easing into it."

Her perfectly shaped brows arch. "I believe the situation is a little more urgent than that."

"We've been dealing with it for two hours. It can wait five more minutes. It's not life or . . ." He trails off as she shoots him another brow arch.

"One of you talk," Dalton says. "Now."

Isabel says. "Your deputy made the mistake of telling Nicole that we're sending her to Whitehorse the moment this weather clears."

"I was examining her," Anders says, "and explaining my lack of proper medical training, apologizing for it while promising we'll get her to a hospital as soon as possible. I was trying to be reassuring."

"Proving your serious lack of *mental* health training."

"Which is why the shrink should have been there, like I asked her."

Isabel looks at us. "It's both our faults. I had an incident at the bar, and I was delayed. I'd spoken to Nicole and knew she didn't want to leave Rockton. I failed to convey that to Will. We had a storm and a crisis and no sheriff." She lifts her hands. "And that's not parceling out blame. It's just fact."

"What's going on with Nicole?" I say. "Obviously she's upset about leaving. Is that what we're dealing with here?"

Anders and Isabel exchange a look.

"She's barricaded herself in the ice shed," Isabel says. "Threatening to kill herself if we don't promise she can stay."

ELEVEN

I make a beeline for the icehouse. Dalton's boots thump on the trod-
den snow behind me as he barks, "Out of her way!"

As I draw near the shed, I see a crouched figure resting against the
door, talking to Nicole.

I slow. "What's Diana doing there?"

"She volunteered as a nurse," Anders says. "And with the storm, we
could best afford to lose the least useful people."

Which described Diana. I've known her half my life. Been her best
friend for years. While I'd ostensibly come to Rockton because
mobbed-up Leo Saratori finally figured out who killed his grandson,
the truth is that I'd been ready to accept my punishment. I'd come
here to help Diana escape her abusive ex. Then I discovered she'd gotten back together with that ex and stolen a million bucks from her
employer, and *that* was why we were here.

"I vouched for her," Isabel says as she catches up. "I won't say therapy
is making Diana a better person, but the only serious danger she poses
is to herself. You'll notice she's the only volunteer at that door. And
she wasn't even the one who screwed up and let her escape."

As I approach, Diana rises. I can't read her expression. No more,
I'm sure, than she can read mine. We've moved beyond the stage
where she vows to destroy me. I'd say that's comforting, but Isabel's

right—Diana's only truly a danger to herself, as she always has been. Nowadays, when we can't avoid each other, we're like two stiff-legged dogs circling and waiting for the other to lunge. Neither ever lunges. Neither submits, either. We just circle.

"He found you," Diana says.

"Yep." I no longer feel the urge to add a smart-ass *sorry about your luck*. To give her credit, she also resists the urge to throw in a snarky comment about Dalton.

Her gaze flicks over me. Hoping to see some damage from two days in the wild? Or making sure I'm all right? I don't even try to guess, just nod at the door and say, "Is she talking to you?"

"No. It's a one-sided conversation. I can hear her in there, though, so she's okay."

I move closer to the door. "Nicole? It's Casey."

"You're back." Her voice drifts out. "Are you okay?"

"I'm fine. Thank you. But I'd really like to speak to you, and that'll be easier if I can come in. It'll just be me. Unless there's someone else you'd rather talk to. Eric's here, too."

"Can I talk from in here, please? I don't mean to be rude, but the moment I open that door, they're all coming in."

I don't mean to be rude.

I feel those words, like I felt the ones asking how *I* was. Her voice is trembling, but there's no rage there. It's as if she doesn't deserve rage. Or simply can't muster the strength for it.

"They wouldn't," I say, "but you don't know me well enough to be sure of that, so we'll talk through the door. Will says you want to stay in Rockton."

"I . . ." Silence. She tries again. "I . . ." Another pause. Then "You're right. This will be easier if I let you in. Can you do me a favor, though?"

"Name it."

"Tell the others to step back five paces and then say something, so I know they're not right outside the door."

They do as she asks. The door opens, and I slide through.

It's dark inside. The walls are several layers thick for insulation.

There's just a hint of light from under the door. I turn on my flashlight and look around. The building is almost empty. Ice has just started being brought in, kept in a pit scraped down to permafrost and covered with our version of hay for the horses.

The roof is low to minimize warm airflow, and even at not quite five two, I can't straighten. I start to sit on a hay bale, but Nicole motions for us to move farther in, where the others can't hear.

When we're seated, she pulls an ice pick from under her jacket. "I will do it," she says. "I just want to be clear on that. I know it'd be more convincing if I were freaking out, ranting and waving this around. But"—a wan smile—"I don't have the energy for that. I just want you to know I will."

"Okay."

She shifts on the hay bale. "I know how I'd do it. I spent a lot of time thinking of that. He made sure I didn't have anything to use, but I got creative. In my head, at least. I'd think of all the things he might bring and how I could use them to kill myself. Once, I even tried swallowing rocks, seeing if I could choke myself and reasoning that even if they passed, they might kill me in my digestive tract. It'd be a worse death than choking. It'd do, though. Anything would do."

She runs her fingers along the ice pick. "I tried dehydration. That seemed to be the one sure way to go. I remembered the sheriff giving lectures before we were allowed out on hikes. He said you can go without food for weeks, but you'll die of dehydration in days." She looks up with that twisted smile. "He made it seem so easy. When I tried, the guy just knocked me out and poured water into me. I didn't choke then either. Unfortunately. But this?" She lifts the ice pick. "This is a no-brainer, as my goddaughter used to say."

"You have a goddaughter? How old?"

She waves a finger. "Uh-uh. I know the suicide prevention tricks. Get me to talk, remind me of my life."

"Actually, I was just making conversation."

"Do you know what I used to dream of in that hole, Casey? Even more than killing myself?" She waves around us.

"The icehouse?"

A burst of a laugh. "No. Good one, though. Lighten the mood.

That's another trick. I dreamed of Rockton. Do you know why I'm here?"

"Eric filled me in. He maintains the privacy of residents unless I need to know more. I needed to know more."

Nicole was the daughter of a cartel accountant. When she was ten, the Feds got hold of her father. The cartel murdered his wife, the message being he still had two children, so he might want to keep his mouth shut. Instead, he took his family into witness protection, which would have worked out better if the cartel hadn't had a few DEA officers on its payroll.

After a couple of close calls, her father withdrew his family from the program, figuring he could hide them better himself. Then, when Nicole was twenty-four, living under an assumed name, the cartel sent photos of her to her father, who did the one thing he thought would finally solve the problem—took his own life. The cartel still pursued, believing her father had had money and information, which he'd bequeathed to his children. When Nicole was twenty-nine, they caught up with her older brother and killed him. A year later, she arrived in Rockton.

"I spent my life not knowing the meaning of *safe*," she says. "For me, safe was that honeymoon period after we moved—yet again. When I felt secure enough to sleep in a bed, not huddled in the closet, clutching a knife, being very quiet so my father wouldn't find me. Do you know what he'd do if he found me there? Cry. I don't think there's anything worse than seeing your father cry."

She shifts on the bale. "When I was little, my father *was* safety for me. Nothing bad could happen if he was there. And then that changed. He'd catch me in the closet, clutching my knife, and tears would roll down his cheeks, and he'd hug me, shaking, and all I could think was *He can't protect me.* He didn't protect my mother. He couldn't protect us. And if your dad can't? Well, then, no one can."

A pause before she continues. "For most of my life, safe was the six months after we ran. That's how long it'd take the cartel to find us. I'd spend one month waiting to see if they followed. Three months being able to sleep. Then I had to start worrying again, knowing they were coming. They were always coming."

She sets the pick on her lap. I don't let my gaze follow it, or she'll know I'm not letting it out of my sight. I just have to grab it—she lacks the strength to fight me. But I won't. She needs to talk. I need to hear what she has to say.

She continues, "When I came to Rockton, I spent the first week sleeping with my back to the wall, holding a stolen knife. I'd listen to people in the street, out having a drink, laughing, flirting, goofing around. Then, one night, there was a knock at the door. It was Petra and Will and a few others wanting to know if I'd like to come out for a drink. And I'm standing at the door, with a knife behind my back, saying no, I'm fine, thanks. Then, after they leave, Will comes back, and I'm clutching that knife, certain this is it—the others are gone, and I'm alone with this guy, and he's going to do something. He tells me I should keep my windows shut at night. The weather's been good, so people are leaving them open, and there's been a rash of break-ins. By ravens."

She chokes on a laugh. "*Ravens.* After he left, I cried. I was ashamed of myself, jumping to conclusions about him, but even more? I was ashamed of myself for being afraid. No one was going to find me here. I was safe. Safe." She looks me in the eye. "Do you know what that feels like? When you haven't felt it in so long?"

I think of all the years I spent waiting for Leo Saratori to find me. Not frightened. Just resigned. He would come, and I would die, and there was no point building a life for myself when it could end at any moment.

"Yes," I say. "I do."

She peers at me, and then nods. "So you understand." She stretches her legs, winces with the movement. "I know this town has problems. But that's what I dreamed of, in that hole. Coming back to Rockton."

Given what happened out here, I would expect Nicole be holed up threatening to take her life if we *didn't* get her back to civilization. And yet I do understand. What happened took place out there. She'd broken Rockton's rules and left the safety of the town. Her sanctuary had not betrayed her. All the months she'd been in that hole, she'd held Rockton as a talisman.

If only I could be there. If only I could get back there.
"I'll speak to Eric," I say.

"She needs medical care," Anders says after I explain the situation. "I am totally sympathetic to her situation, and I'll support her coming back after she's treated. But I am not a doctor."

"What exactly is wrong with her?" I ask. "Besides malnutrition."

He throws up his hands. "I have no idea. Because I'm *not* a doctor."

Diana has been hovering on the edges of the discussion, everyone too preoccupied to tell her to leave. She pipes in with "So what you're saying, basically, is that you don't want to be responsible if she's hurt worse than she seems."

He turns on her. "Yes, Diana. Exactly. You want to fault me for that? Go ahead. But I will not be responsible for missing something critical."

"I'm no expert either," she says. "But it seems to me there *isn't* anything critical. Not physically. What she needs most is care for this." She taps her head. "Which means keeping her calm and seeing what happens. It's not like we can ship her off to Whitehorse today anyway. You guys didn't find her comatose, barely alive. She's not at risk of dying tomorrow or the next day or even a month from now."

Isabel shoos Diana off, politely enough. Diana doesn't argue. She's past that, too, which is probably Isabel's influence, convincing her that being a pain in everyone's ass is only going to—again—hurt *her.*

Once she's gone, Isabel lowers her voice and says, "Diana has a point. Nicole's physical health is stable; her mental health is not."

Dalton rubs his chin. "Any other circumstance, I would send her south, but . . ."

"We're a self-sustaining community," I say. "With no room for anyone suffering serious physical or mental issues, but making her leave after what happened feels inhumane."

"Yeah," he says. "Thing is, though, I can bluster about the weather, tell the council it might be weeks before I can fly out again, but that's all. Nicole's going to want a guarantee, probably for the rest of her term. Which is not happening."

Residents are promised a two-year stay, and they cannot leave sooner than that. They may, however, stay up to five years, if they pull their weight and don't cause trouble.

"She'd settle for a year," I say.

"Also not happening. The council won't let her stay when it'll be months before she's in any shape to earn her keep."

"Leave this to me."

TWELVE

One person who hadn't been included in our "town meeting"? The actual town leader. I've never quite figured out what Val Zapata's official title is. I think no one uses it because that would legitimize her position, and really, she's nothing more than a mouthpiece for the council. We don't deliberately exclude Val. The first time I suggested she be consulted on a town matter, Dalton had snorted and told me to go ahead and invite her. I did. She refused. I've come to suspect she's hiding here, too, unable to leave, resenting Rockton and everyone in it for that.

We're sitting in Val's living room now. Her home is structurally the same as mine and Dalton's, like everyone with jobs important enough to earn their own house. They're comfortable little chalets, one and a half stories, wood, less than a thousand square feet, identical in their construction. There's not much room for architectural flair in Rockton. Inside, though, is where people make the house a home. Unless they're Val. Her place looks exactly like mine did when I moved in, without so much as a decorative pillow on the sofa.

We're on the radio with Phil, the faceless voice of the council. Others are there, tele-linked in, but we never hear them. I have this mental image of a half dozen middle-aged white dudes in suits, sitting in their offices, speakers on, cell phones in hand to text messages to Phil, their gazes fixed on stock exchange tickers. To them, Rockton is just another investment, not worthy of their undivided attention even as we discuss a tragedy I can barely comprehend.

It's just Val, Dalton, and me in that living room. I shouldn't be here—my position doesn't warrant it unless I'm summoned. But I think everyone has decided it's really better for me to act as Dalton's spokesperson. Val certainly prefers it. To her, I am an intelligent, educated, well-spoken professional, and Eric Dalton is a knuckle-dragging redneck barely literate enough to write his own name. If she's ever been in his house and seen the walls lined with books, she must have told herself they're insulation.

When I finish explaining the situation with Nicole, I'm not sure if the council is still awake. No one says a word.

"Obviously, we don't have the medical expertise for a proper—" I begin.

"We are well aware of your current medical situation," Phil says, boredom edged by the faintest note of exasperation, as if we were complaining about the lack of Internet. "You will get a doctor when a qualified one applies for sanctuary."

"I'm not complaining. I'm stating a fact related to this case. Will Anders has assessed Nicole and determined she's suffering from everything you'd expect from someone confined in a tiny cave. Malnutrition. Muscle deterioration. Visual impairment."

"Yes, yes, we know."

"No," Dalton cuts in, "you don't know. She was kept in a hole barely big enough to lie down in. Held captive by some psychopath. Raped—"

"We don't need the details, Sheriff."

"Yeah, you do, and I'm sorry if those fucking details mess up your fucking day, but—"

I cut him off with a look. He might be telling them everything I'd love to say, but it's not productive. We both know it's not.

"Nicole has been subjected to extreme trauma," I say. "The problem is that, as you might imagine, she's eager to leave Rockton and put this whole experience behind her. But we can't let that happen. She's in such a delicate mental state that no matter what precautions you take, Isabel strongly fears Nicole will find a way to tell her story to the world. That would endanger Rockton."

There's a noise at the other end of the phone, as if I finally have his attention.

"Nicole is a good person," I say. "She doesn't want to cause trouble. But she's in deep psychological pain, and she wants her captor caught. To her, that will mean bringing in the RCMP. What we need to do is prove that we can find him. We can punish him. That's all she wants. When she sees that we can do the job at least as well as the Mounties, she'll relax and heal and reach the point where she'll leave happy and stable."

"Can you do that?"

"Find her captor? I—"

"At this point, that's the lesser of our concerns."

Not the lesser of mine. Or anyone who actually has to live here. I bite my tongue, and Phil says, "I meant, can you convince her to stay?"

I take a moment, as if this requires deep consideration. "Isabel believes we can. We'll start by using the storm as an excuse. Then we'll show her that we're on the case, putting all of our efforts into tracking down her captor. I might even be able to convince her that once we find him, she would still be safer here. I think it's best to be upfront about timing. I would say it could be as much as a year, to be completely sure she's fine before she leaves. Does that work?"

"It does. Thank you, Detective. Your diligence and foresight in this matter is appreciated."

I'm back in the icehouse. When I tell Nicole that we've bought her a year, she breaks down in tears. When she recovers, I say that her stay is dependent on her health remaining stable, of course, and if she must leave, I'll do my best to let her return. She doesn't argue—it's obvious we're not going to risk her health. When I confess about the story I had to weave to buy her time, she finds a laugh for me.

"Clever," she says. "You know how to handle them. I'll be sure not to tell anyone that I wanted to stay."

"Thank you. Now, I'd like to keep you under guard for a while. We'll also assign a caretaker, until you're stronger."

"Can it be Diana?"

I hesitate. "We'll see if she can be spared. For now, let's get you home and resting. I'm going to have questions—a lot, I'm afraid. If you're up to it, I'd like to come by in a few hours. I know that doesn't give you much time to rest."

"You're trying to find the bastard who did this. I'm here for whatever you need."

I'm walking with Dalton through the perimeter woods, heading to my place. We're narrowing down local suspects. Yes, we know Nicole's captor might be a hostile or a settler. But presuming it's an outsider is the worst kind of gut-level community policing. The sad truth is that a crime like this is more likely to be committed by a local . . . and someone known to the victim.

"Sex offenders normally shoot to the top of the list," I say. "Except the ones we have aren't the right type. Not for anyone over the age of sixteen."

We have pedophiles rather than rapists, the council apparently declaring the former low-risk, given that we don't have kids here. I could see that as a sign that they care about the residents, but in reality, they're like actuaries, measuring risk and profit, and saddling us with habitual violent offenders of any type just isn't good business.

We're discussing the possibility that one of our pedophiles rechanneled his frustrated drives. If I were having this conversation with some of my co-workers down south, I'd get the a-perv-is-a-perv argument. When it comes to criminology, Dalton is the best-read partner I've had, and it really is an academic discussion—given the nature of pedophilia, what is the chance they'll substitute adult rape?

We're passing the station when Anders catches up. Dalton tells him we're heading to my place for a rest, Anders says, "What about . . . that thing?"

"It can wait," Dalton says.

I sigh. "Let me guess. Crisis number twenty-seven awaits? If someone took firewood and didn't pay again, it's Jen. And if it's not her, she's almost certainly done *something* to deserve a day on snow-shoveling duty, so I'm fine scapegoating her. There. Case solved."

"It's not a case," Anders says. "Eric brought you . . . a thing."

That has me perking up. "A present?"

"It can wait," Dalton says.

"Hell, no," I say. "I could very much use the distraction. Give me the thing. Now."

Anders snickers.

"Get your mind out of the gutter," I say. "If I was being dirty, I wouldn't use a grade-school euphemism."

"Hey, *your* mind went the same place."

"Only when you snickered like a schoolboy." I look at Dalton. "I want the thing. Whatever it is."

"You'll get it. Later. You need to rest and—"

"I need the thing."

"You heard her, boss. She needs the thing. Yeah, it's bad timing, but you have to give it to her sooner or later. You've offered it, and she's not going to rest until she gets it." He pauses. "This conversation isn't sounding any less dirty, is it?"

"It's just you," I say. "Go work. I get the feeling Eric will be a lot more comfortable giving me the thing without you around."

Anders laughs, shakes his head, and jogs off.

I look at Dalton. "In all seriousness. I'm fine with waiting."

"No, it's not something that should wait. It's just . . ." He rakes his hair back and sighs. "Fucking lousy timing. Shoulda waited until spring, but I got ahead of myself, and fuck, I probably shouldn't have gotten it at all without telling you."

"Eric? Babble never helps. Even profanity-laden babble. What you're saying is that you've bought me a gift and you're not sure it's appropriate."

"Yeah."

"Then give it to me now, or just tell me I'll get it later."

He resumes walking but changes direction, and soon we're at Petra's place. He raps on the door, and when she answers, he says, "I'm here to pick up that . . . thing."

She grins. "Ah, right. The thing." She leans against the doorpost, blocking our view inside. "Sorry, Sheriff. I've misplaced the thing. You'll have to come by another time. Maybe next week? I'll have found it by then."

He shakes his head.

"Fine." She looks at me. "I'm keeping your thing, Casey. You wouldn't want it, so I'm doing you a favor."

There's a noise from in her apartment. It sounds like . . .

"Is . . . that a whine?" I say.

"Wine? Not here. Try the Red Lion."

She starts to close the door. Dalton catches it and ushers me through.

"Private property, Sheriff," Petra says.

"It's Rockton," I say. "There is no private property." I try to brush past her, following the faint sound of whining, but Dalton catches my arm and says, "Remember you said we should consider getting animals again? Working animals."

My smile grows to a grin.

"A *working* animal," he says. "Not a pet. We can't have pets here. But she needs a master, someone to train her and live with her so—"

I'm already past him and down the hall. The whining comes from Petra's bedroom. When I throw open the door, a blur of black fur zooms over and stops short when it realizes I'm a stranger.

I see it, and I let out the kind of noise I've never let out in my life, the kind girls in school would make over new shoes or a hot guy, and I'd roll my eyes and think, *Seriously?*

I make that noise.

Behind me, Petra's laughing, and I'm dimly aware that I'm totally ruining my rep, but I don't care. I'm on the floor with this giant mop of black fur in vaguely puppy shape. It's on my lap, wriggling and whining as if it doesn't care that it's never seen me before in its life—I am its new best friend.

It's a black puppy with a streak of white on one ear, and as it licks my face, I spot a black tongue. I stop, my arms still around it, and I turn to Dalton, and I can barely get the words out. "It's a—You got me a—"

That's all I can manage, and I swear I'm going to cry. I never cry. Certainly not happy tears. I've never even been sure those are a real thing, but that's what wells up now.

When I was young, my parents once had to attend a conference just after they'd fired our latest nanny for letting me go inside the corner store alone. My sister went with them to the conference—she was ten and knew how to comport herself in public, a skill I would never master. I stayed with my aunt, whom I barely knew.

My father had been estranged from his family ever since he decided to marry "that Vietnamese girl"—my mother was half Chinese, half Filipino. There'd apparently been some reconciliation after my sister was born. Then I came along and, well, the difference between me and April is that she can pass for white and I cannot, and I guess something was said, and the upshot is that I don't remember ever meeting my paternal grandparents.

But my father's younger sister wanted a place in our lives. So, with a laundry list of rules, my parents let me stay with her while they attended the conference. My aunt promptly threw out their list—at the top of which was "no dogs"—and introduced me to her boyfriend . . . and his Newfoundland.

My six-year-old self fell in love with that dog the way it had never fallen in love with a person. And she loved me back with the kind of unconditional love only an animal can truly give. When my parents came to get me, I was reading in the backyard, using the dog as a pillow. They saw me lying on a dog bigger than me, and . . .

I never saw my aunt again. Instead, I got a solid week of dog-attack photos. I didn't care. In years to come, I might forget weekends with men who passed through my life, but I never forgot the one I spent with that dog. I told Dalton about it when the subject of pets arose in conversation, and now I see this puppy's black tongue, and . . .

"You bought me a Newfoundland puppy."

Petra murmurs something about needing to run an errand. Then she's gone, and Dalton's just standing there, this look on his face that

I can't quite read. I adjust to sit, with the puppy on my lap, and I say, "I know it's a working dog. I just . . . It's a surprise."

"A good surprise?"

He asks that in all honesty, and I have to laugh, shaking my head. I grin at him, and he stops moving, and there's that look again, the one I can't decipher.

"Eric?" I say.

He snaps out of it. "No. Right. Yeah. Good surprise. Okay." He hunkers beside me, and the puppy launches itself at him, going crazy now. It jumps on him and licks and whines like it'd been abandoned for weeks and the only familiar face it's ever known has finally returned. Then it piddles. Right on his boots. And he sighs. Just gives a deep sigh.

I smile up at him. "Not the first time it's done that, I'm guessing."

"Nope." He rises, and the puppy goes even crazier, as if about to be abandoned again. Another sigh, and he scoops it up under one arm and takes it to the kitchen, returning with a rag.

"It's a she," he says. "I did some research. With this breed, females are a better choice. They're mastiffs, which means they're stubborn, and a male would get bigger than you someday. I figured that a war of wills wouldn't go well—for you or the dog."

He cleans the mess as the puppy returns to me, satisfied Dalton isn't leaving.

He continues, "The ideal breed would have been a hound for tracking. But hounds aren't northern dogs. She is. They're supposed to have a good nose, and they *are* used for search and rescue. She'll be big, too, which is good for protection. So a Newfoundland isn't a perfect fit, but hell, no dog's going to be perfect for what we want, and you like them. . . . You do like them, right?"

I grin my answer. Then I tug him down to the floor, and we play with the puppy until it's time to return to real life.

THIRTEEN

When Dalton got me a puppy, he obviously didn't expect us to be launching a major case. There's no way I can have a puppy at my heels as I investigate Nicole's kidnapping. Petra promptly volunteers for dog-sitting duty, day or night. She only works part-time at the general store. Otherwise, she's parlayed her skills as a comic book artist into one of those local "cottage industries." I don't know how much time she'll get for drawing with a puppy around, but she insists.

By the time we leave the dog with Petra, I need to interview Nicole. We walk over, and Dalton stands guard out front. Nicole is upstairs, so I wait in the living room and try not to see Beth in her former home. She's still here. She's in the faint smell of the hospital-strength antiseptic. In a lopsided dream catcher on the front window. In the laugh I hear as she tells me about making the dream catcher, her one and only attempt to be artsy.

She's there too in a still-open novel on the coffee table, where she must have been reading on the futon that used to be Abbygail's bed. Reading and maybe thinking of Abbygail.

I look at this room, and I think of our first lunch here, after Anders set us up on a "date," convincing the shy local doctor to ask the new girl to lunch. I think of the friendship that came of that lunch, quiet and warm and easy, so welcome after the roller coaster with Diana. I think of where it began . . . and how it ended.

When Dalton dropped me at the door, he asked if I was okay coming in here. I shrugged it off. And I was honest in that—standing outside, I felt nothing, my mind consumed with the task of interviewing Nicole.

Then I came into this room, and the very smell of it brought those memories crashing back, the reminder that we haven't been able to clear her house, haven't quite dealt with what she did. Like I haven't dealt with what she did to me. Pick that up, put it in the closet, shut the door, and face the situation at hand.

Last year Nicole Chavez snuck out of Rockton on a warm fall evening, just before dusk. There was a nearby berry patch not quite tapped out, and she wanted berries. That's it. The patch wasn't more than a hundred paces from the town limit, and it was still light, and she was close enough to shout if she happened upon a bear or a hostile. As rebellions go, it was no worse than me as a child, petting the neighbor's dog through the fence.

Nicole snuck from town to gather berries. She found the bush, crouched to pick, and . . .

And that's all she remembers. She woke in that cave, the back of her head throbbing, her brain groggy from the drugs that kept her sedated when the blow wore off.

She woke in that hole. And that's where she stayed.

For over a year.

Fifteen months.

Sixty-three weeks.

Four hundred and forty days.

I knew she must have been taken straight to that cave, yet I kept telling myself that isn't necessarily true. She could have been held captive elsewhere and moved to the cave. Maybe she tried to escape and was relocated. Maybe she was only in the hole for a month, two tops.

It's not as if I imagine her happily shacked up in a cabin with a settler. Her body tells another story. So why does this hit so hard, the confirmation that she's been in that hole the entire time? Because I cannot wrap my head around it. Some primal part of my brain runs gibbering from the thought. If it happened to me, I would go mad. I would literally go mad. I'd claw the flesh from my body, like a wild beast in a trap. Rend my flesh. Rip out my hair. Batter myself bloody on those rocks. My brain could not handle it. This is a test I would fail, and that terrifies me.

But this isn't about me. It is about the woman who did survive.

Nicole and I sit in the living room. The blinds are drawn. They're blackout blinds to help in summer when the sun shines past midnight. She's curled up in a chair. A pair of sunglasses rests by her side—the darkest anyone could find—and as we talk, she periodically puts them on, against the light seeping around the blinds. But then she'll take them off again as she tries to adjust.

There's food everywhere—baked goods and dried fruit and whatever else people have. When tragedy strikes, this town shines brightest. Sometimes a little too bright, people tripping over themselves with "what can I do?" to the point of interference.

As we talk, I catch the occasional murmur outside the front door, and I realize Dalton is really standing guard against those coming by with whatever they think Nicole might need. Food, drink, a wool blanket, a novel, a sweater. Of course, they're hoping to catch a glimpse of her, too, or overhear a tidbit of fresh gossip. That's human nature. The moment they see Dalton, they'll lay their offering on the pile before scurrying off.

Back to Nicole. As she said before, she can't tell me what her captor looked like. He wore a balaclava. When he arrived, her candle went out. That was the rule. He communicated little more than those rules, which meant she often wouldn't hear his voice, and even when he gave her an order, he kept his voice pitched low, gruff, as if he'd rather say nothing.

He *would* leave a candle burning up top. But all she can tell me is that he's light-skinned, not thin, not short.

He is the man in the snowsuit. The general size fits. The balaclava fits. The blow to the back of the head fits. The region where we found him also fits.

What does that mean for Sutherland? I haven't forgotten the

bloodied toque in the snow. For now, the snow keeps falling, and there's no way to search for him without endangering our militia.

When I ask Nicole if she can give anything more, she says, "He watched me. I'd hear him come into the cavern. I'd see the light. I don't know how long he'd sit up there. My watch only worked for a week or so. It's charged by light, which always seemed terribly convenient . . . until you're in a cave."

She smiles, and she wants me to smile back. *See? It's not so bad—I can joke about it.* Joking to make *me* feel better, as I sit here struggling to stay composed, and when she smiles, all I can do is nod.

If I tried to smile, I'm not sure what would come out: a twist of pain or rage. Both impulses war. I want to curl up in a ball of sympathetic agony, and I want to march into the forest, find whoever did this, and—

I look across the room, at that lopsided dream catcher.

Is that what you felt, Beth?

There's no question about me. I have that darkness inside. Absolute darkness. Yet it's not a caged lion, waiting for the gate to be left unlatched. It's just there, in case I need it.

Nicole continues, "When the watch worked, though, I timed him once. He stayed up there an hour, watching, and then he came down, and . . ." She looks at me. "Do you need to know about . . . that?"

"No."

She nods. "Thank you. I know I might have to discuss it if there's a trial. But what can you say besides 'it happened'? I was in no position to refuse. I learned—fast—not to refuse. Just get it over with."

She goes quiet and then says, "I got pregnant. He knew my schedule—he had to bring stuff obviously, this bag of rags I'd keep until my period was done. When I didn't need them, he realized I was pregnant. He hit me until I wasn't. I remember lying there, bleeding, hoping he'd ruptured something critical, that this was the end. But it wasn't. Just the end of *that*. Afterward, he started pulling out." She shakes her head. "Sorry. I said I wouldn't give details."

"You can *give* me any details you want. You just don't need to."

She nods.

We talk for a little more after that, until she's flagging, and I make some excuse to go. As I leave, she says, "I'll be okay."

"I know."

And I think she will be. I'm just not sure I could have said the same if I was the one in a hole for over a year.

Fifteen months.

Sixty-three weeks.

Four hundred and forty days.

FOURTEEN

Dalton and I walk to the office. We don't sit inside. Dalton will, for my sake, but as long as the temperature isn't twenty below, he's happier out of doors. We stop at the bakery to grab coffee and then as we detour through the station, we find a bottle of Irish whiskey beside the machine—a gift from Isabel. Dalton splashes some into our coffees. I carry those. He grabs caribou skin blankets.

We sit on the back deck, drinking our coffee, my hands wrapped around my mug for warmth. It's late afternoon, and the sun has fallen behind the trees, darkness stretching with each passing moment.

"We still need to search for Sutherland," I say. "I know that's probably pointless. The storm will have erased his tracks, and I suspect we're looking for a body. But if it's the same perpetrator, which it certainly seems to be, there's a chance he's holding Sutherland captive."

"You think so?" Dalton takes another swig of his coffee. "From what I've read, with this kind of thing, there's not much point in taking a man."

"Playing devil's advocate, I'd point out that a man can, biologically, serve the same purpose, and also that this is more an issue of control. He watched her. For hours. But, yes, I think it's far more likely this guy killed Sutherland as a trespasser. We still need to look. I also have to go back to that cave, to see what clues I can find."

"First light," he says. "We'll take the horses."

I lean against the wall and sip my spiked coffee. "You haven't said if there's anyone in your book you really like for this."

"Neither have you. Which means there's no one either of us really likes."

"Hmm."

"We've got people who've committed murder, but this guy kept Nicole alive. And the folks we've got mostly killed one person for a reason. Whoever did this enjoyed it. No other purpose. If we have anyone here fitting that description, I don't know it."

"Except, one could argue, the pedophiles."

"Of which we have three, and two don't fit the description. One's a woman. And Lang's too skinny."

"Then that's the only way to narrow the field. Focus on those who could have done it. Right time period. Right gender. Right skin color. Right basic physical size."

"Forty possibilities."

"You're fast."

He looks over. "You gonna pretend you didn't already work it out?"

"No, I was just giving you props."

His brows knit.

"Props. Proper respect. Yes, I have been working it through. My calculations, though, give me forty-seven."

Now his brows shoot up. "You fail math, Butler?"

"Remember that for skin tone she was looking at him in dim light and in contrast to *her*. All she can say is that his skin is lighter. That doesn't make him Caucasian."

"Fuck."

"Yep."

After a moment, he says, "What's your take on Nicole? She seems to be coping well."

"Maybe too well. It might be shock. Which worries me."

"Agreed. We've got Isabel keeping an eye on her, but Isabel did therapy for people having normal problems. Not *that*."

"So you'd like a second opinion?" Isabel's voice precedes her as she walks around the building.

"Yeah, under the circumstances, I'd like a second opinion."

"Then get one. You've got a better source than me here. Someone who can assess both Nicole's physical and mental health. You just need to kick his ass hard enough."

"I wish I could," Dalton grumbles. "If I threaten to put him on shoveling duty for a week, he'll just take off his damn butcher's apron, pull on his parka, and ask me to point him in the right direction. Only person who can get him to do it?" He looks at me.

I sigh. "I'll go talk to Mathias."

FIFTEEN

I push open the door to the butcher's shop. From the back room comes the ominous sound of a saw skritch-scraping through bone. The smell of blood hangs so heavy I can taste it.

Most residents will stop right here and call a tentative "hello?" If they don't get an answer, they'll leave.

I walk around the counter and poke my head into the back room. "Mathias? *Avez-vous une minute?*"

The saw stops, and his voice drifts out, "*Pour vous, oui.*"

Most Canadians my age have taken French. Years of it, the end result of which is that we can travel to Paris and ask for directions *en français* and even understand the response if it isn't too long. Asking for those directions in Montreal is trickier, because what we've learned isn't Quebecois.

I spent a few years working in Ottawa, which vastly improved both my French and my dialect, and I shamelessly "practice" it on Mathias, knowing that while his English is perfect, he enjoys the chance to communicate in his native language. We do have two other Francophones in Rockton, but Mathias doesn't like them. And if Mathias doesn't like you? Don't talk to him. Just don't.

He comes out of the back room, wiping his bloodied hands on his even bloodier apron. At fifty-three, he's one of the oldest residents in

Rockton. If there's a stereotype of a butcher, he doesn't fit it. He looks like a young Ian McKellen, a little less dapper and a little more . . . I won't say dangerous, but there's a glint in his eyes like he's sizing up everyone around him and finding them terribly amusing.

He scrubs up at the sink and takes off his apron. I think the only people he bothers removing it for are me, Dalton, and Isabel, and it's not so much respect as the realization his bloody-butcher routine isn't nearly as much fun with people who aren't fazed by it.

When his hands are dry, he disappears into the back and returns with a plate. On it are three slices of sausage. Without a word, he lays it in front of me. I try each slice, then point at the first piece and ask, in French, "What wood did you use to smoke that one?"

"Birch."

"It's better than the aspen." I point to the second piece. "I like the heat in that one, though. Did I taste anise?"

"Correct. Eric brought me new spices."

"Nice. My favorite, though, is . . ." I pick up the rest of the third and eat it. "You had me at cardamom." I say the spice name in English, which makes him chuckle and say, "*Cardamome.*"

"Close enough."

I get a waggled finger for that, and he disappears, and returns with a package of the cardamom sausage for me.

"You recognize the spice," he says. "But the meat?"

I chew slower. "Is that . . . pork? Wait, is this . . ."

"Your wild boar."

There aren't actually wild boar in the Yukon. Many years ago, though, the town experimented with pigs, importing a Hungarian breed that crossed European boar with domestic pigs and created a winter-hardy pig with a wool-like coat. Great idea. Until they escaped. They've been living and breeding in this part of the woods for generations. A deep-woods hiker once got a picture of one. It was dismissed as a Photoshopped fake. Clearly there are no wooly-coated wild pigs in the Yukon. For imaginary beasts, though, they're delicious.

"So Rockton gets bacon for breakfast this week?" I ask as I eat more sausage.

"*You* get bacon. And cardamom sausage. Eric, too, if he asks nicely. You must make him ask nicely. Which means you will probably get all the bacon."

"Oh, I can get him to ask nicely."

Mathias laughs. "I am sure you can. People keep waiting for Eric to be more pleasant, now that he has a girl. The only difference? He scowls a little less when he throws people in his cell."

I shake my head and push the empty plate aside. "While I appreciate the gesture, I can't take all the bacon. That's not fair."

"Fair is for fools. It is your first pig. It is yours. No argument." He takes the plate. "And it is a bribe, as well. Take the sausage and the bacon, and do not ask me what you came here to ask me."

"Then you need to keep the meat, Mathias. I have to ask."

"No, you do not. I know the question, and I will answer it with a resounding no. Good enough?"

I sigh and lean on the counter. I say nothing. I just wait.

"You are going to tell me that you need me," he says. "You are going to tell me the sad story of this girl I cannot remember."

"Is there any point?"

"No. You are right—her story will not move me, so you will not relate it. Instead, you will remind me of my responsibilities as a member of this community. You will do it subtly. Not like Eric." He switches to English and a dead-on impersonation of Dalton. "You were a fucking shrink, Mathias. That means you have a fucking medical degree *and* a fucking psychiatry degree, and we need both, so stop whining about how you're out of practice, and get your fucking ass over to that house."

Mathias reaches under the counter and takes out a knife and a sharpening stone. He works on the blade while we talk. He does that a lot. Not surprisingly, it freaks people out. Honestly, though, it's just busywork. Mathias isn't good at doing nothing except talking. And, yes, I suspect his choice of task isn't accidental. It amuses him. With me, though, there's no message, other than the one that says this conversation isn't engaging enough to occupy his entire attention.

"Eric is a good man," he says. "I like him. You may even tell him that. He would not use it against me. He doesn't know how. It is not in his nature. You, though?" He waggles the knife at me. "You are different. You are devious. Cunning."

"Coming from you, I take that as a compliment. I'm asking you for a favor, Mathias. I know you never practiced medicine. I know you haven't practiced psychiatry since you got here. I don't care. I just want you to talk to Nicole. Name your price."

"It's not a favor if there's a price."

"A favor implies a future price. I like mine determined up front."

"Good. Open-ended favors are trouble. People will take advantage of you." He resumes sharpening. "You know I like that you speak French to me. And you are interesting. Here? Interesting is the best thing a person can be. You are also very easy to look at. That never hurts. But do you know what's more dangerous than a pretty girl?"

"A pretty girl with a gun?"

He laughs. "No, a pretty girl who is also clever. She knows exactly what to say to make you pay attention, and you are already paying attention because she is pretty. Very dangerous."

"You're prevaricating. Which means I *do* have your attention."

"Always." He sets the knife down. "I will not see this Nicole. But I do want something. My five years will be complete this spring. I wish to stay. I believe I have proven my worth. Isabel stays."

"Isabel *pays* to stay."

"Mmm, I believe Isabel does not need to pay much. Do you know what is even more dangerous than a pretty and clever girl? A pretty and clever *woman*. Isabel knows the most valuable currency in Rockton is secrets, and she holds more of those than anyone. I have money, yes. Secrets? No. But I want to stay."

"Right, well, considering you just told me you won't talk to Nicole, there's no deal to be made."

The shop door opens. Mathias barks, "*Fermé!*" and even if the unseen customer doesn't know what the word means, he decides a hasty departure seems wise.

Once the door has shut, Mathias turns to me. "When I was a psychiatrist, I had a specialty: studying psychopaths, sociopaths, and others with antisocial personality disorder. Do you know the difference?"

"Roughly, but you're telling me this because Nicole is none of the above."

"Unless she *allowed* herself to be kept in a hole for a year. Now, that would be a truly fascinating psychology. I saw something similar once, yet it was not nearly so extreme as this. We will presume, for the sake of argument, that this girl did not give permission. But what you missed in my job description was the keyword, which was overshadowed by the more powerful ones."

I think for a moment. "Study. You said you studied them. Which means you aren't a therapist. But we have Isabel for that. I want an assessment. That's what you did."

"True." He picks up another knife and begins sharpening it. "People take offense when I do this. You do not. Eric does not. Isabel just tells me to put the damned knife away. Do you know why it does not bother you three?"

"Because we don't think you're going to carve us up for tomorrow's *tourtière*?"

He chuckles. "Probably not. As I said, I like you. Also? You do not have enough fat. I am certain some do worry when I sharpen my knife, but for most, they simply do not like me seeming distracted. It is a case of—" He waves his hands. "*Look at me! I am important!* You do not need that. Eric does not need that. Isabel does not need that."

"Okay. . . ."

"I sharpen my blades while I chat, because it is an efficient use of time. Yet I realize how it can be misconstrued. It is the equivalent of checking one's cell phone. It can be read as *This conversation bores me.* When I studied patients, I had to be very careful not to multitask in their presence. Well, not unless it was useful—take out my phone to check messages while a narcissist is speaking, and he will need to regain my attention, which may mean telling me things he had meant to keep secret."

"Uh-huh. This is leading somewhere, right?"

Another waggle of the knife. "Patience. I enjoy our conversations.

Do not rush them. So now, imagine I am speaking to this poor captive girl, and I do this."

"Sharpen knives? Yeah, no. But I think you can give her thirty minutes without getting distracted."

"It is not 'getting distracted.' It is . . ." He puts the knife down and leans on the counter. "How long was she in that hole?"

"Fifteen months."

"How big was it?"

"About five feet across."

"She was down there fifteen months. In the dark. In the cold. Alone except for when a man came and made her *wish* she was alone. Or perhaps she was grateful to have contact with another person. How would that make her feel, if she found herself looking forward to those footsteps? You have thought of what that would be like, yes?"

I don't answer.

"You have. I see it in your face. You think of it, and you feel for her. You empathize. You cannot imagine what it would be like, but you still try."

"It isn't empathy if it's about me."

"That is the definition of empathy, Casey. You feel what she must have. And do you know what I would think, sitting there and hearing her story? How fascinating it is. What an incredible case study in human resilience and the psychology of captivity. That is all I would think, and she would see it, and she does not deserve that. Which is as close to empathy as I come—that I recognize my reaction would harm her and I do not wish to do that."

"But—"

"My offer then is to briefly examine her medically and then consult psychologically. For the latter, you will speak to her—you and Isabel. I will give you questions. You will ask them, and you will respond to her answers with all due empathy."

"I'm not sure I—"

"You will. Neither you nor Isabel is the warm, come-cry-on-my-shoulder type. Your empathy is that you are outraged by her situation, and you will do whatever you can to help her. She needs that more. A Valkyrie to avenge her pain, not tissues to soak up her tears. She also does not need a vulture of a scientist preying on her responses because he finds her an intellectual diversion. If you find the man who did this to her? I will speak to *him*."

SIXTEEN

It's night, well past quitting time. Dalton and I spend dinner and most of the evening hashing through suspects and coming up with a plan of action. Then he's called off to deal with yet another unrelated issue. That's law enforcement here.

I work alone at the station, while Anders is out with the militia. Later I fetch the puppy and stay for tea with Petra.

I don't know Petra's reason for being in Rockton. We are friends. Good ones. Yet I do not ask. I've had enough hints to know there's serious trauma in her past. When she's willing to share, she will. I don't ask Dalton for her story either. If I ever need it for work, I'll ask her first. All relationships are extra complicated in a town like this.

I leave Petra's with the puppy on a leash, which feels silly. She's eight weeks old, barely past infancy. I pick her up, but she whines and wriggles, and it's clear she's happy with tumbling and stumbling if it means new territory to explore.

I still feel bad having her on a lead rather than letting her toddle free. It's not as if I couldn't grab her if she bolted. But when Petra handed me the leash, she said, "Eric insists. I wasn't allowed to even open my door without having her locked in a room, or apparently she'd head for the hills and never be seen again."

Which I understand. If Dalton had his way, we'd all be on leashes.

That impulse thwarted, he'll exercise it on the one creature he can reasonably expect to wear one.

Walking the puppy means it takes a good hour to cross the few hundred feet to Dalton's place. That's not just because she wanders. Most people here haven't seen a pet in years, and this isn't just a dog, but a squirming, shaggy black puppy who instantly adores every last person she meets.

By the time we make it to Dalton's place, I can't feel my face anymore, but she's in no rush to go inside, so I wander to the edge of town. I'm standing near the path, rolling snowballs for the puppy to chase, when I hear, "Casey!" and turn to see Dalton running, hatless, toward me, his jacket undone.

"What's wrong?" I scoop up the puppy. "Is it Nicole?"

"No, I . . ." Deep breath. "I saw you from the station, heading toward the forest with the puppy, and I thought you were taking her in there for a walk."

"After dark? And after what's happened?"

He shoves his hands in his pockets. "Yeah. Sorry. I just . . ."

"Worried?"

"Yeah."

"Here, have a puppy. It helps."

He takes her, and she snuggles in, going from boundless energy to total exhaustion in two seconds flat.

"I was trying to figure out where to take her," I say. "Are we sleeping at your place or mine?"

"I wanted to talk about that. The dog-rearing books say she'll be more comfortable with a permanent home. Like a den, right?"

"Ah, I hadn't thought of that. So bopping between our houses isn't puppy-friendly. We need to pick a place and stick with it."

"Yeah. Is that a problem?"

"Not at all. Petra said you collected the puppy's things earlier. Are they at my place?"

"Uh, no." He shifts the puppy. "I was walking past mine, so I put them in there. Just for now. Unless you're okay with staying *there* until she's bigger or . . . whatever."

"Sure. Your place is closer to the station, and you're more settled in than I am."

"So that's all right? Moving into my place?"

He's studying my expression carefully, and I'm not sure why, but I smile and say, "Completely all right. Let's go make this puppy a den."

An hour later, we're in bed, snuggled up and talking, too tired for anything else and too aware there's a puppy whining on the floor.

"Should I move her bed downstairs?" Dalton asks.

I shake my head. "She misses her mother. She's only been away from her, what, a night or two? You picked her up in Dawson?"

He hesitates. "Yeah, but . . . she came from down south."

In other words, he hadn't just happened to learn that someone in Dawson City was breeding Newfoundlands. I ease back onto the pillow and say, "Did you give her a name?"

"Figured that was your job. She came with one, but it doesn't seem like a real dog name. They said it was for registering her."

So she didn't even come from a hobbyist breeding Newfoundlands in her backyard. He bought me a pedigree dog.

"What's the name?" I ask.

"Uh . . ." He rolls over and reaches for his jeans. It's tucked in his pocket. We don't carry wallets in Rockton, needing neither cash nor ID. Another of those oddities that took a while to get used to.

He unfolds the paper. "Blackmoor Down's Bohemian Rhapsody."

"That's a mouthful," I say.

"Yeah. I tried Rhapsody. She didn't respond to it. So you can call her whatever you want."

I flip to hang over the foot of the bed and ask, "What's your name?"

She bounces up, pawing at the bed. I pet her. "How about Storm?"

"Because she came to you in one?"

"I'll tell everyone that, but actually I'm naming her after my favorite character in *X-Men*."

"Which is the movie with the wolverine guy."

"Comics first. I'll get you those, so you can catch up. Storm dresses in black and has white hair." I pat the puppy's white ear. "We'll have to teach her to control weather. Which would be even more useful than tracking."

I give Storm one last pat and lie back on the bed, and she erupts in a veritable storm of despondency, crying and yowling as if she's been abandoned in the forest while surrounded by wolves.

"Guess I shouldn't have paid attention to her," I say.

"She wasn't settling anyway."

I reach down again to pet her, and she mood swings into utter joy, complete with slobber.

"I remember this about Newfies," I say, lifting my dripping hand. "Drool and fur. Lots of both." I peer at Storm. "You'll be worth it, right?"

She rolls on the floor, sending both fur and drool flying. I lean farther to rub her belly. Then I back up, and the crisis-crying starts anew. I keep retreating. She begins leaping at the foot of the bed.

"She can't come up," Dalton says.

"I know. Once she's in the habit, we're screwed."

"Especially when we're sharing our bed with a hundred-and-twenty-pound dog."

"Oh, I'd regret it even with a puppy." I reach to pat her again. "You're adorable, baby, but no one interferes with my sex life."

Dalton chuckles. Then he says, "Pick her up."

"We just agreed—"

"Pick her up."

I do, and he rolls out of bed and hoists us both into his arms.

"Impressive," I say. "Now let's see you do it when she's full grown."

He carries us downstairs and lays us on the rug in front of the fire. It's bearskin. No head, though. If Dalton has to shoot a nuisance bear, he'll take the pelt to find some good in a bad situation, but it's utility rather than a trophy.

As he starts the fire, Storm sniffs the rug, gets a noseful of grizzly and starts a little dance—jump off the rug growling, do a puppy spin and then pounce back on, sniff the carpet again, jump off growling . . .

I'm laughing, which confuses the poor thing and only makes me laugh more, and Dalton stops what he's doing to watch. Watch me, not the puppy, until I glance over and he busies himself with the fire again.

Once he gets it going, he grabs caribou skin blankets, and by then, Storm has decided I can sufficiently protect her from the terrifying flat predator, and she's snuggled with me, half asleep already. Dalton slides in behind us, and I cuddle up, him on one side, a puppy on the other, and I fall asleep thinking—not of Nicole or the cave—but simply, *This is perfect.*

SEVENTEEN

Once I'm asleep, though, even a warm puppy and lover can't keep the last two days at bay. I dream of the man in the snowmobile suit, of his pipe hitting my head, of waking in that cave and screaming until my throat is raw. I dream of a shadowy figure hunched at the top, watching me. But it's not him. It's Diana. She watches and then rises and walks away. Next it's Beth, doing the same. Leaving me screaming for them to come back, please come back and help me.

Finally I'm alone and huddled on that cold rock floor, not even the comfort of the skins beneath me. I hear a noise at the top. It's Dalton, and I'm sure he will leave too. Of course he will. Nobody stays. Not for me.

Dalton stays.

He crouches on the edge and says something, and I see his lips moving, but I can't make out the words. He drops a rope, but it falls short. I jump, claw at the wall, try to climb, but whenever I get closer, it recedes until it's so far above my head, I can barely see it.

Then Dalton shrugs. Just shrugs, as if to say, *What can you do?* He drops the rope. It comes curling down the hole, and I'm screaming, screaming, *Please, please help, I'll do better next time, just help me.*

Then he's gone. Given up on me. I scream and I scream and then I hear a voice at my ear, whispering, "What did you expect?" It's Blaine, blood on his shirt from the bullet I put through his heart.

Another noise sounds up top again, and I spin, and I'm hoping it's Dalton. He's just gone to find another way, and then he'll come back.

Instead four figures ring the hole. Four faces peer down. The four I've seen in every nightmare for the last twelve years. The last faces I saw before I fell under the rain of blows that changed my life.

"Looks like you've got company, Casey," Blaine whispers. "Maybe they'll do it right this time."

I wake in Dalton's arms. He's holding me, smoothing back my hair and whispering, "Shh, shh, shh." I feel him there, hear him there, and I am both comforted and shamed, as I always am.

I am ashamed that it has been twelve years, and I still have nightmares. That in four months my new lover has already become so accustomed to them that he only has to feel me shaking against him, and he'll wake and hold me and whisper.

I huddle against him and swallow, shivering, and he says, "Talk?" I shake my head and curl up against his chest, and he holds me until I fall back to sleep.

EIGHTEEN

We don't get on the trail at first light. I take Storm out while Dalton makes breakfast, and when I open the door, I'm blown off my feet by a gust of wind. Dalton gets the door shut, and we peer out into the darkness as a storm whips up.

Anders was supposed to join us on our trek, and he valiantly makes it to Dalton's place, but there's no way we're going out. We spend a few hours holed up, working in front of the fire. While the wind dies down by eleven, we've lost too much daylight to hunt for Sutherland.

By the time we head to the station, everyone's walking to work, the shops opening. No one lingers at home with the excuse for a snow day. We can't afford that. Eleven isn't even all that late for opening Rockton in the winter season. The town's schedule accommodates the seasons. Longer summer hours and shifts mean shorter ones in winter, when the town goes into a state of semi-hibernation.

Dalton drops off Storm with Petra and then meets me at the bakery, where I'm chatting with the couple who work there. We take our coffee and morning rolls and nearly collide with Val coming in.

"Fresh sweet rolls," I say, lifting mine as I pass, but not slowing, not opening up a moment of conversation as I would with anyone else. A friendly comment and then move on.

Val says, "The council needs to speak to you." Then she turns and leaves.

I hesitate. Devon holds out a cloth-wrapped sweet roll for Val and giving me a wry smile.

"Gotta try, right?" he says.

Both Brian and Dalton snort, almost in unison, as if to say they don't see why we bother. Not with Val. I take the roll and thank Devon as we leave.

Val's already inside when we arrive. I knock. She opens the door. I lift the sweet roll, and she stares at it as if suspecting a bomb in pastry shape.

"Late breakfast, early lunch—whatever you call it, it's good. And I wouldn't want to eat mine in front of you."

She gingerly takes the roll. Then she sees Dalton behind me.

"The invitation was for Casey, Sheriff."

"And that wasn't clear, so I came."

"Your presence is not required."

I tense, but Dalton only shrugs and says, "Okay. I'll wait," and starts clearing snow from her front porch.

"I'm certain you have better things to do," Val says. "Unless you're concerned Casey will run off on you."

"Nah, she can't run that fast. I always catch her. Throw her over my shoulder. Haul her back to my c—" He stops, and I know how he'd been going to finish that. *Haul her back to my cave.* He resumes sweeping off the deck. "My workload for this morning requires my detective. So I'll wait. Eat my roll. Sip my coffee. Glower at the locals. That's ninety percent of policing, you know. The glower."

I wait for Val to snap something. But she doesn't even seem to hear him. She's already retreating into the house, saying, "Suit yourself, Sheriff," as she motions me in.

We settle in the living room. Val has left her sweet roll on the table. I've put mine down, and I'm waiting, but she just sits there.

"How does she say it happened?" Val asks.

"What?"

"The young—" She stops. Waits a beat, and then says, "Nicole," as if she knew the name but is reluctant to admit it. "How does she say the initial attack happened?"

"She was picking berries when she was hit from behind."

"Where did she say this took place?"

"A hundred feet or so from town."

"She went berry picking at night?"

"It was evening and still light out."

Val plucks imaginary lint from her dress pants. I don't know why she wears dress pants. It's not as if she goes out and meets people. But as she fusses, her hands tremble.

"Val?" I say.

"Was it one man? That's what your report says, but is she certain? Only one?"

Shortly after Val arrived in Rockton, she disappeared while on militia patrol. Dalton was the one who found her, and she told him she'd just gotten lost. She admitted to me that she'd been taken by two men, whom she'd tricked, escaping unharmed. She did not escape unharmed. No one's going to capture a woman, threaten her, and then fall asleep, having done nothing in between. To Val's mind, though, "allowing" anything would be a sign of weakness. So she did not.

"Nicole is certain it's one man," I say, but Val doesn't relax. She just looks up and says, "What do you think of her story?"

"Story?" I try not to bristle. It's just poor word choice, but I've been known to use it myself. "I'm not sure it's possible to think anything other than that it's terrible. Unbelievably terrible. If you're suggesting—" I pause. Rephrase. "We're all concerned, of course, that it could happen again. That her captor knows about Rockton and may take another woman. We've doubled night patrols, and we're going to be careful about letting women outside the boundaries. As sexist as that will seem, I think everyone will understand. We have a predator—"

"What evidence do you have to support Nicole's claims?"

I think I've misheard. Or at least misunderstood, and I answer with a startled "What?"

It takes Val a moment to respond, and she does as if reluctantly. "Nicole claims that she was held captive for more than a year. What evidence do you have to support that?"

I resist the urge to blink at her. Instead, I say, "I found her in that hole. Severely malnourished. She has muscle atrophy and vision damage. If you are suggesting she put herself there . . ." I struggle for words and finally end with, "I'm not even sure what to do with that."

"The council—" She inhales. Clears her throat. "The council would like to suggest that you more thoroughly question Nicole's story."

"She was *raped,* Val."

Her hands start to shake, and she cups them together. "Do you have evidence?"

I stare at her.

"The council would like you to consider the possibility she orchestrated this tragedy herself."

"You're . . . you're suggesting she starved herself and stayed in a pit until her muscles *atrophied*—"

"The council suggests it. They insisted I relay their concerns." Val holds out a sheaf of papers. "I took notes."

"Notes on what?"

"Nicole's true story. The council believes we are the victims of a hoax."

As furious as I am, I should have anticipated the council's response. This case is messy. They don't like messy. This past fall, it took three deaths for them to admit Rockton had a killer.

Dalton and I are back at the station. He starts the fire, and I sit in front of it, on the caribou blankets, with my notebook and Val's papers.

Dalton starts to sit with me and then rises with a grunt. "Better find something to do or I'll be reading over your shoulder."

"I don't mind if it's you."

He sits beside me again, and I shift up against him, and we read in silence until we've finished. I turn the last page and then sit there for at least a minute before I say, "They could be lying, right?"

Dalton doesn't answer. After a few moments, I say, "I want to think they're making it all up. And they could be making *some* of it up. Exaggerating. They probably are."

"Yeah."

I lay my hand on the notes. "This doesn't mean Nicole did this to herself. I can't imagine anyone doing that." I twist to look at him. "I hate even considering it. I know how you operate up here. If a woman comes to you and says she was sexually assaulted, you start from a position of presuming she's telling the truth."

"Of course."

"That's not how it works down south. We try to treat all crimes the same, but a woman claiming assault often bears the burden of proof. Do you know how many times I raged because Diana wasn't believed when she accused her ex of abusing her, stalking her? And then it turned out—"

"Yeah. And you can stop beating yourself up over that."

"I didn't say—"

"You hate that you defended her. You hate even more that she sets a bad example for women who *do* have crazy exes. But half the women here are running from an abusive partner. You know how many others have turned out to be lying? None."

"I know."

"And not to defend Diana—she's a bitch, always going to be a bitch—but Graham was still abusive. They may have staged the last beating for your benefit, but what about the ones that made her leave him? He beat her. He stalked her. She just kept going back, and I don't understand that, but I've read enough to know it happens."

He taps the pages. "Whatever this means, don't think of it as blaming the victim. You believed her until you had reason to reconsider. Innocent until proven suspicious."

"You're right."

"Usually am." He gets to his feet. "Now you need to talk to Nicole. Sort this shit out."

NINETEEN

Dalton takes his spot with the militia guard on Beth's porch. I go inside. Diana is there, and she pauses, as if expecting to give a report, but I just nod and thank her. She leaves, and I walk into the living room where Nicole stands by the front window, looking out at Dalton.

I clear my throat. She steps back, but only half turns, still watching him.

"Why doesn't he come in?" she asks.

"Do you want him to?"

She smiles. "I guess not." She moves to sit on the futon. "Diana says you two are an item. At first, I thought she was kidding. I figured you and Will . . . Well, that makes more sense. You and Will."

I take a seat.

"If he wants to come in . . . ," she says.

"If Eric wants to do anything, he does it. He's fine there."

"Eric. I don't think I even knew his first name. He's just Sheriff Dalton. Or 'yes, sir.'" She smiles again, and it's clear she senses a chill in my greeting, and she's trying to coax a smile, but the silence drags until she's fidgeting.

"I told you that I knew why you came to Rockton," I say. "Eric gave me the official story. Which was not *untrue*. Your father got mixed up with a cartel and took the family into witness protection after your mother died. He later committed suicide, but that didn't stop the cartel from coming after you and ultimately killing your brother."

"Right . . ."

Her tone asks where this is leading, but her expression doesn't echo it. Which means I can no longer cling to the hope that the council has outright lied.

"Why don't you tell me where I'm going with this?" I say.

She reaches for her teacup, but her bony hand shakes too much to risk it.

I see that hand. I see her. How thin she is. Clumps of her hair have fallen out. Sores ring her mouth. Vitamin deficiencies have left her skin covered in a full-body rash.

Nicole swallows. Folds her hands. Unfolds them. Then she blurts out, "I gave them my brother."

"Yes."

She looks at me. Looks me right in the eye, and I don't see defiance. I see relief. She has spoken the words, and I have accepted them, and there will be no outrage, no shock, because this is not news to me. I knew what she'd done when I walked in here. It reminds me of the relief I felt when I realized Dalton knew what I'd done to Blaine.

"May I explain?" she asks.

"If you like."

Hands fold. Unfold. Like a disjointed wringing. She finally places them on her legs and grips her knees as if to hold her hands in place.

"We started moving when I was nine. Garrett was twelve. At first, Dad said it'd just be the one move. We'd live in San Diego, which we both loved. That would be our new home. And it was . . . for six months. Then we moved. We moved, and we moved, and we moved, and eventually Garrett and I stopped trying to make friends at our new schools. We became each other's best friend. Dad encouraged that. It lessened the chance we'd slip up and say something to a stranger. But when I say we were best friends, it's like . . . it's like growing up here. I heard that's what Sheriff Dalton did. That he was born here, has lived here all his life. It's like that, except there's this one other kid, so you have to be friends with that kid because there is no one else."

"You didn't get along with your brother."

"We got along well enough for siblings. I just wouldn't have chosen him as a friend. Of course, I had to pretend otherwise to make my father happy. And Garrett *was* okay with it. He made sure I didn't have other friends, and soon the alternative was to be alone so I *learned* to be friends with my brother. When we hit high school, my father decided dating was too dangerous. So no friends, no dates, no social circle at all, and we were growing up, and . . . When I said I slept in the closet with a knife, it wasn't only the cartel I was hiding from."

She doesn't sneak a look to see if I'm reacting. She just keeps talking.

"When I was sixteen, I read this book. All the girls at school were, and one offered it to me, and I was so desperate for a connection. It was about a brother and sister who grew up locked in an attic. When they became teenagers . . . things happened."

She fists her hands and then forces them open on her knees again. "The other girls thought it was romantic. Forbidden love. I threw up. Every time someone mentioned that book, I started shaking. It wasn't romantic. Wasn't the least bit romantic. But do you know what the worst was? I cared about my brother. Whatever he did to me, I couldn't stop caring. When I finally escaped to college, I'd find myself staring at the phone for hours, wanting to call him, to talk to him. I *knew* him. That's what it came down to. Whatever he'd done, he *was* my friend. My only one."

She shifts on the futon, picking up a pillow, then gazing at it as if not sure how it got into her hands before tucking it back down again.

"I eventually asked Garrett not to contact me, and he wouldn't for months. I think he was trying to break free, too. I wasn't the only one cut off, refused friends, not allowed to date. One therapist said I should forgive him. Another said I was wrong to even *consider* his side of the story. Neither was right. But I don't know what is right." She pauses. "I can give you the therapists' names and any permission needed for them to share their notes. I'll provide whatever you need to prove my story, but the truth is, nothing excuses what I did."

"Tell me about that. What you did."

"Like I said, Garrett would go months without making contact. But that always ended. If I wouldn't take his calls, he'd come around.

Just wanting to talk. Coffee, dinner, a drink. Couldn't we do that? Be brother and sister again. I tried. I wanted that, too. But we'd go out, and it'd seem fine . . . and then it would start. He missed me. No one was good enough. No one else was me." She looks toward the window. "I know there are a lot of women in Rockton who've dealt with abusive partners. Maybe some men, too. My story won't be any different. It's just the ending that . . ."

Her hands squeeze. "I moved a lot. I'd take contract jobs so I could move when I had to—not escaping the cartel but escaping my brother. Then came the night I woke up with him in my bed. Holding a knife. I got away and threatened to call the police. But I didn't. The shame of explaining that my own brother . . ."

She swallows. "That's when the cartel renewed their interest in us. My father *had* taken money. We got it after he died. Garrett bought himself a fancy sports car, and the cartel caught wind of that, but he didn't have a proper job or a permanent address. I was easier to find. When they showed up, I made a decision."

"You gave them Garrett."

"I had a plan. I thought I was so damned clever. I called Garrett and told him I was giving the cartel his location unless he promised to never see me again. He called my bluff. In the past, I'd threatened to report him and never did, so he figured I wouldn't do this. I proved him wrong. I told the cartel where to find him. Then I called him and said I'd done it and that he had to run. He didn't. They caught up with him and . . ."

She starts to shake. "My father used to tell us what the cartel would do if they found us. We thought he was just trying to spook us. He wasn't."

"About the money. You had your share. Hidden. And Garrett didn't tell the cartel that."

Her whole body flinches, her eyes closing, face screwing up. "Yes, he never told them. He knew I'd betrayed him, and he didn't do the same to me. I wish he had."

"But the cartel still came after you a year later. They tortured you and then they threw you in a hole."

She goes still.

"That is what happened, right?" I say. "They put you in a pit and held you captive, but you escaped. Yes?"

The muscles in her jaw work, but her lips stay pressed together, as if holding the words back. Then, slowly, she shakes her head.

"That's not what happened?" I prompt.

"No," she says finally, voice barely above a whisper. "I lied."

"I know."

She shudders as if in relief. "I know how that looks now. I tell a story about being held captive in a pit back home and then I'm actually held in a hole here. It's too coincidental. So I must be lying again." She looks at me. "I'm not. Tell me what I need to do to prove that."

I say nothing.

She fingers the rash on her arm. "This isn't enough, is it? Not after . . ."

"After the last time? When you showed obvious signs of torture—all self-inflicted?"

"I was desperate. The detective in charge of my brother's case wouldn't stop digging. He figured out what I'd done. He was coming for me."

"He kept digging for a whole year? So he could get an accessory charge?" I shake my head. "Never."

"He didn't care about charging me. He just wanted leverage against the cartel. He thought I knew more, and if the cartel found out he was trying to use me against them . . ."

She goes quiet. Then she says, "I didn't care if I went to jail for Garrett. I deserved that. But I would not become my father. I wouldn't live his life. I knew about Rockton from when someone suggested it to my father. He gave me the contact information before he died. So I staged my story about being captured and tortured. Then I called that number."

When I don't reply, she brings up the very question I cannot answer, the one I keep asking myself.

"Why would I fake it again?" she says. "I had a motive the first time. What would it be now?"

"I don't know enough about you to answer that." I glance at the two books she brought back from the cave. "Those are your journals?"

"No, they're just stories."

"Stories?"

"Silly, crazy stories to keep me sane." She walks over and hands them to me. "I almost wish they were journals. That might help. You can still read them. At the very least, maybe they'll help prove I was down there that long."

I take the books.

TWENTY

A flip through the books proves they are just stories. But there's another reason I've taken them, and once they're in hand, I head to the station to examine them further. When Dalton shows up, I hold out the books and say, "What are these?"

"Dunno. Haven't read them."

"I mean the books. The actual physical objects." I put one down and turn the other over in my hands. "I know we sell blank journals at the general store, but these aren't them."

Blank books are among the most popular items in Rockton. When electronic forms of entertainment aren't available, people rediscover childhood hobbies—writing poetry, painting landscapes, playing an instrument. Writing requires only paper and pen, and on almost every supply run, we stop at the dollar store and buy blank journals.

"This is old," I say. "I smell mildew, and that cave system is dry. But it's not just thrift-shop old. It's properly bound, and the pages are yellowing. I wouldn't be surprised if this"—I tap the cover—"is real leather. And . . ." I open the book to the first page and run my finger down a jagged edge on the inner spine. "It's had pages torn out. The first twenty or so. Both of them are like that."

"Conclusion?"

"That they really were journals. Very old ones. A miner or trapper started writing in them and then stopped. Got bored or just didn't have that much to say. When Nicole asked for paper, this is what her captor brought her. Is there anything like this in Rockton?"

He shakes his head. "I only buy the kind you've seen."

"And you've been doing the supply runs for how long?"

"Six, seven years."

"Longer than any current residents have been here. Presumably these didn't come from your place, so the only way a resident would have gotten hold of one would be to find it hidden in his house. Under a floorboard or whatever. Which is not impossible, but you guys do a thorough inspection between occupants."

"Have to. Floorboards and all. That's the first excuse people give when they're found with contraband—must have been the guy who lived here before me."

He reached for the book I'm holding. I hand it to him. He flips through it, frowning.

"I've seen . . ." He doesn't finish, just keeps turning pages, his fingers running over them. "I had books to draw in, when I was a kid."

"You drew?"

He shrugs. "Sketches. Wildlife and whatever." His fingers move across the writing, as if picking up touch memory from the old, ink-dented paper. "My mother used to hang them in the cabin, and this one time, when we had a fire, she tried going back in, and it turned out all she wanted was my stupid—"

He inhales sharply and slaps the book shut. "My father used to get me books. Old ones. I don't know where they came from, but they smelled like that. Looked like that. Ledgers or journals, from miners and trappers, like you said."

I want to backtrack. Hear the rest of his story. Gain insight into a part of his life he slaps as firmly shut as that book.

Tell me about your sketches.

Tell me about your mother.

Tell me anything.

I get as far as "Do you ever—" and he cuts me off with "I don't know where my parents got the books, but it wasn't from Rockton."

He checks his watch. "We're losing daylight fast. I've got a few things to do. I'll meet you in a half hour, and we'll get Storm for a walk."

Dalton and I are walking the puppy. It's twilight, and we're in the forest, taking her farther than she's gone before. I have something on my mind. He knows, and that's why we're here.

He doesn't ask me what's wrong. The guy who usually demands hard answers to uncomfortable questions now walks quietly at my side, murmuring to Storm when she wanders, voice low so he doesn't interrupt my thoughts. The guy who drags people through town by the scruff of their neck now has his glove off, my hand wrapped in his, thumb rubbing every so often, a small gesture of comfort. The guy who doesn't have time for your shit—and no problem telling you so, loudly and profanely—now crouches patiently by the side of the path, holding back undergrowth so Storm can sniff a fox hole. I watch him hunkered there, pointing at spots for the puppy to sample, and I suspect I'll never figure him out entirely, and I don't care. Dalton is like Rockton itself, so many aspects, not all of them easy or comfortable, but the sum total adding up to something unique and remarkable and unforgettable.

When he rises, I tell him Nicole's story. All of it.

"It bothers me," I say when I'm done. "I don't know why. It's not like I have any sense that she's lying . . ."

"That's not it."

Dalton stops, his hand tightening on mine. He scans the twilit forest before glancing at Storm. She's picked up his unease, and she's sampling the wind but seems to smell nothing out of the ordinary.

When we resume walking, he says, "It's her situation. She murdered a guy who did something to her, something that deserved punishment, but not that *severe* a punishment. And she got away with it."

We walk a few more steps, before I say, "She didn't actually kill—"

"Splitting hairs. Yours was bad judgment. Taking a gun to a confrontation? Never a good idea. Nicole made her choice deliberately."

"But she warned her brother. She didn't plan for him to die."

"You confronted Blaine with a gun to spook him, prove you were serious. A threat that went as bad as it can go. In your case and Nicole's. That's what makes you uncomfortable. You hear her story, and you think it's forgivable. Yet if her situation parallels your own, what does that mean for you?"

"I need to separate the cases."

"Or you could—crazy idea—confront and reconcile the problem? Admit that on a culpability scale for murder, killing Blaine only rates about five."

"I need to separate the cases."

He sighs. "Fine, so moving on to the other part that's bothering you . . ."

He's gone still again. He doesn't stop moving, but he's scanning the darkening forest. When I squint into the trees, I sense nothing. Neither does Storm, who's trotting along ahead of us.

Dalton shakes it off and says, "The problem is the fact that accusing her of voluntarily living in that hole is preposterous. Especially without a motive. So you're wondering why the council gave it to you."

"You don't actually need a detective, do you?"

"Sure, I do, because my answer is 'because they're assholes.' I'm gonna guess you need more."

"I do. It's like they expect we'll be so freaked out by this that we'll jump on any other explanation, however flimsy."

"Or *they're* jumping on it."

"Why? Is it just because terrible crimes are terribly inconvenient? Like trying to cover up a murder in a fancy hotel?"

"Maybe."

"It bugs me."

"I know."

I'm about to say more when he tenses again, his eyes narrowing. This time, I ask, "What do you see?"

He takes another slow look around. Then he makes a face. "Nothing. Just jumpy."

"Are you sure?"

Another scan. "Mostly."

I take out my gun. "If you think there's someone out there, we should investigate."

He looks from me to Storm and then back at the forest.

"We're not going to tromp in there with a gun and a puppy when it's just me being rattled," he says. "We should head back. It's almost dark, and we didn't bring a flashlight."

He looks at my gun as I put it away. "Good to see you're okay with pulling that. Proves you're capable of progress. Just very slowly."

I flip him the finger. He tugs the glove from my pocket and holds it out. "Wouldn't want that to get frostbite."

I shake my head and put on one glove, my other hand going into his. As we leave, I cast one last glance around the forest as he's tugging Storm onto the path.

I don't see anyone. Don't hear anyone. Don't even sense anyone. But if Dalton did? Someone's there, watching us. I know it.

TWENTY-ONE

I want to talk to Val. I'm on my way there, alone, Dalton having taken Storm to the station. People are heading home after work, which makes it Rockton's rush hour. I avoid the main street. I'm halfway to my goal when I catch a glimpse of motion between two buildings, and I spin.

It's a woman. Middle-aged. Brown hair. Blue eyes. Unremarkable in every way. The sort of person who fades into a crowd. And, in this case, one person I wish would fade into it.

"Don't shoot!" Jen says, hands going up. "Little quick on the trigger, aren't you, Detective?"

My hand hasn't even dipped toward my gun. "Do you want something, Jen?"

"Just to tell you you're a bitch."

I sigh and resume walking. "Second verse, same as the first. Any particular reason today? Or are you just reminding me that I haven't changed your opinion?"

"You don't give a shit about changing my opinion." She stops in front of me. "You pretend that you're on our side—the women of this town. But you're no different than all the big-shot bitches down south, ready to stomp us first chance you get. Do you actually honestly think Nicki put herself in that hole?"

I go still. "Who told you—"

"I was taking her a care package and spotted your rottweiler boy-friend on the front porch. So I went around back and stepped inside."

"How much did you overhear?"

"Enough."

"You're right—questioning her story is a shitty thing to do, which means I had cause. So, tell me, why did I do it?"

"How the hell should I know?"

"Then maybe you should ask, instead of leaping to the conclusion that I'm evil. You really are a broken record, Jen. You need to find new tracks to play."

"She doesn't know any," says a voice behind us.

I don't need to turn to say, "Hello, Mathias."

He joins us, meeting Jen's scowl with a mocking bow. "Jennifer, it is always a pleasure. May I say you look radiant this evening."

"Fuck off, old man."

He turns to me. "You wonder why Jennifer cannot find new tracks to play? She knows none. Learned behavior. A lifetime of being bul-lied has turned her into one. It happens, sadly."

"What?" she squawks. "You crazy old man."

"You were significantly larger when you arrived, Jennifer, and you carry yourself in a way that suggested you have always been a big girl. Your hair looked like you cut it yourself. And your clothing? You did not shop in thrift stores because it was trendy, did you, Jennifer?"

"You—"

"Crazy old man? Casey is right. You really must find new tracks. I could teach you fresh insults. I know many. I might also suggest therapy, but the only person here who could help with that is Isabel, and you burned that bridge spectacularly. You could not even whore properly."

I bristle, but he cuts me off with, "Yes, yes, that was uncalled for. Run along, Jennifer. You have taken up enough of Casey's time. She is very important, you know. Even I like talking to her. She is a special young woman."

Jen scowls at me and stomps off.

"That was a little heavy-handed, don't you think?" I say, switching to French.

"Jennifer is always heavy-handed."

"I mean your parting shot."

He smiles. "Oh, I couldn't resist. Did you ever see *The Brady Bunch*?"

"Before my time."

"Naturally. Well, there were three girls, and the middle one thought her older sister got everything—all the attention, all the praise, all the advantages. *Marcia, Marcia, Marcia.* That's Jennifer. *Casey, Casey, Casey.* The cry of the chronically dissatisfied. Our Jen has always been an equal-opportunity misanthrope, but in you, she's found something special. You must remind her of someone she hated as a child."

"Great."

"Or it's a secret crush."

"Let's stick with memories of hatred past."

I glance toward the road, and he waves for me to continue and falls in at my side, saying, "So you suspect Our Lady of Captivity may have put herself in that hole? Colluded with someone, that is. To actually *place* herself in a hole without food and water for a year is impossible." He takes a few more steps. "Unless . . . did you say there was a rope?"

"At the top, yes."

"Which she could have thrown up there when she heard you coming."

"Uh, no. Impossible and stupid."

"I accept impossible. There is no such thing as too stupid. Still, to go to such physical lengths to fake an abduction would require remarkable willpower and a truly perverse psychological profile. Dare I ask what her motivation might be?"

When I don't answer, he notices the direction I'm heading and says, "You're going to ask Isabel? No, my dear, that won't help. Isabel counseled those who had temporarily lost their way. I studied those who'd voluntarily left the path and saw no reason to return."

I don't correct his presumption on where I'm going and why. Instead, I say, "You know, I would totally ask for your help . . . if you weren't so out of practice. And if you hadn't promised to assess her and then ducked out of actually doing so."

"I have ducked nothing. I am circling the situation. Assessing from afar and gaining all the facts before I proceed. It is how I have always worked."

"Maybe, but I also wanted your *medical* opinion, and I still haven't gotten it."

"I will see her tomorrow morning."

"Good. Get Isabel to take you. Eric and I need to check out the crime scene and look for Shawn Sutherland."

"That is a waste of time. On both counts. Her captor will have cleared the scene by now, and Mr. Sutherland is long gone, likely in the euphemistic sense, given the weather conditions."

"Even if we're only looking for a body, that will provide closure."

Mathias gives me a look. "The only 'closure' anyone ever truly wants is a miracle, the missing person found alive. Calling it 'closure' is a defense mechanism for grieving loved ones, who fear they will look foolish admitting they still hope for that miracle."

"Sure, that's what families hope for, but at least a body gives them a chance—"

"To grieve? They've been doing that since the victim disappeared."

"I was going to say a chance for justice. To see the killer caught and punished."

"Good. If you had told me that the point of catching the killer was rehabilitation, I'd have been terribly disappointed in you."

I shake my head. "As for Sutherland, waste of time or not, we're going out tomorrow."

"To find his body and punish his killer? I don't believe you can incarcerate Mother Nature. Or does this mean you have reason to believe you will find Mr. Sutherland dead, and *not* from exposure to the elements?"

"Please assess Nicole tomorrow morning, Mathias. I'll get your report when I return."

I knock on Val's door. After a moment, the blackout blinds ripple. Then I hear footsteps, and the door opens.

"I just wanted to let you know I read the council's report," I say. "And I confronted Nicole. It's all true."

She nods, obviously relieved. "All right, then. So she orchestrated her own capture, and we don't have some madman—"

"No," I say. "I mean what they claimed she did down south is true. She fully admits it. But staging her own kidnapping a second time? To what purpose? And for a full year? How much sense does that make to you?"

In anything else, I would expect Val to leap to the council's defense. But I remember how she gave me those notes, her expression, her shaking hands. That's why I'm here. To get her reaction.

She says nothing. Not a single word.

Which tells me everything.

"It doesn't make sense, and we both know it," I say. "You asked whether I believe Nicole's story? I do. Completely."

I turn and walk away.

I've planted the seed. Time to see what sprouts from it.

TWENTY-TWO

Our evening is spent in a staff meeting. Which means the three of us—Anders, Dalton, and me—at Anders's place, talking. We've brought Storm, and Anders is getting her to chase a shoelace he's pulled from his boot. I'm telling them that Mathias will consult on Nicole tomorrow, and Anders says, "Does anyone think it's weird that the crazy Frenchman doesn't want to actually interview Nicki?"

"Suspicious, you mean," I say. "Because you like him for the crime."

"I like him for every crime." When I give him a look, he says, "Okay, I'm kidding. Mostly. Now, if Nicki had been brainwashed into self-imposed captivity, I'd say he's our man. But keeping a woman in a cave hole lacks finesse."

"It's also inconvenient," I say. "That cave is terribly far away. But yes, I'm considering him a suspect, like every guy who's been here since Nicole disappeared."

"Uh-uh. Not everyone." Anders taps his arm. "For once, racial profiling means I am *not* a suspect." He looks at Dalton. "Which is more than you can say."

Dalton shakes his head. "Nicole says her captor last visited the day before you found her. I was in Dawson City."

"Yeah, I'm not even sure this Dawson City place exists. I've heard your stories of it."

"So," I say, "back to the subject. Yes, Mathias is a suspect. No, I don't think his refusal to interview her *is* suspect. He's just being Mathias. He did agree to conduct a brief medical examination, which means he's not going to be hiding behind a curtain. But, yes, given his role in the case, I'd love to know more about him, to be completely sure Nicole is safe with him."

Both Anders and I look at Dalton.

"What?" Dalton says.

Anders sighs and heaves to his feet. "Come on, pup. Time to go piss in the forest with Uncle Will. The adults have something to discuss. Don't give me that look, Eric. Casey's asking about Mathias's entrance story, and I know you won't tell her in front of me. That info's on a need-to-know basis. I don't need to know."

"With Mathias, it's public record, so you might as well hear it," Dalton says. "He's here because one of his subjects didn't much like being under his magnifying glass. Guy was a serial killer in New York. That's where Mathias did most of his research—he lived in Quebec but commuted to the States for cases. This guy targeted teenage girls. Raped and tortured them. Claimed he was at the mercy of twisted urges. Mathias studied him. Two years into the sentence, the guy emasculated himself."

"What?" Anders says. "No. Did I say I don't want to hear this story?"

Dalton waits, giving Anders a chance to leave. The deputy squirms, but says, "Fine. Go on. Just no details, okay?"

"I don't know them. What I do know is that this piece of shit blamed Mathias. Said the doctor brainwashed him or hypnotized him and made him do that to himself."

"Seriously?" Anders says. "I was *kidding* about the brainwashing."

"Well, that's what this guy claimed. As soon as he recovered, he escaped, leaving a trail of bodies. He wrote threats on the wall in blood, swearing to do to Mathias what he claims the doc did to him. When the cops couldn't find the guy, Mathias decided he wasn't spending the rest of his life cupping his balls. He'd heard about Rockton through the grapevine, so he applied for entry while he waited for the guy to be caught."

"Which hasn't happened," I say.

"Nope. I think Mathias is fine with the excuse, though. From what you said about extending his stay, he's in no rush to cut his Yukon early retirement short."

"You said the story is public record?"

"A long paper trail of proof. It hit the news—the guy's crimes, conviction, self-mutilation, escape, vows to kill the shrink he blamed for making him—"

"We get the picture," Anders says. "Well, Casey does. I'm trying very hard *not* to. What you're saying is that you've looked it up and confirmed Mathias has a valid and proven reason for being here, one that says he's on the run from a serial killer, not one that suggests he could be a psycho himself."

"Yep."

"Damn," Anders says. "Well, there goes my career as a detective."

Another hour passes in conversation. I'm lying on the rug, and Dalton has moved down to the floor, his back against the sofa, with my head on his lap. Storm's stretched out in the narrow space between my head and his stomach, squeezing in so she can be with both of us, and I'm thinking of that Newfoundland from so long ago. What was her name? Right. Nana, after the most famous instance of the breed, the beloved "nanny" in *Peter Pan*. I remember how Nana would shift against me as I read, as if making sure I was comfortable and . . .

I wake to a cold nose finding the spot where my shirt rides up from my jeans. It's Storm nudging and whining. I'm on the floor, Dalton lying behind me, his arms around me, the rise and fall of his chest telling me he's sound asleep. Another nudge. Another whine. Then a smell. The distinct odor of puppy piddle.

I rise quickly, my gaze flying to the rug beneath us. Thankfully, that's not where she went. There's a small puddle on the hardwood. A remarkably small puddle, as if she'd peed just as much as necessary before trying again to wake me. We don't have papers set out for her. The breeder had begun housebreaking from near birth and advised us to continue that.

I grab a rag from Anders's kitchen to throw on the piddle. Then I pull on my boots and jacket, and Storm is at the front door, going nuts with the joy of her success. I look out the front window. It's dark, not surprisingly. Silent, too. Moonlight glistens off the snow.

I check my watch. It's barely midnight, but the street is empty, no sound of voices; people aren't in the mood to wander and socialize, which tells me just how anxious they're feeling since we brought Nicole back.

That worry pulls me into the house and over to the guys. Anders is still mostly upright, his head back on the chair, slouched as if he'd closed his eyes for a second and crashed. He's zonked, no hope of easily rousing him.

I walk to Dalton. Storm erupts in a frenzy of anxiety, thinking I haven't understood her current requirements. I bend and lay a hand on Dalton's shoulder, and Storm helps, her black tongue rasping over his bearded cheek. He doesn't stir.

"Come on then, girl," I say, more in hopes of waking him than communicating with her. Still no movement from either guy.

I take Storm to the back door instead, which makes her even happier. The forest is there. The glorious forest. I snap on her lead while she wriggles. The door opens, and she's out like a shot, leaving me stumbling after her.

"We're going exactly this far," I say as soon as I'm off the back deck, shuffling through the calf-deep snow.

Storm disagrees. Vehemently. Voices her disagreement in howls that, while adorable, will not be appreciated by Anders's neighbors.

When I sigh, she senses victory and begins yanking on the lead, straining toward the forest's edge.

"Ten steps." Then I count them, as if she's a child. When I reach ten, the long lead takes her just into the forest. She piddles. Then she does more than piddle, which makes me glad I brought her out.

Once she finishes that particular bit of business, she decides it's time for a walk and begins straining again. I'm reminded of what Dalton said, that Newfoundlands are members of the mastiff family, and I feel it in that pull, the warning that she's going to need to be very well trained, because when she's full grown, I'll lose the war if she decides she wants to go somewhere I don't.

For now, I yank back with a firm no.

We battle it out for a minute before she stops. Just stops, and I feel a momentary thrill of victory. Then I see her, body completely still, nose twitching, eyes wide.

She whimpers. It's tentative, uncertain, and I jog over, reeling in her lead. I enter the forest. I don't think about that. I hear her crying, and I run to her, and she plasters herself to my legs. She's shaking, and I know it's not the cold. I bend to pick her up. As I rise, movement flashes to my left. I spin and see nothing.

It's dark. Truly dark. We can't have outdoor lights. To use indoor ones after dusk, you must pull your blackout blinds to avoid the glow that signals a settlement.

When I'd been standing on the forest edge, the moon had lit the strip of yard to twilight. Now, inside the woods, trees block all but a glimmer of moonlight, and I am suddenly aware of how dark it is. How quiet. And that I left my gun inside.

I'm straining to listen, but Storm is whining and burrowing into my arms, an armful of anxiety and fur and claws as she scrabbles to get closer.

"Shh, shh, shh," I whisper.

What did you hear? What do you smell?

If it was a person, you'd be bounding over for hugs and pats because that is your life experience with humans—love and attention.

And yet . . .

I stand there, in the dark and the silence, and I remember Nana, when my father came across that yard to get me. She'd growled, and that had startled me, and I'd looked up to see him, and there was no outward reason for her growl. He wasn't bearing down on me. Wasn't snarling my name. Wasn't even scowling. My parents weren't like that. Sometimes I wished they had been. Sometimes I even wished they'd just haul off and smack me, because it would have been emotion, and I'd been so starved for any sign that they cared. I'd tell myself they must or they wouldn't try to keep me safe, but their kind of care always felt like putting the car in the garage or jewels in a safe. Protecting an investment.

My father had walked calmly into the yard that day. When he'd asked me to come with him, his voice was equally calm. He didn't lay a hand on me, but Nana had leapt up snarling, which of course, seemed only to prove his point that dogs were dangerous. The truth was that Nana recognized some sign that my father posed a threat, the same way a guy can offer to buy me a drink, as nice and respectful as possible, yet some sixth sense in my gut says to refuse.

Now Storm is desperately trying to hide in my arms from some unseen danger, and I can tell myself it's not human, but I know it is.

I just know.

My back is to the house. I take a step in that direction. Then another. I'm ready to wheel and run, but that means putting my back to him. I imagine the man in the snowmobile suit and that bar raised to hit me, and I know it might not be the same person, but this isn't a criminal investigation, where I need to consider all possibilities. I must seize the worst-case scenario and act as if it's the only one.

I'll be safe in a moment. Only a few steps to get out of the forest and another couple of dozen to the deck, and even if I don't make it that far, I'll be close enough to shout, close enough for Dalton or Anders to hear me.

Another step.

The squeak of snow underfoot. Not a crunch. Just a squeak. It's enough. I'm about to wheel and run, and Dalton's name is on my lips, but the moment that squeak comes, Storm flies from my arms, her back legs pushing to launch herself. She leaps in front of me, growling. I grab for her, but a shape moves in the forest, and she lunges, and I'm not gripping the leash. I don't even realize that until she's running and the lead snaps against my hands as it reels out.

I dive on it. Again, I don't think. I see that leash against the snow, and I dive, and I catch it. Something flashes, winking in the moonlight, like a steel bar flying from the darkness. It's swinging down at my dog, and I yank that leash so hard Storm yelps and flies backward, and I fly too with the momentum. I hear a shout of "Casey!" and footsteps running, and I yell, "Here!" but Dalton's already racing through the yard. No coat. No boots either.

He barrels over as I rise, leash in hand. He stops and exhales, as if realizing I just stepped out for the dog, but then I say, "Someone's out here."

I'm clutching the shaking puppy, and Dalton has his gun out, moving in front of me, squinting into the darkness. I start to step back, and he's so close we're touching, and when I move, he reaches as if to grab me.

"I'm retreating," I whisper. "I'm not armed, and—"

He nods before I can finish, and I turn, walking as he does the same in reverse, keeping our backs together, both of us scanning the darkness. When we reach the yard, he says, "Go!" and I race to the back door. I pull it open and glance over my shoulder, but he's right there. He covers me until we're inside and then I'm hugging Storm, consoling her as he shouts, "Will!" striding toward the living room.

I put Storm down and hurry to get my gun.

"Will!" Dalton says again, but Anders isn't even twitching, and Dalton walks over and says, "Calvin!"

Anders scrambles up, with "Wha—what?"

Calvin is Anders's real name. Calvin James. We don't ever use it, even in private, and it's not just for fear of slipping in public. Here, he wants to be Will Anders. Here, he is Will Anders.

He's up now, and Dalton is telling him to get his gun and his boots, someone's in the forest. Storm whimpers and presses against my legs.

"I'm sorry," I whisper. I lift her, run upstairs, and shut her in Anders's bedroom. She starts to yowl. I race back down. Anders is already out the door. Dalton pauses. He pauses and looks back at me, and I know what's going through his mind, the impulse to say, "Stay with the puppy." It's only a moment, though, and then he's nodding and holding the door open for me to go out.

TWENTY-THREE

We don't find anyone. There are boot prints, though, ones that match the prints from the storm, from the man in the snowmobile suit. You'd think, with snow on the ground, we'd be able to track him. *We* think we should be able to track him, and when we can't, the frustration keeps us out there long past the point where we've lost the trail—when he joined up with sled tracks from an afternoon patrol. We follow those tracks, flashlights shining on either side, looking for an exit point, until Anders finally says, "Guys . . . ," and as frustrated as we are, we know he has a point. We've gone too far from town. We've lost our chance.

On the way back, Dalton says to Anders, "About earlier. What I called you. I shouldn't have done that."

"It's cool."

"No. It's not."

"Yeah, it is. If you need me to wake up, that'll do it. Apparently, my subconscious mind still hasn't made the transition." When Dalton doesn't answer, Anders moves into the lead, slapping his back on the way and saying, "It's cool."

Dalton glances at me, and I move up beside him and take his hand. It still bothers him. He's off-kilter with this case. We all are. And it's just beginning.

Whatever Anders may have said to make Dalton feel better, being called by his real name nudges something deeper. We're sleeping in his living room again, after bringing Storm down and reassuring her, and I wake to a kick in my thigh. Anders is back in the same position as earlier—apparently, sleeping semi-upright is way more comfortable than one would imagine. The kick is from him, twitching in his sleep, and when I wake, he's mumbling under his breath, trapped in a nightmare. I catch a few words, enough to know he's remembering the war. He's telling someone to stay put, don't go out, damn it, don't go out until it's clear.

I lay my hand on his ankle, and he's shaking as hard as Storm was earlier. Sweat gleams on his face, catching moonlight edging through the blinds. When I squeeze his ankle, his eyes pop open and he gasps, as if coming up for air. He sees me and nods, and then he sits there, eyes half shut.

Anders catches his breath. Then he catches my eye, too, not a word exchanged, just a look, a shared understanding that, sometimes, when night comes, we can't be Will Anders and Casey Butler, that those other selves surge and remind us of pasts that won't ever go away. That shouldn't ever go away. Mistakes made. Terrible, life-altering mistakes. And that's who we are, at least when the lights go out, and the world goes quiet, and we can't pretend we've left those old incarnations far behind.

We're on the trail by daybreak. I'm still unsettled from last night, so as we ride, I indulge in self-therapy, mentally counting off things I've already done today that have made me happy. Waking to puppy kisses. Watching Dalton play in the snow with Storm. The gorgeous scenery as we ride, snow lacing the evergreens, steamy heat rising from the horses. My mare, Cricket, interpreting my subtle moves and responding in a way that feels like telepathy. Dalton, ahead of me, scanning the forest, both watchful and at peace, completely in his element. Anders, behind me, telling a story about a caribou encounter. And the reminder that we're going—not to see that terrible hole again, but to solve a crime, find a monster, and stop him. All that makes me happy, even the last, which is to me as soul-satisfying as gamboling with a puppy.

We take the horses all the way to the foothills. There we wait for Kenny, who is following on the snowmobile with Paul, another of the militia guys. They'll stay with the horses while they fill Anders's empty sled and tow Dalton's stuck one.

We climb to the cave. I don't hesitate for a second, beating Dalton up the hill and inside. He isn't fooled—he knows I'm going overboard to say, *See, I'm fine with this.* He also knows better than to question. This is my job. Let me do it.

Anders stands watch at the mouth of the cave. I lead Dalton to the hole. And there's nothing to find. Mathias is right—Nicole's captor has cleared the scene.

We aren't hunting a stupid man. He knew we'd taken Nicole. He's removed the boxes and candles and the skins. I curse myself for not taking a better look at the time, but the only thing on my mind had been the fact we'd just pulled a starving woman from a hole.

I still examine the scene. I check for anything left up top. Then I climb down into the hole. Dalton follows me.

There's blood on the walls. Long-dried blood, and I picture Nicole clawing the rock, trying to get a grip, her fingers raw and bloodied. Dalton's crouched on the floor, rubbing a large dark spot and then lifting his finger. It's red. I bend beside him, and he's looking at that spot, and I can see him mentally measuring the stain, and wondering what could leave that much blood and not kill her.

"She was pregnant," I say. "He ended it."

Dalton jerks back so suddenly he has to brace against the wall for support. He gives me a sidelong look, as if he isn't quite sure how to take this, how to comprehend it.

"It might not have been that," I say, but I look at that patch of blood, and I know I'm not wrong.

I stand. "I'm not getting clues here. Let's head back to Will."

TWENTY-FOUR

With Anders, we're crawling through the cave system. I don't know what I'm hoping to find, but I failed to secure and assess the scene the first time. I must be absolutely sure I've missed nothing now, or I'll wake in the middle of the night certain I overlooked some vital clue.

We're heading down a tunnel, checking every side crevice, none big enough to crawl through. Then, as my head-beam lamp passes through one, it reflects off something white. I pull back and try to get a better look, but the crevice opens into a drop, and what I see down it is a patch of white.

I check the crevice. It's narrow, but I could squeeze through.

Anders is in front of me. He's stopped, watching and waiting. Same as Dalton behind. When I say, "I see something in there," Dalton creeps forward, looks and says, "Got anything to fish it out with?"

"I can go in."

"Nope."

"I can. I'll fit—"

"Can and not. Buddy system. Will and I won't fit. So you aren't going in."

"It's right there. I just need to crawl four feet and then down two or three more. Hell, I can stretch out in there and reach."

"Nope."

"Boss?" Anders says, and when I glance over, he's giving Dalton a look, communicating a message that Dalton very clearly does not want as he pulls back and says, "Nope."

I glare at him. Then I tug off my backpack, making myself smaller, and start into the crevice. His hand lands on my ankle, gripping tight.

"Did I say no? Or are you forgetting who's in charge here."

"Oh, I didn't forget. But I don't think I'm talking to my boss right now."

He returns my glare, his jaw setting.

"Am I?" I say. "If Will could fit in there, would you tell *him* no?"

"This guy we're hunting? He's not going for Will."

"Tell that to Shawn Sutherland. And that"—I point at the patch of white—"is not our guy lying in wait."

"You sure?"

I look to Anders, who says, "Eric . . . ," in that voice that tells Dalton he's being unreasonable. Most times, Anders follows Dalton's lead, the amiable older brother, willing to recognize that the younger guy is in charge. Which means that when he uses the voice, it counts, and hearing it, Dalton rolls his shoulders, glowers at both of us, and says, "Go in and reach down, but stay where I can pull you back."

That's not as easy as it sounds. This isn't a tunnel—it's a crevice, which means I squeeze through. When I try pulling my legs in after me, Dalton gives a warning growl that means I'm teetering on the edge of crossing him. But he *is* being unreasonable. I don't know if it's vestigial panic from me getting lost in the storm, but it's making me testy. I have a job to do, and here he is my boss, not my lover.

So I squeeze through, one leg out where he can reach it. His fingers rest lightly on my ankle, confident that I'm obeying his commands. Once I'm in, I pull my legs in after me, too fast for him to grab, and he lets out a "Butler!"

"I need both my feet. You can still see me."

He starts to say something, but at the rumble of Anders's voice, any demands drop into unintelligible grumbles.

Now comes the tricky part—reaching down into the drop from a crouched position. I do some crazy rearranging, bracing myself between the rock walls until I'm in a weird semisuspended, half-upside-down position. Then I shine my headlamp down on that white patch.

"It looks like fabric. A shirt, maybe."

"Yeah," Dalton says. "From a special tailor who does only custom work and has this guy's address on file."

"You read too many mysteries," I say. "That never actually happens."

"Which is my *point,* Butler."

"I know. I'm just poking you, seeing as how you can't reach in here to poke me back."

He grumbles, but it's lighter as he relaxes.

"Whether this fabric can lead to a killer or not, I need to get it. Just give me . . ." I wriggle and stretch. Still about six inches short.

"It's not going anywhere," Dalton says. "We'll bring something back to fish it out."

"If I can just crawl down—"

"No."

"It's a crevice, not a hole. I can't fall through. I'll just shimmy—"

"No."

"Casey?" Anders says. "Just reach for it, okay? We don't know how deep that drop goes. If you can't get it, we'll come back."

He's right. It's just that I see a potential clue, and I already screwed up, leaving some behind when we took Nicole, and now they're gone, and I really need this one. Except I don't. It's not going to be a shirt with a name helpfully ironed in the collar. Hell, it could be a shirt covered in hairs, and that still wouldn't help. We don't have a crime lab here.

I take a deep breath and wriggle down another couple of inches and stretch as far as my fingers will reach. They brush the fabric. I just need another inch. I wriggle . . . and I slip. I hit a smooth section of rock, and my hip slides, and then I'm unwedged and falling. I hear Dalton's "Casey!" and Anders's curse, and I'm plunging headfirst down the crevice, body scraping the sides, arms and legs wildly trying to get a purchase, but the crevice has widened, and I'm not wedging in again. I'm falling, past that white cloth, past—

"Hands down!" Anders shouts. "Get your hands down!"

Battering the sides, I'm dropping slowly enough that I have time to get one hand over my head, the other rising to block my fall and keep my head from smacking rock.

My hands strike something. My elbows fold on impact, and my head rams into whatever my hands hit.

"Casey!" Dalton's voice booms from above.

I call back, "I'm okay." I think I'm okay. Not actually sure. I just know that I've stopped falling, and there's something below that's cushioned my landing. My helmet is pushed over my eyes, the lamp broken. Pain throbs through the arm that touched down first. Broken wrist? Damn it, no.

And, really, if that's the extent of the damage, I'm lucky, so stop whining.

True, but . . . shit. I'm wedged in a crevice, head down, no idea how far I've fallen and I can't—

I wriggle. Okay, maybe I *can* move.

"Casey!" Dalton's panicking now. He must not have heard my reply. Rock rains down on my legs. Damn it, did he squeeze into that first crevice? Of course he did. I exhale a sigh and then shout, as loud as I can.

"I'm fine, Eric. I'm at the bottom. Just hold on."

Wriggle, wriggle. Okay, there's some room here. Pull my one arm this way. There, it's through, and I find a grip on that side. My other arm is still against whatever cushioned my fall, and when I move it, I'm touching fabric with rocks beneath. Nicole's clothing. What she was wearing when she disappeared. That makes more sense than her captor randomly dropping his own shirt into this hard-to-reach hole. He stuffed her clothing down here to hide evidence.

Except . . . wait. Didn't he dress a corpse in her clothes?

Doesn't matter. Right now, the bigger concern is the guy freaking out at the top of the crevice, calling, "Can you get turned around? Can you move?"

I need to. If I don't, he's liable to try squeezing all the way down, and the only thing worse than being wedged in this crevice would be having Dalton even more wedged in above me, like a cork in a bottle.

"I can move," I call. "Just give me a second. I'm taking it slow."

"Okay, okay." The words come in a rush, as if he's reassuring himself more than me. Which is fine. Right now, he needs it more. He keeps talking, telling me Anders has gone back to get the rope from Nicole's hole, and fuck, why didn't he think to bring rope, and didn't he tell me not to go down this crevice? Didn't he order me not to go farther?

"Well, if you'd let me turn around and climb down feetfirst, I wouldn't be headfirst, would I?"

He goes silent. Then he mumbles what may be an apology, but I won't hold him to it.

I have my arm down now. Butt wriggling, wriggling. Wait, is that a concavity in the rock? Why, yes, it is. Twist, twist, twist. There. My ass is in the depression, which gives me more room. If I grab this jutting piece and then that one . . . Shit, that hurt. Rocks are not soft. Or smooth. I don't even want to know how many scratches and bruises I'll have after this.

Wriggle, twist, wriggle, twist.

"Are you turning around?" Dalton calls.

"Trying," I grunt.

"If you're going to hurt yourself, stop. We can figure this out."

"I'm—" I bite back a hiss of pain as my arm scrapes a sharp spot. "Got it. There's a depression that's just enough for . . . Yes! Almost—" I bite my lip as a muscle pulls.

"Don't hurt yourself. We'll—"

"Got it. Oh, yeah, I've totally got this. Just . . ." A grunt and a heave and twist and—"My feet are down. My head is up. I am properly perpendicular."

"Good. Don't try climbing. The rope's coming."

When I look up, I can see Dalton's light and part of his head. He is indeed inside the first crevice and now peering down the drop. Or I presume that's what he's doing. All I can see is the top of his head.

"Hey," I say. "I see you."

"Yeah." A grunt echoes down the crevice as he does some wriggling of his own, until I can make out his eyes. I realize the light coming down is from a penlight, not a headlamp.

"Where's your helmet?" I say.

"Didn't fit in."

"If mine did, yours would have." I sigh. "You didn't cut open your arm again, did you? The last time you came barreling after me, I had to stitch you up."

"I'm fine."

"Tell me that *fine* means there's no blood."

He doesn't answer. I sigh. "Damn it, Eric. You should have learned."

He still doesn't answer, which means he's not going to learn this particular lesson. If I'm in trouble, he's right behind me. The last time, I'd been exploring a narrow chute with Petra when we'd discovered an arm. She'd screamed—that unknown trauma from her past triggered.

I'm about to joke that at least there aren't any body parts down here. Then I remember who that arm had belonged to—Abbygail—and I stop myself.

"No body parts down there?" he says, and I smile and shake my head.

"Not this time," I say. "Just clothing." Which reminds me that I'm standing on it, and really should be checking that out, not chatting with Dalton. I guess that fall panicked me more than I'm letting on. I'm trembling even now with the relief of having gotten upright.

I look down. It is indeed clothing. A pair of jeans and a shirt. That's all I can make out; Dalton's penlight beam really isn't doing the job. I reach up and smack my headlamp. It flickers on and then off again. Another smack. Nothing. Dalton's stretching his arm down, saying, "You want my light? I'll toss . . ."

He trails off. I'm peering up at him. He says, "Casey?"

"Yep. Still in the hole." I wave. "See me?"

"Okay. Just keep looking up at . . ." He trails off again and says, "Fuck."

"Let me guess. Will can't get the rope?"

"No." He inhales. "I'm going to drop the light for you. Before I do, you need to listen to me."

"That's what I'm doing."

"Look at me until I'm done, okay?"

"Uh . . ."

"There's clothing at your feet."

"I know—"

"Just listen. That clothing doesn't belong to Nicole's captor."

I'm about to ask how he can tell. Then I figure it out. He's still talking, and when I move, he says, "Keep looking up at me until—"

I look down, following the beam of his penlight to see a skull grinning back at me.

TWENTY-FIVE

I'm standing on a body.

I don't panic. That could be because I've seen too many corpses in my life. But the real reason? I decide it's not real. I've hit my head on the way down, the blow penetrating the helmet, and I'm not actually conscious right now. I dreamed of getting upright and chatting to Dalton and joking about not finding body parts, and then looking down and seeing an entire corpse under my feet. It's my brain trying to be amusing and failing miserably.

That's what makes sense. The possibility I'm actually awake, in another cave finding another dead body? Not happening.

So I'm just going to sit and wait to regain consciousness. Plunk my ass down on . . .

A body. I'm standing on a body, a long-dead corpse stuffed into the hole, that "skull" not actually bone but desiccated flesh with hair still clinging to it. Long dark hair. There are earrings in the leathery flaps that would be ears. Small diamond studs.

A lover bought me diamond studs once. The first guy I dated after my attack. No, not dated. Slept with. Because even three years after the beating and Blaine, all I could manage was succumbing to the physical drive to take a lover. He'd bought me diamond studs for Christmas, and I'd ended it then. Left those studs on the bedside table and slipped out in the night, never to return.

I squeeze my eyes shut. Shock. I'm in shock. Or asleep. I prefer *asleep*.

Dalton calls, as if from a mile away, his voice growing sharper each time he says my name.

I need to respond. Reassure him. Even if this isn't real, I must reassure him.

I look up. He's wriggled into that crevice so far I can see his whole face now, eyes anxiously fixed on me.

"It's okay," he says. "We'll get you out."

"I'm fine."

"We'll—"

"Eric? I'm a homicide detective. I'm fine. It was just a surprise. You tried to warn me. Thank you."

There's a too-calm note to my voice. Definitely shock. I reach up to rub my face briskly, and I catch the stink of the long-dead on my fingers. I fling my hands down.

Deep breaths.

Don't let him see you taking deep breaths.

"So we have another victim," I say, in that too-calm voice, and this is what's really panicking me. Not the fact I'm standing on a body, but what that body signifies. Someone who did not get out of Nicole's hole alive.

"We don't know that," Dalton says. "He could have fallen. Done the same thing you did, and if he wasn't with a partner—"

"It's a she."

"Fine. *She* fell. It happens, and it's a tragedy, but people disappear out here. Hikers, campers, spelunkers—"

"She's not dressed for that. She's wearing a sweater and jeans."

He makes that growling sound—I'm annoying him with my logic. This is not the time for that shit.

I try to wiggle my ass down to take a better look at the body.

"Don't—" Dalton begins.

"Homicide detective, remember. Not going to mess up my own crime scene. Except for the fact I am inadvertently standing on the body." I curse and try to shift my feet, which only makes things worse, bones crackling under my boots, the sound making me freeze as I am all too aware I'm crunching a victim, adding insult to injury.

Speaking of injury . . .

Yes, let's focus on that. What did she die of?

It's impossible to even guess, given my angle and the way the body is wedged. I move as carefully as I can to one side, wincing as the corpse shifts with the movement. As it does, though, I see a hand. A brown-skinned hand still wearing a gold wristwatch.

I see that hand . . . while seeing both light-skinned hands of the poor woman I'm standing on.

"Eric?" I call.

When he doesn't answer, I look up, and he's not there, and I'm thrown into my nightmare, where he's at the top of the hole and then he's gone and—

"Eric!"

"Here!" His voice booms, and he scrabbles against rock. "I'm right here. Will's back, and I'm getting the rope from him. Just hold on."

"There's another one."

Pause. "What?"

"There's another body. I'm standing on *two* victims."

We're back in Rockton. We barely made it to the edge of town before Dalton was off his horse, waving the reins at the poor resident who happened to be walking past. She takes them, looking bewildered, and Anders says, "Just lead him behind us." Dalton's making a beeline for Val's. He gets about twenty paces and stops. Wheels. Snaps, "Butler?" and resumes walking.

"That's my cue," I say as I slide from Cricket. Anders reaches for the reins. As he takes them, he whispers, "He's just freaked out."

"I know," I say, and jog to follow Dalton.

By the time I get there, Dalton is already striding into Val's living room, having not bothered to knock, telling her we brought back two bodies and get the goddamned council on the phone now.

Val's gaze shoots my way, as if begging me to tell her this is some terrible joke. But the fact that I'm standing beside Dalton answers that question.

She looks as if she's going to be sick. Physically sick. For once, she does not argue when we demand to speak to the council.

Ten minutes later, Phil is on the speaker. He tells Dalton that, yes, he realizes it's urgent, but Dalton needs to have Val call ahead and set up an appointment time.

"Yeah, fuck that," Dalton says and launches into an expletive-peppered description of what we've found. "We need a doctor," he says. "We have two goddamned bodies and no one qualified to examine them."

Phil sighs. "If we haven't found a doctor in four months, we certainly can't do it in the next—"

"There used to be a guy," Dalton says. "A former resident who stayed on call until we got someone else."

"Dr. Russell. He passed away five years ago. And before you ask, no, we do not have *another* former resident who was also a medical professional and willing to be on call. We've been through this. We've contacted the last two town doctors—"

"Yeah, yeah. They were assholes. I don't want them back."

No one mentions Beth. There's still part of me that might say, in an emergency, maybe she could return, briefly. . . . But after what she did to me, Dalton couldn't get her out of Rockton fast enough. And we don't even know if she's alive.

I can tell myself the council wouldn't execute her for her crimes. For the exposure threat she posed, though? That's why we're stuck with Diana, isn't it?

If I say I'm sure Beth's alive, I'm being naive. Willfully naive? I hate that, but this is how we deal with the bargain we've made. We live in our castle, and we protect those within and pretend not to see that the moat is filled with ravenous piranhas. Yes, perhaps, every now and then, someone falls in, but they swim out and wander off. Yes, that's it. Everyone who leaves is out there, alive and well.

"Perhaps I need to say this slower for you, Eric," Phil continues. "We do not have a doctor to send."

"At all?" There's a note in Dalton's voice that I know well, and I realize what he's getting at, but Phil only sighs and says, "I'm going to blame this misbehavior on stress. I understand you are concerned, Eric. I understand how difficult it must be to have Ms. Chavez return in that condition and now to find two bodies that may be connected. But extenuating circumstances aside, there is a limit to how many times—and in how many ways—I can tell you, no, we do not have a doctor up our sleeves."

"No?" Dalton says. "Not one hiding in plain sight?"

"Phil?" I say. "It's Casey."

A soft sigh, relief at the chance to deal with a rational person. "Detective, yes. Hello."

"I believe what Eric's asking is whether we have a doctor in town that he doesn't know about."

Silence. "Pardon me?"

"Eric is on the selection committee, so he knows who we have here." *Or who you pretend we have here.* "But perhaps there's a resident who asked you not to reveal his or her former occupation. Who was a viable candidate without that professional advantage and didn't want to practice medicine here."

"No," Phil says, "we do not have anyone like that, Detective Butler. For medical expertise you have Mathias Atelier and Deputy Anders. That will, I'm afraid, need to be sufficient."

So we have one psychiatrist who has never practiced medicine. One army medic who has never practiced medicine. Plus one homicide detective who has never even *trained* in medicine. That is who now stands around the bodies of two dead women. They deserve so much better.

Dalton isn't with us. He told me he had "to check something." That's not squeamishness. The day I arrived in town, they'd brought in a mutilated body, and Dalton had been right in there, like it was a high school science project. Anders had been the one most affected, and at the time, I hadn't thought much of it, except that he was a deputy, probably unaccustomed to corpses. But as a war veteran, he *is* accustomed to corpses, and that's the problem. Show him a body in pieces, and he's back in that war, what he saw there, and everything that goes with it.

Now we're looking at these two women, and Mathias says, "The desiccation is interesting. I presume it's a dry cave?"

"That section is," I say. "But I haven't seen anything like this outside a museum."

"I have," Anders says. "Desert does the same thing, if a body's been out there long enough."

I glance over. His face is impassive, and I have no idea what's going on behind those dark eyes, but when he notices me looking, he offers a tiny smile and mouths, *I'm fine.*

"Abbygail's arm was like this," Anders says. "Not quite as preserved, and with more scavenger damage, but it would have ended up similar to this. So . . . let's get to it." He turns to me. "As the only person with forensic experience . . ."

I nod and scrub in.

"Will, can you—?" I look over to see he already has a notebook and pen, ready to take dictation.

I remove the women's clothing, one piece at a time, one corpse at a time. It's not easy. Some of it has fused to their bodies.

"There's evidence of decomposition," I say. "Arrested decomposition, suggesting the killer—" I stop. "Sorry. Detective brain butting in. Just the facts, ma'am."

"These notes are for you, Casey—" Mathias speaks English for Anders's benefit. "I do not think we must stand on protocol. Including interpretations along with the observations may prove helpful. As you were saying . . ."

"Arrested decomposition suggests the first body was not immediately placed in that crevice, but began the process of decay in another climate, and then was moved to the crevice. The second body—" I stop. "Start again. For the purpose of these notes, the 'first' body is the one found on the bottom. That doesn't mean she was killed first, though that does seem like a reasonable early interpretation. I'm going to continue removing garments with the warning that I may damage the tissue of the first body in doing so."

I proceeded slowly, meticulously. Clothing off. Folded. Placed in plastic bags.

"Both bodies are female," I say. "Both in an advanced state of desiccation. I'm going to make preliminary observations, which I will research later to determine time of death. I'll ask Dr. Atelier and Deputy Anders to assist in those observations."

We're making notes on the state of the bodies only. Mathias offers interpretations as well. He's sure I'm right about the order of the deaths, which only makes sense. The first victim dies and is later disposed of in that crevice. When the second also dies, she's immediately dropped there.

As for cause of death? "There is significant damage to the back of both skulls," I say. "All three of us agree death appears to be from blunt-force trauma."

I think of Sutherland's bloodied toque. I think of that pipe, heading for the back of my head.

"Given the state of the bodies, it is difficult to determine lesser forms of trauma. We do see some postmortem injuries, presumably arising from their environment and the manner in which they were discovered." The investigator *landing* on them and then having to squeeze them through very tight passages. "But we do see evidence of a broken and badly healed ankle with the first body. Rib damage with the second. There are also signs of . . ." I'm about to say *enforced captivity,* but I'm extrapolating. Instead, I list my observations. Untreated dental decay. Evidence of malnutrition. Hair and nail damage.

Signs that these women were not captured, killed, and dumped in quick succession. Signs that we are looking at Nicole's intended fate: held in a hole until . . .

Until what? She became too malnourished? Until her captor found a replacement? Or simply until he tired of her?

The door opens. Dalton walks in, papers in hand.

"We're just finishing up," I say. "I was just going to do another check for identifying features. Not that I expect we'll identify them but . . ." I shrug. "It'll help."

He walks to the second body and lifts her arm, his gaze going to her wrist. He rubs his thumb over the skin, smoothing it, and as he does, something I missed in the wrinkled, desiccated skin. Lateral scars. Then I realize he went straight to it. As if he knew exactly what he was looking for.

A chill slides over me. "Eric?"

He walks to the first body and checks the knees. There are surgical scars there—I'd noted them. He takes a closer look and then nods.

"Eric . . . ?"

He lays a photo on the first body. A photo of a woman about my age, brown skin, dark wavy hair. Like the body on the table. On the second he places a photo of a woman about the same age, with long dark hair and blue eyes, matching the corpse beneath it.

He turns to the first body. "Robyn Salas. Disappeared March 20, 2010." Then to the second. "Victoria Locke. Disappeared July 3, 2012."

TWENTY-SIX

We're on the back deck at the station, tequila shots in hand. I've taken one already. So has Anders, leaning against the railing, bundled up and trying not to shiver. He's eyeing his second shot. Tequila isn't really his thing, but it looks mighty good right now, a defense against the cold and the mood, both settling around us.

He downs his. I follow and put my glass aside. Two's my limit, and not for any reason other than that there have been times in my life when a third looked so good. And a fourth and a fifth. I've seen too many cops go down that road, never to return. Up here, restraint is even more important. It's too easy to use alcohol to push back the darkness.

Dalton hasn't poured himself a second shot. Two is for home, when it's just me, and he doesn't care what he says and, sometimes, says what needs saying. Tonight it's one.

He's been talking about the dead women. About Nicole, too. Until now, we haven't spoken much of her as a person. That's not disrespectful. It's oddly the opposite—she's here and alive, therefore it's wrong to talk about her. But now we do, both men giving their impressions of her before she disappeared into the forest.

As I'd already gathered, neither had known Nicole well. She'd been here only about six months, and she herself had said she hadn't mingled much.

"I ran into her now and then," Anders says. "I'd talk for a few minutes, try to get to know her."

"Did you sleep with her?" Dalton asks.

Anders looks at him. Just looks.

"What?" Dalton says. "Valid question. Percentage-wise, you've worked your way through, what, half?"

"At least I'm sociable."

"That what you call it?"

"Guys . . . ," I say.

"Percentage-wise, maybe *ten*," Anders says. "Which is better than your zero." He looks at me. "Sorry. One."

"Ten percent? Math isn't your strong suit, is it?" Dalton says. "If we've got about fifty women here—"

"Whatever. How about the earlier victims, boss? I seem to recall stories about you getting around back in the day. Or am I not supposed to talk about that in front of Casey?"

"Casey is absolutely fine with it," I say. "Casey is grateful for those women who took it upon themselves to school a young man. And Casey would be equally fine if one or both of the women in question had slept with Eric. While she'd like to point out that this is an inappropriate topic of conversation about victims, Casey also recognizes that this is Rockton. It is actually, as Eric says, a valid question. Were either of you *that* close to them? Close enough they may have divulged information there that they wouldn't have otherwise."

"The answer is no," Anders says. "No pillow talk—or sex—with Nicki or Victoria. I postdate Robyn. And by that I mean I arrived after she vanished. There was no actual dating involved."

"And they all postdate my youthful adventures," Dalton says. "But, yeah, let's talk to friends and lovers. For Nicole and the others."

The others.

Robyn Salas. Aged thirty-three. Ballet dancer in Toronto, she'd had an obsessive fan who turned into a stalker. When she took out a restraining order, he lay in wait and rammed her with his car, breaking her knees so badly she'd never dance again. He got free on a technicality and came after her to "finish the job." Someone gave her a line to Rockton and she fled here, where like Nicole, she flew under the radar, just another of the dozens of residents that Dalton knew only in passing. She'd vanished four months after she arrived. When a search party failed to turn up anything, Dalton's father had ruled it death by exposure.

Victoria Locke. Aged thirty-five. Victoria had been one of the white-collar criminals who bought her way in. She'd run a Ponzi scheme with her sister. The sister took off with most of the money, leaving Victoria to the police, with just enough cash to buy two years in Rockton. After she vanished, they'd found her jacket, clawed and covered in blood, and after more searching, Dalton had to admit it seemed like she'd been killed by a bear.

As for her personality? "An odd one," Dalton says. "Not like Nicole or Robyn. They just seemed quiet. Victoria wasn't a whole lot different than some of the guys out in those woods. Reclusive. Kinda paranoid. Just wanted to hunker down and wait out her term. I used to think she'd be happier if we just gave her a damn cave—" He stops himself. "Fuck."

Fuck, indeed.

Three missing women. Two dead bodies. One man presumed dead. Zero leads.

During the murders this past fall, I'd marveled at how the town stayed calm. People trusted Dalton to resolve it. Only when we confirmed Abbygail's murder did that change as the town mourned one of its most popular residents.

This is different.

We have a woman who was kept captive for fifteen months. We went looking for a missing man and returned with two bodies. People have connected the dots. They know what we have out there. And they are not angry. They are afraid.

We go to the Lion for dinner. It doesn't occur to the guys that this might be problematic. I keep my mouth shut, wanting hot food made by someone else and hoping this will be the same as before. Sure, we'll get those brave souls sidling up and saying, *So, about what's going on . . .* but one look from Dalton will send them scurrying.

That's all we get until we're midway through our meal, and it's as if they waited until we were comfortable and unlikely to flee. Then they descend.

Is it true you found two more victims?

Who are they?

What's going on?

Is it someone out there?

Is it someone in here?

What's going on?

Where's Shawn?

Are you still looking for him?

What's going on?

And what are you going to do about it?

Dalton's glowers and snarls send them scattering, but he's like a dog in a rat pit, beset on all sides, snapping at one assailant only to have another leap in from the unguarded side.

I promise a public update at daybreak. Right now, we're exhausted, just exhausted.

But they are afraid. They don't say that. I hear it in their voices, see it in their eyes.

Is it one of us?

Are we safe?

How are you going to keep us safe?

Dalton won't rush through dinner to escape. Like that dog in the pit, he holds his ground. Finally, it's over, and we get about ten paces down the road before someone grabs my arm. Dalton spins, all the anger and frustration bubbling up as he knocks the hand off, sending the person—Trent, one of our local handymen—stumbling back.

"I just wanted to ask—" Trent begins.

"And you think you're the only one? The only fucking person who wants an update?" Dalton's voice rings down the dark road.

"I just—"

"What's our job?"

"I just want to know—"

"I asked you, what's our job? Are we the goddamn local news? Or are we the ones trying to catch a killer?"

"I just wanted to ask Casey—"

"You're not going to stop, are you? Your personal concerns are more important than our detective returning to work on this case."

Dalton jerks his chin, telling me to keep moving. I take a step. Trent's hand lands on my arm again.

"Just tell me—" That's as far as he gets before Dalton's right hook hits. Trent goes down. Then he's up again, hauled to his feet by Dalton, who drags him, stumbling, to the station.

Even with that brief altercation, we've attracted a crowd, those lurking about, not daring to approach, but hoping someone like Trent would and they'd overhear the details and reassurances they want. As Dalton drags Trent through town, people pop out from houses to watch.

The first time I saw Dalton do this, I was horrified. It seemed textbook police brutality. But this isn't beating the shit out of a suspect behind closed doors and then claiming he fell down the stairs. Everyone who watches knows what has happened. Everyone knows this is what will happen if they interfere with our case. Everyone agrees, in silent accord, that this is fair, and as they watch, they roll their eyes and shake their heads at the dumb-ass who crossed Dalton.

Trent gets tossed in the cell, where he'll spend the night. Once Trent's situated, Dalton is up on the station front porch, as Anders and I wait at the bottom. Dalton's gaze travels over the growing crowd. Then he motions to me. I climb to stand in front of him.

"You want answers," I say to the crowd. "We get that. You know we do. But you also know we can't respond to each of you individually. Everyone has the same questions. Everyone will get the same answers. Tomorrow. Nine A.M. Right here. Until then, Eric, Will, and I are still on the clock. Still figuring things out. Still getting you answers."

"As Detective Butler has been doing since she *found* Nicole," Dalton says. "Since she and Deputy Anders went after Shawn Sutherland, got trapped in a fucking snowstorm, found Nicole, and brought her back through *another* fucking snowstorm. And they went back out there today, to that cave, finding two more victims, which they have spent the fucking day studying to get you your fucking answers. Understood?"

"Fuck, yeah," says one of the militia guys, and that gets a laugh, and people relax, easing back, nodding, voices rippling through with murmurs of thanks and offers of help and apologies for the "assholes" who bothered us, because, you know, it sure wasn't them.

"Now, if you'll excuse us," I say. "We have a puppy to pick up. If anyone has concerns unrelated to recent events, Deputy Anders has five minutes to answer before he joins us to continue working the case."

"You bringing him tomorrow?" someone asks.

I look at Anders. "Depends on if we can drag his ass out of bed that early."

"The *puppy*. Are you bringing the puppy?"

"I'll consider it."

Dalton moves forward. "Only if no one else accosts her trying to walk down the damn road. Now—"

Jen steps into my path.

"No," Dalton says. "Hell, no."

"I need to speak to you," she says to me.

"Did you not hear a word I said?" Dalton says. Then he turns to Anders. "I told you we need more cells."

"Jen?" Anders says. "Casey is exhausted. If you want to talk to me, I've got a few minutes. Or you can speak to her in the morning."

"It's about the case," she says.

Dalton is ready to sweep her aside, but I say, "Do you have information?"

"I want to help. I want to join the militia."

"What the hell?" Dalton says. "You haven't wanted to do anything since you got here, and now you want to join the militia? The hell you do. You just want inside information, and you think this is the way to get it."

"No, I want to—"

"Detective Butler?" a woman steps from the shadows. I know who it is, but I stare, as if I must be wrong, because it seems to be Val. Out of her house. At a town conference.

Dalton seems ready to snarl at her, too, but he stops himself and looks at me, silently asking first. Do I feel up to dealing with Val? If not, he's happy to threaten her too—it's not as if their relationship can possibly get worse.

I say to Val, "Sure, I can spare a few minutes. Jen, talk to me about that later, okay?"

Dalton's lips tighten at that last part. He's warning me I shouldn't encourage Jen—since I got here, she's been nothing but a bitch to me, and I have every reason for refusing to even entertain her request. But I'll listen. I have to give her a chance.

TWENTY-SEVEN

I shouldn't have gone with Val. Anders and Dalton weren't exaggerating—I'm beyond exhausted. Mentally, physically, emotionally, each seeming to sap energy from the others. In short, I am in no condition to deal with Val.

We get inside, and she says, "These murders. Do you think they were committed by the same man who took Nicole?"

I open my mouth to give a neutral response and instead say, "Does it matter?"

Val blinks. "What?"

"Oh, sure," I say. "It matters to me. Huge implications for the investigation. And it matters to the average citizen. Are we looking at a serial pattern here? Or are there multiple monsters preying on Rockton women? But does it matter to you, Val? Does anything? You sit here with the blinds drawn and wait for it to all go away. Wait until *you* can go away. What even is your purpose here? You're not the town leader. You're a glorified telegraph operator . . . and we barely send a telegraph a week. It's the worst example of bureaucratic inefficiency in a town that can't afford *any* inefficiency."

She stares at me.

"I'm sorry," I say. "I'm tired. Very, very tired. I'll come back tomorrow and answer your question properly."

I get up and start for the door.

"Wait," she says.

I stop, my hand on the doorknob.

"I know what you think of me, Casey, and I would argue that I do much more than operate the satellite radio, but I suspect you know that. You *are* tired. Tired and frustrated, and perhaps, with me, you have reason to be."

I stay where I am.

"I would like to hear your thoughts on these crimes," she says. "If you have a moment."

I turn to face her. "On the understanding that I may say things I shouldn't?"

Her lips twitch, just a little. "I believe I already know that."

I go back to the living room.

"My gut says one perpetrator," I say as I sit. "But I'm being careful not to jump to that conclusion. I need proof beyond the fact that all three victims were from Rockton and found in that cave system."

"And the condition of the bodies? Would it . . . suggest . . . ?"

"Suggest Robyn and Victoria had been held captive, too? It's hard to tell, given how long they'd been there, but there were signs of prolonged captivity, consistent with what we see in Nicole. I still can't presume it's one perpetrator without proof. That would seriously affect my investigation. First, it would mean he couldn't be from Rockton."

"Here? Why would he be from here?"

Of all people, she should know, but she seems genuinely shocked, and if I explain, I'll tumble headfirst into anger again.

"A single perpetrator means the only locals who've been here long enough are Eric and Isabel," I say. "Nicole last saw her captor the day before we rescued her, when Eric was in Dawson City. And her captor was clearly male, so it's not Isabel. Therefore, one perpetrator would mean an outsider."

"Which it is. It must be."

"If it's not multiple perpetrators, the killer could be someone who is no longer here. Or the captor would be someone still here. That would imply separate cases. More likely, it'd be two perpetrators working together. Mentor and student, their times in Rockton overlapping enough for them to discover their shared interests."

"It's *not* someone from Rockton, Casey. It's one of them. Out there." She straightens her blouse. "I realize we have some people here who have committed crimes. But they are not the kind who'd do this. This is, as you said, a monster. Or *monsters*. We don't have that here."

Does she know that for a fact? Or is she toeing the party line?

The first time I met Val, she struck me as classic middle management, from her attire to her demeanor. In many ways, that's what she is, which means that while she has to know more about Rockton than us mere employees, she may not know the worst of it.

Dalton thinks she knows what we have here—he jokes that's why she never comes out of her house. But looking at her now, something in her expression tells me she believes what she's saying. Or she wants to. Desperately wants to.

"You believe it's hostiles," I say. "Or settlers."

"I don't know why Sheriff Dalton makes the distinction," she snaps. "They're *all* hostiles. No one would choose to live there. No one normal."

I don't argue, fearing that, in my exhaustion, I'll say more than I should about Dalton's own past.

"At some point," I say, "I would like to ask you about your experience with them. The hostiles."

I say it as gently as I can, but she still flinches.

"Not right now," I add. "But if my investigation swings in that direction, as you think it will, I'll need as much as I can get on them, from as many angles as possible. Eric says—"

"You're asking Sheriff Dalton about the hostiles? That's like asking the pot about the kettle."

I bite my tongue. Hard. "I know your experience of them is very different from his," I say when I can speak again. "That is why I'd like to talk to you."

"I don't think that will be necessary, Detective. I appreciate your thoroughness, but I'm sure you can find others to more adequately discuss the topic. I will, however, guarantee that is what you are looking at here. Whether one monster or several, they come from out there. Not in here."

———

My first "press conference" was memorable for being the first one ever to be held in Rockton. I talked Dalton into letting me do it by convincing him that updating a gathering once was more efficient than snarling at an unending succession of citizens.

Otherwise, that conference was memorable only for the sheer unmemorability of it. I'm accustomed to dealing with pushy members of the press and outraged members of the public, all trying to get their two cents in while paying very little attention to what the police are actually saying. That first time in Rockton, they listened to the update, and they accepted it, much the way one accepts the announcement of a minor flight delay—grumble a bit, but trust that the airline has the situation in hand.

When I hold my conference this morning, people are more unsettled. They have questions. Yet they still listen and accept and, yes, trust.

I spin the story to emphasize the likelihood that the killer comes from without. From the forest. I'm careful to warn that might not be the case, and everyone needs to be careful in town too, but mostly, I want them staying out of those woods.

TWENTY-EIGHT

After the press conference, I head to speak to Nicole. Diana is at the house. Despite my reservations, she's doing an excellent job with Nicole.

I don't know what it's like to be in Diana's head. God knows, I've tried getting there. I realize it's not uncommon for people to still love their abusers, to put up with the abuse and even turn against those who try to help them. I know it. I don't understand it. With everything Diana did, it would seem she never truly recognized she was being abused, that she paid lip service to it for my sake, while seeing only the exciting emotional tumult of a toxic relationship.

Yet her patience and kindness with Nicole make me wonder if I'm being unfair. If she did feel trapped in her relationship with Graham, knowing it was abusive but unable to break away. Maybe the sympathy and care she gives to Nicole as a victim is the sympathy and care she couldn't give to herself.

I think that, and then I think of all the ways Diana betrayed me, all the times I thought I understood her motivations and suffered for it.

When I reach the house, Nicole is on the front porch, bundled in a nest of blankets, wearing dark sunglasses as she sits in a shard of sunlight, her face tilted up to catch it. A cat long denied the sun, now basking in it. When she sees me, she sits up and says she'll come inside, but I tell her not to rush, I have to check in with Diana first. Nicole settles back in her sunlight, and I head indoors.

Diana's in the kitchen, making tea. We talk. We're capable of that, though I'm well aware of how odd those conversations are, speaking to my oldest friend as if she were any other resident tasked with Nicole's care. Polite and businesslike, not a spark of warmth between us. No chill either. Just . . . nothing.

Before she leaves, she says, "I hear you have a puppy."

I tense and say, "Eric got her for me. To train for tracking."

"Good idea." She pulls on her boots. "Do you remember when I tried to talk you into getting a cat?"

"Uh-huh."

A brief smile. "You're not really a cat person. A dog's better. I'm glad you have one. I saw you with her the other day. She's adorable."

"Thanks."

"You looked happy."

I pause, tensing again, as I say, carefully, "I am . . . ," and I'm waiting for the inevitable comment, the one that suggests she's done me a favor, tricking me into coming to Rockton, but she only nods and then, before she goes, says, "The next time you come by, maybe you can bring the puppy. Nicole would like that. She mentioned it, and I suggested she ask you to bring her, but she doesn't want to be a pest. It might cheer her up. She tries to hide it, but it's . . . rough. Really rough. Especially the nightmares. I know Will left sedatives, but she's not taking them. I don't feel right sneaking them into her tea at night, but I *am* tempted."

"I'll talk to Will and Isabel."

Diana makes a face at the mention of Isabel. There was an issue between them early on, where Isabel had been convinced Diana was "freelancing." Selling sex, in other words. But I get only that face— no argument—and then she's gone, promising to be back in an hour.

Nicole comes inside, and I set the two books beside a chair. She moves them farther from the fire, giving me a wry smile and saying, "Sorry. That's how he used to keep me in line. Burn pages of my writing."

I imagine that. He could threaten to take away her food, her water, torture her, even kill her, but what good does that do when someone *wants* to die? No, he threatened the only thing she cared about.

I say I'm sorry, but that makes her uncomfortable. Like when she'd apologized over taking the books with her. They would to us seem inconsequential. To her, they'd been the one good thing that came of her time down there—maybe not even the stories themselves, but what they represented, those hours when her mind escaped that hole.

"About the other women," she says. "Are they . . . his?"

"We aren't sure. Did he mention that he'd done this before? Taken captives?"

She shakes her head. "No, but . . . sometimes he'd reference other women. I figured they were girlfriends or such. Now I wonder if he was referring to *them*. Those women you found." She takes a notebook from the side table. "I made a list of everything he'd said about other women."

I move to sit beside her, and we go through her notes. A pattern emerges, one I've read about in serial killer cases. A man searching for a woman who fits a very warped set of criteria. His perfect mate. When each victim fails to meet his expectations, he resorts to shaping—giving his victim hints on how she should behave to make him happy. How she should behave to stay alive.

As for shaping *him,* one woman stands above all others. His mother. Sometimes, in crimes like these, men seem to be looking for that unconditional love. Nicole's captor played out yet another variation on the maternal theme: looking for the kind of woman his mother considered worthy. And his mother was very particular.

"I remember him saying how one woman tricked him. He thought she was single, no children. She had a scar, and he didn't know what it was from. She said she'd had a baby, who lived with his father. He checked me for a C-section scar like hers. Made me swear I'd never been married. His mother said divorced women are whores, and he shouldn't touch them."

Victoria Locke had left her six-year-old son with his father when she came to Rockton.

"He also checked me for tattoos," she says. "Another 'sign of the whore.' He said he'd been tricked about that, too. He'd been with a woman for a while before he realized she had a tattoo on her lower back. Some 'heathen symbol,' he said. Which made it twice as bad. Mother would not have approved."

"Did you get the sense his mother was still alive?" I ask. "Up here? Or down south?"

"He never said. It didn't seem like he ever planned to introduce us. He just had to reassure himself that she'd have approved of the woman he was, you know, raping. He never tried to fancy that up, either. I thought he would. In the movies, guys like him tell themselves they love the woman they're kidnapping. That she'll see he's amazing and fall for him. I kept waiting for a sign of that, so I could use it. I even tried to fake caring for him. Fake . . ." She steels herself. "Fake enjoying it. He didn't like that. He wanted exactly what he had—an unwilling captive. One who met his mother's requirements."

"And you did."

"So it seemed. But that didn't help. He kept looking for flaws. Always looking."

Because he *wanted* to find flaws. That justified the abuse. Justified the murders.

We talk for a while after that. Before I leave, she says, "I'd like to go for a walk."

"Sure, just ask whoever's on guard duty to take you. I'd rather you didn't wander around town alone, but you aren't a prisoner here."

"I mean into the forest."

I sit back down.

"Yes," she says. "I know, that should seem like the last thing I'd want. Which is why I do. I loved the forest. I got captured because I loved it. I said I wanted berries, but I wanted the excuse more. I don't blame the forest for what happened. I blame myself. I knew how dangerous it was, and I didn't respect that."

I understand. That is the lesson my parents failed to impart, the one I now get from Dalton. Whether it's the forest or horseback riding or ATVs or snowmobiles or caving . . . this thing you're doing? It might kill you. But it's amazing too, so take precautions and enjoy it. My parents had stopped at the "might kill you" part. But this is life, isn't it? It's amazing . . . and it might kill you. In fact, someday, it will.

"Yes," I say. "I get that. But—"

"Did you get any of this growing up? Camping? Hiking? Cottage?"

"Some."

"To me 'wilderness' was that stuff between cities. The stuff I saw out a car window. Well, except for this summer camp when I was eleven and my dad was still trying to pretend things were normal. The girls in my cabin complained nonstop. The heat. The bugs. The dirt. Ick, ick, and more ick. I didn't even bother forming my own opinion. Just latched onto theirs, as I always did."

"Understandable, under the circumstances."

"Which doesn't stop me from looking back and thinking, *God, I was a twit*. And in this case, I missed out on what could have been an amazing experience. But I got a second chance when I came here. The forest became my place to escape. My wild paradise. But when we were coming back here from the mountain, all I could think was *get me out of here*. Out of the forest. Whatever peace I found there, he took it from me. I want it back."

"I completely get that, and I agree, but it's only been a few days."

"Take it slower?" She shakes her head. "The longer I wait, the harder it'll be to go in there again."

"Okay, but . . . as much as I agree with the impulse in theory? He's still out there."

"Which means if you take me, you might be able to catch him."

"By using you as bait? No, I wouldn't—"

"Yes, suggesting that it might lure in my captor is an excuse. It's not like he's lurking beyond the town line. If he is, and you're there to shoot him? Great. Otherwise, I'd just like to tag along while you walk that puppy of yours. Let me face the forest, and then I'll get back in here and shut up." She smiles. "At least for a while."

TWENTY-NINE

I'm in the clinic helping Anders put Robyn Salas back on the examining table. We're storing the bodies in the crypt, which is not unlike the iceboxes in our homes—a cold-storage area under the floor, dug down to permafrost.

Body disposal is one of the more complicated problems facing Rockton. We can't send those who've allegedly disappeared home. We can't cremate them without the power needed to run an incinerator. Nor can we practice a more natural method—like placing the body on a platform—when we can't risk anyone discovering it. And the permafrost rules out a mass burial. Instead, not unlike serial killers, we must scatter our dead in shallow graves, spaced out and well hidden. That can't happen until the ground thaws, though. Until then, we have full access for posthumous examinations.

We've already checked Victoria Locke and confirmed that she has a C-section scar. Combine that with the story about a son left with his father, and it seems almost certain Nicole's captor was talking about Victoria.

We unwrap Robyn. She's the one I postulate was stored elsewhere before being put in that cave, which means her body started decomposing and then dried.

"I keep thinking she looks like something out of a horror movie,"

Anders says. "Which feels disrespectful. I'm kind of glad I never knew her."

"That's the advantage to being a city cop," I say. "When I watched autopsies of strangers, I had to remind myself they weren't movie props. At that point, though, it's easier *not* to connect the body to a person."

"But it isn't a person," he says, as we unwind Robyn's wrappings. "That's how I got through it, in the war. I'd remind myself that whatever makes up a human being—spirit, consciousness, mind—was gone, and I was just dealing with the parts they left behind. Which, oddly, doesn't really help when that 'part' is a half your buddy's head landing on you after an IED goes off."

His lips twist wryly, but it's not gallows humor. He's never talked about the war before, beyond what he did at the end, the shooting that brought him here.

"I don't know how you'd deal with that," I say honestly.

"Neither did I, which was the problem. A complete and total lack of ability to deal with pointless death. You're out there, and you're told it's for the greater good, and all the guys around you seem to believe it. So when you don't share their faith, you feel as if you're missing something. Being myopic. Unable to see the bigger picture."

He rubs his face on his shoulder as he keeps unwrapping. "Shit, don't know where that came from."

"Maybe having been to war and then seeing bodies that remind you of it?"

A quick smile. "You think so? Yeah. Okay, refocusing in five seconds."

"I'd tell you to take all the time you need, but you don't want that. I'd also tell you I'd like to hear more, anytime, but you already know that. So I'll rescue you from this awkward moment by instead saying I don't see a tattoo."

"Agreed. On all counts. Including the apparent lack of a tattoo. However, that doesn't rule one out. It just means she doesn't have a garish, multicolored one, which really doesn't work on certain skin tones."

He flexes his arm, where he has a US Army tattoo on one bulging biceps. It's black ink against his dark skin. I take a closer look at Robyn's lower back. Her skin tone is between mine and Anders's. A dark tattoo would also explain why Nicole's captor missed it for so long, given the dim light.

Decomp and desiccation have left this part of her body wrinkled and warped. Before I can even glance over my shoulder, Anders hands me the penlight from the tray.

"Mind reader," I say.

"It's an easy mind to read sometimes."

When I shine the beam on Robyn's lower back, I see a black line, too smooth to be natural. We use our gloves to stretch the skin. Then I trace the outline as best I can onto a piece of paper while Anders holds the penlight. I try not to think about how many tools I could access at home to help me reconstruct this. Except I wouldn't be reconstructing it at all. I wouldn't even be examining her. The coroner and lab techs would do all the work.

I can grumble about the elbow grease and hurdle jumping and imperfect measures that go into lifting that tattoo. The truth is, though, that I love the creative workout that goes into figuring out a solution to problems so easily solved in a modern lab. Victims are usually better served by that tech—DNA analysis has put countless perpetrators behind bars and saved countless innocents from a life there. But there is something to be said for this level of involvement, digging in and doing the work and knowing that the case is mine to win or lose.

When I finish shading in the lines, the shape takes form. It's a raven inside a sun, done in a style reminiscent of southwest Native American art. When Nicole said her captor had called it a "heathen" symbol, I expected something occult. But this fits, being what he might interpret as religious art from a non-Christian faith.

"We've got one perpetrator," Anders says.

"We do."

"Does that help?"

"I hope so."

Dalton and I are having lunch at the station.

"So we have a time line now," he says. "Whoever took Nicole has to have been around at least five years. Which means, since you've eliminated me and Isabel . . ."

The next "oldest" person in terms of residency would be Mathias, who arrived months after Robyn disappeared.

"Val was right," I say. "We're looking at someone from outside. A settler or a hostile."

"Agreed."

"I know more about the settlers. There are a few small communities, plus those who live on their own, like your brother. We'll start by talking to Jacob, get his opinion on who fits the physical description or seems a good suspect. As for the hostiles, what can you tell me about them?"

"They're hostile."

"Uh, yeah . . . says so right there on the label."

"Yep. And that label means I don't know shit about them. I've had encounters only, which I've kept as brief as possible."

"Have you spoken to them?"

"Fuck, no. Most times, I don't even see them. They're like any other predator—the moment I know one's nearby, I put on my threat display while getting the hell off their territory."

"How do you know they're hostiles and not settlers?"

"Well, let's see." He points to a tiny scar along his hairline. "That's the one who slingshot a rock and nearly put my eye out. He was howling and yipping like a feral dog. Then there was the one who charged me. He was naked except for the belt made of bones. He'd painted himself in mud. Or I hoped it was mud, but wasn't getting downwind to be sure."

"And that's proof you're dealing with hostiles?" I snort. "I ran into those guys every time I had to break up a frat party."

"That's the problem with kids down south. They don't have enough to do. Enough responsibility."

"You sound like such an old man. *Kids these days. When I was their age, I had to haul water five miles, chop wood in snowstorms, hunt for our dinner, and do my homework by candlelight.*" I pause. "Oh, wait. You really *are* that guy."

"Yeah, yeah."

"Okay, so we don't have a lot on hostiles, then," I say. "I may need more, town records or whatever, but for now, I'll start by focusing on settlers. In the meantime, Nicole has a request, and you aren't going to like it."

THIRTY

I expect to fight Dalton on letting Nicole into the woods. I have my list of arguments prepared. The biggest one of all? I understand what she's doing and why she has to do it.

After my attack, I spent months battling an even greater enemy: fear. Forcing myself to return to the scene. Walking down alleyways. Going to bars filled with the kind of young men who reminded me of my attackers. Resuming martial arts training and letting people hit me. If I flinched doing any of that, I couldn't become a cop. I wasn't letting my attackers take that dream from me, the same way Nicole won't let her captor take her newfound love of the forest.

But I don't have to say any of that. I ask Dalton, and I explain her motivation, and he says, "Yeah, guy's not going to jump her midday. If she feels better facing it? Storm could use a good walk anyway. Go see if she's ready. I'll finish up here and get the dog."

Nicole has her coat and boots on by the time Dalton arrives. As we walk through town, she asks if Dalton can hang behind when we get into the forest. She might pretend "setting a trap" is only an excuse, but she is hoping to do that. Hoping he's out there and if he sees her, accompanied only by a small woman and a puppy, he will strike. We know that's unlikely, but Dalton agrees.

As we reach the forest edge, Nicole slows, quick breaths controlling obvious anxiety, but when either of us looks her way, she squares her thin shoulders.

Before Dalton leaves, he says, "If this becomes too much, say so. There's no one here you need to impress."

She gives him a weak smile. "Sometimes, wanting to impress is what keeps us moving when all we really want to do is curl up in a fetal position and whimper."

"Okay. Just be warned, if you feel the need to curl up on the path, Storm will think you're playing dead and maul you."

She chuckles. "I'd be okay with that."

He hands me the leash, and as he does, he squeezes my hand and says, "You know."

"Be careful?"

"Yeah."

I squeeze his hand in return and take the lead, and he heads into the forest. The trails are in better shape now. After a snowfall, Dalton has the militia ride over them with the snowmobiles. They aren't bare, but we don't need snowshoes.

Nicole stays quiet for about ten steps. Then she looks over her shoulder, in the direction Dalton went and says, "Where do you get a guy like that?"

"Cranky, sweary, and overprotective?"

"With the guys I've dated, those would be their *good* qualities. Which means obviously I need to change my criteria." Her cheeks flare. "And I can't believe I'm talking about that. As if, a few days after being rescued from one guy, I'm thinking of what kind of man I'll date next."

"You weren't dating him."

She laughs.

"Which means it's not the same thing at all," I say.

She wraps her arms around herself. "It isn't, but it's like I still feel, after that, men should be the absolute last things on my mind."

"Because that's what others will think?"

A pause. A long one. The she nods. "Like others will be judging me, and if I start checking out guys after my ordeal, maybe that means it wasn't so bad."

"Anyone who believes that is an idiot."

She smiles. "Thank you."

"You're separating the two just fine. Don't second-guess, especially not for others."

She glances over. "You sound as if . . . I mean, I don't want to pry. You're a police officer, so you have experience in that way."

"I was attacked," I say. "Four guys. Serious beating. Rape? I don't know. Which sounds crazy, but I'd have been unconscious at the time, and I was in such bad shape that someone decided testing for it wasn't necessary."

"Do you wish they had?"

I walk in silence for a minute, and she starts to apologize for asking, but I say, "I think so. I know I probably was, so afterward I had issues—with men, with sex, separating that from my attack. Like you said, it wasn't so much a matter of *me* having difficulty separating them as feeling like I *should* have difficulty. But I never say I *have* been raped, because that feels like I'm appropriating an experience."

"I don't think there's a club. And if there is, I don't think there are levels of membership."

"True."

"You can't judge someone else's trauma, right? No one has the right to say you're a real victim or not."

"Survivor," I say. "Not victim."

"Right. I've heard that. Now the trick is to reach the point where I feel less like a victim and more like a survivor."

"You will."

We walk in silence. I'm never that open about my past, but I feel almost obligated with Nicole. On the job, I offered sympathy while maintaining professional distance. That's gone here. Or it is with Nicole, as if rescuing her gives me some responsibility for healing her.

"Can I hold that?" she says, gesturing at the leash.

I hesitate. Storm is darting from side to side, chasing whatever snow we kick up, constantly in motion, constantly tugging. Nicole is keeping up, but only because I'm taking it slow, and even then, her breathing says this leisurely hike is the equivalent of a 5K run.

"If it's too much, I'll give her back," she says. "I don't want you to lose her."

There's little danger of that. Even if Storm breaks free, she's still a puppy, with puppy-short legs and a puppy-short attention span. I'm more worried about what she'll do to Nicole.

Nicole has her hand out. "Please."

I hand the leash over. Storm promptly races behind us, twisting Nicole in the lead. I grab for it, but Nicole only laughs and untangles herself. She gives Storm a tug, and we continue on.

We're walking and talking, staying on the trail. I catch glimpses of Dalton—intentionally revealing himself to say *I'm still here*. Even when I don't see him, I feel him there, the sense that I can relax and get caught up in conversation with Nicole. Someone is watching out for me, and yes, I can do that myself, but it's nice to know I don't have to all the time.

I am on alert for one thing, though: Nicole's energy level. As it drops, I say, "I think we should turn back."

"Two more minutes," she says. "You can time me."

"I will." I waggle my wristwatch, and she gets a laugh from that. It's a nice sound to hear, a bubbly laugh, as if she's surprised that she can still do that, too.

I turn to motion to Dalton that we're getting ready to head back. He appears from behind a tree, meeting my gaze, his lips curving in a slight smile.

That momentary distraction is all it takes. Nicole yelps, and I wheel. She's only a few feet ahead, but it seems like twenty, and I'm running even before I realize what's happened. She's falling, and I think she's been shot or attacked and—

She lands flat on her ass in the snow, and she's laughing. I'm still in flight, and Storm is too, launching herself at Nicole. I let out a cry of my own, warning the puppy off her. Then I see a blur in the forest, leaping over brush. I get a split-second glance at the figure's face, and it looks like Dalton. And then I realize he's coming from the wrong direction. I pull my gun, and Nicole shrieks, her arms flying up to ward him off.

He skids into the path and stops short.

"Sheriff," Nicole says. "Sorry, I—" She stops as she sees it's not Dalton. Just someone who looks like him.

"Jacob," I say.

He glances at Nicole, then at Storm on her lap, the puppy's front legs planted on Nicole's shoulders as she licks the woman's face.

"I thought that was . . . ," he says. "What is it?"

Nicole lets out a laugh, and Jacob's face turns bright red. "I thought—It looks like—"

"A bear cub?" Dalton says as he jogs over.

Jacob turns even redder. "No, course not."

"Totally does," Nicole says. "That's what I thought the first time I saw her. But they tell me she's a puppy."

She reaches up for help, and Jacob is closest, but he just stares at her hand. Before I can step forward, he figures it out and tugs Nicole to her feet.

"Sorry," he says. "I thought . . ."

"I was being attacked by a bear, and you came to my rescue. Thank you. That's very sweet. And I *was* in danger of being mauled . . . by an overexuberant dog." She hefts Storm and holds her out. "See? Puppy."

Jacob's expression says he's not entirely convinced, but when she staggers under Storm's weight, he grabs the puppy, who immediately transfers all affection to him, licking and whining and wriggling. I reach to take her, but he keeps holding her, both hands around her body, studying her, not unlike his brother with a new species.

"Eric got her for me," I say. "She's very friendly."

"Friendly? Or hungry?" he says as Storm licks his cheek.

That makes Nicole laugh, and Jacob's lips curve in a tiny smile. He puts Storm down and holds her leash, watching as she trundles off.

"It's cute," he says. "With those paws, it'll get big."

"Huge," I say. "She'll be my tracking dog *and* bodyguard."

"Good idea," he says to Dalton.

"Yeah, I get them every now and then," Dalton says. "What're you doing here?"

"I, uh, was . . ."

When Jacob trails off, I say, "Just passing by? You must have ESP. Eric and I needed to talk to you about . . ." Now I'm the one trailing off, not wanting to out Nicole in front of a stranger.

"Helping find the guy who kept me in a cave?" she says. "Yes, please. That would be even better than saving me from a giant puppy."

"You're the . . ." Jacob's mouth works, and I'm about to cut in when he says a sincere "I'm sorry." And then "We'll find him. But maybe you shouldn't be, uh, out here."

"In the very woods where my captor lives? Sheriff Dalton and Detective Butler were kind enough to accommodate my cabin fever. But we were just heading back."

"I'll take you," Dalton says. He turns to Jacob. "Casey needs to talk to you. I'll come back for her. If she tells you she's fine to walk back alone, don't let her."

"Why don't—" I begin, at the same time Jacob begins *his* protest.

"You guys are talking. Alone. Together. Awkward, I know. Deal with it."

THIRTY-ONE

Before they go, I lead Nicole away, and she says, "Sheriff Dalton has a brother who moved away from Rockton?"

"Something like that." This is the version Anders knows, an easy explanation for a complex situation.

"I won't mention him in town. Also—because you have to wonder—it's not him. My captor, that is. The guy was bigger. Stockier. Sturdier. And his eyes were darker. With the dim lighting, I couldn't say if they were dark blue or brown, but I know they're not as light as the sheriff's or his brother's."

"Thank you. That helps."

"May I introduce myself properly? Or would he rather not?"

I lead her back to where Dalton and Jacob are talking, and I say, "I forgot the introductions."

"And cavegirl isn't really how I'd like to be remembered." She extends a hand and says, "Nicole," and he shakes her hand and says, carefully, "Jacob."

"Pleased to meet you, Jacob. Now I'll say good-bye as Sheriff Dalton escorts me back to Rockton."

Jacob smiles. "Is that what you call him? Sheriff Dalton?"

"It seems safest."

That makes Jacob chuckle.

As Dalton and Nicole leave, I call, "Don't forget to bring Will."

Dalton glances back. "What?"

"We've agreed no one should be out here alone, so when you come back, bring Will. Please. You aren't the only one who worries."

After they're gone, Jacob says, "Thank you. For being with Eric."

I have to laugh. "That makes it sound like a chore."

"Or like I'm thanking you for taking care of a grizzly bear?"

"Yes, and not a bad analogy some days. But trust me, being with Eric isn't a hardship. He didn't exactly have trouble finding companionship before I came along."

"I've heard." His cheeks heat. "I mean, when he was younger. There were women. Not like you, just . . ."

I almost say *for sex* but remember who I'm speaking to and go with a vaguer, "lovers," and his cheeks turn still redder. I don't know how much experience Jacob has with women. I suspect the answer is none, which might also explain part of his discomfort with me.

He looks in the direction Dalton and Nicole left. "Is she okay? She seems like she is. Or like she's trying to be."

"Yes, she's trying very hard to be."

He shoves his hands in his pockets. "After that, it'd take a lot to be any kind of okay."

"It would. She's trying, though. It'll help when we find her captor . . . who is apparently also a killer."

I tell him about the discovery of the two bodies. For a moment, he just looks at me, like he's sure he's misunderstood.

"That's what would have happened to her, then," he says quietly. "To Nicole."

He looks sick as I nod.

"Okay, well, I've been thinking about guys out here. That's why I was close to town, seeing if Eric would come out. I'm not saying any of these guys *could* have done this, but you need to start from somewhere."

He lists names. Fortunately, my jacket holds my notepad, which I always carry, like I used to carry a cell phone. I write down what Jacob tells me. I don't know anyone on his list, but he says his brother will.

We discuss what I have for a physical description, which weeds out six from his twenty. When I say the killer has been here more than five years, that eliminates two more.

"Do you have any gut feelings?" I say. "Anyone who rubs you the wrong way . . ."

"You mean someone I don't like?"

"Right."

"That list is all the guys who live anywhere near here. I only personally deal with a few." He names them, and I make notes. "I don't trust others. People out here . . . A lot of them have problems. Like Brent. You know about Brent, right?"

Brent is our local cave dweller. "Eric says he's mildly bipolar, which—" I stop myself. "He has mood swings that suggest a mental illness."

"Yeah. That's called bipolar?" Jacob tilts his head, looking like Dalton when he processes new information. "Meaning he goes between opposite poles of moods. Yeah, that's Brent. It doesn't mean he's crazy, and I'd say he couldn't be your guy, but you have to consider him. I know that. You even have to consider me." His hands go back in his pockets. "And that's a stupid thing to say. Of course you need to consider me."

"Nicole cleared you. Your eyes are too light, and your build is too small."

"Build? You mean height?"

"Weight. Her captor was broader."

A thoughtful nod. "Okay, then you can strike off a few more names. Guys with light eyes or smaller than me. I'll leave the ones about my size, just so we don't overdo it."

Three more names leave the list.

"So there's no one in particular you'd suggest we focus on?" I say.

He hesitates, then says, "Ty Cypher and Silas Cox maybe. Cypher's from Rockton originally. Eric will remember him. He used to be sheriff. He stays pretty deep in the woods. Hates Rockton, so he steers clear. But he gets around. And he's nuts. Not like mentally ill. Nuts like one of these feral dogs."

"And Silas Cox?"

"He's from down south. I used to hunt with him after he arrived, maybe five years back. He seemed okay at first. Just a guy who wanted to live wild. Only one night, we were drinking—he got a bottle of rye from a miner who trades, in season. So we're drinking, and he started talking about . . . women. Bad stuff that he . . ."

"Things he'd done to them? Things he wanted to do?"

"Things he wanted to do, I think. He brought it up like it was just regular conversation, something guys talk about, and I'm pretty sure it wasn't. I mean, the stuff he talked about . . ." Jacob's cheeks redden again. "It didn't seem like normal . . . relations. He sounded like . . . like a guy who *might* put a woman in a cave."

"Fantasies about unwilling partners? Holding women against their will?"

Silence. Then he blurts, "Ropes. And stuff."

I say, as matter-of-factly as possible, "He talked about restraining women for sex. Was it mutual? Partners playing along for fun? Or actual restraint?"

The look on Jacob's face is sheer horror. "Playing along?"

"So, not mutual. He talked about restraining women against their will."

"Yes."

"Holding them hostage?"

"We . . . didn't get that far. He started talking about women, ones he'd worked with down south, who wouldn't go out with him, and what he wanted to do to them, and I . . . I honestly thought I was misunderstanding, on account of the rye. I'm not used to drinking. But misunderstanding or not, I didn't want to continue the conversation, so I got out of there fast and decided Silas wasn't the kind of person I should associate with."

"When's the last time you saw him?"

"A couple of months ago. I was way over by the big lake, shooting duck. I'd been camping there a couple of days. He came by. Started asking questions about Rockton. I did my usual thing, played dumb, said I'd never seen a town, and he said Roger—" He pauses. "Wait, Roger. You should talk to Roger."

I scan my list. "A trapper, right? Lives here year-round."

"I told Eric he might make a good contact. He'd be someone to talk to about this. He knows both Cypher and Silas better than I do. Brent likes the caves, too. If anyone has seen someone in that system, it'd be him."

"Excellent," I say. "So I've got a list of ten settlers and hostiles—"

"Hostiles? No, that doesn't include hostiles. I don't have anything to do with them."

"Because they're hostile?"

I smile when I say it, but his gaze moves out into the forest.

"I just don't," he says. "No reason to."

"Okay, that's understandable. I'm trying to figure out more about them."

"You want to know about the hostiles. When that woman drugged me—how I acted, what I did? That's a hostile. Except they're like that all the time. Their minds don't work right. They're rabid animals. Like me when I—when I attacked you."

"Could they do something like this? Are they smart enough, sane enough to plan it? Take and hold someone captive?"

He rocks on his heels. I'm reminding him of what he did to me, and he's agitated, so I say, "It's okay. I can talk to Brent."

"No," he says. "They couldn't do this. It's not a hostile. Stay away from them."

I nod, but it must not be sincere enough, because he says, "It's not a hostile. Can't be. Just . . . just leave them alone. If you see one, run. Or shoot. Just shoot."

THIRTY-TWO

We're back in Rockton. I've discussed Jacob's list with Dalton, who has added his opinions. First thing tomorrow, we'll go looking for Silas Cox. That's the frustrating thing about the short days—it might only be late afternoon, but it's already dark, no chance of heading out now.

Dalton takes Storm to Petra's so we can get in a few hours of work. I swing by my place to grab a few things, and I'm upstairs, deciding what to take. Fact is, we don't have a lot of clothing in Rockton, and what is in my closet is what I might pack for an extended vacation. I'm tempted to just toss it all in a bag, but that really says *I'm moving in,* and I'm not sure that's what Dalton intends.

I'm putting a sweater into my bag when a floorboard creaks downstairs.

"Eric?" I call. I'd told him I was coming here, and I'd been relieved when he didn't insist on joining me. I'll accept his concern, but I can't abide hovering. At that creak, annoyance darts through me.

"Eric?" I call again.

Silence answers. With anyone else, that silence could mean he'd caught the snap in my voice and decided to slip off. Dalton would call back, *Yeah, it's me,* and take his lumps if I'm pissy.

I pull my gun and move toward the steps. "Who's down there?"

The squeak of a board, someone putting his weight on it as slowly as possible, trying to avoid making noise. I stand at the top of the stairs. A footstep sounds. I glance down the stairs to see a clump of snow at the base and a partial wet print.

I descend one step. Then two. The riser creaks under my weight, and there's a scuffle below as someone runs for the rear door. I race up the stairs instead. Through my bedroom to the balcony. I throw open the door to see a figure making for the trees.

I jump over the balcony. I've done it before, mostly just to get Dalton shaking his head and muttering about losing his detective to a broken neck. I vault over too fast this time and the deep snow is the only thing that keeps me from breaking an ankle. It twists and pain jolts through my bad leg, but I'm already on the move, gun still in hand.

My target hears me coming and looks back. I see his face as best I can in moonlight through heavy tree cover. Dark bushy beard. Dark wild hair. No one from Rockton. A man of the forest. He notices me looking, and his lips part in a curse, and he wheels and runs.

I have him in my sights. I could shoot. But the memory of Blaine will forever stay my hand if there is any reasonable doubt. I can't say this is the man in the snowsuit. I can't tell if what he's wearing *is* even a snowsuit. So I cannot shoot.

I bear down, gritting my teeth against the old injuries screaming that I'm not supposed to do this. I hear the doctor telling me I might never run, might never walk right again, me nodding while my inner voice said, *Screw that.* But sheer willpower gets you only so far. The man is pulling away and then disappears around a thick patch of trees. When I get there, he's gone, and I stand in the forest, listening to some small creature dash through the snow, and I realize where I am, what I've done.

I'm in the forest. Alone. Far enough from town that I can't hear the laugh of anyone heading home for the evening, can't see the swing of a lantern in hand.

He ran, and I didn't stop to wonder why he was running. I presumed he was fleeing. Never considered that he might be luring me into the forest.

I put my back to a conifer and scan the forest. When something moves to my left, I spin, gun raised. It's the cross fox from my yard, looking up at me, nose twitching as if to say, *What are* you *doing out here?* It has a mouse in its jaws, and as the fox watches me, the mouse revives, giving a mad struggle. The fox chomps down, gaze never wavering from mine. Then it takes off, sliding through the trees, heading for home.

I look around again. The forest remains still. Not silent, though. I catch all the usual noises. Does that mean the man has fled? Or that we've both just gone so silent ourselves that—like the fox—the forest has decided to ignore us?

I take a step away from the tree. Then another. With each movement, I pause and listen for an echoing sound, the suggestion he's masking his movements with mine. On the fifth step, I catch the barest swish of a boot in snow. I hold myself still as I register the direction. Then I take a step that way. Silence. Step. Silence.

A crack, barely audible. He's behind a tree, hidden from sight, watching me.

"I know you're there," I say, my voice echoing. "I have a gun. If you don't want me to use it, step out and identify yourself."

The slow crunch of snow under a boot. He's retreating, trying to do it silently. When I take another step, he breaks and runs, and I take three running steps before realizing I'm falling farther into his trap.

I have to pull myself up short and hold there, every muscle clenched to keep from going after him. To follow is madness. To not follow feels like cowardice.

I grip my gun and hold myself in place, waiting until the crash of undergrowth tells me I've lost my chance. And if that stings, well, then it stings.

I take my time going back, listening for any sign that my target has looped around to halt my retreat. When I catch a sound deep in the forest, I start walking backward, one foot deliberately down after another, eyes and ears straining for that distant spot—

A hand closes around my ankle. I spin as it yanks, and I go down on all fours. I kick and flip onto my back, gun flying up, aiming at—

It's Shawn Sutherland, lying prone in the snow.

"H–help . . ." He can barely get that out, lifting his blood-streaked face and blinking at me as if in confusion. His hand still holds my ankle in a viselike grip. When I reach down to peel off his fingers, he lurches forward on his belly, the movement yanking my foot back.

"Shawn," I say. "It's me. Casey. Detective Butler. From Rockton."

"H–help me. Please . . ."

"I will. You're safe. I'll get you to town. Just let go of—"

"No!" He convulses, both hands gripping my ankle now. "Don't leave me."

"I'm not going anywhere. Just—"

A branch cracks in the forest. My head jerks up. Through the trees, I see the outline of a man. He's holding something in his hand, something long and thin, like a metal rod.

I scramble to get away from Sutherland, but his fingers dig in, eyes burning with fever as he says, "Don't leave. Don't leave."

"I'm not—"

I yank hard, to no avail. The figure approaches. I lift my gun and focus on that. He glances over his shoulder, and I see the beard and know it's the man I chased from my house. He continues toward me, his weapon raised.

"There is a gun in my hand," I call. "I will not hesitate to use it."

He stops. Tilts his head. Seems to consider, his gaze going from me to Sutherland.

"I will shoot you," I say. "Put that down, or I will fire this gun."

He shifts the weapon from one hand to the other. I take aim.

"Shoot him," Sutherland croaks.

I look down to see he's lifted his head, and his gaze is riveted on the man.

"Shoot him."

The man dives into the undergrowth. I scramble after him, but Sutherland still has my foot. As I go down again, the figure rises and starts toward me, and as I'm tangled there, my leg twisted. I kick to get free. Sutherland lets out a howl as my foot makes contact. He finally lets go and I'm on my feet, but the figure is gone. I stand there, poised, my gaze traveling over the dark woods.

"Should have shot him," Sutherland croaks. "Should have shot the bastard."

He collapses.

THIRTY-THREE

I drag Sutherland back to town. When I yell for help, three residents come running. Soon he's at the clinic, Anders attending, me helping, Mathias nowhere to be found, damn him.

Sutherland is badly dehydrated. We don't find any injuries requiring an emergency airlift, but we are, once again, reminded exactly how vulnerable we are without a doctor.

Anders washes the crusted blood from the back of Sutherland's head and examines the wound that left blood in his toque. It's a serious bash. Other than that, we find rope burns on his wrist and lower legs, splinters in his hands, and mild frostbite. He's feverish, regaining consciousness enough to mumble that he needs to get back to Rockton.

My best guess, judging by his injuries, is that he escaped his captor, who came after him. As for why that captor had been in my house, I have no idea.

While we were tending to Sutherland, Dalton examined the footprints behind my place. I take a second look. They're scuffed and indistinct, running prints, impossible to tell if they match the man in the snowmobile suit. There's no way of following them, either. Dalton tried but got about a half kilometer in and lost the trail as it merged with caribou tracks.

Dalton keeps fussing with the trail, and I head to Mathias's place. He has his own house, despite being a nonessential resident. If asked, he'll say, "But a butcher is very essential. Anyone can bake a loaf of bread. Carving meat is an art form." Which is bullshit. Yes, I'm sure there's skill involved in butchering, but that's not why he has his own house.

"No one will share a building with him," Dalton had said when I asked. "He scares them off."

"What does he do?"

"He exists, apparently."

After a few early complaints, the council awarded Mathias his own house, over Dalton's complaints that it broke town law. The council just didn't want to deal with the issue.

When I rap on Mathias's door, he calls, in French, "I'm hiding. Go away."

I lean against the door. "Hiding works a lot better when you don't answer."

"I tried that when you sent Kenneth to fetch me. It did not work."

"Sure it did. It let you duck out of examining Shawn Sutherland."

"Because he does not require my examination. And he bores me. When he ran, I thought perhaps he was showing an unexpected spark of character. But now he has returned. Boring."

"He escaped captivity, presumably from the same guy who took Nicole. Doesn't that make him more interesting?"

"Is his captor still alive?"

"Unfortunately."

"Then no, it does not make him any more interesting."

I sigh. "Well, I didn't come to talk to you about Shawn anyway. I want to discuss the psychology of hostiles."

Silence.

"Okay, so that bores you, too. Fine."

I've stepped off the front porch when the door opens a crack. "Psychology of hostiles?"

"Never mind, Mathias. I'm not in the mood to wheedle for a few minutes of your precious time. I'll talk to Isabel."

"Isabel cannot help you with this. It is my area."

"Which is why I came here. Otherwise I wouldn't bother you."

He opens the door and leans against the frame. "You are angry with me."

"No, Mathias," I say as I turn to face him. "I am tired of you. The dead bodies of two women interested you. The live victims? Boring. Just go back inside and wait for me to bring you more bodies. At this rate, I'm sure they'll show up eventually. I just hope they're *interesting* enough for you."

"I cannot help you with Shawn Sutherland. He is evidently alive and in good health for his condition, or you would have hunted me down. Any psychological effects are better handled by Isabel. The only abnormal psychology at work is that of the killer. Can Shawn add anything to what Nicole has said?"

"Not yet. He's still feverish. But you could have shown up for ten minutes, consulted with Will, and helped him feel more confident in his diagnosis."

He considers and then nods. "You have a point. William is placed in a very uncomfortable position here, which he does not deserve. Note that I say that despite knowing he does not like me very much."

"No one likes you very much. Which is exactly how *you* like it."

"True."

"And one of the people who does like you is quickly changing her opinion."

"I know, which is why I opened the door."

"No, you opened the door because what I said *doesn't* bore you."

"I can have more than one motivation. All the best antagonists do." He threw open the door. "Come in, Casey. Let us talk about hostiles."

"How much do you know about them?" I say as we settle into Mathias's living room. "And don't tell me that you know they're hostile."

"That is their defining characteristic, is it not? Like the savages of yore, defined wholly by the fact they were savage."

"But they weren't. So-called savages were defined that way by people with a very narrow view of culture and civilization. That isn't what we're looking at here. These people aren't just different. They're—"

"*Actively* hostile?"

I glower at him.

"All right," he says. "Tell me more. Have you encountered one? I have not. Very few of us here have. I presume Eric would be the exception."

I tell him about Dalton's experiences.

"Now, that *is* interesting. He is correct that it may not have been mud. Did you know psychiatric patients sometimes smear themselves with feces?"

"I've heard of it."

"It's common enough that there's a term for it. Scatolia. Do you know why they do it?"

"Because it's disgusting."

He shakes his head.

"I'm serious," I say. "My presumption would be that they do it because it is repulsive. It's defiant, and it elicits a reaction."

"Yes, in cases like the ones you may have heard of—likely connected to violent offenders—that is the primary purpose, along with acting as an expression of anger, frustration, and helplessness. It can also enforce social isolation."

"Surprisingly."

"In other instances, scatolia can simply be an act of self-control. However powerless one may feel one always has the power to do *that* . . . while, yes, using it to elicit other responses."

"Enacting control over others in the only way possible."

"Precisely. And yet smearing oneself in feces—or even mud—can serve another purpose. What was Eric's reaction?"

"Get the hell away from the crazy guy."

"Precisely. Which is why some prisoners will do it. Taking off one's clothing. Adorning oneself with random items. Smearing substances on one's skin. It is stereotypical 'crazy' behavior. I have assessed many prisoners who did it. Few were actually mentally ill."

"They just wanted an NCR ruling?"

"Not criminally responsible. Yes."

"Everything these hostiles do could fall into the same category. Acting violent, acting crazy. But what's their motivation?"

Mathias stares at me as if I'm asking why we live in houses instead of just laying out sleeping bags in the street.

"The obvious answer is to scare us," I say. "A threat display."

"Yes . . ."

"But what's the point? How are they being threatened? Look at the settlers—Rockton doesn't bother *them,* and they don't bother each other. There's so much land out here that territorial disputes would be ridiculous."

Mathias leans back, purses his lips. "You are correct. And this is why you make a good detective, Casey. You do not presume the obvious without thinking it through. I have been up here too long, with too few puzzles to solve."

"Well, here's one for you, then. If the hostiles are sane, why act like madmen to scare off nonexistent threats? If they are not sane, how did they get that way? Again, there's a presumption—they leave civilized life and revert. But revert to *what?* This isn't some 'pre-civilized' form of human. That plays right into the old idea that we are all one step from savagery, base and violent creatures. The other explanation is that they left Rockton because of some dormant mental illness. But if so, why does it all seem to present in the same form—primarily, violence? Does it make sense that every hostile out there is suffering from the same mental illness?"

He doesn't answer for a long time. Then it's only to say, "I need more data."

"Such as . . ."

"A live specimen would be ideal." He catches my look and sighs. "All right. For now, I will settle for all reports on encounters. Bring me everything. Then we will speak of specimens."

THIRTY-FOUR

I rap on Val's door. When she opens it, I say, "I warned you I'd eventually need to talk with you about the men who attacked you."

She nods and lets me in. As I head for the living room, she says, "Tea?" and I don't particularly want any, but her inflection tells me she does. Maybe even something stronger.

When she brings it, she says, "I'm not sure how much I can help you, Detective. It really was a fleeting encounter."

"That's more than anyone except Eric has had."

She makes a noise under her breath. Just a small one, though.

She sets the teacups down. I wait until she's settled and then say, "You were out on militia patrol."

"Yes, Phil thought that would be a good experience for me. To more fully experience my new life."

"Phil? The first time we spoke, you said *you* wanted to go on patrol." She'd used almost the same phrasing too, about "more fully experiencing" her new life here in Rockton.

"I wanted to be part of the community. I wasn't sure how to go about that, and Phil encouraged me to join a patrol, to gain a deeper understanding of the landscape and have an opportunity to get to know members of the militia. To show that I supported their work and didn't consider myself above basic tasks. I agreed. It was exactly what I was looking for. Whatever you may think of me, Casey, I came here prepared to immerse myself in this job and this community. Despite Sheriff Dalton's objections."

"What did Eric object to?"

"Me joining the patrol. He said I wasn't qualified." She sniffs. "In short, I was female."

"He said that?"

"He didn't need to. Look at the militia. Do you see any women on it?"

That isn't Dalton's fault. There was a female member, a few years ago, and he wants more women to join, but they haven't been interested. Honestly, I'm not surprised—it offers little more than bragging rights, and that's just not important to women. They can make the same number of credits doing more interesting and less dangerous work.

"What exactly did Eric say?"

She flutters her hands. "You know how he gets. Blustering about the dangers of the forest, and how people don't understand, and if I wanted to join a picnic party, there was one scheduled for the next week. A picnic party? I don't know what you see in the man, Casey. I understand that you may feel you lack power here. Perhaps that seems the way to get it. You may also feel threatened—I'm sure you endured more than your share of unwanted attention when you arrived. Being with the sheriff might seem the best way to protect yourself and further your interests in this town, but there are other ways."

"I am with Eric because I want to be with Eric. Suggesting anything else is insulting, Val. Very insulting."

She stops, teacup clutched between her hands. "I don't mean to be," she says. "I worry. You seem so bright and accomplished, and yet you choose to be with that . . . that—"

"I am well aware of your opinion of Eric, Val. I would like to keep that out of the current discussion, unless it has some bearing on it."

Her hands tighten on the mug, and she goes quiet. Very quiet.

"Val? Does it have some bearing?"

Her finger trembles as she puts the mug down. "Of course not."

"If you have a specific complaint against Eric—"

"I don't."

I eye her. There's more here. Not anything Eric's done—I know him better than that. But there is something connected to her attack and to him.

"Sheriff Dalton did nothing," she says firmly.

"Is that the problem? That he didn't take your attack seriously? You never *told* him you'd been attacked."

"It did not bear mentioning. He organized and participated in the search. His diligence was unquestionable, as always."

Do I detect a twist of sarcasm?

She continues, "You wish to hear the whole story. It was a routine patrol. It lasted longer than I expected, and I . . . needed to slip away. I'd drunk more water than I intended."

"So you told the guys that you had to go to the bathroom."

"That wasn't necessary. They'd stopped to examine a campsite, and I said I wanted to see animal tracks we'd passed on the trail. One of the men offered to walk with me. I demurred. I retreated on the path and then slipped off it. I went farther than I intended in my quest for privacy. After I finished, I started back, heard the men calling, and realized I'd gone in the wrong direction. That's when I was grabbed."

From there, her story progresses as I'd heard it before. She was taken captive by two men, who threatened her and then decided it was time for a nap—because threats are just so exhausting. She escaped while they were asleep.

I ask her to physically describe the men. One could be Nicole's captor, but that would be more heartening if it was a more unusual description. I home in on their appearances otherwise, in hopes of expanding my understanding of hostiles. How did they look? What did they wear? How did they speak?

The first time she told this story, she sniffed about the men communicating in poor English, barely understandable. When I probe, though, it's clear that Val's idea of "poor English" isn't exactly the same as mine. It turns out the hostiles weren't the grunting Neanderthals she first described. They sounded like guys I'd expect to meet in these woods—men who might have been mining or hunting all season and not exactly bathing regularly.

Except they aren't. There's little doubt of that. They were aggressive in a way that goes well beyond a couple of rough miners who find a woman in the woods and act out their dark fantasies. These men had stylized scar patterns. Deliberately blackened teeth. Braided hair and beards. They'd been dressed in cured animal hides, roughly sewn and decorated with bones. They seem like guys who recalled seeing old *National Geographic* magazines and emulated a hodgepodge of tribal customs.

When they spoke, it was understandable enough, but with words that Val couldn't understand, like you might expect from people who spoke only to one another, inventing their own dialect. The gist of their message had been clear, though. *You are on our territory. We are going to show you why that is a very bad idea.*

"And then they fell asleep?" I say.

She could come up with some explanation for this, however implausible. Instead she just looks me in the eye and says, "Yes."

That's my story, and I'm sticking to it.

I don't need details of what happened between the threats and the escape, just like I didn't need details of what happened to Nicole in that cave. Details do not impact my case.

"You know what happened to Nicole," I say. "You know that man didn't just hold her captive for conversation."

"I don't need to hear—"

"And I'm not going to tell you, because that's none of your business. I'm saying that you know what happened, correct?"

"Yes."

"Given the short time you spent with these two men, would you believe them capable of doing that to Nicole?"

"Yes."

"Mentally capable of holding her in a cave and remembering to provide rudimentary care?"

"Yes."

"Earlier, your opinion of their intelligence—"

"I would not attempt to discuss the fundamental theorem of algebra with them, but I have no doubt they could have done this."

We talk for a few more minutes. I thank her, and I'm leaving, and as I reach the door, she says, "Do you believe it could have been the same men?"

I open my mouth, and she says, "Yes, I know, Nicole was taken by one person, but there is no reason two couldn't have been involved, one as an accomplice."

"That's a possibility. Either way, it wouldn't rule out one of your attackers being her captor—and the man who killed Victoria and Robyn."

"That's what I avoided, then," she says, her voice dropping. "If I hadn't escaped . . ."

"You avoided something," I say. "You got away. Which does not mean that Nicole *failed* to escape."

"Yes, I know."

"Well, with the way you talk sometimes, I thought I'd better make that clear."

She flushes. "I don't mean—"

"I'm not interested in hashing it out tonight, Val. Nicole never saw her attacker. He knocked her out from behind, and she woke in that hole. She didn't have the chance to escape."

"Possibly because I had. They learned." She wraps her arms around herself. "I keep thinking of that. Dreaming of it. Waking up in a hole and—" Her breathing accelerated, and she steps back quickly. "I'm sorry, Detective. I'm overtired."

"Would you like me to post a guard?"

"No, of course not. I'm fine."

"I will ask the militia to do extra passes by your house. If there's any chance this is the same guy, he targeted you once. If you want a night guard, just ask me. They don't need to know anything other than that there's a suggestion you could be a target. The only catch is that he'd have to stay in your living room—we can't ask him to stand on your porch all night in this weather."

She says, "Extra passes will be fine." Then she looks at me. "Thank you."

I nod and leave.

THIRTY-FIVE

Before we retire for the evening, Dalton takes Storm for a run through town. And I do mean a run, to the point where he's carrying her back and she's not the only one panting. I may have mentioned earlier that, as much as I love my puppy, I'm loving her a little less at bedtime. Hence the run, and then she's sound asleep in her bed upstairs and Dalton finds his second wind very nicely. Soon we're *both* panting, stretched out on the bearskin, legs still entwined.

"Thank you," I say when we're done.

"I was going to suggest we work from home for a while earlier today, but I know you've been busy."

"I'm never that busy."

"Good to know." He kisses me, and then we snuggle down on the rug, and a few minutes later, as I'm staring into the fire, he says, "Working?"

"Yes, sorry." I pull my gaze away from the flames.

"I'm asking, not complaining."

His fingers tickle down my bare side. He just traces right over my scars. I'm sure other lovers thought they were being considerate by avoiding them, but to me it always felt like they were avoiding the ugliness, trying to see past it. Dalton doesn't even seem to notice them, and I'm so busy enjoying his touch that it takes a moment to see that look in his eyes, the one that means he has something to say.

"Hmm?" I say.

"Anything you want to talk about? With the case? You're working through something. I can see that, and I know you were busy tonight, talking to Mathias and Val, and . . ."

And you haven't told me what it is. You always tell me what it is.

"If you want to talk, I'm here," he says. "Well, obviously. I'm always here." He exhales. "Fuck."

"I love it when you flounder," I say. "It's adorable."

He makes a face. I reach up to push his hair back. It's just long enough to show a cowlick in the front, which is also adorable, but I refrain from saying so.

"I'm not talking about what I'm investigating because I'm still working it through," I say. "And, admittedly, also because it's a subject you don't seem keen to talk about, so I *want* to work it through first. Get it straight in my head, before I bring it to you."

He frowns. "What is it?"

"Hostiles. I know, you don't think the perpetrator could be one of them."

The frown grows. "When did I say that?"

"I got the message when I brought them up and you wanted to move on."

He props onto one arm. "That seemed like I was dismissing the idea? Hell, no. I just didn't know what else to say. It's the same as when we considered the hostiles for Powys's death. It doesn't *get* us anywhere. With residents and settlers, we can consider individuals, interview them, question others about them. With hostiles, it's like saying we think a bear did it. Only way we can stop it is to *stop* it. Trap it. Kill it."

"Is that what the hostiles are to you?"

He rubs his cheek, fingers skritching against his beard. "You mean would I kill one if I found out he did something like this? Not unless I had to. Bad analogy, then. I'd trap and relocate. Same as I'd prefer to do with an animal. If I seemed to be avoiding the possibility, it's because this case is a helluva lot easier if we're dealing with a settler."

"Jacob says it can't be a hostile."

"Can't?"

"He was adamant about that. A hostile doesn't have the mental capacity to pull this off."

That frown again. "I don't know why he'd say that. Sure, I don't have as much experience with them, but of course some could do this. Jacob knows that."

"I think it's because of what Beth did to him. He's equating that with hostiles. He looks back and thinks *he* couldn't have held Nicole captive for a year when he was in that mental state, so therefore hostiles couldn't either."

"I guess so."

Dalton goes pensive, and I can tell he doesn't like that explanation. After a moment, he says, "Yeah, there are hostiles who could do it. I remember this one time, maybe twelve years back, we had a group that left town. Four people. The sheriff . . . my, uh, father . . ."

Dalton doesn't talk about the former sheriff much, and when he does, there's a discomfort with the language. Sheriff, father, adopted father . . . kidnapper. What exactly is Gene Dalton to him? I don't think Dalton knows himself. I don't blame him.

"My father," he says, firmer. "He used to be less understanding of runners than the sheriff before him."

"Ty Cypher?"

"Right. Cypher didn't give a damn if people left, and my father thought that was just Cypher being an asshole, but I think it was more . . ." He shrugs. "If you want to go, go. Cypher saw it as a valid alternative. I disagree, but only because people don't know what they're getting into. It's not Little House on the Fucking Prairie."

"First, there's no prairie."

"Exactly."

"Second, you've read *Little House on the Prairie*?"

His eyes narrow in a mock glare. "You got a problem with that?"

"Not at all, Sheriff. Continue, please."

"People have idealized views of the wilderness. That it's some kind of natural paradise. If they want to become settlers, I try to disabuse them of that notion. But if they insist? It's not as bad as my father . . ." He clears his throat. Shifts. "It's not what he thought."

Because Gene Dalton really had seen all outsiders as savages. He'd "rescued" Dalton from his birth parents, which is like "rescuing" a kid from a family voluntarily living off the grid.

"Anyway," Dalton says, "these four snuck off, and the hostiles got them."

"Killed them?"

"Took them. I found their camp. It was a week later, and it'd been long abandoned, but there was stuff there, from their packs. Personal stuff. Photos and mementos they'd brought from down south."

"Things no one else would have wanted. And things they wouldn't have left behind."

He nods. "I found evidence of a struggle, too. Marks in the dirt. Blood. I followed the trail for a while; at some point, though, their captors *realized* they were leaving a trail and took steps to cover it. I lost it in a stream."

"They deliberately covered their tracks. Which suggests a reasonable degree of intelligence. Are you sure it was hostiles?"

"Yeah." He goes quiet for a moment. "I saw one of the captives. The woman. It was a year later. She . . . she'd become one of them. A hostile. She still wore some of the clothing she took, but it wasn't more than rags. Her hair had been hacked off. One of her ears had blackened from frostbite. A couple of her fingers, too. It was . . . hard to take. I knew her. She'd been a biologist down south, and we used to talk about that. Just talk. She was nice. Smart and kind and nice. And when I met her in the forest? She attacked me. Hitting, biting, clawing. I thought I was going to have to shoot her. Later, I wondered if maybe I should have, if that wouldn't have been—" He squeezes his eyes shut. "Fuck, I don't mean that. I don't. That's not my decision to make. But seeing her like that, it was hard. What she'd been. What she'd become."

I entwine my fingers with his, move against him, and stay close, listening to him breathe.

"How did she get that way?" I ask gently.

He looks at me.

"This is the question I'm trying to work out," I say. "How do hostiles *become* hostile? Was she tormented and abused until she just lost her mind? Can that happen in a year? Someone like Nicole pulls through—mentally intact—and someone else doesn't? And if so, then what about the others? The ones who captured her? How did *they* get that way?"

I tell him about my talk with Mathias. When I finish, he's quiet. Then he says, "I never thought of it. Hostiles just . . . they *are,* you know. For me, there have always been hostiles in the woods. My parents—my birth parents—warned me about them from the time I was able to wander. Asking *how* they got that way would have been like asking why bears or cougars would attack if I got too close."

"Just another kind of animal."

"Yeah. Which they aren't, and they weren't born that way, so . . ." He turns onto his back. "I'm going to need to think about this."

It's the middle of the night when we wake to Kenny banging on Dalton's door. Sutherland is conscious. Kenny takes the puppy to Petra's while Dalton and I yank on clothes and hurry out.

Sutherland is still groggy and feverish. Interviewing him in that state feels almost as cruel as interviewing Nicole, but it must be done. We manage to keep him awake long enough to get a semicoherent account.

After he ran from Rockton—"I can't believe I was that stupid"— he'd heard us coming after him on the sleds and veered into the forest—"I wanted to get back to town on my own, figured I'd get in less trouble." He'd been making his way in the direction of Rockton when someone hit him in the back of the head—"I never heard a thing. Just felt it and then everything went black."

Sutherland woke in a makeshift shelter that offered no more than basic protection from the elements. He drifted in and out of consciousness—"I don't know how long. It was so cold, and my head hurt, and all I wanted to do was sleep." Finally, he woke to realize he was bound and gagged.

His captor watched him. Like with Nicole. Only in Sutherland's case, that's all he did. He watched and then he left, saying nothing, not feeding his captive or giving him anything to drink.

Sutherland found a slab of broken wood on that makeshift shelter and used the sharp edge to slowly hack through the rope on his wrist, which explained the splinters. He escaped and oriented himself by the mountains. Eventually, he stumbled onto one of the paths, followed it, and began to recognize landmarks. That's when his captor found him again. Sutherland fled into the woods, hoping to lose him. He ran until he passed out, not realizing how close he was to town.

I ask if he knows where he was kept, if he could get me back to the spot. It might provide some clues. But while he says he'll try, his tone tells me he has no idea where to go. He'd escaped and run blindly through the woods.

"The guy who captured you," Dalton says. "Can you describe him?"

Sutherland nods. "A little taller than me. Dark hair. Dark beard. I—I'm not sure of his eyes. Dark, I think. He'd wear one of those hats that goes right over your head, with the eye and mouth openings."

"A balaclava," I say.

"Right. One time, when he thought I was sleeping, he raised it to drink, and I saw a beard. Oh, and he wore winter coveralls. What's the word? The things you guys wear on the sleds?"

"A snowmobile suit?" I ask.

"Yes. He wore a snowmobile suit."

THIRTY-SIX

The next morning, Dalton and I are out at dawn, hiking to see Silas Cox, the guy who'd given Jacob the creeps with his bondage fantasies. Jacob said Cox is one of the more settled guys out here, meaning he has a permanent residence and tends to stick to it. That residence is about ten kilometers from Rockton, which we need to do on foot—it's too far off-trail to take the horses or snowmobiles. It doesn't take long for me to realize I really need to get working on my snowshoe skills. Or convince Dalton we need cross-country skis. The forest here is dense enough that it's not like we're trudging through three feet of snow, but it's still slow going.

As we walk, I tell Dalton about my meeting with Val.

"Yeah, I imagine she'd be having a rough time of it," he says. "I hadn't given that much thought. Whether or not one of her attackers is the same guy, she'll be wondering how close she came to ending up like Nicole—or Robyn and Victoria. Maybe see if she has a weapon. I'm not giving her a gun, but a baseball bat might make her feel safer."

"There's something else," I say. "We had some weird back-and-forth in regards to your role in her disappearance."

His brows shoot up. "My role? I told her not to go on patrol. Hell, I forbade it. Council overrode me."

"She did say you didn't want her going."

"Right." He catches my look and groans. "Is this that shit about me treating her different because she's a woman? I told her I don't let anyone go into the woods that soon after they arrive. It was weeks before I let *Will* on patrol, and no one came better equipped to handle himself in a bad situation. The problem was that he wasn't accustomed to *that* situation. The forest."

He walks a few more steps, grumbling under his breath. "I never know what to do with that shit. I can say gender has nothing to do with it. I can give examples to prove my point. But with someone like Val, I just can't win."

"You can't. I'm sorry. If it's any consolation, it's not you."

"It's her?"

"No, it's every man who did push her back because she's a woman. You're just the poor guy who has to deal with the accumulated hostility and prejudice. But in this case, you were right not to want her going into the forest. Look what happened. Your concern was justified. Then you responded appropriately, taking all measures to find her. So why was she acting weird about it?"

"Weird how?"

"She brought you into the narrative, and when I asked if you or your actions had any bearing on what happened, she said no. Repeatedly no. But in a way that said yes, if you know what I mean."

"Holding something back."

"Right."

He exhales. "Fuck. I . . ." Another exhale. "I have no idea, Casey. I really don't. I told her not to go. I wasn't with the patrol party. She's not claiming that anyone lured her from the path. She saw her attackers—and they weren't me. She's not questioning the steps I took to find her, which—if anything—were over and above because she's the council rep and she already didn't like me. I was up all night with the search party. Even the damned council thought I was allocating too many resources to finding her."

"You say she didn't like you before that."

"Yeah, but it was mostly just the sense that she thought I was some dumb redneck, too young to be sheriff. Dismissing me rather than outright hating my guts, like she does now."

"When did that change?"

He walks in silence, thinking. "After she got back. Not right away. At first, she was grateful. She apologized to me. Told me I'd been right to want her to stay out of the forest and thanked me for putting so much effort into finding her when it was her own stupid mistake. I said everyone underestimates the danger out here, and it's so easy to get turned around in the forest. Everything seemed fine. And then it wasn't."

"When did it go wrong?"

"Maybe a week or two after that? I remember she'd taken a few days off, and we still seemed to be okay, and then she started making excuses for skipping our meetings—they were daily back then, me giving reports. I figured it was trauma. Isabel agreed. We decided to give her space, but it only just got worse after that. I never tried figuring out what changed her mind about me. I just thought . . ." He shrugs. "I thought it was me. Our styles clash, I was too rough around the edges, she wasn't accustomed to men like me. Whatever the reason, I sure as hell wasn't going to change to make her comfortable."

"It wasn't you," I say. "Something more happened. After she got back."

"I see that now. I just wish I had a clue what it was."

As we walk, I ask Dalton more about the relationship between Rockton and the "locals." I know the basics, of course, but now's the time to hammer those down to specifics—before I meet Cox and say anything I shouldn't.

The issue, of course, is that Rockton might be hidden from the air, but on the ground, it's not exactly shielded by an invisibility barrier. Well, it kind of is, given the architecture. Sutherland passed out fifty meters from town without realizing how close he was.

The problem is that we don't *stay* in town. We come out to hunt, to fish, to gather berries, to chop trees, and just to get out and move around. When you're in a region with so few people, a passing stranger is going to get your attention.

So how big a secret is Rockton? If you live in the immediate area, you know there's a settlement. You just don't know what *kind* of settlement it is. If you ask Jacob or Brent, they'll pretend it's a commune or wilderness retreat, but the Yukon isn't the kind of place where people like answering questions, so most don't ask. Their own wild imaginings are far more entertaining. Even Brent has a list of conspiracy theory explanations for Rockton, and no real interest in learning the truth.

What about those *from* Rockton? Men like Tyrone Cypher. Cypher hadn't run away. He'd just said "fuck this" and walked out. His "fuck this" had been directed mostly at the new sheriff—Gene Dalton. Like Dalton, Cypher hadn't been above throwing his weight around. Unlike Dalton, he didn't need an actual excuse to do it. Also, as Jacob said, he was crazy. So the council demoted him to deputy and Gene to sheriff. After a few years, Cypher stormed off, declaring he'd rather live among "savages" than the so-called civilized folk of Rockton.

Did *he* talk about Rockton after he left? Maybe. But Dalton figured anyone who spent five minutes with the guy wouldn't have believed a word that left his mouth. Whatever Cypher has said, it's never come back on Rockton. The Yukon wilderness is a nest of interlocking secrets, and if you go after someone else's, they might retaliate by digging up yours.

As we walk, Dalton follows Jacob's landmarks and points them out to me, part of my ongoing survival education.

See that ridge? If you can count two points, you're heading northeast. Three, you're heading east. One? Due north. You want to head back to Rockton? Over your shoulder, you'll see the ridge as two peaks, the smaller one to the left.

There's a lightning-struck tree right up here. Take a good look at it. It's a white spruce, like the lightning-struck spruce over by the lake, but see how this one's split? Right down to the base. That's how you tell the two apart.

This is the language I'm learning. The little things that are, to him, as natural as saying, *Head up to the Tim Hortons, then swing a left at the light and keep going until you hit a one-way street.*

I'm in the lead and have been for a while, my instructor letting me take the wheel. *Keep an eye out for crisscrossed felled pines and then make a left, forty-five degrees.*

When I don't quite get it right, he prods my shoulder blade, steering me. This time, though, his hand falls and grips, and that's my brake.

"We're getting close," he says. "There's a clearing to the right, and I'm going to guess that's where Cox built his shelter. Which means we need to watch for traps."

"Booby traps?"

"That's common for those who hunker down someplace alone and exposed. We had them when Jacob and I were growing up."

That's how Dalton words his past life—"when Jacob and I were growing up" or "when I lived out here." Never "when I lived with my parents." Maybe that's too confusing when he has two sets. But I think it's more that the two sets are confusing to *him*.

After the Daltons brought him into Rockton, he waited for his parents to rescue him. When they didn't, the only way he could deal with that was to reject them and accept what everyone told him—how lucky he was to have been "rescued."

Then he grew up and realized he'd actually been kidnapped. And he still has no idea why his birth parents didn't come for him. If he's ever asked Jacob, his brother didn't have an answer.

I want to help him reconcile this. At least, I want to help him confront his confusion and anger and the scars left behind. But I don't know where to begin. I get chances like this, when he mentions that life, but when I've tried prodding further, he slams that door and moves on.

So I only say, "What kind of traps?" and he resumes walking, up beside me now. "Could be bear, but that's rare. More likely . . . Well, let's see."

We reach the edge of a semicleared area. The ground shows evidence of old fire damage, where sporadic shrubs have managed to take root and a few trees have established a fresh foothold. Almost dead center I see a log cabin, small but decently constructed. Dalton stops me on that clearing edge and eyes the shelter. Then his gaze sweeps the clearing. He motions to a section where the snow dips, no tall vegetation poking through.

"Pit trap," he says. "It'll be covered in brush, but that hollow is a giveaway. There's another one. Can you see it?"

I take a moment. Then I point and say, "About five meters left of that black spruce."

"Good."

"There's another low spot over there, closer to the cabin, but it looks completely cleared from this angle."

"Yeah, that'd be a work area, maybe fire pit. Gotta be careful of the hollows and the dense undergrowth, which could be hiding a snare. Snares are particularly hard to see. I say don't even try—just lift your feet when you walk, so you don't drag through one. Even if you do, it's easy enough to get out of. Most of these just are to warn Cox of trespassers."

"But aren't snares more likely to be set off by animals?"

"Yep. Which means dinner."

"Ah."

We've gotten about halfway to that cabin when Dalton catches my shoulder again.

"Around here, walking up and knocking is *not* considered neighborly. Get your gun out but keep it lowered."

I do, and he calls, "Silas Cox?"

A noise from inside the cabin.

"Cox?" Dalton shouts. "We want to talk to you."

The door swings open. There's no one behind it. Then a voice calls, "What do you want?"

"We'd like to talk."

"Well, you're talking."

"Face-to-face."

A shuffling sound. Then, "Tell your boy to step away from you and put his hands up."

"I'm not a boy." I pull off my hat and then tug out my ponytail band. Dalton hisses under his breath, but I know what I'm doing—getting Cox's attention.

"You brought a girl?" Cox calls. A moment of silence, and I glimpse a head as someone peers out at me. "You Injun, girl? Fuck. You come to tell me this isn't my land? Hell yeah, it's mine, and—"

"We aren't here to discuss territory. Can we just speak to you, Mr. Cox? Please?"

"Tell your buddy to take off his hat, too," he says. "Let me get a look at him."

Dalton does. Silence stretches.

"Step closer. You, boy, not the girl. And put your hands over your head."

Dalton obeys, pocketing his gun first. Cox doesn't seem to notice—or care—that I have one. Dalton takes three steps and says, "There, now—"

Cox cuts him off with a whoop. "Well, look at that. If it ain't the jungle boy, all grown up."

Dalton tenses. "That you, Tyrone?"

"Anybody else call you that these days?" Tyrone Cypher steps into the doorway. He's well over six foot, a big bear of a man. Too big to be the man in the snowsuit? That's impossible to say. He definitely has the dark hair and beard.

Cypher leans against the doorway. "The boy who was raised by wolves. I remember when your daddy brought you to Rockton. You looked like the kid from that cartoon, covered by more dirt than clothes. Always thought the Daltons were fools, taking you in. Shoulda brought you down south instead, put you in a sideshow, made a bit of money."

Dalton's eyes narrow before he throws it off. "Good to see you too, Tyrone."

"Oh, listen to you, boy, talking like a regular person. Put the ape in proper clothing, teach him proper el-o-cu-tion, and he can pretty near pass for human. He even brings along his little Injun Jane."

"That's Tarzan," I say.

Tyrone squints at me, as if the trees have spoken. "What?"

"The jungle boy who was raised by wolves is Mowgli. The book is by Rudyard Kipling. Jane belongs with Tarzan. Raised by apes. Books by Edgar Rice Burroughs. And if I look Aboriginal, you need glasses. Also cultural-sensitivity training. But I suppose they don't offer a lot of that . . ." I look around. "Here."

"Got a mouth on you, huh, girl?" I wait for the inevitable offer to show me other ways to use it, but he doesn't go there.

"Where's Silas Cox?" Dalton asks.

Cypher screws up his face in fake confusion. "Silas's what?"

"Where is Silas Cox?"

"Still can get jokes, can you, boy? I'll talk to your girl instead."

"Silas Cox," I say. "This is his cabin, and we're looking for him."

"Well, then you've found him. Close by, anyway. He's hanging out over yonder." He hooks a thumb behind the cabin.

"Call him for me," Dalton says.

"Well, now, I don't think that'll work. I can try. But I'd be damned surprised if he answered."

I glance at Dalton. His jaw is set, eyes narrowed in a look that says he doesn't quite know how to handle this. I've dealt with enough guys like this that I step forward and say, "Did you kill Silas Cox for his cabin?"

"What? This old thing?" He pounds the wall. "Hardly worth killing a man for, don't you think?"

"Did you kill Silas Cox? Regardless of the reason."

"Nope. I'm a mite insulted you'd ask that."

"So Silas Cox is over there." I gesture. "Is he dead or alive?"

"Alive last time I saw him. But I got the feeling the condition wasn't permanent."

"If you did something to cause his death, that's still murder."

"Oh, look at you, getting all technical about it."

"Take us to Cox," Dalton says.

"What? Hell. I was just settling in with a nice cup of tea and a novel. Was getting to the good part too, about some skinny kid, comes swaggering around, thinking he's all grown up, gonna take on the big bad bully and show him what's what." He rubs his chin. "On second thought, I don't need to read it. I know how it ends. The bully shows the boy he's still just a swaggering kid, sends him crying back to Daddy. How is your daddy, anyway? He make you deputy yet?"

"He's retired. I'm sheriff in Rockton."

Cypher bursts out laughing. Then he looks at me. "Please tell me you're the deputy. Because that's the only thing that would make this story better."

"I'm the detective."

"Nope, I lied. *That* made it better. All right, kids, let me take you to ol' Silas Cox."

THIRTY-SEVEN

Dalton is fuming. As we tromp through the forest, he gives no outward sign of it, but I swear I smell smoke as Cypher strolls this
way and that, saying, "Is he over . . . ? No, wait, I think he's . . .
Or maybe . . ."

I roll my eyes at Dalton, trying to ease the tension. He keeps fuming.

In Rockton, people get the chance to reinvent themselves. Dalton
has done that. He needed it. He was the boy from the forest, and while
I know Cypher is exaggerating how primitive he'd been—Jacob is
hardly a loincloth-clad Neanderthal—Cypher is actually being very
clever in his insults. He's not mocking the way Dalton had been, but
the way Dalton might have *felt*.

No one in Rockton these days knew Dalton as a boy. Everyone
from then is long gone and has done him the kindness of not passing
on his story to newcomers. So for years, he has truly been Eric Dalton.
A child born in Rockton, who grew up there. Even that is uncomfortable, knowing people see him as an anomaly—an "anthropo-
logical study" he calls it when he's in a good mood, a "freak" when
he's not.

He has not been the boy from the forest in many years. With
Cypher, he's thrust into that past, reminded of a time when he probably did feel like Mowgli. It bothers him, and he fumes *because* it

bothers him. He's like any of us cast back into an uncomfortable childhood role, struggling to remind ourselves we aren't that person anymore, aren't that powerless anymore.

"You know what the problem is?" Cypher says. "Trees. The forest is full of them, and after a while, they all start to look alike. I know ol' Silas is here somewhere, but damned if I can find him with all these *trees*." He skirts past a spruce. "I have an idea. Why don't you find him, boy? Your daddy used to say you were better than a hunting dog."

"Silas isn't here, is he?" I say.

"I said he was. That means he is. I am a man of my word. Didn't your daddy used to say that, boy? Ty Cypher might be a crazy son of a bitch, but he's as honest as old Abe Lincoln."

"Really?" I say. "Okay, how about telling us why you were in Rockton in the first place?"

"Well, now, that's a story. Something about a dog and a woman, and three men who didn't take kindly to my treatment of either."

I glance at Dalton, who only shakes his head as if he's heard this before. "Okay, I'll bite." I say. "What did you do to the dog and the woman?"

"Not a damned thing, and that was the problem. See, these three men hired me to take care of a situation. That's what I did for a living. Took care of situations."

"With a gun, I presume?"

"Hell, no. That wouldn't be sporting. I work with my hands. Old-fashioned physical labor. So I took this job, and they neglected to tell me that my targets were this woman and her dog. I said fuck no, and I warned the woman, who grabbed her dog and hauled ass. These three guys took exception to that so *I* hauled ass up here."

"They came after you for warning her?"

"Well, not entirely. See the woman was married to one of the guys, and when I told her what was going on, she was awful grateful. And for some reason, this guy—who wanted his wife *dead*—didn't like me messing around with her. So that's why I was in Rockton. For screwing clients and screwing a woman. But I didn't screw the dog. Just to be clear on that."

"Uh-huh."

"For all my faults, I *am* an honest man. If I say Silas Cox is here, he is. Less than fifty paces away, I reckon."

"On the ground," Dalton says.

"What?"

"I said get on the ground. Searching for Cox means putting my back to you. My father *did* say you never lie, but that doesn't mean you're honest. He made the mistake of presuming a man who speaks honestly acts the same. I remember what you did after they fired you."

Cypher grins. "But I was *honestly* pissed off. And your daddy was *honestly* a sanctimonious ass. And *honestly* kind of stupid, not to have seen that one coming. But I'll give you credit for being a smarter man than him." He plunks himself on the snow-covered ground. "Good enough?"

"Is that how you used to leave suspects?" Dalton says.

"You remember that, huh? Good boy."

He gets into a casual downward dog, poised on his hands and feet. I actually have seen Dalton do this—when he doesn't have handcuff ties, the idea being that he'll see or hear the person scrambling to get upright.

As Dalton searches, I take a few steps in the other direction, one eye always on Cypher. I've gone maybe five when a breeze passes, bringing with it a scent that stops me.

Dalton notices, and when I glance over, he motions for me to pursue it as he watches Cypher.

I go about twenty steps before Dalton says, "Ty? Up. Walk between us."

As Cypher follows, he says, "You forgot to tell me you'll have a gun pointed at my head, in case I try to run."

"If it goes without saying, I don't say it. And the gun's at your back. Head's not a sure enough target."

"You really *don't* get humor, do you? That was a perfect opportunity for an insult, something about even *my* head not being a big enough target."

"Like I said, I don't mention anything that goes without saying."

We travel about another twenty paces, and I stop. I swivel. I inhale.

I head to the right, cutting through thick brush. Then I spot something in the undergrowth. Something raw and bloody, peeking from under the snow. I crouch and brush off a layer of snow to see a skull with half its face torn off, eye missing, teeth clenched in a death's-head grin.

Cypher chuckles. "Well, now, seems you hired your detective for her pretty face. Can't say I blame you, though. That's a mighty fine rabbit you found there, girl. Dig up the rest. Maybe you can *detect* what killed it."

"What's your weapon of choice?" I ask. "Besides your hands?"

"You gonna challenge me to a duel?"

"Snare and knife," Dalton says. "Ty likes to get up close and personal with his prey."

"Then you missed this one." I brush back more snow to reveal the snare on its half-eaten leg. "You left it for the scavengers." I peer around. "Have you been hunting on Silas's property? Was that the source of the dispute? Or did you kill him and then settle in?"

"I said I never killed him. True fact, ma'am. That's my snare, 'cause I was bunking down with Silas for the winter. Paid in advance for the privilege, which is why I figure I can keep living here during his unforeseen absence."

I eye him. I don't buy the I-never-lie bullshit. To pull that off, all you need to do is establish a reputation for honesty while saving your falsehoods for when you really need them.

I rise and say, "Shouldn't waste your food."

"Waste? I was feeding the local wildlife. Act of charity."

"You *tortured* this local wildlife. Maybe someone should snare and leave you, see if you like it. Or drop you in a pit, leave you to rot."

I carefully watch his reaction, but he only says, "Silas was the one who liked trapping with pits. Which is fucking stupid with the permafrost. I always said he should switch to snares."

"Pits can be deep enough if you find the right terrain. Plenty of deep chutes in these mountain caves."

"What would you trap in them? Wood rats? Big critters don't roam the caves. They just use the entrances for shelter." He looks at

Dalton. "You really do keep her around for ornamental value, don't you?"

"This isn't what I smelled," I say, nodding at the rabbit as I continue on. "It's buried under snow. The scent suggests something bigger. Which could just mean a deer or caribou or wolf or bear. If it was, I think I'd pick up the musk, too, but down south, I was in homicide, not animal control."

"Homicide? Seriously? Minority hiring at work, huh? How old are you? Twenty-four? Twenty-five?"

"Thirty-one."

"Huh. That's not so bad. Still young, but I knew a chick in homicide, around your age. Came closer to catching me than anyone else. Always figured it was 'cause she had to be better than the boys to get the job."

When he'd started grumbling about minority hiring, I'd been ready for the usual intimation that I only got my job because I fill both the gender and visible minority quotas—two-for-one special! I can't shove Tyrone Cypher squarely into the asshole box he seems to fit, and that's never comfortable.

Cypher is, well, a cipher. Which makes me suspect he had a say in his new surname.

I keep walking and sniffing. The smell of decomposing flesh gets stronger, and I'm focusing on that and then . . .

And then the smell vanishes. I stop. I turn around, but I still can't smell it, and even when I retreat a few paces, the scent eludes me.

"Want a clue?" Cypher says. "Just ask nicely."

"It's the wind," Dalton says.

"Hey, don't be stealing my thunder."

I ignore him. I see what Dalton means. Facing north, the light breeze blows straight at me. When I turn around, I lose that, which means I've gone too far. I've passed my goal.

I back up and catch it again, but faint, meaning I'm still upwind. I keep going and . . . I get a face full of the breeze and a nose full of the stink of decomposing flesh.

I survey the landscape. Then I walk step by step until the smell just begins to fade.

I turn. I look. I see nothing.

"Red hot," Cypher says. "You sure you don't want that clue? I'll trade you for—"

Cypher takes a step toward me, and Dalton's foot shoots out, kicking Cypher in the back of the knees. The big man goes down, then scrambles to flip over, stopping when Dalton presses the gun to his shoulder.

"That's some seriously bad aim, boy," Cypher says. "Guess that's what happens when you don't go to a proper school. Your sense of anatomy gets all fucked up."

"My sense of anatomy is just fine."

"Why—" Cypher stops and chortles. "Wait. I know this one." He glances at me. "When I was sheriff, I'd grab a guy and twist his index finger. He'd wonder why I did that, instead of twisting his arm."

"Because you might hesitate to break his arm," I say, "but you're not going to mind snapping his finger. It isn't an empty threat."

"Good girl. Seems your boss picked up a few of my tricks. Too bad he also learned from his daddy, with his over-re-li-ance on firearms. A real man would put that gun down and take me on properly."

"Then I guess your idea of a real man is a functional idiot," Dalton says.

Cypher throws back his head and howls a laugh. "Oh, that is good. You just forgot to follow it up with 'and that's not surprising, considering where it's coming from.'"

"That's another of those things that goes without saying."

Cypher grins at me. "The boy's real good at learning his lessons. When I was sheriff, sometimes, I'd give guys the option of skipping chopping duty by going a few rounds with me in the town square. You know how many lacked the brains to refuse? Small brains. Big egos. Plenty of entertainment for all. Now, boy, if you'd given me a second, you'd have seen I wasn't making a move on your cute detective. I was just going to point her in the right direction."

"Up," I say.

"What?"

I squint into the treetops. "The right direction is up. Silas is somewhere . . ." I trail off as I walk, my gaze fixed on the trees until I see a shape. It's so high I need my binoculars. I look through and see what is definitely a man's hand dangling from a branch.

Cypher says, "If you think I put him up there, you've got a very generous opinion of a big man's agility level. I can tell you what happened, but you're going to need to take my word for it, 'cause that's one crime scene you're not reaching without wings."

Dalton hands me his pack. Then he unzips his jacket.

"You're seriously going to climb up there?" Cypher says. "Guess you really are part ape."

Dalton ignores him and hands me his jacket. He's wearing a T-shirt, and as he grips the tree trunk to scale it, his muscles flex. Cypher whistles.

"You got some guns, boy. Not exactly my .45 Specials, but you're not as skinny as I remember. You sure you don't want to take me on? I'm getting to be an old man. You might actually win."

Dalton snorts.

Cypher laughs again. "You really did grow some brains, didn't you?"

Dalton starts to climb. It's not easy—he has to scale the lower trunk like a fireman's pole before he reaches branches thick enough to support him. Once he's up there, across from Cox, he calls down, "Tell me what you need in situ, and then I'll have to bring the crime scene to you."

I ask him to make note of Cox's position along with a preliminary assessment of injuries. He does and then says, "I'm bringing him down."

He manages to lower Cox about ten feet before he runs out of decent branch steps. Then he says, "He's coming express," and I step back. He lowers the body as best he can and then lets Cox fall.

The corpse hits the snow face-first. Resisting the urge to turn him over, I assess his back. He's wearing a parka. Boots, too. One at least. The other is gone, along with the leg that once occupied it. I brush snow away from the severed leg. It's been pulled off, not cut. The flesh is mangled and decomposed enough to tell me Cox has been in that tree for about a week. Which means he's not our man.

Dalton hops down as I move to checking the only other obvious area of injury I see from the rear—Cox's neck. It's been bitten from the back, with perfect puncture wounds on either side of his spine. Bitten and broken, his head at an impossible angle. Dalton confirms the neck was like that before he moved the body.

When I give the sign, he flips Cox over. Here's where I see the real damage, his parka ripped open, chest ripped open, the two mingling in a mess of feathers and fabric and shredded flesh.

"Eaten," I say. "Something stored him in that tree for later. The only tree-climbing beast out here with the power to do that would be a cougar. Which is consistent with the bite marks. That's how they attack, right? Like a cat. Pin and bite the neck, rather than rip out the throat like a canine would."

"Yep," Dalton says.

"And the caching? Is that normal?"

"It is. They'll use deadfall sometimes, but a tree will do the trick, too. Any place to hide their prey."

"So unless I can shape-shift into a big cat, this ain't my fault," Cypher says as he rises to his feet. "Agreed?"

"You knew what happened to him," I say. "You knew where he was. But you had to toy with us."

"Out here, you take your amusement where you find it. And you two were so cute. Hot on the trail of the killer cougar. You gonna go arrest her?"

"You gonna tell us where we can find her?" Dalton says. "This is at least the second person she's killed in the last few years. She's learned we're easy prey, which is no joking matter."

"Nope, it's not," Cypher says. "Which is why you don't need to worry about this particular she-bitch. I've been out here every day, watching for her to come back."

"How long exactly?" I ask.

He eyes me. "That important?"

"It might be."

"I was out checking my traps six days ago when I heard Silas scream. By the time I got here, she was hauling him up that tree."

THIRTY-EIGHT

I'm preparing to leave when Cypher steps into my path and says, "You do realize I used to be sheriff in Rockton, right? Whatever this boy's daddy thought of my methods, I kept the law in that town. I know a few things about police work. Had a lot of experience circumventing it in my former life, if you know what I mean."

I have no intention of walking away without questioning him. But I can't let him know I want something, or it'll be another invitation to a game.

"Well," I say, "if you know police investigations, you know there's a limit to what I can tell you. Short version is that we're looking for a man who held a Rockton woman captive in a cave for over a year. And she may not have been the first he put there—just the first who survived the ordeal."

He looks at Dalton. "She serious?"

"Does either of us seem like the type who'd joke about that?"

"Keeping a woman in a cave? That's fucked up. And you say there've been others?"

"Possibly two."

"Stretching back how far?"

"The first one disappeared from Rockton about five years ago."

"After my time." He nods in satisfaction. "Knew your daddy wasn't up to the job."

"Yeah, well, half as many people disappeared into the forest under *his* watch."

"Mine didn't disappear. They took off 'cause I scared them away. Weeding out the bad apples." He looks at me. "So if we're talking five years, that must cut your in-town suspects down to about zero. That why you're rooting around out here?"

"It is."

"Huh. Well, the problem, as I'm sure our boy told you, is that we don't exactly have a high proportion of stable individuals in these woods. Ol' Silas would have been a damned fine suspect. Other than that . . . Well, now that I think of it, I might have another lead for you."

"Go on," Dalton says.

"I was talking to your girl. I think my information is valuable enough to set a price. Tit for tat." He leers at me. "You show me yours, and I'll show you mine."

"Enough," Dalton says. "You fancy yourself a former lawman? Try showing her a little professional respect."

"Oh, come on," Cypher says. "Just a flash. Make an old man's day. You don't have to look, boy. We'll do it behind the cabin over here."

"Shut the fuck—"

"I've got this," I say to Dalton.

His look says not to play Cypher's game. Which doesn't mean he actually thinks I'll flash my breasts—just that he's had enough of Cypher's bullshit. When I head behind the cabin, though, he only grumbles. It takes Cypher a moment to follow. He does, and we're out of sight, and he glances back around to check on Dalton.

"You trying to make the boss jealous?" he says as he walks to me.

"Why do you think that?"

"'Cause you're sure as hell not going to flash me."

"Then why *ask*? Oh, let me guess—you were just trying to rile me up."

"Nah. You don't give a shit. Him, though . . ." He jerks a thumb toward the front of the cabin and grins. "That boy's got a serious case of puppy love, and I wanted to yank his chain."

"So you don't want to see my tits?"

"Fuck, no. I'm not a perv."

I shake my head. "I called you back here so I can get the answers in a way Eric might not approve of." I take off my jacket. "By beating them out of you."

He laughs. Laughs so hard he has to lean against the cabin for support. Two minutes later, he's flat on his stomach with his arm twisted behind his back.

"Shit," he says.

"The bigger they are . . ."

"Huh." He cranes his neck to look back at me, completely unperturbed. "Where'd you learn to throw down like that?"

"Black belt in aikido. I've also got a boxing championship, but it's flyweight, meaning I can't actually beat the answers out of you. Well, I could pin you down and kick until you talk, but that's unsporting. It will get awfully cold, though, facedown in the snow."

He chuckles, then shouts, "Boy? You listening in?"

"Of course," Dalton says, coming around the cabin. "I don't need to eavesdrop when it's this quiet. I think you should get up, though. Lying like that, you won't see anything when she flashes you."

Cypher flashes Dalton—the finger, that is—but there's no rancor in it. He rises and says, "When you say this woman was kept in a cave, was it Three Peaks or Bear Skull?"

"You're the one offering the lead," Dalton says. "You tell me."

"Well, my lead is for Bear Skull. There's a guy out here, second-generation Rockton departee, like you and your brother, only he's not quick to volunteer that information. You know the First Settlement? The one over by Caribou River?"

"Yeah."

"He's from there originally. Pretends he just wandered in from down south and stayed." He looks at me. "You know how many people actually do that? Most folks in this twenty-mile radius have a Rockton connection. Otherwise, it'd be the most populated stretch of the Yukon wilderness. But folks don't go around saying that. Whatever happened to them or their families in Rockton, they respect the idea of it enough not to take a shit on those still there. Rockton was a safe place for us, and the best way to leave it safe for others is to keep our mouths shut."

"But you know this guy is a second-generation settler," Dalton says.

"Yeah. He let enough slip for me to figure it out. He knows the town exists but doesn't know shit about specifics, which means second generation. He tried asking me more about it years ago, having heard I used to be sheriff. I shut him down. Reason I'm mentioning it is that he's been taking a lot of interest in Rockton recently. Very recently."

"What kind of interest?"

"Law enforcement mainly. What kind you have there, how good it is."

"This guy got a name?" Dalton asks.

"Everyone does. He goes by Roger."

I look at Dalton as his gaze slides my way, both of us recognizing the name Jacob gave me for the contact he thought we should speak to.

"Can you describe him?" I ask.

Cypher does. It matches what I saw of the man in the forest—the one who'd been chasing Sutherland.

"When did this conversation take place?" I ask.

"Few days ago, after that cougar-bitch got Silas. I was out hunting her."

I nod, assimilating that, and then say. "On another note, talk to me about hostiles."

"Rather not. Rather just pretend they don't exist. Better yet, rather *make* them not exist." He looks at Dalton. "Don't give me that look, boy. You know as well as I do that if animals acted that way, we'd put them down. Just like this cougar. At least she mostly keeps to herself, doesn't try to cause trouble."

"Do the hostiles bother you?" I ask.

"Their existence bothers me. Just like the cougar's does. Because it's the same thing. Guys like me will give you a chance to leave if you get on their territory. Hostiles just attack. They're not even killing us for food. I think I'd respect them more if they did."

"So you have experience with them."

"As little as possible. But yeah, I do. Fucking savages."

"Too savage to do something like this? Take a woman hostage and keep her captive?"

"Hell, no. It's exactly the sort of thing they'd do." He looks at Dalton. "Remember those four who went missing? You saw the woman later? What was her name?"

"Maryanne. I told Casey about her. But that seems a case of conversion rather than hostage taking."

"Unless she was captured and escaped. Driven crazy by being held in a cave or whatever."

Dalton nods. "I hadn't thought of that."

"Because you don't think like a fucking lunatic. I do. It's why I made a good sheriff." Cypher turns to me. "Hostiles could do this. The problem is that it's a lot easier if it's someone like this Roger guy."

"Because I can interview him. And talk to others about him. Not so with the hostile."

His eyes glitter. "Oh, but you *can* talk to them. They have networks, too. If I capture one—"

"No," Dalton says.

Cypher says nothing but gives me a look to say the offer stands, give it some thought.

THIRTY-NINE

Before we leave, Dalton gives Cypher a knitted toque, gloves, waterproof matches, and a few other supplies he brought in case Cox proved helpful. When he pulls out the last item, Cypher's eyes light up.

"Fuck. Is that . . . ?"

"Still like your coffee, huh?"

I swear, drool forms at the corners of Cypher's mouth.

"If I'd known we'd bump into you, I'd have brought that powdered creamer shit you like." Dalton eases back. "Course, if—"

"Say no more. If we're talking coffee and creamer, screw pride. You want me to poke around, see if I can get a bead on Roger, and if I do, I get my reward. It's a deal." Cypher hefts the coffee. "How much we talking?"

"If the weather's good, I fly into Dawson City every few weeks."

"You learned to fly? Fuck. I always said that's the one thing I wished I'd done, so I could get out of that town, buy what I wanted, and not rely on some damned delivery service."

"I remember."

"You *were* paying attention."

"I'm guessing you're asking how much coffee I can get because you're going to offer to bring Roger in for me. The answer is yes—

we'll pay for that, too. But I want him in good health and communicating. He's no use to us otherwise."

"I'll make sure he's communicating. Good health, though?" He shrugs. Then he looks at me. "While we're talking trades, you gotta teach me that kung fu shit. Could come in handy."

"I couldn't get you up to speed fast enough to use it on Roger."

"Hell, no. I want it for the cougar. That bitch is going down."

We stop at Brent's on our way back. Brent is a troglodyte, one of those terms you can rarely apply to anyone in the contemporary world. He's both a cave dweller and a hermit, which means he fits the word in every sense except the more modern definition, as someone brutish or deliberately ignorant. He has problems—mildly bipolar was Beth's diagnosis—but he lives here of his own free will. He was a former bounty hunter who followed a target to these woods, got burned— literally, with acid—and decided to retire.

Most people who live in caves use them the way bears will, selecting one with a wide entrance. Humans will then fortify that entrance, erecting a front wall against the elements and wildlife. Brent actually uses an interior cavern, one that takes some climbing and crawling to reach. It's more sheltered and comes with a vent to the outside, allowing him a carefully controlled fire pit.

Inside, it looks like those bomb shelters from the fifties. There's a bed, table, and single chair. Goods are mostly relegated to a separate "pantry" cavern. Dried meat and herbs hang from the ceiling.

If the place resembles a bomb shelter, Brent looks like the guy who crawls out of one after twenty years of thinking the world has ended. He's maybe seventy, fit and wiry, with wild gray hair and a thick beard. Today he wears the Canadiens hockey jersey Dalton got for him. He played on the team for a season. Dalton says he mostly warmed the bench, but it's one of Brent's favorite stretches in a life full of twists and turns, and so when I see the jersey, I ask about his time on the team and we chat for a while. Dalton's fine with that. Brent is more friend than contact, and you don't treat a friend by showing up and interrogating him.

Brent perches on his bed as we talk. I get the chair—he insists on it, and I've learned not to argue. Dalton settles on a hide by the fire.

After we've chatted awhile, I tell Brent why we're there.

"He kept her in a cave?" he says when I finish. He shakes his head. "And people wonder why I stayed up north. The world is full of crazy mother—" He clears his throat, and I try not to smile. Brent likes to watch his language around me, as if I don't hear profanity every waking hour from Dalton.

"Well, this particular psycho is in the part of that world you chose to stay in," Dalton drawls.

"Which is why you won't see me out there socializing. Or visiting that town of yours. I stay in here, safe from *all* the crazy, near and far. Who you looking at for this? Someone out here obviously."

"We're considering our options."

"Which is why you're here. Because I'm an option."

"Yep."

I'd have softened that, but Brent only nods and says, "Well, I didn't do it, but you're free to ask your questions."

"We'd like your opinion on a couple of neighbors," I say. "Tell me about Tyrone Cypher."

"He's a bully and an asshole. Possibly the craziest mother effer up here. But could I see him doing this?" He settles in. "Nah, Ty has his own personal brand of crazy. He's like . . . Put it this way. One time when I was out hunting, I spotted a wolverine at a kill. I was watching, considering taking him down for his pelt. Then along comes this grizzly, thinking she'd like some of that deer. Most animals, if they get a grizzly dinner guest, they clear out. Not this wolverine. He fights, despite the fact he's a quarter of the bear's size. He has no chance of winning, but the mother effer just won't stop. He's bleeding, with chunks torn out of him, and he's still going, like a whirling dervish, all fangs and claws. Grizzly finally says eff this. She's bleeding, and that deer just isn't worth the effort. I decide the wolverine has earned the right to keep his pelt, so I leave. A few days later, I wander by, and what do I find? The wolverine, dead of its injuries. But he drove off a grizzly, and he got to keep his dinner, and so I figure he died happy, thinking it was all worth it. That wolverine is Ty Cypher. You don't cross him unless you're ready to fight to the death. Otherwise, though? If you don't bug him, he won't bug you."

I glance at Dalton, who nods.

Brent says, "This abduction takes a whole different brand of crazy. The twisted kind—and the long-term kind, where someone committed himself to caring for these women. Well, 'caring' is probably the wrong word, but you know what I mean."

"How about Roger?" Dalton asks.

Brent goes quiet.

"Brent . . . ," Dalton prods.

"I like Roger."

"Yeah, I figured that. I know Jacob does, too. But Ty told me he was going around recently asking about Rockton. Did he come to you?"

"Roger isn't your man, Eric."

Dalton's jaw sets. He waits. Then he gets to his feet. "Fine. Casey, come on. Brent's right. This Roger is a nice guy. Nice guys don't do shit like this. And you know, if he sets me on this guy, I'll chase him down and string him up, and to hell with due process. Fuck, I'm not even sure I'd bother asking his story."

"Yes," Brent says. "He came by two days ago asking about Rockton."

"What exactly?"

Brent's on his feet, shifting his weight. "Law enforcement. What kind you had in there. How many people, how well trained, and whether . . ." He inhales. "Whether I thought you guys were capable."

"Capable of what?"

"Catching someone you needed to catch."

FORTY

Brent hadn't even admitted to Roger that he knew Rockton existed. Like Jacob, "I don't know nothing about that," was all he ever gave. Brent had asked where the question was coming from. Roger just said he'd heard things, about the people who lived in there, who used to, and it got him worrying about what if one of them escaped. Should people out here need to worry?

Typical paranoia from a population that leaned in that direction anyway. Or so Brent figured.

The problem will be finding Roger. Brent offers his bounty-hunting skills. While he's still not convinced Roger is responsible, he doesn't particularly want Cypher to be the one bringing him in.

We're tromping back to town, the light already fading, when Dalton says, "What Ty said, how I was when I came to Rockton, it wasn't like that."

"I know. I've met Jacob, remember? And even if it was like that, do you honestly think I'd care?"

He doesn't answer, just walks, gaze fixed ahead.

"Eric?"

"It matters," he says. "I know it does. I didn't grow up like everyone else, and it's all about experiences, right? That's what we are. The sum of our experiences. And mine are so . . ." He trails off and rubs his mouth with his free hand. "Fuck. I don't know what I'm saying."

"Everyone's experiences are different. My upbringing was nothing like yours or Will's or Petra's. But yes, yours was *more* different. I'm not sure where you're going with that, though, so you need to give me a hint. Are you worried I see you differently, knowing your past? You do remember that you told me it *before* we got together, right?"

"Yeah. I just . . ." He shakes his head. "I don't know where I'm going with it either. I'm just . . ." His fingers tighten around mine. "Stuff. You know?"

"About the case?"

He walks in silence for a few steps, and then says, "You're okay, right? With moving in?"

That throws me. I haven't even thought about it—we've been too busy with the case, and it has felt no different from before, moving from house to house. Maybe it's different for *him,* not just having a guest but sharing his home.

I say, carefully, "You weren't counting on cohabitation when you got Storm. If it's not what you want—"

"No, I'm fine with it."

"But if you aren't, you can say that. I'm not going to freak out and interpret imminent relationship doom."

He glances over. "Are *you* fine with it?"

"If I wasn't, I'd tell you. You will, too, right?"

"Course."

"Until Storm's old enough to switch between houses. Or until one of us decides we need our own place. It's not like down south, where I've given up my lease. It's easily undone if it doesn't work."

"Yeah."

He's looking straight ahead again, and I feel like I've made a mistake, but I have no idea what it is. I've bent over backward to make sure he doesn't feel trapped. Neither of us has lived with anyone before, so it seems that giving him space is critical. Keep it simple. Keep it flexible. Let him know there aren't any strings or expectations.

"Anyway, back to what I was saying," he says. "I just wanted to set the record straight about what Ty said. It's disrespectful to my birth parents, suggesting they raised me poorly. They didn't. I had clothes. I could talk just fine. They kept to themselves, but they were settlers, not hostiles."

"I know."

We walk a little farther. Then he blurts, "I don't know why I didn't go back. I tried, at first, but I gave up, and I don't know why. I have excuses, in my head. I didn't quite understand what had happened. I was angry when they didn't come for me. Lots of excuses but none of them good enough to explain why I stayed." He rolls his shoulders. "Fuck, I'm in a mood. Ignore me."

"I don't want to ignore you, Eric." Deep breath. Push forward. "I'd like to know more. It's a complicated situation, and I know it still affects you."

"I don't want it to."

"But it does. Maybe if you talked, it'd help."

He says nothing more, and we walk the rest of the way in silence.

I don't see much of Dalton after we get back to Rockton. Part of that is workload. He has his own tasks to do. Requests for help with minor stuff have slowed—people recognize we're too busy for it. But there's still enough to keep Dalton gone into the evening. It's then, though, as night comes, that I begin to feel I'm being deliberately avoided.

I'm in the station when Dalton brings Storm over. He says since it seems I'll be busy for a while, he picked her up from Petra's. Then he leaves again, and I'm left wondering if I've done something wrong *there*. Is he insinuating I'm ignoring our puppy? That doesn't seem like him—our job comes first.

When it's almost ten and he's still gone, I begin to wonder if he's at home waiting. I take Storm back to an empty house, no sign he's been there since we left that morning. I putter around for a while.

When Storm needs to go out, I take her as far as the back deck, staying on it while she does her business.

Then I play with her. I'm on my hands and knees, rolling snowballs at her when a distant pack of wolves start their night song, and she zooms into my arms. She's shaking, but as I hold her, she finds the courage to listen, ears perked, nose working. I'm holding her, my face buried in her fur as I whisper to her and she alternates between licking me and listening to the wolves. They stop, and as I start to roll another snowball, I see a figure in the window, and I give a start.

It's Dalton. Just standing there watching.

Even when he sees I've noticed him, he doesn't come out right away, continues watching as I roll another snowball for Storm and laugh as she skids and tumbles to catch them, only to have them vanish with a chomp of her jaws.

The door opens. Dalton comes out.

"Um, boots?" I say, pointing at his stockinged feet as I sit up. He just keeps walking, his expression unreadable, and when he lowers himself to the deck, Storm launches at him, but he doesn't even seem to notice. His hands go to the back of my neck, and he pulls me toward him.

I put my arms around his neck, rising to kiss him, expecting a light hello kiss, but when his mouth meets mine, it's a hard, deep one. I jump, startled, but he doesn't notice that either. He kisses me with a ferocity that reminds me of the snow shelter, when he found me in the storm. A wordless, desperate kiss.

I return that kiss, feeding my own worries and uncertainty into it, looking for reassurance he's okay, we're okay, everything is fine. I find it there, in that hunger that promises he's not withdrawing, not angry with me, just unsettled and looking for a way to work out his frustration.

I'm more than happy to give it to him, sliding my hands under his shirt, chuckling when he jumps at my cold fingers. When I try to pull away, though, he presses my hands to his skin. His eyes half close as I run my fingers over his chest. Then his own hands are undoing my belt and tugging down my jeans, the kiss never breaking. One leg free, and that's enough, and his fingers are inside me, making me hiss, his cool fingers against my heat.

I raise my hips and rock against his hand, enjoying before realizing I'm leaving things rather one-sided. I undo his belt and reach inside his jeans, but then he's moving up over me and he pauses, and I know what that pause means. I arch my hips in answer. His hands move to my hips and then he's in me, and it's like the kiss—hard and deep and a little bit desperate—and I reciprocate, beat for beat until another wordless pause, one I know just as well, and I grab his hips in answer, giving him the go, and letting myself follow until we're lying in the snow, panting.

His lips move to my ear, and I'm ready for some wry comment about the snow or the very confused puppy. Instead, his lips press against my ear, breath warm, as he says, "I love you."

I tense in surprise. Then I wrap my hands around his face, pull it over mine and say, "I—" But he cuts me off with a kiss. Before I can get my breath back, he's picking me up, along with Storm, and carrying us into the house.

He deposits the puppy in the living room and then carries me upstairs. Once we're in bed, I try again, lying on top of him, my face over his, and I get as far as "I—" before another kiss shuts me down.

"You don't want me to say it," I say when we finish.

He shakes his head, and I understand what he's really saying. He doesn't want me to echo him, to make the seemingly obligatory response.

"Can I show you instead?" I ask, and that gets the first sign of a smile since he came out the back door. He nods, and I show him.

FORTY-ONE

Sutherland is fully awake the next morning, coherent and asking to speak to me. Dalton and I head there after dropping off Storm.

Sutherland's in his living room, dozing under a blanket. When I walk in, he starts awake. "Sorry. I keep thinking I'm fine, and then proving myself wrong. Got halfway through making breakfast and almost passed out. Kenny had to finish cooking."

I take a seat on the sofa. "Don't push. It'll only slow things down."

He starts to answer. Then his gaze flicks to the doorway as Dalton joins us.

Sutherland straightens fast. "Eric."

Dalton takes the seat beside me. When Sutherland doesn't go on, Dalton says, "Is me being here a problem?"

Sutherland smiles weakly. "Only if you're ready to put me on chopping duty. I'll take my lumps, but I need a bit of time to recover." He turns to me. "I wanted to apologize for running. My timing put you and Will in an awkward position. Kenny explained all that. I appreciate you guys coming after me, though I know it caused trouble with . . ." His gaze slides to Dalton.

"Not going after you wasn't an option," Dalton says. "It's their duty. Which means they had to break my rule. That's fine, though, because I pull rules out of my ass. That's how law works in Rockton."

Sutherland flinches. I'm tempted to ease in and soften the blow.

Then I remind myself how I felt when he took off, how pissed I'd been, how he could have gotten Anders killed in that accident, gotten us both killed in that storm. I keep my mouth shut and leave him pinned under Dalton's gaze.

"I know you have reasons," Sutherland begins. "I'm sorry. I'm really—"

"I don't want your apologies. I just want you to make damned sure it doesn't happen again. Have a little consideration for others. That never seemed to be a problem for you before."

"It wasn't. I just . . . I hit a wall, you know? I'd settled in, adjusted, and then it just . . . struck. The isolation. The boredom. The loneliness. I've heard people talk about cabin fever, but I didn't really get it until the sun was gone before five. It felt like the walls closed in. I got so sick of the darkness and the cold, and I realized it was only going to get darker and colder. I snapped. It won't happen again. I'm responsible for keeping myself busy and entertained. I've been talking to Kenny about a poker game I can join, maybe signing up for chopping duty voluntarily, if only to get me off my ass and out of town for a few hours. I might learn to hunt come spring." A weak smile. "That'd shock the hell out of my dad. He never could get a rifle in my hands."

"Trying fishing instead," I say. "Once you're well enough."

He nods. "That's more my speed. Thanks."

And that's all Sutherland wanted to tell me—to apologize. He tries adding tidbits to his description, but they won't get me any farther in my investigation. I'll ask Petra to stop by, see if she can coax a sketch from him, but I think I'll need a suspect for him to ID. He just didn't see enough for a sketch.

Dalton had told Jacob we'd meet him today at noon, which just means when the sun is straight overhead. Jacob is waiting when we arrive. They trade first. Dalton has brought salt, instant coffee, soap, and two sweatshirts. Jacob has a young buck and a brace of rabbits. In trade, he takes all but one sweatshirt.

"What the fuck am I going to do with this?" Dalton says when Jacob hands back the shirt.

"Bring it next time."

"You realize that means I need to cart it back to town and store it."

"Then bring me less next time."

"You're a pain in the ass, you know that?" Dalton grumbles under his breath. There's no real anger in it, but there is frustration. He wants to do more for his brother, and he's not allowed to.

Dalton reaches into his backpack and passes over a coffee thermos and a box of cookies. "This is from Casey, so don't hand it back or you'll insult her."

"It's from both—" I begin.

Dalton cuts me off with a glower. "You want me to say it's from us so it doesn't look like you're sucking up. Too bad. It's from you; I'm not pretending it isn't."

I sigh. "I don't know why I bother."

"Neither do I." He hands the thermos and box to Jacob. "Take. Sit. Drink. Eat. Give me back the containers before we go."

"He doesn't have to—" I begin.

"He doesn't want to store and cart them back. At least I think about stuff like that. Don't want to inconvenience anyone."

He gives his brother a hard look. Jacob ignores it, thanks me, and finds a log for us to sit on.

We talk suspects. I expect Jacob to balk at us naming his friend as our lead suspect, but it seems "friend" is an exaggeration. Jacob knows Roger. He's hunted with him, traded with him, even hung out with him, yet that only means he's someone Jacob trusted.

"Shit," he says when Dalton tells him what Cypher and Brent told us about Roger. He's crouched in the snow, petting Storm. "He's asked me about Rockton, too. I should have mentioned that, I guess, but it was way back, and I never thought much of it."

"What exactly did he ask?" I say.

"Just the usual gossip-fishing expedition." He pushes loose hair behind his ear. "He acted like he knew about the town. Which he would, if his family came from there, but he never said that, so I figured it was just what people do sometimes. They act like they know all about a thing so you'll think you're not giving away any secrets. Like Cypher a few months back—he tried talking me up about a fishing spot of mine, said he'd been there before but forgot where it was, maybe I could take him next time I went, refresh his memory." Jacob snorts. "Like I'd fall for that."

"Nothing specific with Roger, then?"

"No. I blocked, and he dropped the subject, never returned to it."

"Next topic of conversation," Dalton says. "Hostiles."

Jacob tenses, and I go to cut in, but Dalton continues, "You told Casey hostiles aren't capable of these abductions. That's bullshit, and you know it."

Jacob nods. "I do, and I was going to mention that before you left. Explain. Can I talk to Casey? Alone?"

Dalton's face screws up. "What?"

Jacob speaks slower. "I would like to speak to Casey alone. I want to explain and apologize."

"And I can't be here for that?"

There's confusion in Dalton's voice, but a touch of hurt, too. I look at him and mouth, *Please.*

"If you're worried I'll hurt her again, I'm fine," Jacob says.

"I'm not—"

"She has her gun, but I understand if you're concerned—"

"No, course not." Dalton rises from the log. "I just don't see why—"

My look stops him.

"Fine," he says. "At least you're talking to her. Should be glad about that."

"Stop grumbling," I say. "Go study tree growth or something."

He rolls his eyes and stalks off. When he looks over his shoulder, I call, "Keep going," and I get another eye roll, but he continues until he's out of sight.

I shake my head and turn back to Jacob. "He's not worried about you hurting me. He just doesn't like being excluded."

"I know. I just said that to make him stop arguing." He looks in the direction Dalton went, being sure he's gone. Then he says, "Yes, I lied about the hostiles. I just . . . I panicked. I know how Eric feels about you, and he's not going to want you anywhere near them. I don't want you anywhere near them either. After you left, I realized how stupid that was. What if it *is* a hostile, and he takes someone else because you don't expect it? Or comes back for Nicole?" He pauses. "How is she?"

"Resting mostly. The other day took a lot from her. She's still asking when she can come back, though. Take the bear cub for a walk."

He chuckles at that. "I'm still not sure they didn't sell Eric some kind of bear-dog cross. But it seems tame enough." He sobers. "You asked if a hostile could do this. Like Eric says, the answer is yes. I can't give you much on them, though."

"You stay away from them, like everyone out here."

He shoves his hands into his pockets. "Even more than most. If I think I hear one coming, I take off. I know that makes me sound like a coward . . ." Another glance in the direction Dalton went.

"Eric would think it made you smart."

His expression says he's not listening. Or he hears, but it doesn't make him feel better. He turns back to me. "You need to know if hostiles could do this. If they could take a woman captive and . . ." He inhales. "I know what this guy would have done to Nicole. I know . . . I know it happens. Even out here. Maybe especially out here. Not that I know what happens down south or . . . What I'm saying is that it does happen. And I . . . know that. There was this guy, when I was a kid, maybe fifteen, sixteen. A settler from the first community. I had skins he wanted. I'm good at curing. But what he wanted to trade . . ." He takes his hands from his pockets. Kicks snow off his boot. "He wanted to trade me for a woman. A hostile. He said he could catch one, and I could—But I didn't. As soon as I realized what he was saying, I told him to get the hell away from me. I wouldn't have anything to do with him after that."

"This guy—"

"He's gone or I'd have put him at the top of my list. His father went back down south, and he followed a couple of years ago. The point is that I got the impression he did that, and he didn't think it was a bad thing, that those settlers didn't consider hostiles human. So it happens out here. The question is whether hostiles would do it."

Val's story answers this, but before I can comment, he continues with "They would. I know they would. That's why I panicked when you wanted to consider them as suspects. That'd mean talking to them. You shouldn't. At all. They could do it. I know that. From experience. Which is why I stay away. Far away."

He's holding himself still, tense, waiting for me to make him explain. I just say, "Okay."

He looks over.

"I get it," I say. "That's why you asked Eric to leave. You don't want him to know."

"I—I was a kid. It was even before that guy . . . offered . . . But the question is whether hostiles could take someone captive and do that. They can. They do."

He's got his hands shoved into his pockets so far his parka bunches. When he sees I've noticed, he relaxes and says, "I'm fine. It was a long time ago."

"I understand why you don't want to tell Eric, but I'm going to suggest you need to tell someone."

A humorless quirk of his lips. "Just did, didn't I?"

"It's a start."

"And an ending. Sorry. I don't—I just don't have anything more to say about it."

"Okay."

He looks over, and I check for signs that he's hoping I'll push. There are none. When I don't prod, he relaxes, and I say instead, "The guy—or guys—who did that, are they—"

"He's not around."

"And you're sure of that?"

"Very sure."

Jacob means he killed him. I can tell. I just can.

"That's all I have," Jacob says. "I can tell you that it's possible, but I can't tell you anything more about them. You do need to stay away from the hostiles, though. I was serious about that. Just stay away. Please."

FORTY-TWO

As I expect, Dalton and I barely get out of Jacob's earshot before Dalton says, "What was up with that?"

"He wanted to apologize."

"And . . . ?"

When I don't answer, he shoulders up beside me, pushing aside vegetation to walk in tandem.

I glance over at him. "You are an awesome brother. You know that, right?"

A look passes over his face. Guilt. Worry. Fear.

Before he can speak, I say, "You *don't* know that. I get it. You worry about what you might have done wrong with Jacob. What happened this fall only makes that worse. He has residual anger over what felt like abandonment. But that wasn't your fault—you were taken from him. Kept from him. He understands that when he's not pumped full of drugs. You didn't have a choice, and once you did, you reconnected, and you've done everything you can for him. Everything he'll allow."

A few more steps, and I say, "You do remember that I have a sister. An older one."

He says, "Yeah," but there's a hesitation first.

"You forgot that. Understandable, because I don't talk about her. I have no relationship with April beyond blood. I've been gone four months, and when I told her I was leaving—and might not be in contact for years—she acted like I'd interrupted her work day to tell her what I had for breakfast. You *are* an awesome big brother. The problem is that you can't be everything else for Jacob."

"I know that."

"Maybe, but you still want to be. That's not your job. There are things that he needs other people for. Things he can't share with you, and if he chooses not to, then you need to accept that." I look at him again. "Do you trust me?"

He nods. "Course."

"Then do you trust that if Jacob confided anything that would endanger him, I'd tell you?"

Another nod.

"Jacob's fine, Eric. And like you said, I'm just glad he's actually talking to me."

Back in town, we both have errands to run, so Dalton drops off Storm with Petra. When I go to pick her up, I visit for a while, enjoying a coffee while Storm worries a knotted rope toy Petra must have made for her. Eventually Storm pushes it under the couch, unleashing a torrent of puppy grief. I yank out the slobber-covered thing and take a closer look. It's actually fabric, intricately braided and dyed.

"You didn't make this for her, did you?" I say, as I hold it up.

"No. It was a gift from a suitor. Storm decided it looked more like a chew toy."

"Damn, I'm sorry."

"Yep, you owe me one butt-ugly, useless hunk of braided fabric, which I may have accidentally left on the sofa for a teething puppy."

I dangle it for Storm, and she jumps heroically. "What was it supposed to be?"

"I have no idea. Apparently, since I'm an artist, he wanted to do something artistic for me. I held on to it for three months, which I believe is the appropriate length of time to keep something before you can regift it."

"I've never seen it."

"Just because I kept it doesn't mean I feel obligated to display it. That might suggest the suitor still has a shot. Which would lead to more knotted hunks of fabric. And possibly pity sex. I don't do pity sex."

"You can't in Rockton. It'd be a full-time endeavor."

I toss the toy for Storm, and she tumbles after it as I sit back on the sofa.

Petra sips her coffee. "So segueing to guys who have *never* needed pity sex, how do you like shacking up with the sheriff?"

"I'm not sure we've been home long enough to know."

"Best way to do it. Means you don't have to worry about his bad habits driving you crazy. With my ex, I think marriage and cohabitation took us from *I can't bear another minute without you* to *I can't bear another minute with you* in about thirty days."

"You were married?"

"It really didn't last much more than those thirty days. Well, thirty days of honeymoon bliss followed by two years of postponing the inevitable."

"That sucks."

She runs her finger along the top of her mug. "Actually, it was just the marriage part that sucked. I loved him. Still do. We just worked better as friends. It happens sometimes. You meet a guy, and there's that click, and you mistake it for another kind. It should have been friendship, but you both thought you should try for more and . . ." She trails off and then inhales sharply. "You and Eric are a whole other situation. I'm glad to see you make the leap to single-residence dwelling. I thought it'd take him longer to work up the nerve to suggest it."

"Actually, it was for the dog. So she can settle in one place."

Petra grins. "So he didn't work up the nerve. He found an excuse."

"Eric doesn't need to work up the nerve for anything. I'm not exactly a high-maintenance girlfriend."

"Maybe, but he's still careful not to slam his foot on the gas and send you running for cover. I won't say he *got* the puppy as an excuse to move in together, but I'm sure it was an added bonus. And the dog itself says where he's headed."

When I look at her, she gestures at Storm and says, "Starter baby?"

"What?"

"Right, you never did the long-term dating thing. Pet ownership is the first stop on the kid express. There's even a scale of pets. If it's a fish, it's a very tentative commitment. Dogs, though, are all the way. Toilet training, teething, playtime, lessons, day care. Eric is on the baby train, full speed ahead."

I stare at her.

"Oh, I'm kidding," she says. "Well, exaggerating anyway. It just means he's serious. Really, really serious. Which is a good thing, right? Unless I really misinterpreted, you're not looking for a winter fling."

"No, of course not. I just . . ." I look at her. "*Is* he telling me he expects kids?"

"No, no. Damn, I'm sorry. I was being flip, and I've totally freaked you out. I have no idea whether Eric wants children or not. A puppy just means is that he's committed enough that you guys need to have that conversation—soon. The two biggest things that break up a relationship? Differing financial styles and differing views on kids. Up here, finances are not an issue. Differing views on kids isn't a deal breaker, but it's something you need to discuss *before* things get more serious or you end up with him saying *Let's start a family,* and you saying, *What family?* Been there, done that. It wasn't good."

"I'm sorry."

"Like I said, there was more wrong to my marriage than differing views on children. We just made the mistake of *not* sorting that out, and assuming we knew what the other wanted, and then staying together because of the kid."

"You—you have—"

"Had," she says. "Past tense. Yeah, really didn't mean to go there. Sorry. Anyway, back to you and Eric. Just know that the puppy means he's serious, and if he's serious, then it's time to open those lines of communication on everything, including children."

It's night. Storm is upstairs, sound asleep after an hour-long snow-play session to guarantee puppy exhaustion and an hour of peace and quiet. Well, relative peace and quiet. Fortunately, we've done a good enough job with the playtime plan that any noise coming from downstairs hasn't woken her. Now we're stretched out on the bearskin rug as the fire casts dancing shadows around the dark room.

I prop up on my elbows. "Are you as tired as you look?"

He opens one eye. "Depends on the purpose of the question. Am I too tired to drag my ass upstairs to bed? Yep. Am I too tired to prolong the evening's entertainment? Nope. Just give me a few minutes. And possibly a beer."

I head into the kitchen. When I return with two beers, he says, "Can't believe that actually worked."

"If it's ultimately to my advantage, I'm happy to oblige."

I settle in cross-legged beside him. "While you're recuperating, do you have enough energy to talk?"

"Always."

"It's about . . ." I look toward the steps. "The puppy. And moving in together."

The smile falls from his face. "Okay . . ."

"Nothing bad. I just wanted to discuss—"

Someone bangs on the front door. A double-fisted pounding. "Eric? Casey? It's Kenny."

"Hold on," Dalton calls.

The door flies open. Kenny rushes in . . . with a good sightline to where we're scrambling for clothing. Dalton blocks me and snarls, "I said hold on."

Kenny spins around. "Sorry, sorry. It's Val. She woke up to someone in her bedroom."

"What?" I say as I yank on my jeans.

Kenny starts to turn, saying, "She—" and then remembers why he's facing the door, his memory goosed by a fresh snarl from Dalton.

"It's fine," I say as I yank on my shirt. "I'm decent enough. Just tell me what's going on."

He half turns, facing the wall instead. "Val woke up and started screaming. Paul was passing on patrol. He raced in. Val was hysterical." He glances at me. "I'm not supposed to use that word, right?"

"It works here. Just keep going." I'm at the front door now, yanking on my boots, and Dalton's handing me my parka.

"Val said there was a man in her room. She said it was"—he looks at Dalton—"Eric."

"What?" Dalton says.

"Obviously it wasn't you. It happened five minutes ago, and . . ." He gestures toward the blankets in front of the fire. "So I don't know what's going on, but she's demanding to see Casey. And not . . ."

"Not Eric," I say.

"She's made a mistake. Paul thought he saw the guy in the forest, though. He'd have gone after him, but with the way Val was screaming, he thought she was hurt."

"I'll talk to her."

"Get Will," Dalton says to Kenny. "Tell him to meet us at Val's place. As soon as he's on his way, round up the militia. I want all hands on deck. But no one makes a move without my say-so. Tell them to get to Val's house for further instructions."

FORTY-THREE

Dalton and I head out. As we walk, he says, "This wasn't me."

"Uh, yeah, considering we were having sex for the last hour, I have no doubt of where you were, Eric."

"If she tries to say it happened earlier, I can account for my whereabouts all evening. The last person I spoke to was Isabel. Then I passed Brian heading home, and we talked. He can confirm I was walking straight to my place. Then we took Storm out to play."

"Eric? It's okay."

"I just . . . I don't know what is going on, Casey. Yeah, I'm freaking out. I feel like she's trying to frame me or plant doubt about me, with you or—"

"Eric? Deep breaths."

He makes a face, but he doesn't argue that he's not panicking. I squeeze his arm.

We're almost to Val's when Dalton spots a figure trudging along the road.

"You!" he calls. "I need your—" He exhales a *fuck* as the figure turns, and we see Jen's face beneath a parka hood. "Never mind."

He scans the road, but it's past midnight midweek and bitter cold. The streets are empty.

"What's wrong, Sheriff?" she calls as we continue on. "Am I

disappointing you by not committing a crime? You sure you don't want to strip-search me? I might be carrying something."

Dalton mutters deep under his breath about *what* she might be carrying and its level of communicability.

"Jen?" I call back. "Do you think we could get your help with something?"

"If you're looking for a threesome, I don't do that shit." She points at Dalton. "And I sure as hell don't do *that* shit."

"Val was apparently attacked tonight," I say. "Can you just . . . ?" I motion for her to catch up as we walk. She hesitates, but when she sees Dalton is moving ahead, she joins me.

"Someone broke into Val's room," I say. "Obviously, the big concern is that it was Nicole's captor. I need to speak to Val. Eric and Will have to organize a search party. We need someone to guard the scene."

"You're asking me to guard a crime scene?"

"You did say you wanted to join the militia. Or was that just a way to get information on the case?"

She straightens. "I was serious."

"Good. Then guard the scene, please. If someone broke in, there will be footprints outside, but as soon as people hear a commotion, they'll come gawking and mess up the scene."

"Okay, but no one's going to listen to me."

"Make them. Please. If they argue, tell them Eric said that anyone who ignores you is going ice fishing. Let them interpret that however they want."

She snorts a chuckle, then says, "I want militia pay."

"If you keep everyone away, you'll get double. If anyone trespasses, consider it volunteer work."

Val is huddled on her couch, comforter wrapped around her. When I walk in, I say, "Would you like a tea?" and she shakes her head.

"It was him," she says. "Sheriff Dalton."

"Let's back up to what happened."

She looks up sharply. "You don't believe me."

"We'll get to that. First—"

She rises, comforter falling from one shoulder. "No, *this* first, Detective. I'm telling you that I saw a man in my room, and I can positively identify him, and you're ignoring that because he happens to be your lover."

"This just happened, correct?"

"Yes."

"Eric has been with me for over an hour."

"Sleeping with you. Or so you thought."

"It's barely midnight, Val. We were awake."

"You *think* you were. You don't want to believe he'd do this."

"No, I *know* I was awake, and I *know* he was there, because we were having sex."

She blanches, and her voice sharpens. "I did not need to hear that, Detective."

"Apparently, you did. You weren't listening to me otherwise. Eric got home almost two hours ago. We played with the puppy. Then sex. Then talking. He was there the whole time. It'd have been kind of hard not to notice. He has alibis before that, too. For the entire evening."

"He was quick with that, wasn't he? Giving you alibis."

"Because he's been accused of a very serious offense by someone who actively dislikes him. He's a little freaked out right now. If you think that I'm lying to give him an alibi, speak to Kenny, who came running in when Eric and I were in front of the fire, having a beer . . . and not wearing clothing. That'd be a helluva trick if Eric had just left your house. This wasn't him, Val. Either you mistakenly thought it was, or you're trying to frame him."

"Frame him? Are you saying I made this up? There was a *man* in my room, Detective. In my *bedroom*."

"And the way you're wording that suggests you're no longer certain it was Eric."

She pulls the comforter up again and slides back down to the sofa.

"Walk me through it."

She does. She went to bed at ten and fell asleep quickly—"I haven't been sleeping well, and I had sleep aids from when Elizabeth was here." She dropped into a deep sleep, waking when she sensed someone in the room. She sat up to see a man whom she swears was Dalton, sitting in the chair by her bed, watching her sleep. When she screamed, he left.

"Left?" I say. "You mean he ran out of the room?"

"Ran, walked . . . I don't know. I was getting out of bed as fast as I could, and when I was up, he was gone."

"Could you tell which way he went?"

She can't. It only takes a quick search for me to confirm there's no one still here.

"He left," she says when I return. "I was in a state of shock, and I did not pay attention to which exit he used. I hardly see how it matters."

"It would make it easier to track footprints," I say. "We'll check both doors. All the windows are winter sealed. What about your balcony?"

"That is also sealed. Permanently. I consider the balconies unsafe and have told the council so."

I get a full description of the man she saw. As soon as she claimed it was Dalton, I thought of the guy who could be mistaken for him: Jacob. I can't imagine why Jacob would do this, but I have to check. Yet Val is adamant that the man had short hair and a close-cropped beard.

She is adamant it was Dalton.

Jen does keep everyone away from the scene, but it's soon apparent I'm not going to find evidence there. There are few prints, and none match the snowsuit man's.

It's been over an hour, and I'm still painstakingly examining every footprint within a ten meter radius of Val's house. I'm on my second round and I'm crouching, my flashlight beam illuminating a set of prints, as Anders walks over.

"Anything?" he asks.

"Lots of prints, but none near the back door, and I can identify the ones at the front. Mine. Val's. Kenny's. Paul's. That's it. As for the person Paul thought he saw in the forest, he took me to the spot. There are fresh deer tracks. That's it."

"Yeah, we didn't find anything in the forest, either. So there's no proof anyone broke into her place. Yet she not only claims someone did, but that it was Eric—even when she knows he has a bulletproof alibi. That's just weird. If she's trying to frame him, at least wait until the actual middle of the might, when you'd be asleep."

"I think it's more likely a nightmare. She dreamed he was in her room and then woke up screaming and never realized it was only a dream." I straighten. "I don't know if that's plausible."

"Actually, it's totally plausible. I had about a year where I couldn't sleep without pills. If I actually managed drift off, I'd hallucinate something almost exactly like that. I'd see my buddies who got killed by the IED. Or the officer I killed afterward. They'd be standing by my bed."

I'm rubbing my hands against the cold. He plucks my gloves from my pocket and gives them to me without even pausing his story.

"Thing is," he continues. "It never *felt* like waking up from a nightmare. It felt like I hadn't fallen asleep and they really were in the room. I never believed in ghosts, but that seemed the only explanation. Turns out it's a type of hallucination that comes right when you've fallen asleep, when you're still conscious enough to think you're awake. Probably explains a lot of ghost stories."

"Maybe. She did take sleeping pills. But even if it was a nightmare, why Eric?"

He doesn't have an answer. But I'm going to get one.

FORTY-FOUR

Val is at her living room window when I come back. I climb the porch, and she's got the front door open.

"We need to talk—" I begin.

"Yes, we do." She brings me inside and closes the door. She's dressed now, as if she's given up all hope of sleeping. On the table, one of her notebooks is open. I glance at it and see not words but numbers. A page filled with algebraic equations.

"One of Hilbert's problems," she says.

"Ah," I say, as if I have any clue what that means.

She pushes the book aside and sits. "I do not know what happened tonight, Detective. There was a man in my room. I am certain of that."

Her tone is too firm, telling me she's actually not certain, not anymore, but Val isn't the type to back down from an embarrassing mistake.

"I misidentified him as Sheriff Dalton," she says. "I withdraw that accusation. I understand that you might have reason to believe I intentionally misidentified him, but I assure you that is not the case."

"I don't think it was."

"Thank you." She folds her hands on her lap. "I would not do that. When I realized my obvious error, I sat here working on an algebraic problem, attempting to set my mind at ease, and I realized I should not set it at ease. That my uneasiness was my subconscious telling me

I have been making a grave and unforgivable error. You have treated me fairly, Detective. You clearly do not agree with many of my choices and opinions, but you have been able to rise above that in a way I find admirable."

"Okay."

"And I have not been equally fair in return. I have been keeping something from you. A secret that I did not reveal because I feared—" She clears her throat. "I feared—and still do—that you will take his side in the matter, and perhaps even go to him with it, and that will place me in danger."

"By *him,* I'm guessing you mean Eric."

She tenses even at his name. "Yes."

"If he's done anything—"

"Nothing that can be proven. That is the problem. I have reason to believe he is at the root of a larger conspiracy. That his actions—or inactions—led to my attack and to the attacks on the others. He did not play any direct role in them, but he allowed them to happen."

"In what way?"

"I believe Sheriff Dalton permits and even encourages the hostiles to strike against our citizens as a method of control."

It takes me a moment to unpack that. Even then, I have to respond with care, my incredulity kept in check. "You've said before that you think Eric should take action against the hostiles. You think he's wrong to let people into the forest, and he should exterminate the hostiles for the safety of the town."

"If they were animals, we would do it."

"Putting aside that for a moment." *Please.* "It seems to me that you're accusing Eric of more than failing to take action."

"That is why I saw his face on my intruder. I have reason to believe he actively encourages the hostiles, through his interactions with the so-called settlers. A conspiracy to maintain order in Rockton in the most heinous manner, one that allows residents to suffer as a warning to others."

I don't respond. Can't for at least a minute. Then I find my voice with "You keep saying you 'have reason' to believe this. You have evidence."

"If anyone had evidence, Sheriff Dalton would no longer be in this town. What we have is conjecture."

"We?" My gaze moves to the radio receiver across the room. "The council suspects Eric of this? *Phil* is the one who told you to go on that patrol, Val. Eric warned you off and was overruled by the council."

"They were testing him. Phil explained the situation later, in expressing his horror and regret at the incident I suffered."

"So the council knows you were attacked?"

"Yes, as does Sheriff Dalton, who denied it happened. According to him, I didn't wish to admit I'd simply gotten lost, so I made up a story."

"Whoa. Hold on. You *told* Eric you'd been attacked?"

She smooths her blouse. "The council did. Initially, I decided to say nothing. Phil realized I was upset and persuaded me to tell the truth. He said he would handle it with the sheriff, to avoid any further embarrassment on my part. Given that I was recanting my earlier account, I could see how Sheriff Dalton might have been reluctant to believe the new version. That's when I got the entire story from Phil— the council's fears that the sheriff was more deeply involved. He counseled me not to discuss the matter with Sheriff Dalton for fear he'd realize the council was suspicious."

I get up and walk to the door. Val bleats something I don't hear. I throw it open and see Kenny on guard duty.

"Kenny? Can you find Eric for me? Tell him to bring the patrol logbook."

FORTY-FIVE

I'm watching at the window when Dalton appears, moving quickly, with none of his usual swagger and stride. He looks like a schoolboy who's been summoned to the principal's office and has no idea why, only knows he's in trouble.

I open the door and lean out to whisper, "It's fine. We're just going to straighten something out." He nods, but that look stays in his eyes.

Val waits in the living room. She sits ramrod straight, and when we enter, she fixes me with a look that says I am a grave disappointment. She doesn't argue, though. Hasn't said a word since I summoned Dalton.

As he walks in, he says, "I know you think I broke into your place, Val, but I didn't."

"She realizes she was mistaken," I say.

He nods, but his gaze shoots to her, apprehension lingering. I motion for him to sit. Then I say, "A few months ago, I mentioned that Val had been attacked in the forest. What did you say?"

His brows furrow.

I continue, "I said she'd been attacked, and you said . . ."

He takes a moment, as if struggling to shift mental gears. "I said I knew she'd gotten lost. I was there when they found her."

"But she didn't mention an attack."

"No."

"Phil had a private talk with you a few weeks later. About what happened to Val. Do you remember it?"

Another moment, as he thinks back. "Okay, yes. He told me not to make a big deal of it, that Val was embarrassed over getting lost and I was to drop the matter entirely. I said I never *did* make a big deal of it. Getting a scare like that is lesson enough."

I glance at Val. She's not leaping in to correct him, just sitting stiffly, chin raised, prepared for battle but waiting for the first volley.

"Did Phil tell you she'd been attacked?" I ask.

"What? Fuck—" He stops himself. "No. The first time I heard that was when you told me. Otherwise, I'd have needed details. Of the attackers, that is. So I could see if any of my contacts recognized them."

"And what would you have done if you'd found them, Sheriff?" Val asks.

"That's up to the council. Same as with any major crime."

"Before Val went on that patrol," I say, "you strongly advised against it."

"Hell—" He stops again. Restarts with a quiet "Yes."

"You have forbidden others to do the same. Including Will when he first arrived."

"Yes. I can bring in a half dozen guys who wanted to go out on patrol too soon. They'll confirm I told them the same thing."

"Exactly what did you warn them about?"

"What *didn't* I warn them about?" He looks at Val. "It was the same lecture you got. Everything from the threat of wildlife to the hazards to getting lost."

"Hostiles?" I ask.

"I warn about people in general. I don't talk about the hostiles specifically—I don't want to scare anyone like that. But I'm very clear that there are people out there and that encounters with them can be fatal."

I turn to Val. "Is that what he told you?"

She nods.

"With no particular emphasis on the people over other dangers?" I ask.

She nods.

"If Eric was using the hostiles to frighten people, don't you think he'd hammer on that point?"

"What?" Dalton says. "*Using* the hostiles?"

"The council believes you facilitate—possibly even orchestrate—hostile activity as a form of control over residents. Frightening locals so they don't wander or run off."

"What?"

"They believe you use your contacts to help you. That you . . ." I look at Val. "I'm not clear what exactly. Lure the hostiles close enough to town for sporadic attacks? Or have our excursions pass hostile areas in *hopes* of attack?"

"Both," she says.

Dalton stares like he's landed in an alternate reality. Or like we've all been smoking things we found in the forest.

"The patrol logbook, Eric," I say. "That's where patrols log signs of human activity so you can go out and evaluate, correct?"

"Yes, but if the council says that proves I'm tracking hostiles—"

"Can you open the logbook and tell me the entries for the last week of October? Particularly the one about a campsite the patrol found."

He does. It's nothing unusual—the patrol found the remains of a campsite a few kilometers in, and Dalton investigated.

I take the logbook and read. "Appears to be settler, approx three days old, canceling lake trip."

I look at Val. "The lake had frozen, so we were taking a group for a twilight bonfire. A winter celebration party for those who win a spot by lottery. Eric had the militia scout the main path to the lake for the three days leading up to the party, to be sure it was clear. They found this on their first pass. Eric canceled the event." I look at him. "You concluded it was settlers, so why cancel?"

"I can't take the chance. Not with something like that—a nighttime event for citizens who don't spend a lot of time in the forest. What looks like settlers could be high-functioning hostiles, and just because the campsite was three days old didn't mean they weren't still in the region."

"Did you tell people that?"

"No. I said the ice wasn't thick enough, so I was postponing it for a week."

"Complete with a rant about how if you caught anyone sneaking down that way, they'd be on chopping duty all winter."

"A month. Never say all winter because I won't follow through." He pauses. "It wasn't really a rant either."

"Totally was." I sneak him a smile. Then I turn to Val and lift the logbook. "This is full of that. Patrols or other excursions see signs of human activity, and Eric goes out to evaluate, and if he concludes anyone was in that area, that region is on lockdown. He is meticulous. Even a little paranoid."

"I wouldn't say—" Dalton begins.

"Totally are. And I don't argue because as upset as people get over having an excursion canceled, it means attacks—like the one on Val—are *extremely* rare. Hostiles are like cougars—most residents pass their entire time here and never even catch a glimpse of one." I turn to Val. "But you had a full-blown encounter. After Eric tried to keep you out of the forest and the council encouraged you to go."

She says nothing.

"I don't understand," Dalton says. "I tried to stop you. They encouraged you. But *I'm* the one using hostiles?"

"It was a test," I say. "If you tried to keep the new council rep out of the forest, it proved you were responsible for hostile encounters."

His face screws up. "How?"

"Because you wouldn't want the new rep to be attacked. Except you keep all new residents out . . . and can prove that. And there are extremely few hostile encounters . . . and we can prove that. Oh, plus the small fact that Val actually *was* attacked."

"Did they try to claim I set that up?" Dalton mutters.

When Val doesn't reply, he looks at her. "They *did*?"

"No, I did. I started thinking perhaps, if they were right about the sheriff using the hostiles, then he decided to teach me a lesson. When I mentioned it to Phil, he said no, very strongly no, that whatever else they thought Sheriff Dalton was capable of, they couldn't imagine he'd ever do anything like that. But . . ."

"The idea had already been planted, and the more strenuously Phil insisted Eric couldn't be responsible, the more it seemed as if *he* was in denial. Phil and the council."

"Yes," she says, and her voice is low.

"So you thought Eric was responsible for your attack. At best, he cultivated an environment that allowed it to happen. At worst, he actually set it up."

She nods.

"And the council set *that* up. Led you to believe Eric cultivated that environment. Led you to believe he denied your attack. Even, in a roundabout way, led you to think he may have orchestrated it."

Val shakes her head. "What possible motivation would they have?"

"What was the end result? When you first arrived, you thought Eric was too young and uneducated for his position. Right?"

She nods.

"Eventually, you'd have realized you were wrong. That Eric does his job very well. That he's just more volatile—more difficult to control—than the council would like. The best way to manage him? Have a rep who thinks he's dangerous. Who will report his every misdeed. The council made you their dedicated anti-Eric spy. And your reward? The result of what they told you, and the fear and distrust they instilled in you?" I wave around the chalet. "A prison cell."

FORTY-SIX

We don't talk after that. Val needs time to digest it. Dalton does, too, and he's so quiet on the walk back that I turn to him a couple of times and say, "You do understand that no one thinks you actually did any of that, right?" He nods but says nothing, just walks, until we're at his place. We take Storm out to do her business, and he remains quiet. Back inside, I put her to bed and find him sitting in front of the fireplace, staring into the glowing embers.

"Mind if I light that?" I ask softly.

He gives a start and then rises, reaching for the timber pile. I lay my hand on his and say, "I've got it," but he hovers there, as if thrown by the sudden loss of purpose. When I say, "Unless you'd rather," he nods and starts rebuilding the fire.

"I could be wrong about the council," I say as he arranges logs.

He lets out a half-stifled laugh and shakes his head. "Nah, I'm just an idiot for not seeing it."

"It was a very carefully constructed misunderstanding between you and Val, the result of that misunderstanding being a level of animosity that ensures you'd never actually *talk* and resolve it." I move to sit on the sofa. "I know this hurts, Eric. You think you're immune—that you understand what you're up against with them—and then it gets worse. That hurts."

"Yeah, but . . ." He pauses, crouched on his haunches, and rubs his mouth. "Before all this tonight, you wanted to talk about moving in."

The change of subject throws me, and I go silent, as I process. He turns away and lights a match.

"Yeah, that's what I figured," he says.

"What you—?"

"It was too fast." He retreats to the other end of the couch. "When I got Storm, I wasn't thinking it'd mean we had to move in together, but I sure as hell jumped at the excuse. Here's a puppy. Now, if you want it, you'll have to move in with me."

"It wasn't like—"

"Yeah, it was. I didn't just jump. I pounced. One more way to tie you down. Tie you to me. Make sure you won't leave."

"I'm not—"

"I think about what happened to Nicole, and I feel like that's what I'm doing, in a way. Putting you in a place. Confining you. Locking you up."

"Eric, you're not—"

"But I want to," he blurts. "Figuratively. Lock you in. Keep you safe. Keep you here. Fuck, yeah. First a dog. Then moving in together. Tying you to me, to Rockton, because I'm afraid you're going to leave."

Before I can speak, he says, "I'm afraid, Casey, and I *hate* that. I hate how it makes me feel. This is Rockton. People come; people go. If I knew them and liked them, then sure, I miss them. But that's life here, right? Everyone is temporary. Even when my parents moved down south, it was just something I had to adjust to, and fuck, it's not like they were even my real parents."

He rubs his face, as if he can scrub those thoughts away.

I think of Nicole, and the way life on the run affected her. For Dalton, it's not even that. Every relationship—right back to his birth family—has been temporary. It is a life of abandonment, and yet it's such an intrinsic part of his world that he doesn't *feel* abandoned. That's just what they do. What they *must* do in Rockton. People must leave. He stays.

I crawl into his lap. His arms tighten around me, and he buries his chin in the curve of my shoulder.

"That's why I freaked out over Val saying I broke into her bedroom," he says. "Even if I had a perfect alibi, I just . . . panicked. When we found out Nicole's captor had visited her while I was in Dawson City, all I felt was relief. You wouldn't have to consider me as a suspect."

"I—"

"You might think I'd never do that, but every time I'm a suspect, it's going to make you reevaluate. How well do you know me? How much can you trust me? I'm a guy you met a few months ago, and now you're living with me, sleeping beside me, trusting me, and maybe that's too much. Maybe it's all too much, and it's just not worth it."

I put my hand under his chin and bring my face to his. "It is completely worth it," I say, and press my lips against his. "I have no intention of leaving, but that's not really what this is about. It's the reality that I could. That you'd be hurt if I did."

He nods, and I curl up in his arms.

"I'm hardly an expert," I say, "but I think that's just part of falling in love. You realize you don't want to lose someone. That it would hurt if you did. I'm not used to that either. When I walked away from my life, there was only one person I regretted leaving, and even that was just regret. Losing you would hurt—really hurt—so I just . . . I try not to think of it."

"I can't stop thinking of it. I obsess over it. And the worst thing? Feeling like it's not totally about me. It's not under my control. What if you decide it's not safe here? What if you miss being down south? What if the council makes you leave?"

He shifts to look at me. "Remember when you helped me deal with their threat to kick me out? Come up with a game plan? That helped—a lot. That's what I need to do with this. Have a strategy in case you need to leave, and it's not about me. I've decided I would give it a try. Life down south."

"What?"

He leans back and shrugs, like this is no big deal. As if this isn't the very reason the council's threat works. As if this isn't the reason he backed out of relationships before they got serious. Because he has no intention of leaving the north. Ever.

"I could do it," he says.

"No," I say. "Absolutely not. I would never ask—"

"But I'd do it, if I wasn't the reason you were leaving. I can't promise it'd work. But I could try."

I want to keep arguing, but his expression warns me not to. He's made this decision, and that's as much a relief as his backup plan for building a new Rockton.

Instead, I say, "If you're honestly worried about me being *frightened* out of Rockton, that's bullshit. Being a homicide detective isn't a safe or easy job anywhere. I knew that when I signed on—down there *and* up here."

I continue, "As for that talk I wanted to have earlier, it wasn't about moving too fast. Not at all. It was something Petra said about Storm. She was joking about a puppy being a starter baby."

"Huh?"

"That having a pet together was a trial run for a baby."

"What?" He shakes his head. "That's not the same thing. Not even close. Yeah, I'm not going to lie, saying Storm is a work dog was mostly an excuse. I gave her to you because you wanted a dog. But starter baby? Hell, no. Do couples actually do that shit down south?"

"I have no idea." I pull my legs up under me. "What I really wanted to talk about, though, wasn't whether you intended Storm as a baby trial run, but to just . . . discuss it. We're living together. We're in a committed relationship. Petra suggested it's better to have the baby conversation sooner rather than later. She's right. Especially in this case." I take a deep breath. "I can't have kids."

He nods. "Sure. I get that. If you don't want kids, you don't want them, and no one should try to change your mind."

"No, I mean I *can't* have them."

He looks at me, and under that look, I feel my tears prickle. This is another of those things in my life that I deal with through avoidance. Just don't think about. Now I have to. And it hurts.

"The attack," I say. "The damage. I can't . . ."

"Fuck," he says. "Fuck, I'm sorry. I wasn't getting it. Just wasn't getting it. I'm so sorry. Fucking stupid."

"You're never stupid." I kiss him and say, "Also, for the record? I love you."

He hugs me tight, and we sit like that for a while. Then I say, "We could try. Not now, obviously. But at some point, we could, if that's what you wanted. The doctor says there's a chance I could get pregnant. It's a very slim chance, though, so I just tell myself I can't. That makes it easier."

He hugs me again, saying nothing for a few minutes, and then, "Having kids has never been one of my goals. I always figured it wouldn't happen, and I'm fine with that. But thank you for telling me."

I manage a wry smile. "Saves us from a really awkward conversation later?"

His arms tighten. "No, I'd just want to know. Whatever you're dealing with, I want to know."

FORTY-SEVEN

We don't hear from Val the next morning. Am I hoping to? Yes. I want her to call us in and tell us she's made a horrible mistake. I want that for the town—for Val to step up and be a true leader. And, yes, I want it for Dalton, one less force he's working against.

But she stays in her house, blinds pulled. When I comment to Dalton, he shrugs it off, like he expects no better and he won't let Val spoil his mood today. He is in a good one. Calm, more secure in his footing, getting back to himself. When Jen stops by to collect her militia credits, her snarky jabs bounce off him. He just hands her the credits and tells her if she wants more militia work, talk to Anders.

A late night means an equally late start to our day. That may have had something to do with forgetting to set the alarm. By the time I've finished writing up my report from last night and helping Dalton with a few minor issues, it's early afternoon.

I find Mathias in the community hall weight room. It's a popular spot in Rockton, not unlike in a prison complex. People living in relative confinement with few entertainment options often decide to use the time for self-improvement. The library and weight room get a lot of use. Today, though, it's empty except for Mathias, bench-pressing an impressive amount.

"You do realize you'd be a lot scarier if you did this in front of an actual audience," I say.

"That would promote entirely the wrong image," he says, still lifting. "A strong man may be intimidating, but the truly frightening one is the man who can kill without lifting a finger."

"Like with hypnosis?" I settle on the bench opposite him. "Yes. I know why you're here. It's need to know. I needed to know."

"He did not die."

"In retrospect, I bet you wish he did."

Mathias sits up and reaches for his towel. "I do not regret needing to come to Rockton. I do regret the lives he took in his quest for misguided revenge. Hypnosis to make a man cut off his own genitals?" He shakes his head. "If such a power existed, why would the world need soldiers? Simply brainwash the enemy into killing themselves."

"So brainwashing Rockton residents to turn them into hostiles would be a nonstarter."

"And the detective deftly swings the conversation onto the desired topic, having spent exactly the required amount of time on small talk, so the subject does not feel undervalued on a personal level."

"One, you aren't a subject. Two, talking about brainwashing a man into castrating himself is no one's idea of small talk."

"I wouldn't say *no* one's . . ."

"You want small talk? Let's discuss the fact that you are violating . . ."

I point over his head. Dalton posted a notice saying *Use of the bench press or squat rack without a spotter is strictly prohibited.* Someone had altered the handwritten sign to read *Use of the fucking bench press or the fucking squat rack without a fucking spotter is punishable by one week of chopping duty during fucking blackfly season.*

"Eric and I have an arrangement," Mathias says. "If I die pinned under the weights, it is my own fucking fault." He pauses. "Or was that goddamn fault?"

"So, hostiles. You've read the reports."

"I have."

"And your conclusion?"

"I would like a hostile. Alive, preferably." He purses his lips. "No, definitely alive. Dead men are very hard to interview."

"I'm not bringing you a hostile, Mathias."

"Then I cannot provide you with a proper answer."

"Guess."

"That would hardly be scientific."

"Neither is psychiatry."

"Ouch."

"I'm not looking for an irrefutable answer. I want possibilities. What turns residents of Rockton into hostiles? Is it simple psychology?"

"Psychology is rarely simple. But that is not the response you want. You wish to know how likely it is that people of otherwise sound mind leave Rockton and quickly 'revert' to some bestial form. I would use the word 'impossible,' if I did not know better than to place absolutes on any aspect of human behavior. Extremely unlikely, then. Even in the case of the woman Eric knew, who changed so significantly within a year."

"So it wouldn't happen?"

"*Shouldn't* happen. Not without other factors. Brain trauma or chemical interference."

"A serious head injury or drugs?"

"Not necessarily drugs as you think of them. It could be environmental. Ingesting something that altered her mental state."

"Is there anything up here that would do that?"

"I do not know everything that is up here. I would need to speak to Eric."

Dalton is too busy to meet with Mathias today, and it's not urgent anyway. It's just a theory I'm mentally playing with at this point. The question of how we came to have hostiles has little bearing on the question *could Nicole's captor have been a hostile?* I'm not even sure where to begin answering that. As everyone has been telling me, it'll be a whole lot simpler pursuing settler culprits. But that doesn't mean I can't try narrowing it down, which is why I'm at Nicole's place an hour after leaving Mathias.

Nicole has just returned from the community center. I've given her guards orders to let her move about the town while accompanied, with outings logged so Isabel and I can be sure Nicole isn't overdoing it in her desperation to prove she's okay.

Kenny's on duty. I speak to him and then go inside to find Nicole making tea in the kitchen.

She looks over and grins. "You brought me a bear cub."

"Thought you might like that," I say as she bends to greet Storm. I walk over to finish making the tea. When she rises with a quick "I can do that," I pretend not to hear her. Once it's ready, I carry it into the living room.

"I can carry a teapot," she says. "I've been working out."

"That better be a joke."

"Kind of." She takes a dumbbell from the coffee table. "Just picked these up." She does a biceps curl. "One whole pound. In a month, I get to move up to two."

"Impressive."

"I wanted to start with the fives, but Dr. Atelier made me take these. Something about muscle damage. He showed me a few exercises I can do with them, too." She puts the weight down and sits. "I remember when I was here before, I stayed away from the butcher shop. He just seemed . . ."

"Weird?"

She laughs. "To put it bluntly. He's definitely different, but he's been kind to me." She sips her tea. "So, before we get down to business. I'd like to discuss *business*. I want a job." She lifts a hand. "Don't tell me my job is getting better. I've heard it from Diana."

"Who is correct."

Nicole shakes her head and pats the sofa to get Storm over. The puppy looks at me, making sure I don't want to claim petting rights. When I motion, she bounds to Nicole and jumps up, front paws on her knees.

"Down," I say to Storm, and then to Nicole, "Push her down firmly, please. That won't be nearly so adorable when she's over a hundred pounds."

Nicole nudges the puppy down, mock-whispering, "I know. People trying to rein in our enthusiasm. Spoilsports."

I roll my eyes.

"I'd like a job," Nicole says. "There must be something I can do, even if it's just taking inventory at one of the shops. Makes me feel like I'm pulling my weight."

"I understand—"

"Yes, you do," she says. "You totally get it because it's the same thing you'd want. Which doesn't mean you think it's healthy."

"I don't think it's *unhealthy*. I just . . ." I shake my head. "I will find something for you. But it will be a part-time job and probably boring as hell."

"I spent a year in a hole. Anything is more interesting than that. Now let's drop the subject of Nicole needing to slow down and switch to Casey trying to solve an impossible case, finding a killer in a thousand square miles of wilderness. You have questions."

"One, and I'm going to preface it by acknowledging that it's going to sound like the dumbest question ever. But bear with me."

"Shoot."

"Your captor. Was there anything odd about his behavior?"

She sputters a laugh, startling Storm, who zooms back to me and leaps onto my lap. I give the puppy a hug and put her down as I say, "Yes, beyond the part about holding you captive, and everything that went with that. Like I said, it sounds like a dumb question. Clearly that's not normal behavior. And yes, it's not like I can ask if his behavior seemed typical for psychos who keep women in caves—"

"Yeah, he's my first kidnapper. Hopefully my last, too. But I think I understand what you're asking. Were there any signs of mental impairment or pathology beyond the obvious."

"Right. Did he speak proper English? Accented? Any indication of education level? Anything odd in word choice?"

She thinks and then says, "He disguised his voice enough that I couldn't tell if he had an accent. His speech didn't strike me as particularly uneducated or well educated—it didn't stand out either way. I never heard him use dialect I didn't recognize. Or words that just weren't right, like you sometimes get in mental illness. He didn't talk a *lot*. But it was normal. Well, as normal as you can get under the circumstances."

"When he spoke about women, his requirements, how they tricked him. What was his tone? His affect?"

"Were they crazy rants? No." She pauses. "Have you ever gone out with a guy who complains about his ex? Who's still bitter about the whole thing? That's what it was like."

"You said he burned pages of your books. That seems like a very deliberate punishment."

"Oh, it was. Trust me. He wasn't going into a frenzy, ripping out pages. He'd slowly burn one page in front of me, then warn that next time, he'd do ten. Honestly, Casey, while I can laugh about the question, in every possible way, he was as normal as you could expect. Creepily normal. Which is why, in the beginning, I thought I could reason with him. But I couldn't, and it wasn't because he was too crazy to be reasoned with. He knew exactly what he was doing, and he didn't give a damn. That was the scariest part. That someone who seemed sane could do that to another person. That he could fully understand his actions . . . and just didn't care."

I'm woken that night by a pounding at the door. I lift my head and see Dalton propped on his elbows.

"Fuck," he says. "You hear that, too?"

"I'm telling myself I'm dreaming."

More pounding. Storm whines, nails clicking as she gets out of her bed.

"You're dreaming, too," I say.

She whines again. Dalton grumbles under his breath and swings his legs out of bed, saying, "If it's Val again—"

"If it's about Val, we'd better go down together, prove we're both here."

I follow Dalton down the stairs and pick up Storm as he opens the door. There, on the porch, is Shawn Sutherland, dressed only in his sweatpants.

"Shawn?" I say.

His mouth works, but he's breathing too hard to form words.

"Come inside," I say, and I take his arm and pull him in as Dalton flicks on the hall light. That's when I see the bruises. A ring of them around Sutherland's throat.

FORTY-EIGHT

Someone has tried to strangle Shawn Sutherland. We get him to the couch and try to ask what happened, but he's in shock and just keeps saying, "I thought I was safe. I thought I was safe."

I tend to Sutherland while Dalton pages Sam, the militia he'd left on guard. After last night with Val, we've pulled out the radios. There's no answer, which could only mean the damn thing isn't working. I tell Dalton to go. Then I call Anders. It's 2:00 A.M., and it takes a lot of punches on the call button, but he finally wakes. I've just hung up from that when Dalton calls from Sam's radio.

"He's out cold," he says. "Someone hit him from behind."

"Is he okay?"

"Yeah, I'm—" His voice cuts out. "—Kenny at Nicole's—not answering—once I wake Sam up."

"I'm on my way as soon as Will's here."

I lock Storm in the bedroom. Then I get out onto the porch, and I'm still zipping my jacket when I see Anders coming at a run. I jog to meet him. We pass without pausing, me calling, "I'm going to check on Nicole. Kenny's not picking up."

"Shit. You want me—"

"Shawn needs you. I'll be fine."

He calls back that he'll catch up.

I'm racing to Nicole's when Dalton shouts, "I'm here," from behind me. Not *wait for me,* which I appreciate.

I race between two buildings, and there's Nicole's house . . . with Kenny sitting on the front porch. He sees me and stands.

"Radio?" I say.

"Huh?" He lifts it and hits buttons. There's only static.

"Shawn was attacked," I say as I climb the steps. "When's the last time you heard from Nicole?"

"Before she went to bed. But Diana's on duty." He opens the door. "Di?"

Silence answers. I push through. Dalton catches up, and he's shouldering past Kenny, gun in hand.

We move quickly into the living room. Diana is lying on the futon, curled on her side, blanket pulled up. I let out a sigh of relief. There's no sign of a struggle. No sign of trauma. She's just asleep.

Dalton heads for the stairs as I walk over saying, "Di?" I reach out and shake her shoulder. "Di? It's me."

She doesn't stir. I try harder. One good hard shake, and she topples to the floor, head lolling.

"Eric!" I shout as I drop beside her, my hands flying to her neck, searching for a pulse.

"Nicole's gone," he says as he thunders down the stairs. His wet boots squeak as he draws up short behind me. "Her bed's empty."

I take one running step toward the stairs. Then I glance back at Diana.

"Nicole isn't there," Dalton says. "Stay with Diana. Is she knocked out?"

I drop beside her again. "I don't know. Damn it. I can't tell."

He's on the floor, hands going to her neck as I check her wrist.

"I think I feel something," I say as I pick up a faint pulse. "Do you?"

He shakes his head and yanks a picture frame from the coffee table and holds it in front of her mouth. A light fog of condensation forms on the glass.

"Kenny!" he shouts.

Kenny's right there. He's been here the whole time, in the doorway, watching and waiting for instructions.

"Get Will, right?" Kenny says.

"Please," I say. "As fast as you can. Then get everyone. Nicole's gone."

He takes off. I check Diana's vital signs again, as if that breath-fog was a trick of the light. It wasn't. She's breathing. Her pulse is weak, though.

I shine my light on her neck. No signs of strangulation. I look around. Dalton has backed onto his haunches, and he's holding out a teacup. I lean over and sniff. It's an herbal blend, which makes it impossible to tell if it smells as it should.

"It's almost empty," Dalton says. "The cup was teetering on the edge."

As if she'd been falling asleep fast, with just enough energy to put it back on the table.

"Sedative," I say. "But it's too much."

He sedated Diana to kidnap Nicole.

Nicole's gone.

We couldn't protect her. He's taken her again.

Diana twitches, reminding me I have to focus on her. Her breathing is dangerously shallow. I start CPR. Between bouts, I try to get her to regain consciousness. She doesn't.

Our first thought is that she's been given the sleeping pills we left for Nicole. Anders knows where they are, though, and when he arrives, he checks. Nicole's supply hasn't been touched.

We get Diana next door to the clinic, and as he's assessing her, I'm digging through the drug locker. It's secured with a heavy-duty lock, and there's no immediate sign that anyone has broken in. I go straight to the sedatives. The box looks fine, but when I grab the stock chart, I can see exactly what's missing.

I run back into the examination room. "You haven't given Nicole or Shawn any benzo without marking it down, right?"

He shakes his head. "So that's what we've got? Shit."

I know enough about overdoses to understand his curse. Too many sleeping pills is rarely fatal. An OD of benzodiazepine is another matter.

"I'll . . ." He trails off and then exhales. "The only remedy I even know is to pump her stomach, which I've never done."

"We have instructions," I say, grabbing the binder from the shelf. After Beth left, Dalton and I went on a research binge.

"Manuals are awesome for figuring out a new car stereo," Anders says as he scrubs in. "Life-saving procedures are not exactly the ideal time to learn a new skill."

"Sorry," I say, squeezing his arm as I walk past. "Stomach pumping is one procedure you just weren't getting volunteers for."

He lets out a ragged chuckle and then says, "I had a beer after work."

"Hmm?"

"I know you can smell it on me, and you're trying to decide if you should ask how much I've had. You can always ask, Casey."

"I don't need to because you'll always volunteer."

Anders does drink too much. It never interferes with his job—Dalton wouldn't allow that—but we do wish he'd cut back a little. Yet we also know why he drinks and that, maybe, if it doesn't become a problem, there are worse ways for him to silence his demons.

We pump Diana's stomach. Then I need to go work the scene. I don't want to. Whatever she's done, when I saw her unconscious on that floor, it felt the same as when I'd found her passed out from her ex's supposed beating, right before we came to Rockton.

I still care. I've never pretended I didn't, but that heart-in-throat terror reminds me how much. It won't fix anything. Things might never be fixed, probably *should* never be fixed. But I care. I always will.

Next door, Dalton is hunting for Nicole's trail. It should be easy. It's not, because her captor isn't stupid. He realizes snow on the ground will make it very easy to track him, particularly with a captive in tow.

He's left a very clear trail from the back door—boot prints combined with uneven drag marks, as if he'd put Nicole on a tarp or a sheet and hauled her. That's easy to follow. He lets it be easy. There's nothing else he can do. But his trail goes directly to the main groomed path. And then it is lost. We continue on with our lanterns, hoping to find footsteps leaving the trail, but only see those from people zipping off for business best not done on a path.

"She's out here," I say.

"I know."

"It can't be this hard. There's snow. We just need to get farther along the groomed paths. Past the logging sites, past the lake, past everything." I take a deep breath and when I look around again, the forest seems to shimmer through a veil of exhaustion.

"We can do this," I say. "We have to."

"We will."

I squeeze my eyes shut. "Okay, so methodically tackling it, we start with the old logging path. That's the shortest. Get to the end of that and . . ."

A flake of snow lands on my arm. Then another.

"No," I whisper. I look up at the sky to see snow falling.

"No. No, no, no!"

Dalton's fingers wrap around my arm. "Let's do what we can. Quickly."

FORTY-NINE

We barely get to the old logging site before the wide path is covered. We try another direction, in case heavier tree cover keeps the ground barer, but by the time we reach that, it too has been blanketed in snow.

I want to keep searching. Blindly searching. Stumbling through the dark and the snow. I think I might have, too, if the wind hadn't whipped up, a true storm blowing in, Dalton all but picking me up and carrying me back to Rockton.

"We'll go out at first light," he promises. "The first *hint* of light, and we'll be out on the horses, searching."

Searching for what? I don't even know. Nicole's captor isn't going to set up camp right off a main path. He's not going to light a fire and call attention to himself. He's not going to take Nicole to the same cave where we found her.

Back in Rockton, Dalton doesn't even suggest sleep. I have a witness to question and a scene to process.

First, I talk to Sutherland. The marks around his neck tell me it was a soft ligature. Manual strangulation leaves very different pattern. The thick mark and lack of abrading suggests a fabric, like stockings, rather than something rough, like a rope. I notice fibers and remove them.

Anders found no sign of serious injury. Just a very traumatized victim. He escaped his captor, made it back to Rockton, thought he was safe . . . and he wasn't. We promised safety and failed to deliver on that promise. Failed him, failed Nicole. She's back out there. Back with her captor, her tormenter, her rapist.

Like Val, Sutherland woke to someone in his room. Someone strangling him while holding a bag over his head.

A surge of adrenaline let Sutherland throw off his attacker. By the time he clawed free of the bag, he was alone in the room. That was when he'd grabbed a knife and raced outside to find Sam unconscious. He'd left him there and run all the way across town to Dalton's place.

That's all he can tell me.

On to the scene of the main crime: the poisoning of Diana and the abduction of Nicole. I find the tea blend in the kitchen. There's only one, making it easy to dose. I bag that as evidence. Then I pour Diana's leftover tea into a jar.

Upstairs, I stand in Nicole's bedroom doorway and visually process. Dalton says he only came as far as the door, so the scene is intact. I sketch it. Then I go straight for the teacup on the nightstand. I pick it up and sniff. It's nearly empty, and it smells the same as Diana's. There's no sign of struggle in the room, suggesting Nicole was unconscious when she was taken.

I hunt for further clues but find nothing.

I'm at Sutherland's place, piecing together the evidence with his story. I find the ligature used to strangle him. That doesn't exactly take skilled detective work—there's a ripped length of sheet lying beside the bed.

A strip from a sheet seems an odd choice until I think about it. His attacker undoubtedly made a choice not to use rope. It would abrade the attacker's hands, leaving marks. It also isn't easy to stuff a suitable length of rope in your pocket. For this, all Sutherland's attacker needed to do was rip a length from his victim's spare set.

I'm back at the clinic. Anders and Dalton are talking to the militia and volunteers, preparing for tomorrow's search. Diana is being watched by Sam, who's back on his feet and eager to prove himself. Jen's assisting.

"So, you guys screwed up," Jen says as I walk into the room where Diana is still unconscious. "Val has some lunatic break into her place, and the very next day, Nicki is taken. Again."

I'm about to answer when Dalton's voice drifts in from the hall, punctuated by footfalls. "Yeah, I fucked up. Now go make yourself useful."

Jen turns on him. "You *did* fuck up, Sheriff."

"Didn't I just say that?"

"No, *we* fucked up." I turn to Jen. "All evidence suggested Val's intruder was only a nightmare, but we should have proceeded otherwise. Added extra guards. Maybe moved both Shawn and Nicole into a place with a single entry point."

"Happy?" Dalton says to Jen. "Or do you want us to sign a confession, too?"

Jen's eyes narrow. "I was just pointing out—"

"That we fucked up. That Nicole is gone. That Shawn could have been killed. Yeah, we're disappointing you by not arguing, but we don't have time for that. We take responsibility. Now move on, so Casey and I can figure out how to *find* Nicole."

"I want to help. As permanent militia."

"Does this seem like recruitment time? I've told you that I'll pay you for what you do now, and after this is over, I'll consider your application."

"Bullshit. You'll never hire me. You hate me."

"Hate?" He snorts. "Too much effort. I just don't like you much, which wouldn't stop me from hiring you. You know what would?

The fact you've got a longer infraction record than anyone in this town."

She crosses her arms. "I've done my time."

"Still, getting hired might not be in your best interests. Militia are subject to triple penalties for all infractions."

"You just made that up."

"Yep. Now go think about it, and if you still want to apply, see me next week. In the meantime, if you join the search, you'll get militia pay."

She still grumbles as she heads to the door, saying, "I'm going to be right outside, and I'm coming back in to watch Diana when you're gone. You're not ripping me off halfway through a shift."

"Thank you," I say. "We appreciate the dedication."

She snarls a *fuck off* over her shoulder as she leaves. When she's gone, Dalton and I collapse into chairs beside Diana's bed. A few minutes later, I'm sound asleep.

FIFTY

We're on the trail at first light, as Dalton promised. Out all day on horseback, in hopes that the quieter ride will help us hear anything untoward. We don't.

We return to the cave. As much of a long shot as that might seem, that's exactly why we have to go back. It's like when I played hide-and-seek as a girl—my favorite trick was to return to a spot I'd used earlier because no one ever checked those. We're dealing with a smart man, in full control of his choices and actions. He might do the same. He didn't. We comb through that cave system and find no sign that he's even visited it again.

Late afternoon, we return to join the general search. The hunt is both organized and controlled—the last thing we want is for Nicole's captor to grab a second victim.

There's no shortage of volunteers. Too many actually, more than we can afford to have in the forest and keep the town running. I used to hear about searches like this down south. Someone would go missing on a hiking trail, and I would always wonder at that. How could you leave groomed trail—often to go to the bathroom, as Val had—and get lost? The search would be organized, with hundreds of volunteers and tracking dogs and search helicopters—every tool available to modern search-and-rescue. Yet they'd find nothing. How was that possible?

I've already discovered how easy it is to get lost only a few steps from a path. Now I see a massive search effort, how flawless it seems, how futile it feels. Nicole could be bound and gagged under a fallen branch, and we would pass right by her.

Which does not stop us from searching. All day. Into the night. Up the next morning. Out again. Endlessly searching.

I overdo it. I can't help that. I found her. I brought her back. And I let her be taken again.

I finally understand exactly how Dalton felt when Abbygail disappeared—that devastating level of guilt. For him, it was a girl with an unrequited crush, threatening to go into the forest to get his attention . . . and then disappearing. For me, it is the woman I brought home from an unimaginable ordeal . . . only to let her captor take her again, right from under our noses.

We talk about that, as we're out there, searching. Shared guilt. Shared reassurances that we'd done our best. Shared fears that we hadn't, that we couldn't, that when it comes to keeping another person safe, there is never going to be a point where you feel you did all you could.

Here, part of doing all we can means taking the plane up as soon as the wind dies down. It also means recruiting every human resource. That morning, Dalton tacks a piece of yellow cloth to a tree. It's a sign for Jacob to meet him when the sun is high.

From there, we go to Brent, and Dalton asks him to use his bounty-hunting skills to help us. He doesn't offer payment. That is implied, and even then, it'll have to be worked into a trade so Brent won't feel insulted.

We head to the marked tree just before noon. Jacob is already there and waiting. I tell him about Nicole.

"But how? Did she go into the woods again? I know she wanted to walk the dog but—"

He stops short of saying anything that could sound like an accusation.

"She was taken from her bedroom," I say.

"And, yeah," Dalton says. "She had a nurse, a guard, heightened patrols—"

"I'm not saying—" Jacob begins.

"We are," I say with a weak smile. "Trust me, we're saying it."

"This guy came right into Rockton, though? That's . . ."

"Ballsy," I say. "We know. Then the storm hit, and we lost their trail. We were wondering if you could help."

"Of course. Just tell me what to do."

Dalton gives him a region he's familiar with, and Jacob nods, and then says, "We'll find her. It might seem like this forest goes on forever, but someone's going to see something. This guy won't kill her. If he wanted to do that, he'd have done it in town, right?"

When I nod, Jacob seems relieved, as if he hadn't been stating a fact as much as posing a question.

"She's tough," he says. "She knows we're looking for her, and she'll stay alive. That's how she'll beat him. She'll stay alive until we find her."

I hope so. I really hope so.

On the way back for lunch, we meet up with Anders. We're walking and talking, heading toward the station.

"I'll round up a hot lunch," Dalton says. "You two . . ." He trails off as he sees Jen parked on the station front steps. "Fuck."

"Why don't I go get lunch?" Anders says.

"No, I—"

"I insist."

"I'll go with—" I begin, but Dalton's hand lands on my shoulder. I sigh, and we walk over to Jen.

"This isn't a public rest stop," Dalton says. "It's also not the way to get yourself hired."

"Huh," she says. "You sure? I kinda thought that making myself useful and helping your halfwit detective might *be* the way to prove myself."

Dalton says nothing, just stands there, looking at her. Finally she rises and says, "What?"

"I'm waiting for you to rephrase that without an insult attached. Though I suspect that might be physically impossible."

"I was just—"

"Reflexively insulting Casey. The way you do to everyone. Because everyone needs to be knocked down a few pegs, and that's your job. Which means you aren't ever getting a job *here*, Jen. As militia, you'd need to show both of us basic respect. That's how policing works, just like in the army."

She crosses her arms. "Do you want my tip or not?"

"Come on inside," I say. "And if you really feel the need to insult me, at least do better than 'halfwit.'"

Dalton stays outside. Because at ten below freezing, it's really just too warm to be indoors. Jen plunks into the chair behind the only desk in the station. My seating options then are to kick her out of it or take another chair, as if I'm the witness and she's the cop. I stay standing.

"What's the tip?" I say.

"I'd like a coffee. Black. Cookies, too. I know lover boy smuggles in chocolate chips for you."

"Leave."

"That wasn't an insult."

"It actually was. Nicole has been kidnapped—by the psycho who kept her in a cave for a year, after he murdered two other women. Making me take time to fix you coffee insults everyone in this town who actually gives a damn."

Her lips tighten. "I've been out there, pulling double shifts on the search parties—"

"Because we're paying you."

"For one shift. The second is volunteer. But I want a hundred credits for my tip."

"We don't pay for tips."

"Time to start."

"No, it's not, because that would set a precedent. The payoff is that I use your tip to catch a killer, which helps everyone. It's a community effort."

"Fuck community. I want credits."

"And you honestly expect to be hired as militia with that attitude?"

"My attitude is adjustable. You know what adjusts it? Money. You don't want to 'start a precedent' by paying me for this tip? Hire me now. Then I'm on the payroll, and I'll do my damn community service."

My palms thump onto the desk, cutting her short. "You are wasting my time, Jen, and I'm starting to think that's your end goal. Stall my investigation so you can tell everyone what a shitty job I'm doing."

"I wouldn't do that," she says, her voice tight as she straightens. "I have a valid tip. I'm just not sure you're competent enough to use it."

"Oh, for god's sake." I stride to the door and grasp the knob. "Get out."

"You don't want my tip?"

"Yes, I do, but it's obvious I'm not going to get it. I can't pay you. I can't hire you. I can't even convince you I'm competent—apparently solving a quintuple homicide wasn't enough."

"If you'd solved it faster, Mick would still be alive."

I go still. Completely still. Then I say, as quietly as I can, "Get out."

She rises. "You couldn't save him. Just like you couldn't protect Nicki. You—"

"Get out!" I roar, and she stumbles back.

The door flies open, and Dalton is there.

"Yes," Jen says. "I've upset your little girlfriend. Bad, bad Jen. Fine. You want the tip? You were right about Val. She dreamed up her intruder. I investigated. There's nothing to suggest anyone was at her house that night. I delivered her breakfast today, and when I asked about the intruder, she got all flustered. I'm thinking it was a repressed-chick wet dream. She woke up while fantasizing about Dalton, flipped out, and made a mistake. There wasn't an intruder."

I'm not sure this qualifies as a tip, but I need to get to work so I just say, "Okay."

"With Nicki gone, it might seem like it was the same guy and Val could shed more light on it. But it's a whole separate thing. You can skip Val's story. Concentrate on the rest."

"Thank you." I struggle to say that as sincerely as I can. I'd already requestioned Val and put to rest any worries that she really did have an intruder. But Jen doesn't know that and seems to have honestly been trying to help. I'd just wish I could have gotten that without the ridiculous preamble.

I tell Jen to add an extra hour on her militia time card.

"An hour?" she says. "I spent half a day on that."

"Consider it volunteer work," Dalton says. "Part of your application for a position."

"Fuck you, asshole," she says and stomps out.

When the door closes, I say, "I can't learn my lesson with her, can I?"

He walks in and stokes the fire. "There used to be this feral cat that'd come around. Must have lived with settlers at one point. It knew people. It'd slink about, and folks would feed it, try to coax it inside. If you walked past, it'd meow and roll, like Storm does when she wants attention. It'd even rub up against you, purring. But if you reached down, there'd be bloodshed. Every goddamned time. Folks knew that. You think they stopped?" He shakes his head.

"Did you try?"

"Fuck, no. I wasn't falling for her bullshit."

I smile. "Which makes you the smart one. But I suppose it's not really about intelligence. It's ego. We want to be the special one. The one that breaks through. The cat might attack everyone else—but me? I'll be different."

"Some people, yeah, it's ego. Others? It's a genuine desire to help."

"Only the cat doesn't want help. It wants bloodshed. To lure you in and then lash out and punish you for trying."

"Yep."

A commotion erupts outside, and we hurry out to hear voices.

"Get that fucking gun out of my face or you'll eat it," a voice booms. "I'm here to see your fucking sheriff, and if you stop me, you'll find out why that's a fucking bad idea."

We see Anders is on his way back with lunch, and he stops short and looks toward the porch, as if Dalton is somehow projecting his voice down the road.

True, the profanity is classic Dalton. As is the second threat. But the booming voice and the first threat clearly aren't our sheriff's style. I know who it is, though, and Dalton winces as he realizes it, too.

Dalton heads down the steps. He's not rushing but not dawdling either. That could be dangerous for whoever gets in the newcomer's way.

We round the station to see Tyrone Cypher striding into town.

Paul follows with his gun still out, as if trailing a bear, waiting to see if it'll need to be put down. It's an apt analogy. Cypher looks like a massive grizzled brown bear stalking in from the forest. People spill out of homes and businesses to watch, and from the way they stare, I wonder how many thought the "people in the woods" stories were fairy tales meant to keep them inside town borders, those wild men no more plausible than the trolls and witches of the brothers Grimm.

"Finally," Cypher says when he spots Dalton. "Would you tell this fucking yahoo to put his gun down or I'll stick it where he ain't ever going to get it unstuck." He wheels on Paul. "And inform him that's no idle threat."

"It's fine, Paul," Dalton says. "He's a former resident."

"Former fucking sheriff, you mean," Cypher says.

Anders falls in beside me and whispers, "Oh, this explains so much."

"This is Tyrone Cypher," Dalton says. "He was the sheriff before my father took over and a deputy after."

Cypher's lips tighten, annoyed by the reminder of his demotion, but Dalton continues as if he was just being thorough with the intro-duction. "Ty is permitted in Rockton, but only if I'm informed of his arrival." He looks at Cypher. "And only if he remembers he's no longer the sheriff."

Cypher snorts. "You like that, don't you, jungle boy?"

I step up to Cypher and say, under my breath, "No."

He raises his brows.

I meet his gaze and say again, "No."

There's a moment where he studies me. Then he claps me on the shoulder and says, "Get your back down, kitten," and turns to Dalton with "Eric, I've got something for you." He emphasizes Dalton's name, telling me he understood my message and might even comply.

Dalton jerks his head. "We'll take it inside."

"We were just about to have lunch," I say. "Looks like we have enough for four."

I glance at Anders, which prompts Dalton to say, "This is Will Anders, my deputy. Will, Ty Cypher."

Cypher looks Anders up and down and then flicks a glance at me. "Can't escape that minority hiring quota shit even up here, huh?"

"Nah," Anders says. "After you, the council just got really skittish about hiring dumb-assed white dudes. It's actually just the dumb-assed part that was the problem, but you can't blame them for being overly cautious."

"See?" Cypher says to Dalton, pointing at Anders. "*He* knows how to make a proper comeback."

"I just have a lot more experience dealing with dumb-asses. And racists."

"Hey, who you calling racist?" Cypher points at the boxes of food. "I'm not the guy who sent the black dude to fetch his lunch."

"Actually, I volunteered—"

I cut Anders off with a wave. "Don't even bother. Tyrone is still convinced I'm Aboriginal."

Cypher screws up his face. "What?"

"First Nations," I say.

"First . . . ?" He rolls his eyes. "Oh, fuck. Are you offended 'cause I called you an Injun? Fine. Are those the currently fashionable terms? First Nations? Aboriginal? I'll use those, then. Happy?"

Anders looks at me, one brow cocked. "Then I should warn you about lunch, Case. It's probably not something you've tried. Chicken chow mein. Chinese. But it's pretty good."

"I've heard that."

Dalton shakes his head and escorts Tyrone into the station.

FIFTY-ONE

Cypher has found Roger. Found his camp, at least.

"I'd have brought him in," he says as we eat. "But he knows something's up. He's hunkered down in an open patch right up against a cliff side. No way of getting close without him seeing me coming. I'm no fucking good at subtlety."

Anders snorts under his breath. Cypher doesn't catch it and continues, "I considered waiting for nightfall, but I figure I'm about as likely to spook him as to bring him in. If I spook him, he's gone. Seemed safer to just come and get you folks."

I thank him for that. Then Dalton and I exchange a look. While it's a sensible decision, it's also worrisome. I'd have kept my suspicions to myself. But Cypher isn't the only one in the room who lacks subtlety.

"You setting us up, Ty?" Dalton asks as he reaches for another helping.

"What?"

"You heard me. I appreciate that you didn't risk spooking him. It's the right move. Not a Ty Cypher move, though."

Cypher's eyes narrow. "You calling me stupid, boy?"

"No, but given that you'd get a bigger reward for bringing him in, I'd have expected you to try."

"Maybe because you knew a younger man, one a helluva lot more willing to wager good money on a shitty bet. I want my fucking coffee. I'm not going to risk that. I want supplies, too. We've got a bad winter coming. You spend time out in those woods, you learn that big gambles are the sure way to guarantee you won't spend much *more* time in those woods. That's something I'd expect you to know all about."

I make a noise in my throat, but Cypher doesn't push the jab further, just refills his mug and adds enough creamer to make my teeth ache.

"If you don't want Roger, that's fine," Cypher says. "But you still owe me for scouting him."

"You know I'll come with you. I'm just letting *you* know that I don't trust you, and I'll be bringing Will and Casey."

"You sure you don't want the full fucking militia? An honor guard to keep you safe?"

"An honor guard is ceremonial. The term you want is 'security detail.' I don't need either. I want backup, and if you think mockery will make me say 'fuck that,' and come alone, you've got the wrong sheriff. Now pour that coffee in a thermos, and let's move while we still have daylight."

We've been hiking for maybe ten minutes when Cypher says, "Seems tense back in Rockton. Everyone running around with guns, jumpy as hell. A bit of professional advice. You're obviously thinking Roger is coming back for the girl. I'd say the chances of that are slim to none."

I think he's making a really bad joke, but when I look over, he's perfectly serious. He doesn't realize Nicole is gone. Those who escorted him in wouldn't have mentioned it, and we'd been too focused on Roger.

"It already happened," I say.

"What?"

"He came and took her two nights back."

"Came *into* Rockton?"

I nod.

Dalton says, "And before you ask, yes, she was under guard. A caretaker inside. A guard outside. Double night patrols."

"So he's a smart fucker. Not a hostile, then."

"On the surface, it seems like their sort of crime," I say. "But his captive says he was frighteningly normal, and the fact he took her again, from Rockton, suggests we aren't dealing with a madman. He even attacked another former victim to distract us."

Cypher looks over, brows rising.

I continue. "My guess is that he got Nicole into the forest but didn't dare take her far with the added security. He hid her and then went back to strangle the guy who escaped him. In the resulting confusion, he spirited Nicole off."

"He could have just been silencing a witness," Cypher says. "But yeah, the fact he failed to kill the guy—and that he must have grabbed the girl *first*—means it was likely a distraction. Smart. Not one of those freaks, then. Hostiles aren't big on planning. And they wouldn't think they could slip into Rockton unnoticed. The smell alone would give them away."

We walk a little more, and then I say, "Honestly asking your professional opinion, what else could we have done to make sure this didn't happen?"

"Stick that gal's ass on the plane and get her out of Rockton."

"Which would seem like the first thing she'd want. It wasn't. To her, Rockton was safety. We still tried to talk her out of staying, but she . . ."

"Threatened suicide," Dalton says. "Even if we'd managed to force her out, she could have retaliated. The council agreed she should stay."

I expect Cypher to say it didn't matter what Nicole wanted—get her on that plane and let the council deal with the rest.

Instead he says, "Hell, yeah. If the council thinks she's a threat, *nail* her ass to Rockton."

"I'm not sure she would have actually—" I began.

"Doesn't matter what she'd do. What matters is what the council *thinks* she might. In those circumstances, if you put her on a plane, you sign her death warrant."

I look over sharply. "Have they done that?"

"Fuck if I know. But given what I did for a living, no one knows the low value of a human life better. Except maybe soldiers."

When Anders tenses, Cypher glances at him and says, "The army doesn't give a shit how many grunts die. Only person who cares is the guy standing beside you. To them, you're a person. To some government pencil pusher? You're a tool. An expendable one. That's what we are to the council. Only even *less* useful than tools. You ever hear those stories about rich people who leave all their money to their dogs or cats? Their heirs need to pamper the fucking animals, or they lose their inheritance. That's what we are. Those dogs and cats. If we're rich ourselves, then the council doesn't get the final payout until we make it home alive. If we're one of the charity cases, the *real* power behind the council—those folks who pay to keep Rockton running—don't like seeing their precious pets mistreated."

As he's talking, I'm thinking of Beth, and when he finishes, I can barely bring myself to ask. But I have to.

"What about those who get kicked out? For crimes?"

"They're threats, aren't they?"

Dalton shakes his head. "My father said the fact they've committed crimes is enough—it's blackmail material, should they ever become a threat. He says the council monitors them and, yeah, if they do something suspicious, maybe they act. Otherwise, no."

"Well, if your daddy said it, then it must be true."

Dalton's jaw tightens. "If you have any proof—"

"Proof? No. But I've got a brain in my head, and I know how people like the council think. Made my living working for their sort. All that matters to them is the bottom line. There was this one time they were going to send a guy back south, blamed for something I was sure he didn't do. So I took him into the forest, gave him supplies, and pointed him in the direction of the nearest town. Did he make it? Probably not. But I figure I gave him a better chance than he'd have had on that plane coming to pick him up. Hell, after I left Rockton, the council tried to recruit me."

"Recruit you for what?" I ask.

"No idea. They sent some guy to find me out here, make me an offer I couldn't refuse. I refused it. By hauling him into a tree like that she-cat hauled Silas, tying him to a limb and handing him his fancy satellite phone. Came back a few days later, and he was gone. I figure they sent someone to fetch him. Didn't really care one way or the other, as long as they didn't bother me again. They didn't."

"And you have no idea what they wanted you to do?"

"Hell, yeah, I have an idea. I just didn't bother asking him to con-firm my suspicion. Thing is, kitten, I wasn't a bad sheriff, but a man like me? He's got one real skill. One real talent. And it ain't chop-ping down trees."

We've been walking for almost two hours, and the mountain is finally getting close when Dalton slows, his head tilting in a way I know well.

"You hear something, boy?" Cypher asks.

"Wondering if we're going to get there before nightfall."

"You afraid of the dark?"

"Just cautious."

"Too fucking cautious. You get that from your daddy. Always looked ten times before he leapt, and by the time he did, there was nothing left to leap at. He—"

"Boss?" Anders says. "I need a piss break."

"You gotta announce it, too?" Cypher waves at the side of the path. "No one's stopping you." When Anders glances my way, Cypher says, "Seriously? You think you got something she ain't seen before, boy?"

"Go on," Dalton says. "Just don't wander far."

Cypher's what-the-hell look turns to what-the-fuck when it's not Anders who lopes off into the forest—it's Dalton. Anders pulls his hood up, shielding his face.

"What—" Cypher begins.

"Ty?" I say. "While we're waiting, I've got a question for you. Eric says you claim you once took down a grizzly with your bare hands. He thinks it's bullshit—don't give me that look, Eric, you know you did—and I say it's possible. So how did you do it?"

I watch the wheels turn in Cypher's head, as he tries to figure out what's going on. But whatever his act, he's not a stupid man. He glances in the direction Dalton went and then eases back, saying, "You calling me a liar, boy? Fuck, yeah, I took down that bitch. Your daddy was there. Just ask him. We were out hunting, and this new idiot decided—"

A yelp resounds through the forest. Then Dalton's "What the hell? Shawn?" followed by a stream of indecipherable babble. Anders and I jog toward the voices as Cypher lumbers along behind us. We get about twenty paces. Then we see Sutherland lying in the snow with Dalton standing over him.

When Dalton reaches down, Sutherland balls up like a hedgehog, earning a grunt of disgust from Dalton as he pulls Sutherland to his feet.

"What the hell are you doing out here?" Dalton says.

"I wanted to help. I heard you were going after the guy who tried to kill me, and I wanted to be there."

"We have no fucking idea if this *is* the guy."

"Which is why I came. So I can ID him. If it isn't, that'll save you bringing him back. If it is, then you can make him tell you where he's holding Nicki."

"How will you ID him?" I say as I walk over. "You never got a decent look at your attacker."

"I saw him in the forest, when he chased me back to Rockton."

"I saw that guy, too. Which means I can ID him . . . as the guy who chased you back to Rockton. Not necessarily the person who attacked you last night or the one who took Nicole."

He stares at me. "But it's the same person. There's no way it *can't* be."

Dalton lets him go. "There are a hundred fucking ways it might not be the same person. That's why we have a goddamn detective in Rockton. To make sure it's him before we ship an innocent man down south, and then the real guy takes another victim."

"He killed two women. Held Nicki captive in a cave. Tried to kill me—twice. And is that all you're going to do? Ship him down south?"

"And what do you suggest?" Dalton says.

"If I can ID him?" He nods at Anders. "I hear Will's a good shot. Accidents happen."

Dalton wheels with a snarl that sends Sutherland staggering back. Cypher grabs Sutherland by the scruff of the neck.

"You want to take a swing at him, Eric? Aim for the kidneys. It'll hurt like hell but he'll be fine."

"If I wanted to take a swing at him, I would have, and I sure wouldn't do it with someone holding him."

"Good answer. The second part, at least. Not so sure about the first. At the very least"—he gives Sutherland a hard joggle—"maybe we can shake some sense into him."

"I was just saying—" Sutherland began.

"Fucking bullshit is what you were saying," Cypher says, tossing him aside. "What'd you do down south? Some damned office job, I bet. Push papers all day, go home and watch a cop show, see them send the bad guy to prison and tell yourself they're cowards, a real man woulda put a bullet through the fucker. Which only proves you've probably never even thrown a punch in your life, got no goddamn idea what it means to take a life. You think you're a man? You don't go telling a cop he should 'accidentally' shoot a perp. You do it yourself. I see that knife in your pocket. We catch this guy, we'll hold him down, let you take care of his worthless ass."

"Hell, no," Dalton says. "We are not—"

"I was making a point, boy. I'd be happy to hold Roger down for this office drone. He'd drop his damned knife and run. The point—" He grabs Sutherland before the other man can escape. "The point is that you don't ever call someone else a coward for not pulling that trigger. You want it done? You do it. Otherwise, *they're* not the fucking coward."

"Sun's dropping," Anders says.

Dalton nods. "I know. I'm going to need to ask you to escort Shawn back . . ." He trails off and murmurs, "Fuck," under his breath. He glances at me. I subtly shake my head. We can't afford to lose Anders, in case this turns out to be a trap. Nor, however, can we bring Sutherland along.

"I'll hang back," Sutherland says. "I'll be fine." He pulls that sheathed hunting knife from his parka pocket. "Whatever this jerk says, I'm not going to just stand there while someone attacks me. I made the choice to come out here. I'll live with the consequences."

"Or die with them," Cypher mutters. "Which all things considered, might not be the biggest loss in the world."

FIFTY-TWO

Sutherland is lagging behind, and he's acting as if he's being respectful, but there's a hangdog quality to it, like a kid dragging his feet because he's been scolded. It's pissing off the guys. These aren't men who can muster much sympathy for a guy like Shawn Sutherland. Cypher can obviously be a bully. Dalton isn't, but he can play the part. Anders can't even fake it, yet like Dalton, his problem with people like Sutherland is not that they can't throw a punch—it's that they seem incapable of looking after themselves and unwilling to learn. They really are, as Cypher said, the average citizen who expects the police or the army to protect them, that being their tax-given right, and any failure in that task leads to armchair-quarterback griping.

It isn't about physical strength. It's about being capable. Being able to protect yourself by strength or speed or wits or sheer resourceful-ness, and if you can't do any of the above, then don't come running into the forest, where others have to take care of you, diverting them from their task.

I do feel sympathy for Sutherland. He's been through hell, and he's trying to be helpful. He's just not cut out for it. But then I wonder whether I'd be as quick to cut a woman the same slack. I have no patience with damsel-in-distress syndrome, and if a woman pulled this crap, that's what I'd accuse her of—getting attention by putting herself in harm's way and making others look after her. And maybe, if it was a woman, the guys would cut her that slack while I got pissy, a weird co-gender bias, where we have less patience for weakness among our own.

Even if I do feel bad for Sutherland, I don't fall back to chat and make him feel better. There's someone else who needs my support more.

"The militia aren't trained for this," I say to Dalton as we walk. He glances over, and I continue, "That's what you're thinking. That they have, once again, failed in their duties, this time letting Sutherland escape."

"Goddamn comedy of errors," he mutters.

"Because they've trained to guard the town, not individuals."

"Then the fault lies with the fucking idiot in charge—"

"That'd be me," Anders says.

Dalton glances over. "What?"

"I train the militia, Eric. I'm their direct supervisor. That makes me the idiot. Yes, I know, you meant yourself. You hire them. You *help* train them. But they report to me. They're my responsibility. So unless you were going to say I'm the idiot—"

"Course not."

"Then shut up. This isn't about blame. Well, not unless we can blame the dumb-ass who escaped protective custody without stopping to think he was going to cause trouble for the guys trying to look after him. Casey's right. The militia isn't trained for this. *We* aren't trained for this."

"You know what your problem is, boy?" Cypher says to Dalton.

I wince. "I'm pretty sure he doesn't want to know."

"Like I'm pretty sure you're going to tell him anyway," Anders mutters.

"Your problem is a lack of options," Cypher says. "How many people in Rockton have actual law enforcement background? Anyone besides her?" He hooks a thumb at me. "Dollars to donuts, the answer's no."

I open my mouth to say Anders does, but he shakes his head, telling me not to bother. Cypher has a point, and, damn it, he's going to make it.

Cypher continues, "You don't get a lot of cops in Rockton, and that's not because they need protection less than the average person. It's a matter of statistics. For every cop, you're going to get five office drones, four shop clerks, three factory workers, two schoolteachers, and a fucking partridge in a pear tree. And of the lot of them, you know who'd make the best militia goon? The goddamn partridge. Hell, when I came to Rockton, there wasn't a cop in the entire town. That's why they made me sheriff. A fucking hit man was the closest thing they had to someone with law enforcement experience."

"Hit man?" Anders says. "Tell me that's a joke. You . . ." He trails off, as if remembering Cypher saying he knew the value of a human life and had worked for people who didn't give a damn about it.

"Shit," Anders says. "A damn hit man."

"A damn *good* hit man. Like I said, I got one talent. But general talent of the criminal variety? That's what you need more of on your team, boy. If cops aren't an option, get yourself some guys who've spent time on the other side of the law. They know how to do the job. Am I right?"

"Why are you looking at me?" Anders says slowly.

"Oh, come on. Is it that big a secret? I saw those biceps of yours in the station. Saw part of that tat, too. Both are the product of some leisure time courtesy of the Canadian penitentiary system."

"No, both the product of some *hard-assed work* time courtesy of the *American army.*"

"Ah, so that's why you gave me that look when I talked about soldiers. Didn't argue, though, did you? You avoided jail by joining the army."

Anders's eyes slit now. "I beg your pardon?"

"Get your back down, boy. You know what I mean. Escaped the streets to make a life for yourself in the army. You get my respect for that more than if you'd spent time in jail. Only idiots get caught."

"The streets I grew up on were in a suburb," Anders says. "And the only gang I ever joined was the hall-monitor club in middle school, which I quit after the first month because they abused their power."

"Yeah, hall monitors can be nasty little pricks. First job I ever pulled was on one of them, back in grade eight." When Anders and I both stare at him, Cypher chuckles. "Oh, I'm kidding. Might have, though, if someone had offered me lunch money. But what you need to hire, Eric, is a few good criminals. No shortage of those in Rockton. And on that note, it's time to pipe down. We're almost there. Don't want Roger to hear company coming."

We spread out. Dalton goes into the woods, me following and taking up a position between him and Anders, who stays on the trail with Cypher. We walk about another hundred meters, until we can see a dip at the foot of the mountain, where Cypher claims Roger has set up camp. That's when Dalton signals Anders, who falls back temporarily to tell Sutherland to stay behind.

We get another hundred meters. I still can't see down into that dip, but Dalton motions for us to stop. Then he scales a tree. As he's going up, I gesture, asking if I can do the same. He nods.

I was never much of a tree climber in my youth. On my parents' list of approved childhood activities, it ranked just above trampolines, which they declared the greatest menace to children since the invention of the motor vehicle. But climbing is useful for doing exactly what Dalton was—getting a better vantage point.

I shimmy up the trunk until I reach a branch big enough to support me. By that time, Dalton is already stretched on a limb. He's alternating between looking at his target and glancing at me, to be sure I don't tumble to my doom. Once I'm stable, he turns his full attention to the scene below.

There is a campsite down there, with an old army tent, heavy canvas and low to the ground. The trampled snow suggests someone's been there for a while. Is that someone Roger? Or is this a well-constructed trap?

There's no sign of Roger himself. The campfire looks cold, no wisps of smoke or burning embers. I see none of the scattered detritus I expect at an active shelter site. Just a dead fire and a tent.

Dalton climbs down. I do the same, and by the time I reach the bottom, he's waiting.

"No sign he's there," I say. "The tent's closed, so I can't see inside. Like Tyrone said, it's a strategically located campsite, with no easy access for an ambush. If that means Roger is worried about an attack, he's not likely to nap midafternoon. I see plenty of foot trails coming and going. They seem to come from average-sized boots, and Tyrone does not have average-sized feet. But there's no way I'd call that solid evidence."

"Yeah," he says. In other words, he concurs and has nothing to add.

"I'm taking Ty and closing in," he says. "You and Will stay behind. Keep a wider view of the situation."

Dalton and Cypher begin a direct approach on the camp. If Roger's there, that'll trap him between the mountain and two lawmen.

When Dalton and Cypher begin down the dip, I move forward, keeping an eye on Dalton's back. If Cypher is going to attack, he'll swing behind and tackle him, getting Dalton on the ground as fast as he can.

I'm watching for that move when I hear a rustle behind me. Anders is standing ten meters away, poised and scanning the forest calmly, having heard nothing. I'm turning back to Dalton and Cypher when I catch a louder crackle and realize what it is.

Sutherland.

I madly gesture for Anders to stop Sutherland from getting closer. Anders nods, and he's taking off when I see a blur in the forest. A blur that is not Sutherland.

Someone is between Anders and Sutherland, and I can't run to find out who because that's not my priority. I have Dalton covered, and I cannot turn my back on him while Tyrone Cypher is at his side.

Anders picks up speed. He's spotted the third party. My gaze swings from Anders to Dalton, still creeping up on that tent, too far away to hear what's happening back here. Cypher is close beside him. *Too* close beside him.

Damn it, Eric, move away. Pay less attention to that tent and more—

Dalton wheels. He shoves Cypher hard, and the big man staggers, and I run forward, my gun out. Cypher lunges at Dalton with a roar. Dalton dives out of his way and comes back, ducking Cypher's swing and grabbing his arm, wrenching it behind his back, which would be the perfect move—if Cypher was in any mood to consider the ramifications of a broken arm. But he's a bull seeing red, and when Dalton gets his arm in a lock, he heaves, bucking.

Behind me, Anders shouts, "Stop!" Of course it doesn't work—there's no way the two men can hear him. I'm running. Dalton has Cypher in a headlock, down on one knee, and the big man is still bucking and writhing, and Dalton's shouting at him to stop, just fucking stop, you goddamned idiot. Cypher doesn't stop, and Dalton shoves him to the ground, one foot on his neck. I race down the incline, mouth opening to tell Cypher I've got a gun on him—not that I expect he'll care. That's when Cypher does stop. Completely stops. And says, "Huh."

I follow his gaze and see a snow-covered metal bear trap, jaws wide.

"Yeah," Dalton says. "*Huh.* I saved your foot, you idiot."

"You coulda said that."

"I tried, but you were bellowing like a damned—"

"No!" Anders's shout rings through the forest. I turn and scramble back up the incline. I see Anders running, and I realize he wasn't yelling at Cypher to stop—he was yelling at the guy he'd been chasing. Who has stopped. He's looking in Anders's direction, and behind him is Sutherland, running toward him as fast as he can, knife drawn.

"Shit!" I say, and I break into a run, but I know it's too late. Anders is only about twenty meters from the man, and even he's not going to make it in time. Sutherland is almost on him, and Anders shouts, "Don't you dare! He's standing down. He's not—"

Sutherland tackles the man, who's been staring at Anders in confusion, trying to figure out what the hell Anders is yelling. Sutherland and the stranger go down. Sutherland raises his knife, and Anders shouts at him to stop. Then Anders is slipping, trying to run faster than he can in snow, and he goes down hard on one knee.

Sutherland stabs the man. The blade rises and falls over and over, blood arcing, red dotting the snow. I'm yelling, Dalton's yelling, and then Anders is back on his feet, and he's running, and Sutherland just keeps stabbing. I see Sutherland's face, and I shout instead for Anders to stop. Please stop. Stay back.

But there's no way Anders *can* stop when someone is being murdered in front of him. He grabs Sutherland, and the hysterical man swings the knife. Anders says, "Hey!" and avoids the blade. He backs up, one hand extended as Sutherland snarls, frothing mad, hunkered down and dripping with blood.

"Hey, now," Anders says, his voice low, soothing. "You don't want to do this, Shawn." He keeps one hand up, warding off Sutherland while the other hand slides to his holstered gun. "Just put the knife down and—"

Sutherland lunges.

FIFTY-THREE

Anders tries to back away, but he slips in the snow again and falls flat on his back. Sutherland raises the knife. I fire. The bullet whizzes past Sutherland, but it's enough to startle him.

"Yes," I say, as I keep advancing. "That was a warning shot. You won't get a second, so put down that knife."

He's heaving breath, blood dripping down his face, and my mind shoots back to high school, reading *Lord of the Flies*. Is this what we truly are? Always one step away from this. From cracking. From losing whatever keeps us from attacking anyone who comes between us and what we want.

Standing over a man with a knife. Walking up to a man with a gun. It's all the same really. For some, that barrier is harder to crack. Not with me.

I say, "I'll shoot you, Shawn. If you even twitch in Will's direction, I will shoot you," and that's no idle threat. I will. I must.

"It's okay, Casey," Anders says. "Everything's under control."

"No," I say. "Everything will be under control when he drops that knife. Throw it toward me, Shawn. Or I will shoot."

"Shawn?" Dalton calls behind me as he runs up. "Do as she says, okay? Will was just trying to help."

Sutherland doesn't see us. Doesn't hear us. Not really. All he sees is the deputy who tried to stop him, and that makes Anders a threat.

"Drop the knife," I say. "On the count of five, you will drop that knife, or I will fire."

"No one wants to hurt you," Dalton says. "Drop the knife and step away from Will."

Sutherland only adjusts his grip on the knife, his gaze fixed on Anders.

"Five," I call. "Four—"

Anders kicks Sutherland in the leg and rolls fast as his attacker drops, knife stabbing down, hitting the ground right where Anders had been.

Dalton and Cypher are both on Sutherland in an instant. He slashes, catching Cypher in the sleeve, but they get him down, spread-eagled, as Anders pulls the knife from his grip.

"You're lucky," I say to Anders. "That could have gone all kinds of wrong."

Anders shrugs. "Worth a try. I didn't want you shooting him."

"I wouldn't have aimed to kill."

"I don't give a shit about him. I didn't want you having to shoot." He squeezes my shoulder with his free hand as he jogs over to the man on the ground.

Dalton says, "Just get him out of my sight," presumably to Cypher about Sutherland, as I run with Anders to the downed man.

"You said I couldn't do it," Sutherland says, his voice rising. "You said I couldn't, and I did."

"Fuck," Cypher mutters. "Me and my big mouth."

"Is this Roger?" I ask Cypher.

"Yeah."

"I did it," Sutherland says. "I got the guy. It's him. Casey, look at him."

I *am* looking at Roger. What I see is blood. So much blood. I glance at his face in passing, assessing the worst injuries as I drop beside him. Yes, it is the man from behind my house, the one I saw the night Sutherland escaped back to Rockton. And I don't care. There are bigger issues to worry about. Namely the fact that his chest is perforated with stab wounds.

"It's him," Sutherland says as Anders and I scramble to get Roger's jacket off. "It's the guy. He took me. He took Nicole."

"And if you killed him?" Dalton says. "Then you killed her, too."

"What? N-no. I . . . I . . ." Sutherland trails off in a stream of babble. There might be actual words in it. I don't hear them. I'm completely focused on Roger, and even if he's our killer that doesn't matter because, as Dalton said, he is also the only one who knows where to find Nicole.

Dalton lowers himself beside me to help. "Fuck. He's a mess. *Fuck.*" He inhales. "And that's not helpful. Tell me what to do."

"Roger's in shock," Anders says. "I need to get him stable and get him out of here. The first step is to stop the bleeding, which right now . . . shit, I'm not even sure where to start." He inhales. "No, I've got this. Get his shirt off. We need to assess and triage."

Between the three of us, we manage to peel off Roger's blood-sodden shirt, and when we see the extent of the damage, Dalton lets out a fresh curse.

Anders freezes. He's crouched in the snow over Roger's prone body, hands gloved with blood, more dripping down his arms. Roger's chest slick with blood and stippled with gore. It's slashed open, muscles and intestine poking through. I've seen photos of servicemen ripped up by shrapnel, and that's what it looks like, and Anders stares at his blood-covered hands and this man's blood-soaked torso, red seeping into the snow around us.

"I don't see any bubbling," I say. "That means his lungs may be okay. There's nothing near his heart either. So the first thing we need to do is—"

"Yes," Anders says, snapping back to himself. "I've got this. Eric? I need the first-aid kit. I put my pack down over there. Casey? Hold this right here. We can't worry about internal injury. This is triage. You can stitch, right?"

"I can."

"Then help me with these two worst ones, and then we'll divide the rest. Get him stable and pray he survives long enough to tell us where to find Nicki."

———

We're back in Rockton. I have no idea what time it is, only that it's dark and has been dark since long before we returned. We found a makeshift sled at Roger's tent and managed to get him here alive, which is a massive accomplishment. *Keeping* him alive will be an even tougher one. We've been working on that for hours, Anders and Mathias and I, with Dalton and Diana ready to grab whatever we need.

We have to reopen some of the stitches to access what we couldn't mend in the field. That's probably the last thing Roger's system needs, but we have him doped up on enough morphine that he's out cold, and we hope that forfends shock. There's no sign of serious internal injury . . . which only means no one attending him has the know-how to make that call unless one of his systems fails. And if it does? Well, he's screwed, because we don't have the know-how to *fix* it either.

If there is any saving grace, it is that Sutherland stabbed wildly, his blade often slicing only through the skin. Roger's chest is a mess, and maybe that in itself will prove too much, but by the time we're done, he's stable and resting.

Anders goes next door for a shower. I stay in the clinic, sitting on the cleanest piece of floor I can find. Dalton's quietly mopping up, giving me room to breathe.

"We need to get him to a doctor," I say.

"I know."

"Is that possible? What's the contingency plan here?"

He hands me a glass of water. "Val contacted the council. They're 'considering the matter.' Which means we do need a contingency plan, in case they say fuck it and tell us to let nature take its course, considering he's probably a killer."

"And Nicole?"

"I made that clear. We're not asking to keep a killer alive for humanitarian reasons. We need him alive to find out where he's put Nicole."

"If he hasn't already killed her."

Dalton lowers himself onto the floor. "Jacob's right, Casey. There's no point in taking Nicole only to kill her. He'd have saved himself the hassle and killed her in bed. A big 'fuck you' to us."

"What if it wasn't her captor who took her? What if it was someone else?"

"Someone else?"

I close my eyes and lean back against the wall. "Ignore me. I'm tired and rambling."

He moves closer, until his legs brush mine. "No, you're not. Something's going on in that head of yours. It's been going on for a while, and now it's clicked."

"I've just been . . . I don't know. Trying to figure out where the hostiles come from. Whether there's a connection to the council. How coincidental is it that Val was attacked after they encouraged her to go on patrol? Then they covered up what happened, so you couldn't investigate."

"You think they did what they accused me of? Orchestrated it?"

I rub my face. "It doesn't matter. Not right now. Hostiles didn't take Nicole. It just made me wonder what else the council could do. What *would* they do, if it's to their benefit? Tyrone said it's a good thing we didn't let Nicole leave. He seems sure they'd have killed her. Except she wasn't threatening to tell anyone about Rockton. I made it up. I thought I was so damned clever, beating them at their own game. What if I . . . ?" I look at him. "What if I did this? I made them think she was a threat so they took her and attacked Shawn to convince us it was our guy?"

"But Nicole *wasn't* an exposure threat, Casey. She was staying here."

"Maybe the council couldn't take that chance. If she raised enough fuss, you might fly her out. If we discovered injuries we missed, you might fly her out. Regardless of what they said, you might fly her out. They can't trust you. You'll put the residents first."

He's quiet, face drawn, eyes clouded with worry, and that's not what I want. I want arguments.

I continue, "Jacob was surprised that Nicole's captor would dare come into Rockton and take her. Tyrone was, too. It is ballsy. Incredibly ballsy. Especially for someone who isn't from Rockton, doesn't know how the town works, what the house layouts look like, how to get in and out, how to access our drug supply. Roger wouldn't know any of that. He's a second-generation settler."

"But he was asking about law enforcement."

"And not getting any answers. Not enough to let him break in and take her." I run my hands through my hair. "I'm not saying Roger couldn't have done it. But we know the council has people here. Spies. The only one we can identify . . ."

Dalton shakes his head. "It's not Will. Yeah, I know, consider all options. Not Will, though."

Anders is indeed one of the council spies. Planted to keep tabs on Dalton, but he abandoned that long ago, his loyalty firmly with his sheriff.

"Will was at home and in bed moments after Shawn was attacked," I say. "Whoever did this can't be anyone we'd roust to help with the search, not if he had to get Nicole out of Rockton."

"The boot prints . . ."

"They were roughly the same size as Nicole's captor's. But in that kind of snow, it wasn't possible to say the tread was a match."

We go quiet. Then Dalton says, "The plan with Nicole—telling the council she might be an exposure threat—we agreed on that. You came up with it, but we all agreed. Not one of us thought it could put her in danger. You never said Nicole threatened to expose us, only that you feared she might report the crime, which could endanger Rockton. That's pure conjecture. And what about Diana? She *is* an exposure threat, but they haven't taken any action except making her finish her term." He looks at me. "You had no reason to think your suggestion would endanger Nicole."

I don't answer.

"For now, focus on Roger," he says. "We need to wake him up and speak to him."

FIFTY-FOUR

Roger is awake. Awake and yet not alert, floating in that semiconscious state where he can respond to questions but isn't fully aware of what's happening. Not aware enough to formulate a lie. Questioning him in that condition violates his rights, but no one here gives a shit.

The only problem with Roger's condition is that he isn't entirely coherent either. We're left sifting through the flotsam and jetsam his muddled brain throws out.

"He attacked—he attacked—he attacked—" That's how it begins, when I ask Roger what he remembers. He gets stuck there, like a record unable to complete a revolution.

"He attacked you," I say. "Do you know why?"

"Girl. The girl." He finds my face, and his scrunches up. "You? Yes, you. In the forest."

"You saw me in the forest. During the storm. You attacked me."

"Attacked? No. The storm . . . Yes. But not then. After. With him."

I struggle not to put words into his mouth. "Where were you when you first saw me?"

"In the forest. During the storm. You had her. His girl."

"Whose girl?"

"His."

"You saw me during the storm."

"Yes. You. With him." He nods toward Anders. "You had her. You'd found her. In the cave."

"Did you see me later, during that storm? Alone?"

He shakes his head. "Went home. Needed to sort it out. What I heard. What I saw."

"What did you hear and see?"

"You two. With her. In a cave. He put her in a cave."

"He? Who is—?"

"You got her out. You two. Saw you."

"And the *next* time you saw me?"

"Behind the village. In the forest. With a dog. A puppy."

"What were you doing there?"

"Chasing him."

"The man you were chasing?" I word it carefully. "When's the last time you saw *him*?"

His face screws up. "When he attacked me. You were there. I heard you. Saw you."

"*That's* the man you were chasing?"

"Yes."

"Why?"

"To catch him."

A grunt of frustration from Anders. I nod, echoing the sentiment.

"Why were you trying to catch him?" I ask.

"Because he took that woman. Kept her in a cave. I saw him in the storm. Running from you and him." He glances at Anders. "Then he disappeared, and you found the girl. The one he took. I heard you say she'd been kept in a cave. So I knew that's why you were chasing him."

My heart sinks as I realize what's happened. I say, "And then *you* chased him. From where?"

"The forest. I went looking. For him. To help you. I saw him. He ran."

"You chased him here?"

He nods. "He was already heading this way. By accident. So I helped.

I'd asked around. I knew that was the right thing. You'd handle it here. You have police here. This is where he needed to go."

"Shit," Anders murmurs.

Shit, indeed.

I keep interrogating Roger, but after that brief spurt of semilucidity, he fades fast. I try to ask if he was the one in my house that night. I try to ask if he has a dark snowmobile suit. I try to ask every damned question I have, but he falls into drugged confusion, mumbling about someone named Benjamin and, yep, that's where I lose any hope of getting something sensible from him. I'll have to wait until tomorrow.

We're in the Red Lion eating dinner. It closed nearly an hour ago, but when we walked in with no clue about the time, the staff insisted on staying to make us dinner. Now they've gone home and the three of us are alone in the restaurant, eating venison steaks by the light of a single flickering candle.

"So, it seems we have a tragic case of mistaken identity," I say as I cut into my meat.

Dalton grunts.

"Double mistaken identity," Anders says. "Roger sees us chasing Shawn and then later escorting Nicole. He overhears enough to know she was being held captive and jumps to the conclusion *that's* why we were chasing Shawn. Because Shawn must have taken Nicole. Then Roger spots Shawn escaping from Nicole's real captor and goes after him. Shawn figures *Roger* is his captor and keeps running toward Rockton, which is conveniently where Roger wants him to go. Roger figures he's saved the day, turning in a killer. And what does he get for it? Attacked by Shawn. Which leaves us . . ."

"Absolutely fucking nowhere," Dalton says. "The real culprit is still on the run. Nicole's still missing. And we still have—" He stops himself.

"No idea whodunit," I say. "A detective who's running in circles, ending up nowhere."

"No." He catches my look as I reach for my beer. "*No.*"

"We've had a setback," Anders says. "That's all. What we need is another round of these"—he points at our beers—"and then a really good sleep."

I'm sitting on the deck off Dalton's bedroom. He's asleep inside. I managed to shore up my spirits after my pity party at the Lion. He kept watching for a relapse, but we finished the meal and the second round of beers and retrieved Storm, and if I seemed to have moved past that, he wasn't going to bring it up.

I hadn't moved past. I just don't do pity parties very well. So I fake-crashed into sleep, and once he'd drifted off, I crept out to the deck. Storm followed, and now we're huddled under a mountain of blankets, listening to the sounds of the forest.

Only about ten minutes pass before the door squeaks. I start to rise, but Dalton lowers himself beside me.

"We'll go inside," I say. "I just needed a minute."

He puts his leg over mine, keeping me in place. "Seems like you need a few more than that."

"I don't. I'm sorry. I hate whining and complaining."

"Yeah, you do a lot of that. It's hard to hear myself think, much less sleep. You gotta keep it down." He pushes against my hip, arm sliding behind me, leg still over mine, Storm adjusting to lie over both our laps. "Your idea of whining, Casey, is a split-second whimper, followed by five minutes of apologies for disturbing anyone."

"I feel like I'm whining."

"That's a whole different thing." He shifts closer, pulling me against him. "Back at the Lion, I was venting. You gotta let me do that without twisting it into criticism. You know it's not."

I nod.

"You ready to come inside?"

I hesitate, staring at the slowly falling snow.

"Yeah, okay," he says. "That's a good idea. You sleep better out here."

He starts rearranging the blankets into a bed and moves Storm to the foot of it. When she tries to sneak back up, a soft growl of warning makes her lie down, sighing. He lays a blanket over her.

I shake my head. "It's cold. You won't sleep."

"Then you'll just need to find a way to warm me up," he says and pulls me down under the covers.

I wake to someone banging on the front door, and I decide I don't hear it. I'm warm under the pile of blankets, curled up with my head on Dalton's chest, Storm draped over his stomach, my one hand on her, feeling her heartbeat as I listen to Dalton's. Even the bite of winter's chill on my nose is almost pleasant, as if reminding me how good I have it otherwise, snuggled up under these blankets.

The banging continues.

Dalton doesn't stir. Neither does Storm. And I decide that's proof enough, it doesn't exist. I've been woken twice this week by someone at the door. A third time is statistically impossible.

I bury my icy nose against Dalton, and his arms tighten around me. He murmurs in his sleep, no words I can make out, but it's a contented murmur. When I shift, Storm sighs but again, it's a contented sigh.

See? No one's at the door. I'm dreaming, and when I wake, it'll be morning, and I'll sneak inside to make coffee and start breakfast, and Dalton will smell both and come down to take over the cooking and let me curl up in front of the fireplace. I'll sip my coffee and warm myself by the fire with my puppy and watch my lover cook for me and marvel at what I could possibly have done in my life to deserve such good fortune.

That's how my morning will go. It will be peaceful and perfect and—

"Answer the goddamned door!" Jen's voice shouts. "I know you're both in there."

I squeeze my eyes shut.

Jen shouts again. Storm jumps up and joins in with an answering howl. I lunge to grab her. Dalton grunts and half opens one unfocused eye.

"Is that . . . ," he begins.

"No," I say. "Go back to sleep, and when you wake up, she'll be gone."

"Good." He pulls me down, still holding the puppy, and drapes an arm over us as he closes his eyes again.

"You're on the balcony?" Jen calls as she tramps around the back. "What the hell are you doing on the balcony?"

Dalton rises on one arm to glower down at her.

"You're naked on the balcony?" she says. "In the middle of winter? Is this some kind of weird Northern sex thing?"

Dalton yanks up the blanket over his shoulders. Storm leaps past him and growls at Jen.

"What the hell is the dog doing—" she begins. "No, forget I asked. *That's* a weird sex thing you guys can totally keep to yourselves."

"We are sleeping," Dalton says. "Where we choose to do it is our own goddamn business."

"Sleeping on the balcony? In winter? When there's a warm bed a few feet away? I guess congratulations are in order, Sheriff. You found a girlfriend who's as weird as you."

"Get off my fucking—"

"You need to come to the clinic."

I scramble up, keeping a strategically held blanket in place. "What?"

"I was on watch duty. Something's . . . wrong. I'll meet you there."

FIFTY-FIVE

We don't get a chance to ask Jen what happened. Or tell her that if it's a medical emergency, she should be getting Anders.

We dress fast and take off. Dalton detours to fetch Anders as I race into the clinic. Jen waits in the back room. Roger is where we left him, on the examining table, which comes complete with a removable foam mattress, sheets, side rails and restraints. In Rockton, everything serves a dual purpose.

"What's the emergency?" I say as I walk in.

Jen points at Roger.

"He seems fine." I walk over and gently peel back the sheet, careful not to disturb his sleep. "Did his bleeding start again?"

"I'm not a doctor, but I think that'd be a medical miracle."

I look at her. She jabs a finger at Roger.

I turn back to him. His eyes are closed. His color's fine, but I lay my hand on his forehead, in case he's running a fever.

His forehead is cool.

No, his forehead is cold.

My hand flies to the side of his neck and then down to his wrist.

"He . . . he's . . ."

"He's dead, Jen?" she says.

I glare at her.

"Not a *Star Trek* fan, I take it," she says. "Your kind never are."

"I got the reference. The man is dead, Jennifer, which is really not the time to be cracking jokes. Or to be testing my powers of detection. *Goddamn it.*"

I grab the stethoscope to listen to his heart.

"Yeah, that's not going to be beating," she says. "The whole being-dead thing."

"Just because he appears to be dead doesn't absolutely mean he is."

"So he's only mostly dead?"

"Get out."

"I—"

"You sauntered across town to bring us some cryptic message, when maybe—just maybe—fetching Will instead could have saved this man. But no, it's really more fun to stand by his body and mock me with cinema lines."

Her jaw sets, and she says, "I didn't saunter. I ran. And it wasn't a cryptic message. I just didn't know what to say. As for getting Will, I used the stethoscope. I knew there was no point."

Anders runs in, Dalton right behind him. "What's the—"

Anders stops short and says, "Shit," seeing Roger, now lolling to one side, an arm dangling. He hurries over and checks for a pulse.

"I was just telling Jen that she should have gotten you first. In case there was a chance to fix this."

"Yeah, no," Anders says. "I can't fix dead."

He gets my glower now but meets it with a quarter smile. "Sorry. But no, he's been gone for a while."

When Jen opens her mouth in victory, he shoots her a look and says, "Though she still should have gotten me first. That's proper protocol, which she'd know if she'd read the handbook I gave her. You want to be militia, Jen? It's about more than standing guard. It's following procedure. It's *knowing* procedure. And it's getting off your ass to check your charge once in a while. Whatever shit you've been spouting about my guys this week? None had their charge *die* on them."

I brace for a sarcastic retort. She just stands there and takes it.

"Can you tell us what happened?" I say, as calmly as I can. "Walk us through it."

"I got in and talked to Paul—I was taking over from him. He said Roger was fine, and he did seem okay, so I sat down and read. I had my watch set to check him every hour, like the schedule says."

She waits, as if expecting a head pat. I allow a grudging, "Good. And then?"

"On my first check, he wasn't breathing. I thought I was mistaken. But I checked his pulse and used the stethoscope, and it was clear that he was gone. Succumbed to his injuries. If it was a natural death, I'd notify Will, as the coroner. But I figured, since the guy didn't fall on that knife twenty times by himself, that makes it homicide. Which goes to the detective."

"You would still get me first," Anders says. "Both as head of the militia and the coroner. Okay?"

She nods.

"Did anyone else come in during your shift?"

She shakes her head, and we dismiss her.

Roger does indeed appear to have "succumbed to his injuries." Naturally, we still check him, and the answer appears to be confirmed when we discover bloody froth in his mouth, which suggests his lungs actually *were* damaged. We open him up. I leave the cutting to Anders, but as a cop, I was known for my iron-clad stomach, which means I've attended enough autopsies that I could practically conduct one myself. Which is what I do here, leading Anders through the steps.

One of Roger's lungs has collapsed and filled with blood. That's what killed him. A cut pierced a lung. Which means "succumbing to his injuries" is not the cause of death.

It's murder.

There's no way we missed that injury. It doesn't take twelve hours for a punctured lung to collapse. And we didn't give Roger nearly enough morphine to sleep through a collapsed lung. But according to Jen, he never even gasped, and when I found him, he looked as if he had indeed passed in his sleep. You can't fake that level of post-mortem peace.

When we check the morphine drip, it's been cranked up high enough that he'd have slept through another stabbing. Which he did, in a way, as someone inserted a thin blade and slid it into his lung.

The big question was *when* it happened. There's only one likely possibility.

We get Paul to the clinic without telling him that Roger has died. I start by asking exactly when Jen took over the watch shift and how the handover occurred.

He tries to say she came by as scheduled, no issues, but I keep pressing and—with Dalton standing there, arms crossed—Paul finally cracks.

"She was late," he says. "I didn't want to get her in trouble. I promised I wouldn't."

"This is important," I say, and add a lie with, "We already knew she was late, so you aren't tattling. You're clarifying. How late was she?"

"Will told her if she wanted a second shift, she had to get some sleep and come back at three. Three thirty came and went, and I started drifting off."

"Did you?"

"No way. I stepped outside to get some cold air, and I saw her coming."

"So you waited for her."

I phrase it as a statement, and he nods. When I ask how far away she was, he seems confused. I'm trying to establish how long no one was in the room with Roger—I just don't want Paul realizing that and fudging his answer.

"Was she definitely heading here?" I ask. "Or just wandering after a night out?"

"Oh, okay. She was heading here but taking her sweet time. Even when she saw me waiting, she didn't kick it in gear. I gave her shit when she finally got here. I told her she was nearly forty-five minutes late, and that's not how militia act, and it was my duty to report it to Will."

"But instead you promised to cover for her."

Paul shifts his weight. I keep pressing until he says, "She felt bad, and she wanted to make it up to me, so she, uh, gave me a hand."

"Gave you a hand with what?" Dalton says.

We both turn to look at him. It takes a second. Then Dalton says, "Fuck."

"Nope," I say. "Just a hand."

Paul reddens. "I didn't pay for it. I wouldn't. I know Isabel hates Jen freelancing. I mean, not that I'd pay for it anyway. But since Jen was offering it free, and I *was* kind of stressed, I didn't see any harm in accepting. It was quick."

"How quick?"

He goes even redder. "Not that quick. But she does know what she's doing and—"

I raise a hand. "No details required. I'm just establishing a timeline. Did this take place on the front step where you met her?"

I don't think it's possible for him to get redder. I'm wrong.

"It . . . started there. I mean, she, uh, reached in on the porch and then—"

Dalton cuts in. "Like Casey said, we don't need details. We know the mechanics of the operation. So it began on the porch and then continued inside where it was warmer. In the room where the patient was sleeping?"

"What? No. That would be wrong. We, uh, completed it here, in the front room. The door was closed, so even if he woke up, he wouldn't have seen anything. That'd be disrespectful."

I don't continue pressing for an exact timing. I doubt he had a stopwatch running. Dalton dismisses him, watches him go and then says, "Way more information than I needed."

"But just the amount I needed," I say. "String it all together, and Roger was alone in that room long enough for someone to break in the back and do the damage. Which works with the time line. Jen took over, and he seemed fine, but by her first check, he was dead."

"Murdered," Dalton says. "And I *quadrupled* perimeter patrols last night. Which means we can be almost certain no one snuck in from the forest to do this. And if this was a local, then Nicole's capture probably was, too."

"I think we can stop saying *probably*. We have a killer in Rockton. Again."

FIFTY-SIX

A few hours ago, I'd pictured my perfect breakfast. Hot fire, hot coffee, hot boyfriend cooking over a hot stove. I get all of that. Dalton has forbidden me to join Nicole's search party at first light. We'd be taking spots better given to people who are physically rested and mentally alert.

So I get a quiet start to my day. I even have the warm puppy nestled on my lap. What I don't get, though, is perhaps the most important part of that fantasy—the peace of mind to enjoy it all. I'm petting Storm and sipping my coffee and watching Dalton, and I'm barely registering any of it, my brain immersed in Roger's murder, the implications and the possibilities.

"There's something we need to discuss," Dalton says as he slides an egg onto my plate. "An issue we probably should have discussed four months ago."

"Personal or professional?"

"The intersection of the two."

"Ah, the tricky kind."

He finishes serving breakfast, and we sit on the sofa and eat half of it in hungry silence before he says, "When we got together, you said me being your boss would be a problem. I didn't understand why. But now I get it. Here"—he motions around the room—"we're equal partners. I'm better at cooking, so I do that. You've got a different idea of what 'tidy' means, so you do that. It all works out. In the office, I'm in charge, and you don't seem to have a problem taking orders from your boyfriend."

"Because I'm not—I'm taking orders from my commanding officer. And when we leave the office, you never keep trying to give me orders. We're good at separating those roles."

"But sometimes that separation isn't so easy." He takes a bite of his toast and chews. "As sheriff, I'm entrusted with secrets. Some would be helpful to your job, and I'd like to share them because knowing you as *more* than my detective, I know I can trust you with them."

"Except they aren't your secrets to share."

"That's the problem. But there is discretionary wiggle room. You've read my notes on what I suspect about residents. Those here under false pretenses."

"Which are secrets you uncovered. Not ones you were entrusted with."

He takes another bite of toast. Chews slowly. "So by that token, am I obligated to tell you everything I've uncovered?"

"You aren't *obligated* to tell me anything, Eric."

"Ethically obligated." He stops, shakes his head. "No, that's still the wrong phrasing. *Ethically,* I can tell you, because I uncovered it myself so it's become my secret to share. But there are things I uncover that aren't in that book. Just stuff I stumble over and file away here." He taps his forehead.

"You can't be expected to share all of that." I put down my fork. "I know we're circling the theoretical, slowly approaching a specific."

"Just get to the damned specific?" He puts his plate down. "Yeah, I'm still feeling this shit out. I'm used to being in charge. Sheriff *and* detective, the only person who needed to know anything until I was damned well ready to share. I wasn't deliberately withholding. I just never considered telling you this until I realized, fuck, I should have said something and now—"

"Absolution comes *after* confession, Eric."

"It's about Mathias. I told you and Will why he's here. There's more. Something I found a couple years back while double-checking his story."

"A hole in it."

"Hell, no. I'd have shared that right away. This is just additional information that didn't seem pertinent until I thought about who could have killed Roger."

"Mathias fits. I've been thinking that myself. He had access to Roger. He has the medical know-how to pierce that lung and crank up the morphine drip. A practicing doctor would know we'd see through it, but he's never practiced medicine."

He nods. "When I was researching Mathias's story, I came across one of those . . . what's the word? When someone writes online about a subject they're interested in? Essays and such?"

"Blogs?"

"Right. I found this blog by a guy who liked weird crime. He covered Mathias's story about the patient who emasculated himself, and he linked it to another of Mathias's patients."

"Another guy who—?"

"No, not that. This guy was convicted of cannibalism. Fucking psycho. Hunted and killed people on the streets, homeless ones no one would miss. Cooked and ate them. The court found a shrink who got him committed. When Mathias studied the guy, he argued he wasn't insane at all. Just a sick bastard. Mathias wanted him retried on some loophole. Court refused. A month later, the guy disemboweled himself with a homemade shiv."

"And he claimed Mathias made him do it?"

Dalton shakes his head. "He died from his injuries. Never implicated Mathias. But this blog guy tied the two cases together as incidences of vigilante justice. He said Mathias brainwashed his patients into committing acts of self-mutilation befitting their crime."

"The cannibal slicing open his own stomach and the rapist cutting off his own genitals."

"Yep. Which is crazy. Unless . . ."

"Unless it's not." I finish my toast and then say, "I'd believe it if the victims claimed Mathias physically forced them to mutilate themselves. Hell, I'd even buy drugs as the answer. It's the brainwashing part that bothers me."

"Can't be done," Dalton says. "Mind control doesn't exist. The CIA sunk a shitload of time and money into chasing that pipe dream."

When I raise my brows, he says, "It's a matter of public record. I don't trade in Brent's crazy conspiracy theories. The CIA admitted to it. They were trying to build the perfect assassin, someone they could order to kill, who would then forget it, allowing full deniability. They couldn't do it even *with* drugs."

"So this is impossible."

Dalton takes the whistling kettle off for fresh coffee. "*That* is impossible—forcing someone to do something and then forget it. Which isn't what we're talking about. The guy who survived remembered. He fingered Mathias."

"So it's possible to control behavior? Just not reliably erase memory?"

"I don't know. I didn't study those CIA files. Just found a reference in a book so I chased it down. Satisfying my curiosity. There are ways to influence behavior. The power of suggestion and shit like that."

"Hypnosis," I say, remembering Anders's joke about Mathias. "In university, I went to a demonstration. I was curious, like you. It seemed more like people letting themselves be put into a suggestible state and then playing along. Which I guess is the power of suggestion. And I have seen shrinks pull up repressed memories with hypnosis so . . . I don't know."

"Neither do I. But is it *possible*? Put a guy with Mathias's training in a situation where he has total control over his subject, where no one's going to question his methods or drugs or whatever. Could he make a guy slice open his own guts, thinking he was butchering a deer?"

"I won't say it's *im*possible."

"Okay, so let's pretend Mathias did those things. He exacted fucked-up poetic justice on two pieces of scum. That'd be his motive for killing Roger. Taking justice into his own hands."

"But his MO is punishments befitting the crimes. Straight from Dante's *Inferno*. The Mathias we know would need his drama. He'd wait and figure out the perfect punishment. He'd also wait until we had Nicole."

"Fuck," Dalton has stopped making coffee and stands there.

"If you get stuck on motive, though, you stop seeing the facts. The fact is that Mathias fits for Roger's death. He even fits for Nicole's second capture. He made a point of being kind to her, which is unusual for him. He has access to the benzo and a reason to be in her house to dose her tea. Forget revenge. If we're looking at a council spy who got rid of Nicole and Roger, Mathias fits."

I lean back. "With a stretch, he fits for *all* of it. We decided he couldn't have taken Robyn because he arrived after she disappeared. But it was only a few months later. What if she left to live in the forest, and he found her there? The timeline isn't impossible, and that timeline was the only thing that kept him from being a suspect. He's thinner than Nicole reported, but size is easy to fake with extra clothing. He could also have faked the dark hair Sutherland saw. Mathias spent his life studying criminals. He would know how to do this and get away with it. Part of it could be him."

"Or all of it."

FIFTY-SEVEN

Dalton joins the search party after breakfast. As much as I want to, I have something else to do.

I'm at Val's. We haven't spoken of my theory about the council. When Dalton asked her to contact them about medical care for Roger, she didn't flinch or give him a hard time. She just took his request and reported back afterward.

Now she brings me in without a word. We sit in that damned living room, and it's like some kind of recurring nightmare where I keep looping back to the same place, with the same goal, making no progress. Like Dalton and that cat analogy. I keep trying to pet the cat, be the one person who treats it well in hopes I'll break through.

"I need to know if Mathias is one of the council's spies," I begin.

She tenses.

"I'm not asking you to give me a list," I say. "This is very specific and tied to the case."

"Until our discussion the other night, Casey, I wasn't aware that anyone acted in that capacity. Which sounds naive of me."

I point at the radio. "That is the one method of communication with the council. Which means those messages go through you."

"Yes, there are people who make reports, for various reasons. But I hear those, and I can honestly say that they aren't spying on anyone."

Like Anders, reporting on Dalton, which would seem like a backup account of police activity. The real purpose, of course, was to see where Dalton lied or hid acts of rebellion.

To Val, those reports would seem like simple checks on Dalton's power. If we do have true spies, whatever secrets they impart must be in encoded in their message. And yes, even thinking that makes me wonder if I should join Brent in his cave, swapping conspiracy theories.

But I still ask, "Does Mathias submit a report?"

"Yes. He provides psychological evaluations. General reports give his opinion of the overall mental health of the community. Specific ones deal primarily with an individual's propensity toward violence. That is his area of expertise, though, so it seemed proof that the council was indeed safeguarding citizens."

"*Seemed* proof? You're not so sure now?"

A pause. Then a quiet, "I'm not so sure of anything anymore."

And that is, I suppose, the best I can hope for. That Val is questioning. But questioning isn't the same as *questing,* trying to get answers, to take action. I'm not sure I can ever expect that from her.

"You said the specific ones deal *primarily* with violent tendencies. What else?"

"Various things. If Sheriff Dalton is having a problem with a citizen—one who seems particularly rebellious or difficult—council requests Mathias assess whether that person is a danger here or elsewhere."

"Elsewhere?"

"Once they leave. Or, if the council decided to cut a difficult resident's stay short, would that prove problematic."

"And by *problematic,* you mean whether they're an exposure risk."

"Yes."

"Let's say they are. In that case, as with Diana, they might not let them leave early. But what if they were at the end of their term? What if Mathias decides they'd be an exposure risk?"

"All residents are monitored after they leave Rockton. If Dr. Atelier found them to be a threat, I would presume they are more strictly monitored."

"Do you play any role in that monitoring? Receive feedback on how a resident is readjusting to life down south?"

She shakes her head. "Other areas of the council manage past residents."

"One more question, completely off topic. How did Nicole's brother die?"

She blinks. "Nicole's brother?"

"I know he was taken by a cartel. I know he was tortured. Do we have any indication that captivity was involved?"

More confused looks.

"I know it sounds like a strange question," I say. "But there is a point to it. Is there anything in the council's report that would indicate whether his torture happened quickly or over a period of time?"

"I believe he was held and tortured for several days, which is why she faked a similar situation herself."

"That's all I need. Thank you."

As I head for the front door, Val stays in the living room. I'm reaching for the doorknob when she says, "I know you are disappointed in me, Casey."

She appears in the living room doorway.

"You expected more," she says. "Better. I can only tell you that I need time. I *am* considering everything you said."

"Okay."

"You may also be disappointed because I haven't apologized to Sheriff Dalton. Please remember, however, that I believed what the council told me, and therefore my response was appropriate."

"So you feel you don't owe him an apology. Sure. Nor does he owe you one for the way he insulted and belittled and patronized *you* in response. Oh, wait. He didn't."

"I—"

"You already had preconceptions about Eric. What the council said only endorsed them. But Eric didn't mistreat you in return. So you can tell yourself you did nothing wrong, but the fact you feel the need to defend your decision proves you know better. For the record, though, he doesn't want an apology. He just wants you to do your job."

She lets me leave after that. Not a word of denial. Not one of acknowledgment either. She just lets me leave.

Dalton and I are in the clinic with Roger's body. Mathias is there. Anders is not. Our deputy doesn't have the acting skills for this. I'm not sure our sheriff does either, but he's behind Mathias, sitting and observing, saying nothing.

I've asked Mathias for a second opinion on the cause of death. All he knows is that we have a theory.

"Collapsed lung, obviously," Mathias says. "You have exposed the lung, which makes your findings easy to determine."

"I'm not making a game of it, Mathias. You can see what we've found. I'd like you to confirm it as cause of death."

"Cause of death is clearly that lung, given the fact it is collapsed and there is bloody froth in his mouth." He flips open Roger's eyelids. "Bloodshot eyes suggest suffocation. The fact he did not fight means he was receiving too much morphine. Which could suggest . . ." He checks Roger's lung. "There is a puncture lining up with a stab wound. Someone exacerbated the injury. Used a lancet or other thin object to bypass the ribs and puncture the lung."

"How do you figure that?"

"The wound has been stitched, yet it is open slightly at this end. There was no injury to the lung yesterday. I was here. There is also tissue damage consistent with a blade being inserted and removed." He points it out. "It may appear the killer knew what he was doing, but he was really only making an educated guess. Anyone with basic knowledge of anatomy could do the same."

Mathias taps the morphine pump. "This has been tampered with."

"How can you tell?"

"I cannot. But we know he slept through suffocation. I watched you and William pore over your notes, discussing exactly how much morphine this man needed. I know enough about sedatives to have agreed with your dosage. Someone increased it. Does that concur with your findings?"

"It does."

"Which would suggest I did not kill this man."

"I only wanted—"

He switches to French and puts his back to Dalton. "Playing coy doesn't become you, Casey. You didn't need a second opinion. You wanted to see if I would argue that you and William missed that damage to the lung. That this man did, indeed, die of his injuries."

I glance at Dalton, but he doesn't insist Mathias return to English. Mathias will speak more freely to me.

He drops the probe back on the tray with a clack.

"If you expect me to deny you're a suspect," I say, "you know better. I'm sorry if you're offended—"

"Not at all. Nor are you sorry, so you should not say so. It cheapens our relationship. You believe I may have killed this man. My only question is whether you also believe I am guilty of the rest. Of the kidnappings and the deaths. I believe you do. You have determined that the timing of my arrival in Rockton does not completely absolve me. Your suspect only needed to be present at the time of Robyn Salas's death. Which I likely was."

I open my mouth, but he keeps going. "The death of this man removes him as your former top suspect. It also suggests your killer is almost certainly a local. No one could enter Rockton twice and not be recognized as a stranger."

"Fine," I say. "You're a suspect. Thank you for your time—"

"Before I go, I must ask . . . what do you consider as my motivation?"

"Motivation is the last thing I consider. Facts come first."

"So you presume I'm simply a garden-variety sociopath, a man who rapes and tortures women for fun? No. Again, you insult our relationship by lying."

"This isn't about our relationship. It's about my job."

"You have a motivation in mind. You will. It is how your mind works."

He moves around the examination table, coming toward me. Dalton tenses, but Mathias stops out of reach of me.

"You know why I am in Rockton, yes?" he says. "I presume Eric has told you."

"The moment anyone becomes a suspect, that information is no longer privileged."

"I am not whining about privacy, Casey. We surrender that when we come here, and the fact we retain any privacy at all is a courtesy. So you know what happened to me. What that poor excuse for a human accused me of."

"Yes."

He studies my face. "You know something more. Or you think you do."

"I know there was a second case. One that wasn't officially tied to you. A disembowelment."

I have to switch to English for the last word. My French vocabulary isn't *that* extensive. It catches Dalton's attention. That's intentional. I could have found another way to phrase it, but this is me letting him know what I'm sharing, asking if he wants me to stop. He stays quiet.

"The council did their homework. I am impressed." Mathias considers. "Too impressed. They are not that thorough. It was Eric, I presume? Checking our stories."

I say nothing.

"It would be Eric," Mathias says. "He is the only one who cares enough to be thorough. And his uneducated hick-sheriff routine is quite possibly the least convincing performance I have ever seen. So you have two cases suggesting I somehow persuaded killers to commit terrible acts of self-mutilation." He leans against the examining table. "But how would that relate to Nicole and the others? I know one could say Nicole caused the death of her brother—yes. He was held captive, wasn't he? Held prisoner and tortured. If I believed in retributive justice, I might give her a true taste of what her brother went through. Yet the *entire* scenario does not fit. Her captor tormented her for personal pleasure."

"Maybe outrage over a perceived miscarriage of justice was just the rationalization."

He eyes me before he relaxes, pulling on a smile. "Perhaps, as you say, for whoever would do such a thing, there is more to it. There is gratification. A sublimation of desire. But not in the way you think. That would make the predator no better than his prey. I did not murder this man here. I did not capture Nicole. I am not the killer you seek. As for the rest, I am no threat to you. No threat to Eric or to the job you both perform, protecting the safety of those here."

I look at Dalton. We're still speaking in French, and he's been watching my body language. When I look over, he tenses, ready to rise. I shake my head.

"Your theory is sound," Mathias says. "But there is a missing piece, a part you are not able to resolve. The other women. You don't know how they'd fit the pattern of retributive justice, and you are too good a detective to decide that doesn't matter."

"Tell me about the reports you make to the council."

That throws him; his composure ripples.

"I know you report on the psychological well-being of the community as a whole, plus assessments of specific individuals at the council's request."

"Yes," he says slowly.

"Why you?"

"Do you mean, why not Isabel? She is more a part of the community, which would seem a natural choice, but it is actually a hindrance. That, and the fact she is now a businessperson first, a community worker second. If she had minor concerns about a well-paying customer, would she raise them? Perhaps not. I have no such restrictions, not for business or personal reasons. As well, their concerns over violence are far more my area than Isabel's."

"They also ask you to assess exposure threats."

"I can see that my reporting concerns you, Casey, but I am not understanding the source of that concern. I am well aware that the council's primary interest is not altruistic. It is financial. Even more so than Isabel, who despite her veneer of avarice, does actually care about this town. But it is in the council's best interests to keep the town safe, which is what my reports do."

"Fine, go back to—"

"Not until I understand this new line of questioning. You are interested in my reports, and you highlight exposure threats. The connection, then . . . Ah, back to Nicole, who posed a threat." He taps a probe against the table. "But she did not. You suggested she may be a threat to allow her to stay. I did not tell the council that. I kept your secret."

"Great, so—"

"Yet you believe I may have 'silenced' her, to use the vernacular. Very 007 of me. I *am* flattered. You will notice that I am not, however, mocking the underlying suggestion—that someone could have kidnapped Nicole at the council's behest. I do not say they would. I do not say they would not. I will only admit this—if I believe a good person represents a small risk of exposure, I see no need to trouble the council with my thoughts."

"Have they ever suggested they've acted on your reports? To squelch threats?"

"If they did, I would stop giving any reports. And possibly relocate to the forest. As for what I report, I keep copies. You and Eric are welcome to see them. I would have shared them with Eric sooner, if I did not fear adding my observations might cloud his own judgment."

"I'll take those."

"Good." He looks me in the eye. "I understand why you might suspect me of this, but I did not do it, Casey. I am certain you have already ordered militia to keep an eye on me, but I can assure you, I will not leave Rockton. I trust you to find the correct answer, and I know I am not it."

FIFTY-EIGHT

I'm at the station. Writing. Spelling out what fits and what doesn't. It's past noon when the door opens and Jen walks in.

I keep writing. She drags over a chair. It's light enough to lift, but she drags it, legs scraping on the rough wood floor. Then she plunks herself onto it.

"Has anyone ever said you're a phony bitch?" she asks.

I don't raise my gaze from the paper. "Only you."

"Oh, I'm sure others have said it. Just not to your face. You can talk the talk. Act like you're some hard-ass feminist, but it's all for show."

I set down my pen. "I don't know what a *hard-ass* feminist is. I'm a feminist, which only means that I think men and women deserve equal treatment. Hardly a groundbreaking concept. But I'm sure you're about to give an example of where I failed in that."

"About last night. I've been waiting for you to come and get my side of the story, but apparently, that's not happening. You got the man's side. That's enough."

"Yes, that must be it. It has nothing to do with the fact that one of you has proven trustworthy and the other has not. It may also be because I'm still mulling through Paul's story. You were late. That got him out of Roger's room. Then you further distracted him, giving the killer time—"

"No," she says, and there seems to be genuine horror in her eyes. She covers it quickly with "So now I'm a suspect? Of course I am. I'm always a suspect."

"Then you disagree with my reasoning?"

"I was late for my shift, but it's not like Paul says, me sauntering in whenever I felt like it. I'd worked a double shift. I got three hours' sleep and missed my alarm. I woke up, chugged cold coffee as I dressed, and then *ran* all the way to the station. Paul threatened to report me to Will, wouldn't listen to my excuses. So, yes, I bought my way out of it with sex. If you want to judge me for that, go ahead. I did it to shut him up because I want the goddamn job and I didn't trust you to listen to my side of the story. If I'd had any clue you'd actually think I was an accomplice—"

"Again, look at the facts. If it was anyone else, you'd berate me for *not* considering her. I'm sorry you felt you had to buy off Paul."

"You know what you sound like, Butler? When I was a kid, I got into a fight at school. My stepdad said I needed to strike back at the bullies. So I did, and do you know who was sent for counseling? Not those bitches. Me. You sound just like my counselor. *I'm sorry you feel that way, Jen. You're mistaken, Jen. I understand your frustration, Jen.*" She curls her lip. "Sanctimonious bitch."

I walk over and add more logs to the fire.

"I gave you a chance," she says. "I tried to help. You shit on me."

I turn and look her in the eye. "I'm sorry you feel that way."

She takes a swing at me. I duck it, grab her arm, and wrench it up, forcing her over the desk.

"Sorry," I say. "But you walked into that."

She struggles beneath me.

"You didn't give *me* a chance, Jen," I say. "If you feel like you tried to reach out and I smacked you down, then I *am* sorry. Maybe I should have been quicker to ask for your side. But I was still investigating the possibility you were involved, and I needed to do that before I spoke to you. I will interview you when I'm ready."

"Bitch."

"Yes. I am. But I'm a bitch with a murder case to solve and an innocent woman to free, so unless you can help with that—"

"I'm not sure anyone can help you with that. You're screwing up this case so badly, I have a better chance of solving it."

"Awesome," I say as I release her. "Go solve it."

She shakes herself. "Do you know why else I was waiting for you to come talk to me, Butler? Because I have information that'll blow your case wide open. A suspect you haven't even considered."

I turn on her. "And you were just sitting around, waiting for me to *prove* myself by coming by and *earning* your tip? While Nicole sits in a—"

"No," she says. "I just figured it out, and when you didn't come to me, I came to you."

"Okay. . . ."

"Shawn Sutherland."

"What about him?"

She stares at me and then shakes her head. "You really are thick. He's your killer. Shawn Sutherland."

"You're serious?"

Her jaw sets, telling me she is.

"You've been here almost three years," I say. "That means you got here before Victoria disappeared. But Shawn arrived *after*. Long after."

"Well, duh, he didn't take *them*, obviously. That's a whole separate case. He just took Nicki. This is why you are a lousy detective, Butler. You get hung up on a presumption—in this case, the presumption that one guy is responsible for all three women."

"We have proof."

"Then your proof is wrong."

"It isn't. So that's your big revelation? That you think Shawn—the guy who was *taken* captive—is secretly the killer?"

"He told me he taught school down south. I asked what grade, since that's what I used to do, too, and he blew me off, changed the subject."

"You were a schoolteacher?"

"Are you listening to me, Butler? He wouldn't even tell me what grade he taught, like it was some kind of state secret."

"Because he probably didn't teach. People lie here, Jen. When you said you were a teacher, he realized he wasn't going to get away with his story, so he changed the subject. How exactly that makes him a killer—"

"He attacked that Roger guy to shut him up. Why is that not obvious to anyone but me?"

"Because you weren't there. You don't know what happened, and even without that, the timing doesn't fit."

"No, Detective, you're just too *stupid*—"

"Ah, Jennifer," a voice says as the door opens and Isabel walks in. "Never graduated from elementary school, did you? Still stuck with those playground insults. I'm sure Casey is terribly hurt when you accuse her of stupidity. What did Beth say your IQ was again, Casey? I can't quite recall, but whatever it was, I think you can spare a few points for poor Jennifer and make all our lives easier."

"Bitch," Jen says and walks out.

Isabel sighs. "Someone really needs to teach her a wider vocabulary of insults."

"Did you know she was a schoolteacher?"

"I try to forget it. I might not have much use for children, but I still shudder to think of their ordeal, learning under that one."

"The first time I met her, that's actually what I thought she looked like."

"Then she started punching you, and you decided you must be wrong? Sadly, no. Now let's forget Jen as quickly as possible and move on to less dismal subjects, like murder. Eric says you wanted to speak to me. I was popping in to tell you to come by the Roc when you have a minute. I'll be working in the back."

Have I considered Sutherland as a suspect? Yes. The thought had flitted through my mind, back when I theorized we might be looking at multiple perpetrators. But I'd had far more likely suspects, and then the evidence proved the same man who took Nicole also murdered Robyn and Victoria, which meant it could not have been Sutherland.

Yet I can't seem to dismiss the idea. Maybe it's the lack of other suspects. Maybe it's the fact that my self-confidence isn't quite where I'd like it to be, and someone like Jen can poke holes in it.

I hate admitting that. It's like being hurt by the comments of an online troll. That's what she is—a real-life troll, someone whose only pleasure in life comes from dragging others down. I know that, and therefore, it does not reflect well on me to say that her words have any impact.

I know I'm not stupid. I know I'm not incompetent. I know that Shawn Sutherland cannot have killed two women years before he even arrived in Rockton. It does not make any logical sense.

Yet it bothers me enough that I put aside logic and assess the case otherwise, working through each aspect as if he could be the perpetrator.

I don't finish the exercise. Anders comes in, and I check my watch, see that it's been nearly forty-five minutes since Isabel left. I hurry off to meet her. The wild theories can wait.

FIFTY-NINE

The Roc is locked. I expected that and brought the master key. It's one of the few places in town that's kept well secured. The sheer quantity of booze on hand could make even the most upright citizen consider taking a free tipple if the door was left open.

The Roc used to be open afternoons, but since Isabel's lover—Mick—died opening time was postponed to 5:00 P.M. during the week. She says she needs to train someone to take his place, but she's ignored everyone who asks about the job. She's still grieving, in her way, and that way means she's in no rush to find a new bartender.

While the Roc has a bar, I've never come here to drink. That would be unwise. Guys have no problem coming by for a beer even if they don't wish to partake of the other offerings, but any woman who does the same sets up a dangerous expectation.

Isabel and I argue about this. I call it discrimination, if in a town with only two bars, women can't comfortably frequent one of them. Isabel says I could fix that by frequenting it myself. It's not like anyone's going to think *my* time is for sale. She might have a point. I'm just not willing to grant it yet.

Inside, the Roc looks like an old-west saloon, and I *would* like to have a drink here now and then, the atmosphere being more my style than the fussier Red Lion.

I walk behind the bar toward the storage room, presuming that's where I'll find Isabel. The door is locked. My key won't open it, making it perhaps the one place off-limits even to us. The door is thick, as close to a vault as you get in Rockton. When I rap, the wood swallows the sound. I bang my fist against it.

"Hold on!" Isabel's muffled voice calls.

A moment later, the door opens. And "vault" really is the word to describe what I walk into. It's the size of a walk-in closet, thickly lined, each wall covered in shelves. And on those shelves? The true gold of the north. Booze. The curse of the north, too—of living in a place where entertainment options are limited, and this one easier to come by than most. Which is why it's so tightly regulated, and why the council allowed Isabel to build this vault and not supply us with the key. Here is the real source of her wealth and power in Rockton. She controls the booze.

Dalton might gripe about that, but he never offers to take on the task himself. He'll grudgingly admit Isabel does a good job and earns her profit. Alcohol is still a concern in Rockton, but it causes far fewer problems than in many isolated towns.

"Your growing collection of bottles is up there." She points at the small collection of tequila. "Seems every time our sheriff does a supply run, I get another one. That boy is worse than a teenager with his first girlfriend. Except instead of flowers and candies and sappy Hallmarks, he brings you tequila and puppies and chocolate chip cookies."

"I'm not arguing."

She glances over her shoulder. "You would have four months ago. You're making progress."

"Thank you, Dr. Radcliffe, for the free psych eval."

"Oh, it's not free. You can pay your tab at the bar."

She's at another door, one that must lock on exit, because she's using a key. She holds it open to usher me through. I step inside . . . and get my first look at the heart of the Roc. Isabel's brewery.

Bottled alcohol is flown in, as evidenced by that stockroom. But booze takes up valuable cargo space on supply runs, space better used for staples. Our beer is locally brewed. By Isabel.

This room is more than twice the size of the one we just left. Vats line the walls, batches in progress. At the end, there's an old hand-operated bottling press. Crates of recycled bottles wait beside it. Like the hard alcohol, beer is only available from the Roc and the Red Lion, sold in single servings. The exception would be the tequila bottle in Dalton's house and the half dozen beers in his icebox. But he *is* the exception in almost everything here—the guy who is allowed to skirt the rules, partly because he can be trusted to and partly because no one dares refuse him. It's good to be king. Or at least virtual dictator.

"Today, I'm bottling one keg of lager, one of pale ale, and my first-ever batch of stout. You get to sample the stout."

"I'm not really a fan of—"

"Too bad," Isabel says. "Your task then is to tell me whether it tastes even worse than stout you've had before."

"And if it does, you'll dump it?"

"I don't dump anything, sugar. I just sell it at a discount. You're going to test the lager, too. I've made an adjustment to the recipe."

I hop up on a stool at a high table. "Eric won't love that."

"Oh, I made the usual, too, just for him. I know better than to annoy him over the trivial. Save it for the things that count. Like convincing him to bring in a case of champagne for New Year's Eve."

"You're going to treat the town to champagne? That's so sweet."

She doesn't even dignify that with a response.

"If you're asking for my help persuading him—" I begin.

"I know better. I'll handle this."

"If your plan involves telling him I'd love champagne for my first New Year's in Rockton, I don't actually care for it."

She hesitates, a glass in hand.

"And yes," I said, "he knows that. He saw it on the menu last time we were in Dawson City. He offered. I said I'd rather stick to wine. You'll need a plan B. Preferably one that doesn't involve playing on his new-relationship insecurities."

"But his new-relationship insecurities are adorable. And terribly useful."

I give her a look.

"Don't worry. I consider you a friend. Which means I will refrain from exploiting your lover any more than absolutely necessary. Now, let's get to this sampling so I can bottle these kegs. Business has been very fine since the rydex supply dried up."

"You really think it *has* dried up?"

"No more than you do. Eric is hopeful, but the dear boy has far too little experience of the world. We know better. When our purveyors of fine opiates passed on to the great drug lab in the sky, the supply began to dwindle, until poor Will had to beg the council to double our buprenorphine shipment to deal with withdrawal symptoms. And yet . . ."

"It's too convenient," I say. "There had to be more people involved. And someone on the council itself had to have gotten the base supplies to Rockton. The rydex has just dried up while they retool the plan."

"And in the meantime?" She lifts a sample glass. "My business is booming." She sets the glass in front of me. "Drink up."

I do and then say, "Tastes like shit. Which means, yes, it tastes like stout."

"Excellent. Take the coffee on your left to clear your palate, and we'll move on."

"I must bear a striking resemblance to a guinea pig. Mathias did this to me just a few days ago, with sausage."

"You know, that's something that never fails to amaze me. The man makes people terribly nervous, and yet everyone eats the sausage without question. Then they wonder what happens to those bodies we supposedly dispose of deep in the forest."

I roll my eyes and sip the lukewarm coffee.

"Oh, come now," she says. "You can see it. Mathias running his own little enterprise on the side. *Dear Sheriff Dalton, why don't you let me dispose of those bodies for you? I know just the place for them.*" She hands me a second glass. "The only reason we don't seriously consider it is that we know Eric wouldn't let anyone dispose of those bodies except him. Otherwise? We'll all admit, Dr. Atelier does have an air of the Demon Barber about him."

I take a swig of the lager.

"Which is what you're here to discuss?" she says.

I look up.

"Not whether Mathias is grinding dead people into sausage. He has become a suspect, and other than Eric, no one has known him as long as I have. Arguably, I know him even better."

"Not as well as he'd like, I suspect."

"Oh, I have not missed the doctor's interest, but I have never reciprocated. That seems unwise."

"Why?"

She smiles. "Ah, so here is how you'll do it. Rather than ask what I think of him in general, you'll ascertain why I've never succumbed to his interest in me. Which may answer your question better than the general response. How's the lager?"

"Well, it's a good thing you made Eric's usual, too."

"What's wrong with it?"

"Not a thing. It just doesn't taste like Eric's, which means he won't want it."

She fills my glass, pours one for herself and pulls up another stool.

"There was a time when Mathias would have fascinated me," she says. "He still does, in his way, but the woman who'd have let herself be seduced by Mathias Atelier was a much younger Isabel, one with a regrettable taste for . . ."

She considers. Sips her beer. Considers some more. "I could say bad boys, but that's not entirely accurate. These days, when one speaks of bad boys, one means a certain subtype. A young man who rides a motorcycle, knocks heads together on Saturday night, and is as faithful as a tomcat. My interests, as a younger woman, leaned toward men like Mathias, who is none of those things and yet more dangerous in his way than a dozen of those young men. I learned my lesson down south, one that taught me I'm much happier with men like Mick. Good men. Undemanding men. Men who are easy to understand and easy to love and easily return that love. But I suppose you were hoping for a more specific answer."

"Will I get one if I ask?"

She adjusts herself on the stool. "I find you interesting, Casey. That's a safe version of the fascinating men I once fell for. In you, I can have a friend whose company I enjoy, with whom I can engage in a lively debate without potentially sacrificing any of myself, as I do if I indulge in that with a lover."

"I'd argue that you can lose some of yourself in a friendship gone wrong, but I understand the gist of what you're saying."

"You're referring to Diana, of course. Yes, that's true, but in regards to us, if I'm going to share anything more personal with you, I need to know it's safe."

"That I won't tell Eric? That depends. If you confess you've caught Mathias doing or saying something that would prove he's my perpetrator, then I have to tell my boss."

"I'd have told you that already. I may trade in secrets, but I know which ones I shouldn't keep. You ask me why I reject Mathias. What I see in him that makes me wary. I'll give you a story for an answer." She takes a deep gulp of her beer and then makes a face. "Poor excuse for an alcoholic beverage."

"Because it has less than five percent alcohol. Which means it isn't really beer at all."

"Agreed. But that's the responsible thing to do." She drains her glass. "I'll pretend that was enough to loosen my tongue. When I was completing my doctorate, I had an affair with one of my professors. Yes, terribly cliché of me. Worse, he fit the cliché to a tee. Middle-aged and married. Told me his wife didn't understand him. And I never felt a moment's guilt. If she couldn't keep him happy, I was welcome to him." She shakes her head. "Do you ever look back on your younger self and just want to slap her?"

I smile. "Sometimes."

"I cringe even remembering myself back then. I was so smug. It didn't help that he'd pursued me. Not unlike Mathias, he made me feel like I was the perfect woman: bright, confident, attractive, interesting. At that age, I bought it. I fell for him so hard that I even started slowing when I passed wedding shops, torn between *What am I thinking?* and *Oooh, that cream-colored one would look amazing.* I never told him any of that, but when he'd hint at divorce, I wouldn't argue. Then he got an opportunity to teach overseas. We talked about me going with him, but in the end, he set me free. That's what he called it. Setting me free. He may have even said something about me spreading my wings." She makes gagging noises, and I laugh.

"I ate it up," she says. "I fell even more in love with this man, who was willing to give me up for my own good, my own growth. He would come to visit, and I remained faithful to him. Three years passed. Then through complete happenstance, I came across his name . . . attached to a university in Washington State. He'd been living there for over a year while letting me continue believing he was thousands of miles away. He was still married and had a new girlfriend, too. I went from being the love of his life to his backup mistress. For years I let him lie and manipulate me into honestly believing that everything he did, he did for my sake, my freedom, my happiness."

"Bastard."

"Total bastard. And do you know what he said when I confronted him? Told me he'd only given me what I wanted, and it was my own fault for letting him. Not one moment's remorse. I'd been a trifling amusement. A conquest. Even after he found a new girlfriend, he kept me around because, as he put it, he felt sorry for me, not having anyone else in my life."

She takes a deep drink of the beer. "And that, Casey, sums up Mathias. To him, we are all trifling amusements. Bit players in his life drama."

She's right, of course. Mathias exists in an alternate reality of his own making, where the rest of us aren't quite human. Does that make him someone who'd kill without remorse? Possibly. Kill like this? That's harder to say.

SIXTY

I'm standing on the edge of the woods with Storm as she paces the confines of her leash. Something scampers through the newly fallen snow, and she bolts, yanking my arm hard enough to remind me it may be time to start training or I'll be taking up leash-sledding as my new sport.

"We have to wait for Eric," I say, which of course she doesn't understand, but I say it anyway, as if offering up my excuse to the universe.

Storm whines and tugs and gives me a reproachful look, and I feel the full weight of that reproach. We shouldn't need to wait for Dalton. It's barely four in the afternoon, and I'm armed.

I'm learning to hate the darkness. By midafternoon, it has stolen my day, forcing me to behave as if it's midnight instead. But with a killer loose, I wouldn't want Dalton wandering the woods alone after dark, so I'm not going to do it myself.

When Storm yanks again, I plunk my ass down in the snow. I'm wearing a snowmobile suit, in preparation for puppy gamboling and, yes, inadvertent leash-sledding. So I get comfortable there, earning me looks from Storm that pass reproachful and slide into full-out glower.

"Wait." That's a word she's going to need to add to her vocabulary so I might as well start now. "Wait."

She resumes wandering. I stare into the forest, letting my mind slide to my day. I'm working through Mathias as a suspect, tallying the plus and minus columns, yet another name, another face, keeps sneaking in.

Shawn Sutherland.

This all began when Anders and I left Rockton to chase Sutherland. Then the storm hit. We saw a man in a snowsuit. He dropped Sutherland's bloodied toque and walked away. We took shelter and found Nicole.

The puppy circles, spinning me on my ass, the nylon suit whispering over the snow. The sound reminds me of the man.

Could Sutherland have *been* the man in the snowmobile suit?

I know now that the man in the snowmobile suit was not the one I'd seen behind my house. The second man was Roger, and he was the only one I'd gotten a good look at. So I needed to separate that part of my killer's ID from my mental picture of Roger.

Imagine the man in the snowmobile suit. Size, weight, build. It could be half of the guys in Rockton, but it does fit for Sutherland.

Back to the beginning. Sutherland leads us into the forest. The storm hits, and he changes into the snowmobile suit and returns to drop off his bloodied toque. A few days later he "escapes" back to Rockton with the injuries to support his captivity story. But none of those injuries are impossible to self-inflict. Rub his wrists raw with rope. Add splinters. Knock his head against something hard. Let himself suffer a bit of exposure. Then come back to Rockton.

Having Roger chase him only added an unexpected—and helpful—flourish to his story. Yet when he discovers we've found Roger, he must act. Sneak out and follow us. Vent his victimized rage on his supposed captor, silencing him before he can talk. When Roger survives, he sneaks in and finishes the job.

As for his nighttime attack, it's easy enough to rig up a ligature. Easy even to use it in a way that'll leave marks.

In this case, I would have been wrong about the reason for Sutherland's attack. He would have already gotten Nicole away and stashed her someplace. Then he came back and feigned his attack to give himself an alibi.

But if Sutherland is the kidnapper and killer, why would he get cabin fever and run into the forest? He unnecessarily drew attention to himself. And what is the chance that we just happened to find Nicole while chasing her captor? It would only make sense if we'd caught him sneaking into the forest and pursued at enough distance to track him to his lair. But that's not how it happened—at all. He declared his intent to leave Rockton.

Which brings up the timing issue, the biggest problem with this whole theory. I can't make the timing work. Sutherland arrived in Rockton barely a year ago. He's one of Rockton's white-collar criminals.

Which explains his cover story. For most people, teaching is a career they know enough about to fake it. Unless they're talking to an actual teacher. Jen says she only asked which grade he taught, but I suspect there was more to it. Anyone could have fudged that answer. I'll have to speak to her.

As I consider timing, something in Isabel's story pokes at the back of my brain. Damned if I can pinpoint it, though.

Think outside the box.

I'm trying to do just that when something moves in the forest. I hear it first, and when I look over, Storm's already on alert. Then she goes wild, yanking on the leash and whining and yelping. I think it's an animal, and I shine my flashlight and instead catch the flash of an arm as a figure moves past a tree.

Someone in the woods.

Yeah, Butler, there are lots of someones in the woods.

Not near Rockton, though. Yet that's what I think of, the settlers in the forest, and my mind snags on that thought, and I'm not sure why—

"Better drop that leash before she drags you."

When I say, "Oh, it's you," Dalton steps into my flashlight beam, shielding his eyes and saying, "Yeah, I thought you saw me. Didn't mean to spook you. I saw someone I really didn't want to talk to—stupid fucking housing dispute—so I cut through the woods."

He walks over as I drop the leash, and Storm goes running to Dalton. He grabs the lead as he pets her, then he draws closer and peers at me. "You okay?"

"Sure. I just . . ."
I was thinking something.
Isabel's story.
And settlers.
Why was I . . . ?
Shit. Yes. Exactly.
"We need to talk to the council about Sutherland," I say. "Now."

As we walk to Val's, Dalton fills me in on what he knows of Sutherland's life down south. He does have a connection to teachers—as a fund manager for their union. He'd been suspected of taking significant kickbacks for investing the teachers' money in questionable ventures. Given that he was able to buy his way into Rockton, it was obviously more than a suspicion.

"And before you ask," Dalton says. "I didn't investigate his claim. Never got around to it."

"Because you had no reason to. It's a common enough story for Rockton, and unless he crosses your radar, you aren't going to dig deeper."

"Yeah. But if you're asking for his backstory, that means you're considering him as a suspect. I'm guessing you have new information that suggests we're looking at multiple perps again."

"No," I say. "Just playing a long shot. A very long shot."

I explain my theory to Dalton before we arrive. Then I tell Val I need to speak to the council. She nods and leads us inside.

"What do you need from them?" she asks me.

"I have to ask questions about Shawn Sutherland's situation down south."

She frowns. "You're considering him for these crimes? I don't mean to second-guess you, Casey, but he's only been here a year." She looks at Dalton. "Have you forgotten that?"

"He hasn't," I say. "Which is why I didn't consider Shawn a suspect before now."

"But he's a victim, isn't he? He came back badly injured. I'm sorry, Casey, but I really don't see how he could be responsible."

"Nicole came back in worse condition," I say. "If we suspected her, we can't ignore Shawn. Otherwise, we're saying that all women who are victimized may have been complicit in—"

"No," she says quickly. "That would be wrong. Of course we need to consider everyone. I don't keep admission files here, but Shawn's entry was recent enough that I might be able to help."

SIXTY-ONE

Val's version only confirms that Dalton isn't misremembering. What I want to know, though, is how thoroughly the council researched Sutherland.

"He brought in a significant sum of money," she says. "And the teachers' union had only begun to raise suspicions. They hadn't actually accused him. It's an ideal situation, like in your own case, where no charges have been filed and no formal accusation made."

"So what research does the council do in those cases?"

"In yours, they would have confirmed that the young man's death occurred as you claimed and that the attack on your current boyfriend happened as you also claimed. But that's a case where there's the threat of violence and no financial gain."

"Because I wasn't buying my way in."

"Yes. You brought special skills, though, so they likely didn't do more than a basic check."

"Would the council have confirmed that the teachers' union *was* investigating bad investments? Or would they just take Shawn's word for it?"

"If no accusations were made, it would be difficult to follow up without further alerting the union."

"What about Shawn himself?" I ask. "What background checks would have been done on him?"

When she hesitates, I say, "In my case, for example, I had to submit my passport and supporting identification."

"It's standard procedure to request at least two forms of government-issued ID."

"What I think Casey's really asking," Dalton says, "is not whether it's the normal routine, but whether the normal routine applies to everyone."

"It is supposed to but . . . They do run a criminal background check. I know that much. Also, they will run an online search, to alert us to potential problems. That is a serious concern, naturally—that someone could *claim* to have committed white-collar crimes when it turns out he's the prime suspect in a serial-killing spree. The council takes steps to ensure there are no outstanding criminal issues."

In other words, though, they run searches that may very well come up empty. That they *hope* will come up empty. That might prove someone hasn't been accused of any crimes, but what it doesn't prove? That Shawn is who he says he is.

Val contacts Phil. I put my questions to him as delicately as possible. He still tries to claim they ran basic background checks on everyone, but his blustering says that's bullshit. Sutherland's check cashed. That's the only 'check' that mattered. Which means we're going to need to be a lot more suspicious of every white-collar criminal in Rockton. It's a helluva loophole.

What I'm postulating, then, is that Shawn Sutherland isn't a funds manager who cheated a teachers' union. He's just a guy with enough cash to buy his way in, one who wants to come to Rockton for another reason.

So how does that blow apart my time-line issue? It doesn't. It's just step one in a theory that I have to wait until morning—and daylight—to pursue.

———

The next day, Dalton and I are out on the sleds just before daybreak. His brother has been camping where Dalton can find him. We pick him up and spend the next four hours driving farther from camp than I've ever been. Farther than Dalton has been in years.

We have to hide and leave the snowmobiles for the last few kilometers, to avoid alerting everyone within earshot.

Dalton walks in silence, looking calm and focused. But I can hear his breathing, a little ragged, as if his heart's beating faster than it should be on a casual hike.

"Jacob and I could do this," I say. "Right, Jacob?"

"Sure," Jacob says.

Dalton shakes his head. "I've got it."

"Or you could go with him and I'll stay behind," I say. "If that's better."

"It's not."

We continue in silence, but his gaze starts moving, as if seeing things that tweak half-forgotten memories. It's like walking through a house you lived in as a child and think you've forgotten, but then you catch a glimpse through a window and memories spark. His gaze will catch on something, and then he yanks it back to the path, breathing accelerating.

I watch Dalton anxiously, worried this dredges up uncomfortable memories. His brother is watching him too, but for an entirely different reason. There's hope in Jacob's eyes, and they light up when Dalton notices something. It's going through that old family home with the brother he lost in a divorce, and hoping he remembers, because it's not just about a place, but a time, a shared time, a shared bond. And every time Dalton tenses, I do too, afraid Jacob will pick up on his brother's unease, will realize this walk through their past isn't what he wants it to be.

I'm trying to think of a distraction—for both of them—when Dalton slows, his gaze fixed on the ruins of a very old shack.

"You remember that?" Jacob says. "It was your hideout when we wintered around here."

When Dalton doesn't respond, Jacob falters, and I cut in with, "Eric had a hideout?" and Jacob turns to me.

"He did. See the right side there, where it's a little higher? There's enough of the roof left that Eric was able to hollow out a room for himself. He didn't think I knew about it. It was his secret spot for when I drove him crazy. Which I could."

"That's what younger siblings do," I say. "Or so my sister always claimed."

He nods. "When he'd had enough of me, he'd hang out here. And I'd sit over there." He points to a thicket. "I'd sit, and I'd wait. Then, when he came out, I'd go in myself. I'd try to figure out what he'd been doing, play with his stuff, pretend I was him. Then I'd put it all back so he wouldn't notice."

Others would say this wryly, maybe roll their eyes, embarrassed to admit how much they'd idolized their older sibling. Jacob's smile is genuine. He has no sense that such a thing is worthy of embarrassment. That's what it means to live out here all his life. He never experienced those adolescent years when peers change how you see the world, leaving you rolling your eyes at anything that is simple and innocent and childlike.

Jacob's watching Dalton and grinning, waiting for a reaction. Waiting for his brother to roll *his* eyes, make some comment about what a pain in the ass he'd been and how he was lucky he never caught him in his secret spot. That's the guy we know. But Dalton's eyes fill with panic, as if he knows Jacob is sharing something meaningful and he wants to reciprocate. But he can't. He's spent too long locking down those memories, and maybe he isn't even sure why they're locked down, why this makes him so uncomfortable, but he can't get past it.

"And he never caught you?" I address Jacob, shielding Dalton from a reply. Jacob answers, and I engage him in that, asking what kind of things Dalton kept in there, how old he'd been when he found it. Innocuous questions. Just a girlfriend trying to get a better sense of her lover as a child, interested in his past but not digging too deeply into the personal.

The diversion works, and Jacob doesn't seem to notice Dalton isn't participating in the conversation. He's happy to talk about his brother, maybe tease him a little, livelier than I've ever seen him. And I'm grateful for that. I just wish it was under other circumstances.

"We wintered over there," Dalton blurts out, cutting Jacob off midsentence, as if he didn't realize his brother had been talking. We turn to him, and there's silence. Long silence, and I can see him ready to withdraw again.

There. I commented. That's enough.

He takes an audible breath and then points. "See that line of trees? That's where we wintered. It's a sheltered spot. We'd build a simple cabin. But our parents always dismantled it in the spring, before we left, so no one else would move in."

"You spent summers someplace else?" I ask carefully, uncertainly, and I direct it to Jacob, but it's Dalton who answers, saying, "Spring, summer, and fall, yeah. Once the weather cleared, we were on the move. Winter's easier if you stay one place. Easier, too, if you're near others. But this was as 'near others' as they dared get."

"As close to the settlement, you mean."

"It wasn't ours," Jacob says.

Dalton's voice changes, the strain dissipating as another note takes its place. A note I know well. Switching to lecture mode, the easy comfort of a teacher who knows his subject well enough to recite lessons in his sleep. "What we're coming up to is the First Settlement, the one founded by the original group who left Rockton. There are others, each built by a distinct group that left at the same time. Our parents weren't with any of those groups."

"It was just the two of them," Jacob says. "Our mother's time in Rockton was up, and our father hadn't put in his two years. She couldn't stay; he couldn't leave. So they took off together."

"It was a lark, I think, in the beginning," Dalton says. "They were younger than most people we take these days."

"So it was like running away together," I say. "Except into the Yukon wilderness rather than eloping in Vegas."

"Yeah. I don't know if they just decided to stay after a while or if they weren't allowed back. Anyway, they weren't from a settlement, which doesn't mean you can't join one. They just never did."

"It isn't easy to join," Jacob says. "You start at the bottom doing the crappy jobs, and if you've been living on your own, that's going backwards. Sometimes when we'd go in to trade, there'd be problems. There aren't a lot of women, and our mom was younger than most and . . ." He shrugs. "There were problems."

"The kind that end in black eyes and bloody noses and the elders telling our parents they can't come back until they learn some manners. And by *manners*, they meant learn to put up with guys grabbing our mother and offering our father trade for a night with her—right in front of me and Jacob. Our parents stayed close to this settlement in the winter. But that was it." The path crests and rises, and Dalton peers down it and says, "And there it is."

I look down the slope and see it. The First Settlement.

SIXTY-TWO

The settlement looks more like a temporary camp than a village. Ten cabins, loosely scattered, at least fifty meters from each neighbor. Poor for defense, but I suppose that's not really an issue up here, where the only thing you need to defend against is the wildlife, and you're close enough to your neighbor to shout for help if a grizzly ambles into your living room.

Not that a grizzly would fit in these living rooms. The cabins probably share the same size footprint as our chalets, but without a second story. Intentionally small, Dalton explains, for conservation of heat.

Our boots crunch on the snow, and it's not loud, but in a place like this, it's enough. A door opens. Then another. Dalton moves closer to me, and I'm not even sure he's aware he's doing it, he just shifts over, shoulders squaring.

No one looks my way, though. I'm between the two men, a head shorter than either, a slight figure in an oversized snowmobile suit, with the hood drawn up, scarf wrapped in a muffler, only my eyes visible over it. If they notice me, they mistake me for a boy, like Cypher did. It's Dalton they're looking at. Sizing up. They know Jacob—he trades here, as his parents did. Dalton, though, is a stranger, and he's young enough and big enough to earn wary looks.

"Is Edwin in?" Jacob calls to the person nearest, asking after the town elder—as much to check whether he's present as to let people know he's following proper protocol, escorting strangers directly to the guy in charge.

The man nods. He doesn't say anything. Doesn't bother to stop staring either. People watch us as we proceed to the center of the settlement. By the time we arrive, the door to that central cabin is open. A man stands in it. He's not much taller than me, stooped and wizened, at least eighty. His brown skin and eyes suggest he's Asian, but given his age, I honestly can't tell if he is or that's just the result of fifty years of living out of doors.

"Edwin," Jacob says and bows his head. "May we come in and speak to you?"

Edwin nods and backs up. We walk inside. The cabin is smoky, fire blazing too hot, as if his old bones can no longer take the cold. There are two chairs. Real wooden chairs, as good as anything Kenny would make at his carpentry bench. One is oversized, blanketed with thick furs. Edwin lowers himself into that. We stay standing.

"Edwin, this is—"

"I know who he is," Edwin says. "I'm old. I'm not senile. I recognize your brother's face."

Disconcertion flickers through Dalton's eyes. He blinks it away, but not before Edwin catches it and snorts. "You think you've changed that much? You haven't, and you look too much like your brother for anyone to miss the connection. I remember you, Eric. Yes, even your name. I remember the hell you put your parents through, too, when you took off."

"He didn't—" Jacob begins, but Dalton silences him with a look. He's not going to explain more than he has to. Like in Rockton, secrets are valuable out here. They're weapons that can be used against you.

The old man's gaze flicks to me and then back to Dalton. "You think you need to hide your girl from me?"

"Well, considering I seem to remember—" Dalton cuts himself short, presumably before bringing up his mother's treatment.

I unwrap my scarf and lower my hood. Edwin eyes me, not like an old man looking at a young woman, but the hard, assessing study of a stranger.

"What's your name?" he says.

"Casey."

That snort. "I meant your family name."

"Butler."

A harder snort. "Your *other* family."

I give him what he wants. "My maternal grandfather's family name is Zhao." He nods, apparently satisfied that he's guessed my heritage correctly. I add, "And my maternal grandmother's family name is Navarro."

"Spanish?" There's a thread of hope in his eyes that disappears when I say, "Filipino," and the sneer that follows isn't disgust for the law that forced Filipinos to adopt Hispanic surnames. It's racism, pure and simple.

He says something in Mandarin Chinese. I just look at him, long enough that he shifts in vague discomfort, and then I say, "I was born in Canada. I didn't take Mandarin lessons growing up because my mother believed in full assimilation. I did study it in university because in spite or—or maybe because of—my mother's attitude, I am interested in my cultural heritage. But I'm Canadian. I know French better than Mandarin. I know English better still, so we'll stick to that. I came here to inform you of the death of one of your people. A man named Roger."

I don't know how much of my speech he paid attention to, but that last part gets his attention.

"I don't know his surname," I say. "He was a second-generation settler—"

"I know who you mean. He'd left the settlement, but he was still one of us."

"Then I offer my condolences. He was badly injured in the forest. We took him to Rockton and did our best to save him, but he succumbed to his injuries."

"Injured how?"

"He received multiple deep lacerations to the torso."

Edwin grunts. "One of those damned dogs, I bet." He glowers. "That town of yours should have put them down. What was it thinking, turning them loose? That it was doing them a kindness? A kindness would have been a merciful death."

I open my mouth, but he waves me to silence. "Yes, yes, I know it was before your time. Yours, too," he says to Dalton, and then adds, "So that's where you ended up? Rockton?"

"Yes."

"You like living as a slave to the man? Good thing your momma and daddy didn't live to see that. Or *did* they know where you went? Decide if you were that stupid, they didn't want you back?"

Dalton tenses so hard a vein pulses in his neck.

"My brother didn't choose—" Jacob begins.

"But I choose now," Dalton says, opening his jaw just enough to get the words out as he steadies his tone. "It's my choice. Living here, apparently, wasn't Roger's. He moved out, as you said. I hear he kept in touch, though, so we wanted to see if he had family or anyone who should be informed."

"His daddy passed a few years back. Sister took off down south. But everyone here knows him. I'll inform them of his passing. I appreciate you telling us yourself, Eric. Now if you want something to eat before you go, you're welcome to it. Just mind that you're civil while you're here."

"I'm not the one—" Dalton begins and then bites it off. "Actually, there's one other thing." He looks at me.

"Roger mentioned another settler before he passed," I say. "A man he grew up with. Someone named Benjamin. If he's here, I have a message to convey from Roger."

"I know who you mean. He's not here. Took off like Roger did, and in his case, we haven't seen him in about two years."

"Does he have family here? Roger mentioned something about a mother, but he was in rough shape, so I don't know if she's still alive. . . ."

"She is. She hasn't seen Benjamin either, but if it'll make you feel better, passing on Roger's message to someone, I'll take you to her."

We're in another cabin, and it's only once we're inside that I realize how nice Edwin's had been. His hadn't been much different from what I'd find in Rockton. Small, tidy, and decently furnished. This one is the kind of place that—before I arrived in the Yukon—my prejudices might have led me to expect from someone who chose to live out here. It smells of body odor and human waste, and I spot a bucket in the corner that obviously isn't emptied as often as it should be. The wood walls are thick with soot. The wooden floor is filthy enough that for a moment, I think it's dirt.

Edwin won't even come inside. He just opens the door and says, "Mary? You've got guests. Be nice to them." Then he totters off and a woman's voice says, "Close the goddamned door!"

We step into the darkness. The windows are shuttered, and the only light comes from the fire. A woman sits on the floor in front of it. She's stitching something, but it's too dark to tell what.

When she looks up, she peers at us and says, "Do I know you?"

"Jacob, ma'am. I don't know if we've met. My parents were Steve and Amy. They—"

"I remember them. Your mother was a whore."

Both men stiffen. We *all* do, but she just keeps going, saying, "She'd come here and parade around with her blond hair and her big blue eyes and then get all offended when the men leered at her. A whore, just like—" She mutters something and stabs her needle through. "Is that your brother? The one who ran off?"

"He—"

"Boys," she sniffs. "They all run off. Find some whore and leave. Boys and men alike. All the same." She squints at me. "You're a girl, though, aren't you?"

I lower the hood I'd raised for the walk through the settlement. She eyes me and says. "You're pretty. Boys prefer blondes, but blondes are whores. Course, having dark hair doesn't mean you're not a whore. Are you one?"

Poor Jacob is bug-eyed by this point. He keeps sneaking me looks, wondering why I'm not appalled, perhaps thinking he's missed a few nuances of female greeting rituals. Dalton's watching, too, but mostly to see if this woman's particular brand of crazy is going to result in physical violence. Yes, we're not dealing with a model of mental health, which is what I expect, if my suspicions are true.

I walk over to crouch beside the fire. "That depends on the definition of the person asking, doesn't it? I don't think I am. But everyone has their own way of identifying a whore. For some, it's skin color. For others, hair. I've even met people who say they can tell a woman's a whore if she has tattoos or piercings."

"Nothing wrong with pierced ears," Mary says. "Piercing in *other* places might be a problem, but I'd say it all depends on where. Tattoos, though? That's a sign. You got any of those?"

"No, ma'am."

"How about husbands? Leave one behind down south?"

"No, ma'am. I've never been married."

"Ever steal one?"

"Steal another woman's husband, you mean? No. What would I want with a guy who'd do something like that? It just means he'll do the same to me someday."

She cackles. "Smart girl." Another sizing-up look, this one a little kinder. "You're probably not a whore. Hard to say, but you don't seem the type. Now, what'd you come here to talk about?"

"I need to ask you a few questions about your son, Benjamin."

SIXTY-THREE

On the way back, we run into our old nemesis—the shortening days of winter. We've barely reached the snowmobiles before the sun's falling. We're prepared with sleeping bags and emergency shelter materials in the saddlebags, but I'm really hoping we don't need to use them. I have my answer, and every minute we delay is another minute we've left a killer in Rockton. And another minute Nicole is out there, trapped by the ever-increasing danger that this will all go to hell and we'll never find her again.

The snowmobiles have lights, though, and that's our saving grace. We take it slower on the way back, our headlights illuminating the trail we'd cut coming in. It's not exactly a four-lane highway from Rockton to the First Settlement. There's not even a direct path—we need to cross a kilometer-wide thickly wooded gap between trails, which was difficult in the daylight and is absolutely treacherous now. Dalton leads, with Jacob on the back, me following. My brightly colored scarf from Anders, flutters from around Jacob's neck as a target to aid my headlight.

We drop Jacob off near his camp. He's going to stay there, in case he has to positively ID a man he's met before—a man he'll never forget. But I don't think we'll need that. Jacob has provided a description that makes me sure we have that positive ID already.

It starts to snow again after that, but it's not a storm, and we're close enough that we don't need to follow our own tracks. We're just coming up to Rockton when Dalton hits the brakes, and I see Anders approaching along the dark path, two militia guys behind him.

"Nice scarf!" he shouts to Dalton as we kill the engines. "It matches your eyes."

Dalton flashes him a gloved middle finger. Anders motions for us to get off and walk, and the militia will take the sleds. Once they've roared off, Dalton says, "Problems?"

"Yeah," Anders says as we start walking. "We've got a situation." He looks at me. "Did you get what you were looking for?"

"Shawn Sutherland is really Benjamin Sanders, a second-generation settler. That's how Roger knew him. They hadn't hung around together since they were kids—some falling out—but Roger recognized Benjamin as the man who attacked him."

"He's our killer," Anders says.

"Seems that way."

"Actually, that was a statement, not a question. It's Shawn—Benjamin—whatever his name is. There's no doubt of it because *that's* our situation. Shawn figured out he'd been promoted from victim to prime suspect and that you two had gone digging into his past."

"Shit," I say and turn fast, looking out at the forest. "He bolted? Goddamn it. We need—"

"Really, Case? You think I'd be sauntering to town, filling you in, if Shawn was on the run?" He looks at Dalton. "At least my boss knows better."

"Figure you've got it under control," Dalton says. "He bolted. You caught him."

"Mmm, not exactly. I've had my eye on him all day, like we discussed. He *did* try to sneak off, but I was close enough to call an alarm. *Not* close enough to actually grab him. He's taken a page from his victim's playbook and locked himself in the icehouse."

"Fuck," Dalton says.

"My sentiments exactly. We're going to need to start padlocking that thing, because apparently people have figured out it's the one place they can run that we can't get to them without coming through the front door. Of course, that's also the only way they can exit unless they manage to burrow through permafrost."

"So he's safely contained," I say.

"Yep. He's taking a second page from Nicki's playbook. He's threatening to kill himself if we don't do what he wants, which in this case is to let him leave Rockton. He's just waiting for you two, making sure his goose is cooked."

"How'd he figure it out?" I ask.

"It wasn't me."

"I never said—"

"Hey, considering you thought I let him run while I sat on my thumbs . . ."

I bump his arm. "I apologize, okay? Momentary panic. I'll buy you roses next time I'm in Dawson City."

"Buy me a steak—a real steak—and we're even. As for how Shawn found out . . ."

He trails off. We've just reached the edge of town. There's a figure up ahead, seemingly just milling about.

"Hey, Jen!" Anders calls. "Casey's wondering who tipped off Sutherland. You got any insight into that?"

She turns, and in the moonlight, I see her scowl. "You couldn't even let them get into town before calling me out, could you?"

"Uh, no. We couldn't even get into town without finding you skulking around the path, waiting to confess. You gonna do it? Or am I?"

She doesn't respond.

"Guess I am," Anders says. "She's only waiting on her escort to the cell. Saves the bother of getting dragged out of bed for it. So, yesterday, Jen tells you that you've missed the obvious suspect. You told her the time line doesn't work—which it didn't. But if she believed that, she wouldn't get the chance to tell the town how incompetent you are."

"Fuck," Dalton says. "Seriously, Jen?"

I expect her to crow that she did *find* the killer. But she only stands there, jaw set, her gaze down as she says, "I didn't tell the *town*. I . . . had a couple of drinks and told a few people."

"Who informed her that the fact Shawn wasn't even *in* the Yukon until last year provided him with an ironclad alibi," Anders says. "Unfortunately Shawn himself got wind of it, from someone who thought it was hilarious."

"I'm sorry," Jen says.

Dalton and I both stare at her.

She squares her shoulders. "I fucked up. I'll just go let myself into the cell. You guys need to handle this."

I think she's joking. Or being sarcastic. She just turns and starts toward the station. After a moment of silence, Dalton calls after her, "Get your ass back here and follow us. We need all hands on deck, in case he finds a way to bolt."

We continue on, and she falls in behind us. She straggles out of earshot, and Anders says, "It wasn't entirely her fault. Jen's wild accusations just got Shawn asking questions. He wondered where you two had gone, and someone said you were following up on something Roger said before he died. Someone else told Shawn you guys had been talking to Val last night. It was enough for him to decide to vamoose, leading to . . ."

He gestures at the icehouse, just ahead, where Kenny and two others are on guard. Dalton orders them back, and we move up to the door.

"Shawn?" I call. "It's Casey. Will says there's a problem."

Ten seconds of silence. Then, Sutherland says, "I know you think I killed those women. And I know how that works up here. I remember Doctor Lowry. No judge. No jury. No trial. Sheriff Dalton put her on a plane, and we're all supposed to think he took her back to Dawson City. No one actually believes that. Just like no one believes she was guilty."

"If anyone honestly thinks Beth was innocent," Dalton says, "we need to have a town meeting. She confessed. In front of a half dozen people."

"*Your* people. You, your detective, your deputy, Val, Isabel—"

"Beth confessed. I took her to Dawson City. Put her on a plane. Your conspiracy theory is just a last-ditch, piss-poor effort to save your ass."

"Eric's right, Benjamin," I say.

Silence.

"Yes, I know that's your real name. Benjamin Sanders Junior. Son of Mary Parsons and Benjamin Sanders Senior. We spoke to your mother."

"I don't know what—"

"You were born in the First Settlement. Your mother didn't want to leave Rockton, but your father talked her into it. Then, twenty years ago, he met a hiker. He helped her out of a jam and fell in love. Went back down south with her, leaving you and your mother behind."

"You've got me confused—"

"I do feel bad for your mother, Benjamin. Betrayed and abandoned. But I feel worse for the kid who had to bear the brunt of that. Who grew up with a mother whose bitterness drove her mad, obsessed with the so-called 'whore' who seduced her husband. I got the full tirade. The list of things that make a whore, which apparently corresponds to the things she remembers about your father's mistress. I know *you* got that list. Over and over, you got it."

"I don't—"

"When you were a teenager, she caught you with an older woman who didn't meet her standards. Your mother locked you up in an old shack for two months. When you were twenty, you fell for a girl from another settlement, a girl your mother approved of. But the girl wasn't interested in you. She disappeared, never to be seen again. Any idea where I might find her, Benjamin?"

"I have no *clue* what—"

"Your mother suspected you took her. She told you if you did, that was fine—you had needs and eventually, the girl would come around and be your wife. I'm guessing she didn't come around. So you killed her."

"I did not kill her. She—" He stops. "I didn't kill anyone. I don't know this Benjamin person. I think you've been out here too long.

That's what happens—you go nuts. The only reason that sheriff doesn't fire you is because it'll cut off his supply. Gotta keep his woman happy. Keep her spreading her legs."

"Which is a skill you never actually mastered, did you?" I say.

"Because women are all whores," he spits. "Whores who think they're too good for men like me. Even you, Detective. That first day you were here, you got caught in that bar brawl, and I ran in to help out, and you never even noticed. But when Will and Mick came to your rescue you sure noticed *them*."

He's talking about the fight Jen started at the Roc. Anders and Mick hadn't rescued me. They'd just joined in for crowd control as the brawl got out of hand.

"Tell us where Nicole is," I say.

"How the hell should I know? I never touched her. Never touched any of them. How could I? I was down south when the first two disappeared. I *came* from down south."

"No, you didn't. You were here, in the First Settlement, until a couple of years ago."

"Then how did I take those two women?"

"After that first girl died, it wasn't safe to grab someone else from a settlement. But you knew about Rockton from your parents. So you staked it out. Waited for women to go into the forest. You took Robyn. Kept her; killed her. Then you came back and took Victoria. At some point you discovered the cave was a better place to hold them. Also, at some point, you started thinking Rockton looked a lot cozier than the First Settlement. So when Victoria died, you decided it was time to reunite with dear old dad. You knew from his stories that he came from a wealthy family. You found him down south and blackmailed him into giving you the entrance money and a decent story. Then you bought your way into Rockton, as an actual citizen. That's why the time line doesn't work. You were in the forest when you took Robyn and Victoria but living here when you went after Nicole."

This is the idea Isabel's story had ignited. The tale of her lover who'd left and then returned, moving a few hours away while Isabel presumed he was still across the ocean. What if our killer was a settler who'd seemed to leave and then come back as a Rockton resident?

He would know both worlds—able to navigate the forest and the caves, while living in Rockton.

"Do you realize how crazy—?" Sutherland begins.

"You just had to keep to yourself and hope no one asked too many questions. But even something as innocent as Jen wondering what grade you taught was problematic. A dead-easy question to answer . . . for anyone who grew up down south and knows the education system."

"You really think I did it, don't you?" he says.

"I *know* you did. Your mother described you. She even said you've got bad scar tissue on your left foot, from where she held your foot to the fire, literally. If you want to prove you aren't Benjamin Sanders, just let me see that foot out the door."

He laughs. "Right. I don't trust *anyone* in this goddamned town of whores and liars. If you've decided I did it, then I'm dead already. The only revenge I'll have is that when I'm dead, you'll see your mistake. You'll realize you had the wrong man."

As he's ranting, we're getting into position, Anders and Kenny at the door with a log battering ram. Dalton beside it, ready to swing in. I'm poised with my gun, in case Benjamin attacks.

"There!" he yells. "It's done, damn you. It's done. I've just ingested enough dope to put me to sleep, and I'll never wake up."

Anders and Kenny ram the door. It holds fast. Inside, Sutherland is laughing hysterically. "And what good do you think that will do? I'm dead. Don't you get it? Dead man walking. Dead man talking. You've killed me. Murdered an innocent man."

The ram hits again, and this time the wood cracks. They rip away at it until it's clear. Sutherland is across the room, sitting on the floor, grinning as wide as he can.

"Too late," he says. "Too little, too late."

Beside him is a syringe. He waggles an empty bottle at us. "Gone. All gone. And in a minute, so am I."

Anders, Kenny, and Dalton run over and grab Sutherland as he collapses.

SIXTY-FOUR

We're in the clinic. Dalton and Kenny have gotten Sutherland's limp form onto the examining table. Anders is taking out the stomach pump. I'm undoing Sutherland's left boot.

"You don't need to check," Dalton grunts as he heaves Sutherland into place. "He had the benzo."

Which is true. He didn't just randomly grab an overdose of sleeping pills or painkillers. He's got the very drug someone dosed Diana and Nicole with. That should prove it. The rest should prove it—the story fits, the description fits. Jacob's description too, of the guy who'd once "offered" him a hostile woman, the guy who'd followed his father down south a couple of years ago. A guy he'd known as Benjy.

Benjamin Sanders.

It still isn't enough. I keep thinking of his last words, declaring his innocence, and it's easy to check, so I must.

So I pull off that boot. I pull off that sock. And there it is. The burn tissue, just as Mary described.

"Satisfied?" Dalton says. "Now, get up here and help us keep this bastard alive."

I get into position to assist Anders, and Dalton moves across the room, staying out of the way.

I'm struggling to focus. Part of my brain stays stuck on the pointlessness of his final proclamation of innocence. All I had to do was check his foot.

Focus, damn it. If we lose him, we lose Nicole.

I have the tube, and I'm getting into position while Anders presses his fingers to Sutherland—

No, not Sutherland—*Benjamin.*

I have to remember that. This is not the guy we knew. Not the victim I hauled in from the forest. This is a killer who doesn't deserve another name to hide behind.

Anders presses his fingers to Benjamin's neck, a quick vitals check. I'm reaching to open Benjamin's mouth when Anders frowns. He's got his fingers still pressed there, and he's frowning, and I'm saying "What is it?" and he's reaching to open Benjamin's eye. His fingers touch the eyelid as Benjamin springs up. His arms sweep wide, knocking everything from the tray, and there's a moment when I think Anders's fingers on his eyelid jolted him back to consciousness.

That's what we all must think, because there's frozen shock as Benjamin springs up and those instruments clatter, and then Dalton's leaping in, shouting, "Restrain—"

Benjamin has my upper arm in an iron grip as he's rolling off the table. I lash out. I feel pain. A sharp jab. It's not enough to stop me. It is enough to startle me. That's all he needs. I'm distracted for a split second, and then there's a gun at my head—my own damned gun— and Benjamin's backing up, shouting, "I'll kill her. You know I'll kill her."

I back up with him. I have to. There's a gun at my head—an unsteady one—and so I stay with him, doing nothing to make him pull the trigger.

Across the room, Dalton has his gun out. Anders doesn't. He's off to the side, assessing. His gaze drops to the table, as if trying to see what he can use. The tray of instruments is on the floor, and there's nothing left on that table. Nothing useful.

"You can't get out of here," Anders says. "People saw us rush you in, and it doesn't matter how cold it is, they're curious, so they're hanging around, hoping to hear what's going on. If you run, there'll be thirty people between you and the forest."

"That's why I've got her," he says. "She'll come along peacefully. I know she will."

"Detective Butler isn't some innocent bystander," Anders says. "Even without her gun, she'll take you down before you reach that forest."

"No, she just thinks she will. That's why she'll come along peacefully. She's sure she'll get the jump on me, so she's not going to fight." The gun barrel presses cold against my scalp. "Am I right, Casey? That's what you're doing right now, isn't it? Playing good hostage. Waiting for me to make a mistake. Knowing I will, because no one's as clever as you. Except . . ." He lowers his lips to my ear and whispers, "There's a problem, isn't there?"

There *is* a problem. I feel it coursing through my veins. Literally coursing. That jab when he grabbed me. He's injected me with something.

I glance over at Anders. He's still assessing, working through scenarios. It's a good thing he's there, because Dalton is paralyzed with indecision. There's a gun to my head, and that's all he sees, a wobbling gun at his lover's head, and he's holding a gun himself and that seems to be the answer, but he knows it's not. Yet he can't bring himself to lower it, as if that would be surrender.

"We're going to back down this hallway and out the rear door," Benjamin says. "The sheriff and the deputy will go on ahead to clear the way. They'll warn that any sudden moves will seal Casey's death warrant. I'll fire and run."

"If you take her into that forest, she's dead," Anders says. "You'll kill her as soon as the way is clear."

"No, I'll keep her, like I kept the others. That's why she'll come with me, and it's why your sheriff will let her leave. Because they're both arrogant enough to think they can get out of this. She thinks she can escape. He thinks he can find her."

"Kind of tipping your hand, aren't you?"

Benjamin chuckles. "I could show my whole hand, and they'll still think they can beat me. That's what happens when you're thirty years old and run your own town. Thirty years old and a big-city homicide detective. A guy like me doesn't stand a chance against them."

He shifts the gun. "You're going to find out what a man like me can do, Casey. What an ordinary man can do. How he can outwit you. That's how this whole thing started, a test of wits you never even realized you were having."

"How's that?" I ask, and like Anders, I'm not really hoping for useful answers—I'm just stalling as I struggle against the sedative.

"The cave," he says. "You were going to explore my cave."

I glance at Anders, my brow furrowing.

"Bear Skull Mountain," Dalton says, his voice cracking as if it's been hours since he spoke. "I promised to take you spelunking on Bear Skull Mountain."

It takes a moment. Then I remember—we'd been having drinks at the Lion after a caving expedition. I'd declared I wanted to explore new territory. Dalton suggested we head over to Bear Skull next time.

"You were there," I say to Benjamin. "In the Lion. You overheard us. Bear Skull is where you were keeping Nicole and the bodies, and you were worried we'd find them. So why not just move Nicole?"

"Because I liked where I had her. And I wasn't going to let some stuck-up whore make me do anything. So I engaged you in a battle of wits. You were just too wit*less* to realize it."

"You were luring me," I say. "That day of the storm. You made a point of running when Eric was away. You knew I'd still go after you."

"Arrogance, like I said."

"I'd go after you, and you'd lure me in that direction. Then you'd take out Will or separate us. That's why you led us toward the cave. Get me close, make it easier to transport me. Only you didn't anticipate the storm."

The gun barrel rubs against my scalp. "Of course I did. I knew it was coming. I used it."

Which is bullshit. The storm disrupted his plans. He still managed to get into his snowmobile suit and balaclava, and bloody his toque, but I recall him standing there—just standing there, watching. We'd had our guns on him, and we were alert and unharmed enough that he'd seen no way of taking me.

So he'd dropped the hat and withdrawn. I don't know if he lost us after that or if he'd been keeping an eye on us the whole time—and just never saw a window of opportunity he could use.

We hadn't even known a game was in play, and we'd still won.

"That was you in the forest," I say. "During the storm when I was alone. You attacked me. I—"

"It wasn't the time. I realized that, which is why I let you go."

Not quite how I remember it, but I let him have that and then say, "It was you in my house, too." My words are starting to slur, but I push on. *Keep him talking.* "You planned to fake your escape and show up in my house and take me captive from there. Yet it wasn't that easy, was it?"

"Again, I made a slight misstep. Roger's fault. I decided it was too risky, grabbing you *and* getting past him. I also decided I was missing an opportunity. The chance to snatch Nicole back from under your nose. You've been beaten, Detective. Leave it at that. Now you'll come along quietly, confident in your ability to escape."

"No."

The gun going still. "What?"

I struggle to speak clearly. "I saw that hole. There's no way I can go with you and expect to live. I'll die slowly and horribly in a cave somewhere, and Nicole will die, too. I'm her replacement. So, no, I'm not going with you. For her sake."

This isn't what he expected, and he's thinking fast.

"Will?" I say, fighting to keep my words clear as the drug threatens to silence me. "I'm going to ask you to take the shot. Benjamin will try to kill me. He might even succeed. But shoot to wound him and then keep him alive and in pain—horrible pain—until he tells you where to find Nicole. Can you do—"

Benjamin shoves me. Hard. I'm stumbling, trying to right myself. A gun fires. Something hits me in the back. Hits me hard. Another shot. Shouts. Footfalls. I'm falling, and I hear shots and shouts and then . . .

Darkness.

SIXTY-FIVE

I wake in bed. My brain feels like a poorly tethered balloon, threatening to float off.

There's a voice. It seems to be coming from miles away. I can't quite make it out, but it sounds urgent, anxious.

Huh. Something must be wrong.

A face appears in front of the ceiling. It's Dalton. He looks worried. Shit. What happened now?

"Casey? Can you hear me?"

I close my eyes.

"No! Wait! Casey!"

I drop back into dreamless sleep.

The next time I wake, I bolt up like an alarm is screeching in my ear. Which it is—the screech of my inner voice telling me to get up, Benjamin's on the run, and what the hell am I doing, lying here—

Pain. Blinding, gasp-inducing pain blasts through my shoulder. Hands grab me. Hands lower me back to bed. Push me back to bed. Dalton's voice saying, "Relax. Just relax. You're okay. Everything's okay."

I blink hard to clear my vision. I'm in his bed. He's there, over me, fussing with my pillow and saying, "You've been shot. You're okay, but you've been shot."

He's measuring out painkillers. I say, "Not that."

"Yes, this. You're in a lot of pain—"

"I can't think on meds."

"You can't think if you're in pain, either."

"Eric, please. You know I hate taking—"

He shakes the bottle and says, "Tylenol three. Yeah, Will gave you morphine at first, but now it's just these, which you *are* taking. You've been shot in the shoulder."

"You got Benjamin?"

He hands me the pills and busies himself pouring water.

I lift my head. "Eric? If you're here, that means you got him, right?"

"It was chaos. Fucking chaos. He shot you, and—"

"And that's *why* he shot me. Because he knew you'd help me rather than run after him. Tell me Will ran after him."

"You'd been shot, Casey. Then you fell and hit your head, and yeah, we did exactly what he wanted, but I'm not going to apologize for that. Will got the militia on him right away. I went to try to find his trail, but it was a mess. Tracks everywhere, from everyone running around, thinking they saw him here or there, but it was just another damned militia guy. Will's out there now with the whole team."

I wait a moment. Then I say, "Eric?"

He pretends not to hear. He knows what I'm going to say.

"Eric?"

"Yeah, I fucked up in the clinic," he says. "When he took you captive, I froze. If Will hadn't been there . . . *You* were more useful than I was, and you'd been drugged and had a gun at your head. I just seized up. I couldn't figure out what to do, so I didn't do a god-damned thing, and you got shot, and he got away."

"The point isn't what you did then, Eric. It's what you're doing right now."

"Someone has to stay with you."

"And that someone shouldn't be the best tracker in this town. Anyone can play nursemaid."

He shakes his head. "Will didn't know how the painkillers might react with whatever Sutherland—Benjamin—gave you. He said I should stay with you."

I don't respond. His jaw works, and he says, "Yeah, he was telling me what I wanted to hear. Letting me do what I wanted to do."

Which is true, and I could give Anders crap for that, but the truth is, if Dalton was freaked out over me, I'm not sure he'd have been much good out there anyway.

"You need to go," I say.

"I know." He exhales. "I'm fucking up in every direction tonight, aren't I?"

"I wouldn't have done any different if the situation was reversed."

"Yeah, you would have."

He's wrong. If Benjamin had been holding the gun on Dalton, I would not have been able to see it as a regular hostage situation and react accordingly. That's a huge problem, professionally. I can't let my emotions get in the way of my job. But personally?

Personally, I think maybe it's not such a bad thing if I've reached the place in my life where I have enough emotion to *let* it get in the way of my job. Where I care enough about someone that I could lose my cool at the thought of losing him. And to have someone feel that way about me? As much as I know Dalton made a mistake, it's not a mistake I ever expected anyone would make for me.

I catch his hand. "No, I wouldn't have done any different." I bring him down into a kiss. "We'll need to work on it."

"Randomly put ourselves in death-defying situations to inoculate the other to the danger of our imminent death?"

"Others put us there often enough that we'll be immune any day now."

He snorts a laugh. "No shit, huh?" He kisses my forehead. "I'll go. Get some sleep. I'll bring him back for you."

I drift in and out of fitful sleep. Petra's there at one point. When I wake again, it's Diana.

"Where's Petra?" I ask, and as soon as I do, I regret it, seeing Diana's expression, my words a slap I didn't intend.

"I thought she should get some rest," she says. "Others volunteered. I can go grab Brian."

"No, no. I was just confused. It seemed like I closed my eyes for a second and she turned into you. Damned drugs."

I'm not sure she buys the excuse, but she gives an awkward smile and says, "You're due for more Tylenols soon."

"Has it been that long?"

"It's technically morning." She waves at the darkened window. "As you can tell."

I groan and slowly pull myself up to a sitting position. It hurts, but it's manageable. My actual gunshot wound isn't that bad.

"Is anyone back?" I ask.

"No."

When I frown, she says, "What's up?"

I shake my head.

"I know you, Case. I see you thinking at breakneck speed."

It snowed. That's what I'm thinking. That it snowed a day ago, and that should make tracking Benjamin easy.

Still something about that niggles at my brain, the same way Jen's accusation had, the same way Isabel's story had, the same way Benjamin's "final" words had, when he'd declared his innocence.

Something about this isn't right. The snow . . . the trail . . .

"Tell me what you're thinking," Diana says. "Maybe I can help."

"It's nothing."

She pulls back, rejected again, and I fight the urge to give in and tell her. It's so hard breaking those habits. For years, she was the one I'd talk to. The only one I talked to. Even now it goes beyond mere habit. She's sitting here looking like a whipped puppy.

I haven't overreacted to her betrayals. I can't trust her. I don't ever want to be best friends again, and that's self-protection, not bitterness and spite. But when she gives me that look, I feel like I'm the one who's done *her* wrong.

I've never been able to understand why Diana stayed with Graham.

As a female cop, I was often called on to speak to victims. So intellectually, I understand. Emotionally? No. Despite my confidence issues, I cannot imagine staying with a man who treated me like shit.

How many times has Diana—like a fickle lover—wandered off to greener pastures only to come crying back to me? How many times has she used me? Abused our friendship? Yet I've taken her back, and now seeing her flinch when I refuse to share my thoughts, that wounds me. Makes me feel like I'm kicking that whipped puppy.

And in that analogy, I find a distraction and pounce on it.

"You know what I really need? Some puppy therapy," I say. "Petra said Storm was downstairs. Do you mind bringing her up?"

Diana goes still. I sit up, ignoring a stab of pain.

"Is she with Petra?" I ask.

More silence. Then, "She . . . It happened right after Petra left. Or maybe when Petra left. I'm not blaming her. Not blaming anyone."

I tense. "Storm's gone."

"Devon is looking for her. He came by with cookies an hour ago, and I was freaking out about the puppy, so he went after her. Mathias is looking, too—he joined after I sent Devon to the butcher for scraps to lure the puppy, and Mathias joined the hunt. We'll get her back."

I push off the covers. "I need to—"

Diana stops me. "No, you don't, Casey. People are searching. It's only been a couple of hours. She slipped out somehow, and she's having a grand old time running around out there, I'm sure, but she's a puppy." She gives me a wry smile. "She's going to want her mommy soon."

"Exactly. She doesn't know Devon or Mathias well enough to come to them. I'm not running off into the forest, Diana. I'm just going to step outside and call."

"Fine. Do it from the balcony. You aren't ready for the stairs."

SIXTY-SIX

Diana's excuse about the stairs is bullshit. I've been shot in the left shoulder; I can walk just fine, even shoot just fine. That's what I argue when ten minutes of calling from the balcony doesn't bring Storm. Diana is adamant. I'm not going out into the forest.

"If she smells Eric, she might get lost trying to find him," I say. "And she has no idea how to defend herself against predators."

"No, Casey."

I lean over the balcony railing. Paul is patrolling the yard, making regular circles around the house, and as he passes again, he waves again and calls, "They'll find your pup, Casey. She's just off playing in the snow."

Snow.

My brain snags on that and again, I feel the reason should be obvious, but between the sedative and the painkillers, I feel like I'm slogging through mental molasses.

Snow. Puppy. Benjamin.

What am I miss—?

"Yes," I murmur. I turn to Diana. "Exactly how did Storm disappear?"

"We don't know. Petra said she'd put Storm in the kitchen because she kept trying to get upstairs. When I arrived, I went straight up to check on you. You seemed warm, so I took your temperature, and it was fine. Then I settled in. It was maybe a half hour later before I remembered the puppy. I'm sorry about that."

"Your priority was me, and you thought Storm was safely in the kitchen. Except she wasn't, right?"

Diana nods.

"And the backdoor was closed and locked?"

She hesitates.

"Diana . . . ?"

"I'm walking a minefield here, Casey. You know how I feel about Petra. When I arrived in Rockton, Petra and I hung around. Then you came along, and it was just like with Will—Casey arrives, and I'm persona non grata."

I squeeze my eyes shut.

"Don't give me that look," she says. "It's true. You're the interesting one. You're the messed-up one. Somehow that combination is catnip. You came along, and suddenly Will isn't interested in a return visit to my bed and Petra's found herself a brand new friend."

Which is bullshit. Anders had a one-nighter with Diana, but even before I showed up, he'd made it clear he wasn't interested in more. He'd seen her damage and decided to steer clear. As for Petra, it was Diana who'd given her the cold shoulder, and then she got pissy when Petra and I started hanging out. But all the council-mandated therapy with Isabel isn't ever going to convince Diana she's not the wronged party.

"The back door . . . ," I prod.

"That's what I'm getting at. You know I don't like Petra. You came here for me, and then when we had hit a rough patch, she jumped in. It's like stealing someone's husband during a trial separation. You just don't do that."

I'm not even sure where to begin untangling that mess of self-delusion.

She continues, "If I tell you that the back door was cracked open, it's going to sound like maybe I opened it and let your puppy out, just to be spiteful."

"So the back door was open."

"I would never let your dog out, Casey. *Never.* Whatever I've done, I haven't ever *hurt* anyone."

I stay silent. This isn't the time to rehash history. But she knows what I would say and responds with, "Kurt was a mistake. I didn't like the guy. I thought he was using you. The ex-con and the cop? It was an obvious setup. Either he was planning a crime and wanted your alibi or he knew you had money and was conning you."

"Neither. He was just a guy trying to put his life back—"

"Whatever. The point is that I didn't hurt him. I didn't plan for him to get hurt either. Graham hired that guy. He told me he was just supposed to scare you, wave a gun, fire a warning shot. I told myself that thug shot Kurt by accident, but you know what? I don't think it was a mistake. I think that's what Graham hired him for. He lied to me. He was playing me the whole time."

"Okay . . ."

"I would never hurt your dog. It's a *puppy.* I'm not going to open the door. Let her get eaten by bears? Hope you find her mangled corpse? That's sick. You and I have been friends for fifteen years, Case. As angry as you are you know I would never do that to any animal."

I rub my temples, trying to push back the drug fog.

"If you honestly think—" she begins.

"Diana? Stop. Please. I haven't accused you of anything. I'm *not* accusing you of anything. I'm trying to think. You found the back door ajar. By how much? Enough for Storm to squeeze out?"

"No. She might be a baby, but she's a *big* baby. It was only open a couple of inches. I figure maybe Petra didn't quite close it, and Storm nudged it open. Then it must have shut partly behind her. There's a wind today."

Maybe so, but "wind" in Rockton is never the kind that'll slam a heavy door shut. The town's too small, hemmed in by trees.

I walk to the balcony railing and shine my flashlight down.

"If you're looking for a trail, there isn't one," Diana says. "That's the first thing I checked. But the porch is covered in prints. Paw *and* boot prints from people taking Storm out all night."

"Her leash gives her ten feet of room," I say. "The trick is just to find where her paws lead and no boot prints follow." I head back into the bedroom and grab a sweater and Dalton's backup gun.

"You're not—" Diana begins.

"Yep, I am. Sorry."

I head down the steps. While I'm still woozy enough that I use the railing, I'm too drugged and preoccupied to feel the pain. As I pull on my parka, my shoulder does protest, but I cover my wince.

"She must have joined up with a human trail and followed that," Diana continues. "To find her that way, you'd need a tracking dog. Which is what you will have this time next year, Casey. You'll find Storm, and you'll train her, and this will all be nothing more than a lesson learned. Devon says we need to get her a tracking implant. Which wouldn't be a bad idea for *everyone* here. I don't know why they haven't thought of it."

"Eric tested one. It works about as well as our damned radios." I glance over at her. "Speaking of radios, does Eric know Storm's out there?"

"I wasn't sure if I should tell—"

"No, you're right. Better to not distract him."

I'm standing in the kitchen, one hand on the back door. I stop. Benjamin. Snow. Puppy.

I turn to Diana. "There's no actual proof Storm took off, right?"

Diana gives a slow look around the tiny kitchen. "Even a dog can't hide in this place. I think you need to go back to bed and rest—"

"I mean there's no proof she left on her own."

I walk to the window and look out. When I catch the flicker of Paul's flashlight, I back up out of his line of sight. He passes without seeing me at the window. I check my watch and then continue, "The evidence we're seeing could be equally explained by someone taking her. Lots of prints on the porch to cover footprints. Door left open enough that she might have snuck out, but not so wide open that Paul would notice in his patrols. Someone could time Paul's patrols, lure Storm to the door, grab and dash."

"Given everything that's going on, Casey, I don't think even Jen is a big enough bitch to steal your puppy right now."

"He never left."

She peers at me. "Who?"

"Shawn Sutherland. That's why they haven't found him. He never left Rockton."

"How?"

"It was nighttime. Add in the chaos of me being shot. Everyone expects him to run for the forest. They fan out to the edges. He follows footprints back and ducks in someplace."

"Ducks in *where*?"

"There's no shortage of places empty here at this hour," I say. "He knows Eric and Will and the whole damned militia will be in those woods looking for him. And I'll be here, recuperating. I'll have a guard, though, and probably a nursemaid. So he needs to lure me out. What better way to do that than to steal my puppy."

She's quiet for a moment. Then she says, "I know I just complained you always seem to be the focus of attention, but are you really sure he's *that* obsessed with you? If he's got a chance to escape, would he really risk it to kidnap you?"

"It's not me. It's what I represent. He targeted me at first to stop me from finding him. Now he wants to punish me for it. Someone bested him and—worse—that someone is a woman. He needs to put me in my place. My place is in a hole."

"Okay," she says, and then, "Sorry. I didn't mean . . . You don't normally . . ."

"Have an overinflated sense of my own importance? I know exactly what this guy sees in me, and it's not that I'm not the cavegirl of his dream, okay? I'm an adversary." I see the wavering beam of Paul's flashlight as it rounds the corner and I turn mine off, withdrawing from the windows. Once he passes, I check my watch. Three minutes.

"I agree with your reasoning," Diana says. "The evidence does strongly suggest your dog didn't escape. It also makes sense for Shawn to stay in Rockton. If he wants revenge, yes, he'll snatch you before he runs, thumbing his nose at Eric and Will, too. And the best way to lure you out is by taking Storm. You're doped up on painkillers, so he expects you'll go charging into the woods to find her, the capable cop turned panicked puppy-mommy." She opens the back door. "Pa—"

I slam it shut before she can finish.

"What are you doing?" she says.

"I'd ask you the same thing."

"Getting Eric on the line. Presuming the radio works. If not, we'll have to send someone to find him. We need to get his ass back here with Will so they can turn the tables on this bastard."

"Sutherland will be watching for that. Waiting for them to return. If he figures out I called Eric, he'll abandon his scheme. We'll find Storm dead outside my back door, and a few days later, we'll find Nicole's body, too. If he can't kidnap me, he'll cut his losses and punish me that way."

She's quiet for a moment. Then she says, "This is the point where I should ask you what's the alternative. But I already know it. You're going after him. Which only proves exactly what he's counting on—that you're too doped up on meds to think straight."

"I've figured out what he's up to. Where he is. What happened to Storm. You agree with my reasoning, which should prove I'm thinking just fine. That's how I catch him. By stepping into his trap . . . knowing it's a trap."

I back up as Paul comes around again. Another watch check. "Three minutes. I have three minutes to get out that door and into the forest."

"You need backup."

"I would love backup. But Paul is loyal to Eric first. Same as everyone in this town."

"Except me."

I look over. Her face is half hidden in shadows.

"I don't give a damn about Eric Dalton," she says. "And you need backup. You just admitted that."

"You have zero experience providing it," I say. "I can't hand you a gun. He already managed to get mine away from me."

"I'm not letting you go into that forest alone, Casey," she says. "You take a step out that door alone, and I'll scream for Paul."

I glance at her.

"And don't think you can take me down first. You've hurt your shoulder."

I walk to a drawer and pull out a sheathed hunting blade.

Diana smiles. "Now, that's a knife. I'll take it."

"No." I hand her the knife from my pocket. She flicks the button. A three-inch blade pops out. She looks at the hunting knife.

"No," I say. "Be glad I'm arming you at all."

I take a penlight from the next drawer and hand it to her. Then I say, "I have a plan. That plan does not involve you getting within twenty feet of this maniac. If he grabs me, you will follow at a distance and see where he takes me. Note landmarks. Big rocks. Downed trees. Anything distinctive. Eric can find them."

"Okay."

"Dress warm. If he grabs me, he's going to take me a long way."

"I'm hoping this plan doesn't involve *letting* him grab you."

"It doesn't. I'm just covering the bases. Now, here's the plan. You don't agree? You don't come with me. You may not think I can get you into cuffs and a gag in my condition, but you don't want to test that. You know you don't."

SIXTY-SEVEN

I'm in the forest. I easily avoid Paul. We really need to give our militia serious guarding lessons, but I'm grateful for their inexperience now.

I'm out there "hunting" for my dog with low whistles and the occasional "here, girl." Diana stays in a nearby clump of bush with her penlight off. I don't like having her out here. I really don't. It seems a scenario custom-made for the obvious switcheroo—where Benjamin decides to grab my friend instead, leaving me forever blaming myself for having done something so incredibly stupid.

There's no sign of Storm or Benjamin, and as I hunt, my anxiety over Diana grows. Is my judgment more impaired by the drugs than I thought? If anything happens to her—

A figure moves behind a tree up ahead. I freeze and say, "Storm?" though it obviously isn't. I'm playing my role. Even adding a waver to my voice.

When the figure doesn't answer, I say, "Girl? Is that you?"

The figure steps out and gestures wildly, as if telling me to be quiet. Then he pulls back his hood, and there's just enough moonlight for me to recognize him.

Mathias.

I groan under my breath. I turn in Diana's direction and motion that it's okay, this isn't Benjamin. Then I gesture for Mathias to come closer as I slide into a thick grouping of trees.

He glances around and motions me down, and I move into a crouch. He does the same as he reaches me.

"I hope you are not out here alone," he whispers in French. "No, you aren't that foolish. Diana is near, I presume?" Again, he doesn't wait for an answer. "This is a very bad idea, Casey."

"Storm will come to me. She knows me."

He gives me a hard look. "Do not insult me by pretending you are looking for your dog. You're out here for the person who took your dog. Our killer."

I start to protest, but his look only hardens, and I say, "I have to. It's the only way I'm going to catch him."

Mathias scours left and then right, and the look in his eyes . . . I watch them and I feel as if I'm not seeing Mathias. No, I feel as if I *am* seeing him, for perhaps the first time.

In Mathias's gaze, I see the eagle-eyed attention Dalton or Cypher gives the forest. The apex predator surveying his domain.

But it's *not* the same. In Cypher, it's the look of a grizzly, the lone bear who thunders through the forest, relying on sheer might to scare everything from his path. In Dalton, it's the look of an alpha wolf, more cautious, always aware of the pack at his rear, those he's sworn to protect. And Mathias . . . ?

If I asked Dalton and Cypher what's the most dangerous predator in those woods, neither would hesitate. That cougar. The big cat that prowls, silent and invisible, leaping unseen through the treetops. The one you won't see until she's the last thing you see. That's Mathias. I see that look in his eyes, and every hair on my neck goes up.

"Yes," he says, and it takes me a moment to remember what we'd been talking about. "Yes, it is the best way to catch him. Also, the most dangerous. He already shot you, Casey. Already escaped from Eric."

"That's because—"

"It's because he's very good at what he does. And it's more. It's because he's not like the killers you're accustomed to. Not like Elizabeth Lowry. Not like William Anders. Not like you." Those hairs seem electrified now, a solid jolt of genuine fear coursing through me.

"I would never hurt William," he says. Then he meets my gaze.

"That's what you're thinking, isn't it? Not, *My God, Mathias knows* my *secret, and he'll hurt* me. That isn't your first concern. Like for Eric and William, others come first. With Eric, that is natural instinct. For you and William, it's penance—you don't deserve to be first. Whatever the reason, it's why you cannot catch this killer. He cares for nothing but his self. His self, not himself. Do you know the difference?"

I shake my head.

"He cares only about serving his id and his ego, even at the possible price of his life. He will do anything to win. To defeat you. To punish you. To salvage his sense of self."

"So how does that help me catch him?"

"It doesn't. It only means that he *can* be caught. That he'll fall for your trickery, and honestly believe you're stumbling through the forest in search of your lost puppy. It also, means, though, that Diana is of no use to you. He'll target her if he can. But me? No. Our Mr. Sutherland is afraid of me." Mathias smiles. "Perhaps for good reason."

"So you're offering to be my backup?"

"Yes. But you don't trust me, not after I just admitted I know what you have done. I might not have killed these women, but what if I turn my attention on you, decide you deserve to be taken by this man? That makes no sense, though. If I have done what you think I have, then I would not decide your crime warrants slow death in a deep hole."

I meet his gaze. "And what does my crime deserve?"

"Exactly what you're doing to repay it. A life in service. Same as William. A life using your skills to protect others."

"What exactly do you know?"

"Not a thing. I'm merely guessing."

That's bullshit. The council must have told him our backstories, as two of those potentially violent offenders he's supposed to monitor.

He continues. "I will help you catch this imposter and get Nicole back. That is more in keeping with what you believe I've done, yes?" He doesn't wait for an answer, just says, "Go send Diana back. Tell her to enter through the rear and come out the front door and talk to Paul. Keep him occupied."

SIXTY-EIGHT

I tell Diana that Mathias is taking over. The odds that Diana will be targeted by Benjamin are exponentially higher than the odds Mathias will be. The odds Mathias could escape harm if he is targeted are substantially higher than the odds Diana could. And the odds that I'd feel suffer a lifetime of guilt if Diana got hurt helping me? Much higher than the chances I'd suffer that over Mathias. He understands what he's getting into.

I'm back in the forest now. I pass Mathias, who's where I left him. I resume my careful wandering as I call for Storm, my voice low as if I'm trying not to attract the attention of anyone from town. With every few steps, I stop and listen. Once he hears me, he'll let me hear *her.* Allow her to whine or make some noise that'll bring me running.

I hear nothing.

I circle the town, and I'm about two-thirds of the way around, passing the icehouse and the rebuilt lumber shed. I'm thinking I might have been wrong about Benjamin taking Storm. Yes, Diana agreed with my logic. Mathias did too, having figured out the same thing independently. But there's been no sign that we're right.

I'll go as far as the main path. If I bump into militia there, I'll take my lumps from Dalton. I just need to be sure—

A figure ducks behind a tree. I'm shining my flashlight beam toward town, and there's someone in the strip between me and Rockton. I stop and hunker down, whispering loudly, "Storm? Is that you?"

It could be a local. Someone who saw my flashlight, came to investigate, and ducked behind that tree because, well, there's a killer loose. If so, whoever it is should hear me calling for Storm and come out.

He doesn't come out.

I make a show of looking to the left and right of where he's hiding, bending and squinting and shining my light. I'm hoping he makes the next move, to save me the decision. The question is whether I pretend I can't see him and lure him farther from town. That's what I'd like to do. He's too close and that worries me, fearing someone will come to my "rescue" and get caught in the middle.

Presumably Benjamin still has my gun. If I turn my back, I take a risk. Possibly a huge one.

Part of my brain tells me to take the risk. The only danger is to myself, and I'm doing it to protect others. That's my thing, isn't it? Others' lives are worth more.

Except . . .

Maybe it's Dalton's brutal-honesty therapy. Maybe it's Dalton himself. Dalton and Rockton and everything I have here. For the first time in my life, I see a future, and seeing a future means I'm in no big rush to cancel it.

I step toward where the figure hides. "Is someone there? It's Casey. I'm looking for my puppy, and I'll warn you that I've got a gun and I might have taken a few painkillers, so it's probably not a good idea to play hide-and-seek. You're not in any trouble for coming into the forest. Eric isn't around. Just step out."

I don't honestly expect it's a random resident. I'm trying to put Benjamin at ease. Also letting Mathias—wherever he might be—know I'm approaching a shadowy figure.

You said you've got my back, Mathias. You damned well better.

I take two steps. "You shouldn't be out here. I don't know if you slept through the commotion, but—"

The figure breaks from hiding . . . and runs toward town. That gives me pause. It looks like a man. I see jeans and boots and a parka, the standard winter uniform for everyone in town.

I break into a run regardless. I'm calling, "Hold up!" and "You're not in trouble!" Then he glances over his shoulder. And it's Benjamin. Looking right at me as he runs.

He wants me to see him. There's no doubt of that.

So why the hell is he heading *into* town?

It's still dark, but it must be nearly eight, and I hear the sounds of the town waking. I smell the smoke of wood fires and hear someone shouting, "Hey, wait up!" to some resident walking to work.

Benjamin's running into town. Holy shit, he's running *into* town. With my gun. While people are sleepily wandering about, heading to work.

I kick it into top gear, gritting my teeth against the old pain in my leg.

I have a clear bead on him. I can make the shot. I have no doubt of that. I can shoot and pray I don't kill him, but if I do, that's the chance I have to take. I'm sorry, Nicole. I'm sorry, Storm. I have an armed and desperate man running into a town full of people, and I must weigh the odds. Coldly and calculatedly run those odds, knowing I'm damned to a lifetime of nightmares either way.

I take out my gun. Aim low. I can do that. Take him down but keep him alive just long enough to tell us where to find his captives.

It's no guarantee. I know that. But it's a chance I must take and—

Benjamin veers. I don't expect that, and I skid as I change direction. He's running for the lumber shed.

Why the hell is he running for the lumber shed?

He's changed his mind. Lost his nerve. Realized he's as likely to get caught as to take a hostage.

He throws open the lumber shed door and races inside.

I stop. I stand there, gun in hand, watching that half-open door.

Come on in, Detective. So I can blow your brains out the moment you step through.

I look around. There's no one in sight—we're too far from the bakery, which is where most people up this early are heading, grabbing breakfast and coffee.

I glance over my shoulder and spot Mathias. He's on the edge of town, hunkered down. Then he darts for the icehouse, on the other side of the lumber shed.

Mathias is covering me, so I have to take Benjamin's bait. Maybe it's the damned drugs. Maybe it's just adrenaline pulsing through my veins, saying, *You have him. He's right in there.*

I circle out of the line of the doorway and approach the lumber shed. I smell the new wood, both from the construction and the fresh-hewn contents. I also swear I smell smoke from the fire that gutted the building four months ago. A reminder to be careful.

I creep toward the door. Then I stop and listen. I can hear Benjamin moving inside.

I count to three and run through, slamming open the half-closed door as hard as I can and racing past and then dropping and rolling behind a pile of logs. I quickly shift to a crouch, gun poised.

"I'm not going to come looking for you," I say. "I can stay right here, guarding the exit, until Eric returns."

"Then why come in at all?"

Because he's armed, and this building isn't constructed like the icehouse. Benjamin can easily find a crack or knothole and open fire into the town. I don't say that; I'm not giving him any ideas.

"You've trapped yourself," I say.

"Huh. You're right. Well, that was stupid of me."

"You lured me in here. So what do you want, Benjamin?"

"To talk to you. You're a good conversationalist."

"Not really, but I am a good negotiator. Better than Eric, who *doesn't* negotiate. Like you said, I'm sleeping with the guy in charge, and if he pisses me off, he loses access to what might be the most precious commodity in this town. So I'm here to negotiate the terms of your surrender."

"Dalton will kill me. We both know he will."

Actually, I know he *won't*. I can't say the same for the council.

"I don't know what will happen to you," I say. "But neither Eric nor the council will let you walk away. I might."

He goes quiet. Then he laughs and says, "Like hell," but I detect a note of hope in it.

"Here's the deal," I say. "You give me back my gun. I lead you into the forest. You take me to Nicole, and I'll let you go, with your promise never to come back to Rockton. Oh, and I want Storm, too."

"Storm . . . What sto—You mean that mutt of yours? You really *were* looking for it?" A short laugh. "I thought that was a trick to make me think you had a reason to be out. I don't have your damned dog, Detective."

That gives me pause but only for a moment. Storm really must have slipped out in the chaos.

"Nicole, then," I say. "That's all that matters to me. Nicole. Slide over my gun—"

Something chitters across the wood. I take out my flashlight, put my fingers over the lens and turn it on, giving off just enough diffuse light to see.

There's my gun. Five feet away. Between me and the door.

He's luring me into the open. He must have found a second gun somewhere.

I eye my weapon. I look around and spot a pile of sticks drying for tinder. I take one and crawl over, staying behind the logs. I snag my gun and tug it toward me. The lumber shed stays silent until I have it and then Benjamin says, "Happy?"

It's a trick. It must be.

I turn the gun over in my hands. It's clearly mine. Unloaded, naturally. I stick it in my holster.

He must have a second gun. He thinks I'll come out now, confident that my scheme is working, and then he'll shoot me.

"If we're doing this, we need to go before sunrise," he says.

"I want to see you. Lift both hands over your head."

I raise the diffused light until I can peer around the semidark. I see his hands. Raised and empty. Ten feet away.

"Keep your hands up and come my way. Walk past me and stand in front of the door."

The hands start moving. "Just remember, Detective, if you shoot me, you lose Nicole."

"I'm well aware of that."

Those raised hands move toward the door. Are they definitely his hands? Could he have taken another hostage?

I see a head. The hood is raised. Yes, that's it. He has a hostage—

The figure looks over. It's Benjamin. I give a start, and he smiles.

"Jumpy, Detective?" he says.

I clench my teeth. It must be a trick.

Yet what is he doing? Exactly as I say. Staying calm. Following orders. That's good, isn't it?

He's a desperate man. He may not believe I'll let him go, but this gives him a chance. Lead me into the forest, let me think I'm in charge, and then, when we're safely away from Rockton, turn the tables. Take me captive.

That's the answer. It's always been the answer. He accused me of being arrogant, but that's him projecting his own hubris onto his opponent. He's going to walk into that forest for the same reason he thought I would—confident we can escape.

"Good enough?" he says, standing in front of the open doorway.

"Stay where you are."

"Yes, Detective."

I walk two steps. A bird calls outside, and I look over, startled. Benjamin's foot flies out sideways, and I'm trying to figure out what the hell he's doing, when the stack of lumber beside me gives way with a roar and a crash. Logs smash into my legs. He leaps at me as I stumble.

We go down, my gun skittering across the wooden floor. I'm face-down, and I go to flip over, but the cold steel of a blade bites into the back of my neck.

"You knew it was too easy," he says. "You knew, but you couldn't resist. So damned predictable."

"Now what?" I say.

He hesitates, as if he expected more, maybe a sob or a plea for mercy. I know what comes next, and I'm not terribly concerned. The moment he pushes me outside that door, Mathias will be on him. Or at least on our trail.

"Now what?" I repeat. "If you think I'm going to go with you, I answered that one already."

His thumb digs into the back of my shoulder. Into the gunshot wound. I hiss in pain. That's what he's looking for, and he gives a small grunt of satisfaction.

"No, Miss Casey," he says. "This time I bow to your will. You're not going anywhere."

"You're going to kill me? Is that why we're chatting? So you can give me the gory details before you do?"

"You're the one who started this conversation. I'm not going to kill you, Detective. You won't die today. You won't die tomorrow. Nor are you leaving this lumber shed." He pauses. "No, technically, I suppose that's not true. You are leaving it. In a way."

Before I can respond, he says "Crawl to your left. I'll guide you. Try anything, and I still won't kill you. I'll just cut the back of your neck. Do you know what happens with that? Ask Roger. Well, not now, I suppose. He and I were out hunting with his brother. Bear got the kid. Clawed the back of his neck. Roger scared the beast away, but his brother couldn't walk after that. The settlement put the kid out of his misery. Roger didn't like that. Didn't like the fact I didn't help with the bear either. I don't know why I would. His brother was a whiny brat. So Roger left the settlement. Which is the long way of saying that I know what happens if I put this blade through the back of your neck."

"Just tell me where to go."

He directs me left and walks behind me. I'm thinking of ways to take him down, ways to alert Mathias, weighing odds, when he says, "Stop," and I see that he's removed a couple of boards, opening the floor to the permafrost gap below.

Before I can react, Benjamin drops on me, hard, one knee in the center of my back, pinning me to the floor. The blade moves to my neck, and as his lips lower to my ear, something pricks my neck. I think it's the blade, but he murmurs, "Did you feel that, Casey? Bring back memories?" and I know he's sedated me. I buck, but he pins me harder, his thumb digging into my shoulder injury.

"You have about sixty seconds before you pass out. You could scream. In fact, I'd recommend it. You won't, though, because you still hope to escape this on your own. Calling for help? That's for cowards. Casey Butler is not a coward. Which means she's about to suffer for her pride. That sedative will kick in and then, when you wake up, you'll find yourself in that hole, under this building, the floor sealed up again. You'll try to escape, but you won't be able to move, and you'll think you've just been bound, until you realize I've cut your spinal cord. And do you know what I think you'll do then? Not a damn thing. You'll be free to call for help, but you won't, because you couldn't hack life like that. You'll want to be put down. You're not weak, like Roger's brother, blubbering for mercy. Death is mercy. You'll see that, and—"

I shoot him.

He howls and falls to the side, and I scramble up, already woozy but fighting it, and he's lying there, clutching his bleeding leg, his eyes wide, as if he doesn't quite know what happened, how I could have shot him when he emptied my weapon.

"Did you really think I wouldn't bring another gun?" I say.

The door opens with a bang. Someone's heard the shot. Someone's come. I send up a word of thanks, because this sedative is kicking in fast, and right now, my options would be to kill Benjamin or risk him carrying out his threat. Given that choice, I'd kill him.

I'm sorry, Nicole. So, so sorry.

A figure rushes over. It's Mathias. He grabs Benjamin in a choke-hold and presses into his neck as the younger man struggles. When Benjamin goes limp, Mathias turns to me and says, "Can you walk?"

"He drugged me. Again."

Mathias's lips purse. "For the best, I suppose. It saves me having to do it."

"Wh-what?" I swing up my gun. "You son of a *bitch*."

I try to train the gun on him, but my hands are shaking now, shaking so bad I can't even aim, the sedative hitting hard. I try to find the trigger. Mathias walks over, turns the barrel aside and takes the gun.

"No," I say. "No, no, no."

Mathias crouches in front of me and pushes loose hair back over my ear. "You still think I'm going to hurt you. Never. I will fix this problem for you. You have won the match. I am here to mop up the blood. When you wake up, this garbage will be gone, and you will have your puppy back and, as soon as I can manage it, Nicole as well. Just leave this part to me."

My mouth works. Then I start to drop, and I feel his hands slide under my head, lowering it to the floor as I lose consciousness.

SIXTY-NINE

I wake to Storm licking my face and whining and nudging me. My flashlight is above my head, turned on, and I look around to find I'm still lying on the floor of the lumber shed. That open hole beside me has been covered with boards. I rise, hearing, "Casey!" shouted so loud the voice cracks.

"Eric," I say, scrambling up as Storm races around me in circles, hearing his voice, trying to figure out where it's coming from.

"Casey!"

I say, "In here!" but it comes out as a croak. I rise, wobbling. I make my way to the door, Storm dancing around me.

"Careful," I murmur. "I'm a little shaky."

I manage not to trip over her, and I'm about to pull open the door when she jumps on it, reminding me that yanking it open probably isn't wise. I bend and hold her with one arm, as I open the door with the other.

"Eric! I'm in here! The lumber shed!"

Storm barks. A woman yells for Dalton. It's Anders who appears first, running around the back of the shed. Then Dalton shoulders past and throws open the door as I stagger back, saying, "Storm!" when the puppy charges for the open doorway. Anders grabs her and then Dalton's grabbing me as I collapse, everything going dark again.

When I open my eyes this time, I'm staring up at Dalton's bedroom ceiling. I sigh and say, "Look, next time I pass out, can you put me somewhere else? Just for a change of scenery?"

Anders chuckles. "You woke up in the lumber shed an hour ago. That was different."

Dalton's face appears over mine. "Or you could just not get yourself into situations where you're *likely* to pass out." He sits on the edge of the bed. "I'm guessing Benjamin's gone. Did he take Mathias?"

"What?" I blink, trying to orient myself.

"I know you're not up to questions, but they're both missing."

"No, Mathias took . . ." I bolt upright. "Mathias took Benjamin. I shot Benjamin, and then Mathias came and he said . . . he said was going to get Nicole back."

"Well, let's hope he does," Anders says. "Right now, they're both gone. We're just glad you're not. Diana told us what happened—Benjamin luring you out by taking Storm, and you going after him with Mathias."

"Diana . . . ," I say. "I need to speak to Diana."

"Did he threaten you?" I ask as Diana walks in.

She slows. "Good to see you, too, Case. Up and questioning already. That's a good sign."

"Mathias threatened you," I say. "Not physically. That isn't his style. He has something on you. Knows something. He threatened to tell if you didn't go along with his scheme. If you didn't take Storm and give her to him."

"Did you get hit on the head or is that just the drugs talking?" she says. "I'm the one who tried to *stop* you."

"Only because you knew I'd be suspicious if you jumped on my go-after-the-puppy scheme. You played it exactly right. Resist but let me talk you into it. Insist on being backup, knowing I'd worry and leap at the chance to swap you for Mathias."

She watches me, and I can't read her expression. No, I can. It's just not one I usually see on Diana, a careful assessment. She sits on the edge of the bed.

"Yes, Mathias took Storm. It was all his idea. But he doesn't have anything on me. He convinced me."

A shiver slides down my back. "How? Hypnosis?"

She stares at me and then bursts out in a laugh. "You really are *well* drugged, aren't you? We talked while I was watching Nicole. He doesn't like me much. He thinks I'm weak. I can tell. You fascinate him. Old story, huh?" Her lips tweak in a smile. "Don't worry—I won't harp on that. But we talked about you. Or I did. That's all he needed."

She adjusts her position on the bed. "That's all it takes, isn't it? To get people to do what you want. Understand what *they* want. He knew I wanted to help after you'd been shot. I wanted to get Nicole back, too. I wanted you to take down that sick bastard. Mathias convinced me he could help you do that, safely. Which he did, right? Mathias rescued you."

"Not exactly."

That same semismile. "I'm kidding. I'm sure you rescued yourself, as always. But he would have, if you hadn't."

"And now?"

She settles back. "Now he'll get Nicole for us."

"And her kidnapper? Do you know what he plans for him?"

"Nope," she says. "I don't care. Neither should you."

SEVENTY

It's been two days since Mathias and Benjamin disappeared. Two days of scouring the forest from before dawn until after dusk. We're all out there, hunting. Me, Dalton, Anders, the militia, Brent, Jacob . . . even Cypher just "happened" to bump into us and agree to join the search in return for more coffee and creamer.

I haven't spoken to Diana since I called her into my room. What she did could have gotten me killed—horribly. If I hadn't shot Benjamin, there's no way of knowing whether Mathias would have arrived before Benjamin cut my spinal cord. But Diana is convinced Mathias was watching over me, and that's all she needs to justify what she did.

She can say it was for me, but she also said coming to Rockton was for me. You don't make life-altering decisions for a friend. You just don't. I keep looking for ways to redeem Diana. Redeem her or condemn her completely. It isn't that easy. It may never be that easy.

I'm tramping through the forest with Dalton. We set out on sleds to expand the search area, and now we're on foot, hunting for prints in pristine snow. He has one glove off, hand wrapped around mine.

What happened two days ago hasn't done anything to ease his fear something will happen to me, and he's hanging on even tighter, sticking closer, not sleeping well. We'll deal with that. For now, if this helps, I'll leave my glove in my pocket, hold hands and let him know, in that small way, that I'm safe and I'm not going anywhere.

We round a stand of trees and see Mathias pulling Nicole on a makeshift toboggan. I break into a run, and Dalton doesn't drop my hand—won't drop it—just holds tighter and runs with me.

"She is fine," Mathias says, in English, as we approach and see Nicole lying motionless on the toboggan. "Her captor was not kind to her, nor as careful as he was before, but she is fine."

I still drop beside her and check. She's sleeping soundly, bundled tight, her face bruised. I reach for the back of her neck. That's all I can think about, seeing her so still—what he threatened me with. But there's no damage there, and when my cool fingers touch her neck, she moves, just enough so I know she's fine.

I rise. "Where's Benjamin?"

"I have no idea. He escaped from me. I knew we were in the area where he put Nicole, so I decided to search for her rather than pursue him."

Dalton nods. "Okay, first priority is getting her back to town. Tomorrow, you'll come out with us and show us where you found Nicole."

"That's the problem, Eric. I do not remember where I found her." Mathias rubs a gloved hand over his face. "It is so cold, and I have been out for two days, and I did not prepare properly. I have been eating snow for water, and I have not slept, and my mind . . . It may be hypothermia. It may be lack of sleep. I cannot think straight, and I did not pay attention to my surroundings."

"That's fine," Dalton says. "You've left a decent trail. I'll follow that. Casey will take you back—"

"Is that safe?" Mathias says. "I am disoriented. Casey is wounded. Nicole is unconscious. And there is a killer roaming the forest, one who wishes revenge on all of us."

I glower at Mathias. Diana's right—he does know exactly what to say. There's no way Dalton will leave me now. He says we'll come back tomorrow and pick up the trail, and we head to Rockton.

It's night. Nicole is resting comfortably. We've talked. This time I was absolutely certain she'd want to get on a plane out of Rockton at first light. But she wants to stay. Her father ran, and trouble pursued, and all the running did nothing but screw up her life. So she is determined to stay and fight, even if what she fights now is only her fears. Sometimes, that's the greatest threat of all.

If she changes her mind, Dalton will sneak her out of Rockton and accept whatever consequences that brings. It's what we have to do for now. Hope that no one is forced to leave, no one who might pose an exposure threat, not until we know what happens when they go.

While Dalton and Anders deal with other issues, I go to the butcher shop, where I find Mathias cutting up rabbits.

"It'll be easier if you just tell us where he is," I say as I walk into the rear room.

"What do you mean?" he says in French. He's lucky he doesn't give me his sly smile, the one that says we both know the truth. If he did, I'd be tempted to use that cleaver on him. But as Diana said, he knows people. He knows their limits. So he just takes another rabbit and begins slicing it up the belly.

"Eric has to search," I say. "He has to keep searching, wasting his time and letting people worry that we're not safe, that Benjamin will be back."

"He won't be. He is badly injured, from your shot, and has wandered off to die."

"And fallen into a hole?"

Now he smiles, but it's one of genuine satisfaction. "I would like to think so, wouldn't you?"

"You left him in that hole. You took Nicole and put him in, leaving him to die."

"That would be . . ." He pauses, knife raised. "I should say 'wrong,' but somehow, I keep thinking the word I want is 'fitting.' Let's imagine that is what happened to him. That he fell into the hole where he put Nicole, and he has just enough water that he will be in there for days, suffering, praying someone will come. Sadly, no one will."

"Eric will be able to trace your tracks."

"He can try. I believe I may have wandered. The mental confusion. And it seems as if it is going to snow tonight."

"Eric shouldn't have to search—"

"But he will. Even if he suspects the same thing you do. He must search. It's in his nature. And you will not try to talk him out of it because you like his nature. He will search, and you will accompany him, in support."

Mathias flips over a rabbit. "To understand another person—to accept them and want them to accept themselves, without changing who they are—is a rare thing to find. You are both very lucky. I was never so fortunate. But in my case, acceptance might have been too much to ask."

He cuts into the rabbit, his gaze fixed on it. "It is too much to ask, isn't it, Casey? I know that."

I don't know if I'm supposed to say something here, to tell him I'm okay with what he's done.

"If I knew you'd done it—" I begin.

"Then you would need to tell Eric, and he would need to act. He would have to punish me, try to force me to tell him where Benjamin is, whether he wanted to or not. I understand all that. Which is why Benjamin has simply wandered off." He looks at me. "Yes?"

I pause. Then I look him in the eye and say, "Yes."